CH

It reminded Belinda of a play she'd seen: the king being arrayed for battle. Of course, she didn't have gauntlets or plate armour to arrange. Her maid Sawyer was helping her on with crochet gloves and a dark shawl. The big black hat had been brought out of its spring retirement, drooping its wide brim and feathers; hardly comparable to a helmet and cowl. But Belinda almost wished she *were* preparing to face violent hordes. The weapons she had to contend with were more insidious; they slipped in between the cracks when least expected.

'I hate to do it, madam,' Phoebe the nursemaid droned on in the background. 'I'm ever so sorry. Going up to The Bridge for a few weeks each summer is one thing, but my sister's ill… If I couldn't pop over and help her on my half-days, I don't know what would become of her children.'

Belinda had endured this conversation so many times that it was difficult to put any feeling into her response. 'Do not upset yourself, Phoebe. I half-expected you to tender your notice.'

'I just hope Master Freddy won't be too unhappy to see me go! I've a great regard for him, madam.'

'I am sure the feeling is mutual. I will be certain to have your reference written up before we leave next week.'

The nursemaid bobbed a curtsey. 'Thank you, madam.'

Belinda waited for Sawyer to dust the hair powder off her shoulders before inspecting her reflection. Propped along the bottom of the mirror were notes of condolence from the ladies in her circle. She'd spent so many years cut off from the world that these marks of friendship she'd managed to cultivate were truly precious. How typical that she was being forced to quit society at the height of the Season, just as she was making headway. And now all the staff she'd grown comfortable with were peeling away too, unable or unwilling to relocate their lives to an estate so far from London. Mrs Marsh was staying on as housekeeper to oversee the town property in their absence, but that was all. The little kingdom Belinda had painstakingly built seemed to be crumbling to dust.

It was true she'd wanted change and the chance to become mistress of a family seat. She wanted it still – but the timing was wrong. These events had a habit of pouncing on her too soon, before she was prepared for them. First marriage, then motherhood, and now an inheritance had been thrust into her hands, and it was never in her power to refuse any of them.

'Come then, Sawyer. Let us be going.'

Creswell the footman opened the front door. Outside the day was mild, the streets rinsed clean by recent rain. People were venturing out in thinner fabrics and lighter colours. A hint of pale blue peeped from behind the clouds. Birds called from the blossom-laden trees in the square as white petals drifted this way and that in the breeze.

Belinda steadied herself against the black iron railing and descended the steps. Neighbours twitched their curtains aside to watch her. She shouldn't be leaving the house at all this soon after her father-in-law's death,

HOUSE
OF
SPLINTERS

HOUSE
OF
SPLINTERS

Laura Purcell

RAVEN 🐦 BOOKS
LONDON · OXFORD · NEW YORK · NEW DELHI · SYDNEY

RAVEN BOOKS
Bloomsbury Publishing Plc,
50 Bedford Square, London, WC1B 3DP, UK
Bloomsbury Publishing Ireland Limited,
29 Earlsfort Terrace, Dublin 2, D02 AY28, Ireland

BLOOMSBURY, RAVEN BOOKS and the Raven Books logo
are trademarks of Bloomsbury Publishing Plc

First published in Great Britain 2025

A catalogue record for this book is available from the British Library

ISBN: HB: 978-1-5266-2723-0; TPB: 978-1-5266-2724-7;
WATERSTONES: 978-1-5266-9807-0; EBOOK: 978-1-5266-2726-1

2 4 6 8 10 9 7 5 3 1

Typeset by Integra Software Services Pvt. Ltd.
Printed and bound in Great Britain by Clays Ltd, Elcograf S.p.A

To find out more about our authors and books visit www.bloomsbury.com
and sign up for our newsletters
For product-safety-related questions contact productsafety@bloomsbury.com

For the readers of *The Silent Companions*,
with heartfelt thanks

1774

visitors were supposed to come to *her*... But what could be done? As always, Mamma had left her with no choice. And there were small mercies. She was glad for an excuse to be out in the soft March air with everyone else.

A young lady of perhaps sixteen years old sat on a bench in the square. She wore no shawl, and her stays pushed her bosom up outrageously high. Belinda saw her flutter her eyelashes at a buck strolling past. Bold. But then again, the Season was approaching its Easter zenith. Perhaps the poor child was growing desperate to make her match. To escape from some situation at home.

The footman heaved her into the carriage. Sawyer climbed in opposite and closed the door. 'I do wish you'd let me go alone, ma'am. She'll only upset you.'

'It's kind of you to offer, but I cannot delegate a message like this. I must face up to my duty.'

Sawyer sniffed. 'It seems to me your duty is to your husband now, and to your children. Servants can run around after Mrs Kipling and bear with her scolding. You shouldn't have to. Not any more.'

Belinda let the words hang. Sawyer was so much more than a servant to her, but one could not voice these sentiments aloud. The carriage jerked into motion, startling the baby. She rubbed at her belly.

For a while, she watched the world scroll past – fine equipages, shops and couples strolling arm-in-arm – her window open a crack to hear the rhythmic clop of the horse's hooves. There was a twinge of the old excitement to be going somewhere, *anywhere*. But as the carriage drew towards the City, ever nearer to the river, she could no longer pretend that this was a pleasure trip. Open-top phaetons gave way to plain wagons and carts. Traffic slowed. She was forced to close the window against noisome smells of brine and sewage.

No, this carriage was not taking her away to freedom: it was reversing time, winding her back like a seamstress gathering thread onto a bobbin.

She glanced at Sawyer. The maid had a talent for keeping her face impassive, but she could not be as comfortable as she looked; she *must* feel the net tightening too. Returning always seemed like a strange dream. Not visceral enough to be a nightmare, just unpleasant and off-kilter. Everything almost the same. Belinda spotted a new iron railing, a freshly painted door, and a streetlamp in a slightly different position to where she remembered it being before.

The driver stopped in front of a respectable three-storey house with white-framed windows, Ionic columns and a pediment on top. Once, it had been the finest on the street, but years of soot had tarnished the brickwork, and a pall seemed to hang in the air, even on a bright day. Papa could afford a far superior residence to this now. He'd rented better rooms for Paul and for Luke. But the present occupant would not shift until... When? Belinda couldn't say. Part of her believed Mamma would linger in this house long after her death.

The footman was climbing down from his perch, unfolding the passenger steps. Sawyer pulled her own shawl tightly around her shoulders. 'Are you ready, ma'am?'

Belinda nodded, but she wasn't. The carriage door swung open regardless.

The Kipling servants must have seen her clambering out of the coach and struggling up the short front path, yet they waited until Sawyer knocked before springing into action. Clare, the moon-faced maid, opened the door a slit, releasing a waft of the misery fermenting inside. Distantly, a parrot screeched.

'Please come in, Mrs Bainbridge.' Clare shuffled back, widening the gap just enough to let Belinda, then Sawyer slip by, single file.

It took a moment for Belinda's eyes to adjust to the dimness. As the door snapped shut behind her, she glimpsed a shadow hovering at the end of the hallway. 'Mamma.'

Mrs Kipling hurried forward, grasping Belinda's fingers and pulling her further into the house. 'My dear! I have been watching for you this last hour at least. I was sure your carriage must have overturned. What kept you?' Her papery lips fluttered against Belinda's cheek. She did not wait for a reply before rushing on. 'Oh, what a to-do with poor Mr Bainbridge Senior! The grief has struck you. You look pale and thin.' An extraordinary claim, given that Belinda was pregnant and bigger than she'd ever been with Freddy. But Mamma relinquished her and moved across to Sawyer instead.

'There, now! Are you well, child?'

The maid curtsied. 'I am in good health, thank you, ma'am.'

'I praise God for it.' For a moment, it looked as if Mamma would embrace her too. But another bird squawked and she stepped back. 'Where is my grandson? He isn't ill, is he? Clare said they had the scarlet fever in the next parish over...'

'No, nobody is ill. Freddy wished to stay at home.' Seeing that poor Clare was squashed against the coat stand, Belinda removed her hat and gloves and set them on a side table herself. 'Come, Mamma, let us sit down. I am fatigued.'

'Go on upstairs then.'

Casting a rueful glance at Sawyer, Belinda placed her hand on the banister rail and began to climb the stairs.

They must part to their separate worlds again. Clare would take Sawyer to the kitchens to sit by the fire and catch up on all the servants' gossip. The task of managing Mrs Kipling would fall to Belinda, and Belinda alone.

The parakeets grew louder with every step, but other birds were twittering alongside: canaries and sparrows. The eldest of the parrots, the ones Belinda had sat with day after day throughout her girlhood, had long since died, yet there seemed to be a steady stream of newcomers. Gently, she opened the door to the parlour. Wings fluttered and feathers drifted. Cages hung from the ceiling at various heights, confusing the eye. Each hopping occupant glowed in vivid colour: acid green, cobalt blue, the scarlet of a regimental uniform. Trophies of Papa's voyages, filling the void of his absence.

'I've ordered tea.' Mamma was entering the room already. 'Clare will bring it straight up.'

'Might we open a window? The air is dreadfully close in here.'

'Goodness, no! The smell out there makes me choke.' She chivvied Belinda towards the sofa. 'Then the gulls start calling and upset my poor birds. No, no, no.'

Belinda had never once heard a seagull in all the years she'd lived here. 'Surely you are too far away from the wharves and quays for that?'

'Oh, no, I assure you! I can hear the gulls very well, and those uncouth lumpers, plying their dirty trade!'

That was not physically possible, but Belinda held her tongue. She'd have to pick her battles carefully today. She sat in her accustomed spot and the cushions seemed to remember her, moulding around her contours as if she'd never been away. The baby squirmed. Belinda rubbed her stomach again, partly to comfort the child, partly to comfort herself.

Mamma resumed her seat and the birds settled along with her – yet maybe 'settled' was the wrong word, for Mamma's hands were always in some kind of motion. Often she picked at the skin around her fingernails; today she sat with her palms pressed together, one hand kneading the other like dough. 'Oh, I am *so* glad to have you here. Poor Wilfred has gone off already, has he, to get everything in order for the funeral at The Bridge? Dear, dear. And little Freddy did not wish to come and see me? How is that possible?'

'Freddy does not feel... equal to company at the moment,' Belinda said tactfully. 'He is upset about losing his Grandpa Bainbridge.' That was untrue. At five years old, Freddy had barely known his grandfather. If anything, he'd been a little afraid of him. But he was even more afraid of his Grandma Kipling with her noisy birds and jittery hands. He'd rather have a tooth pulled than come to this house.

Mamma tutted. 'The poor child is grieving, and you left him? I am surprised at you, Belinda. That was badly done.'

'I *would* have stayed by Freddy's side, but you implored me to come and visit you. I could not very well do both, could I?' Mamma paled at the edge in her voice. Belinda had seldom dared to put one there before, but the trials of pregnancy were shortening her temper.

'It is a trying time for everyone,' Mamma acknowledged. 'I shall not detain you here for long, my dear. Only I have felt *so* unsettled! You cannot imagine how this death has affected me.'

A tap at the door. One of the new parrots, yellow-bellied with an azure coat, opened its mouth and croaked, 'Tea.'

Belinda laughed in spite of herself. 'How clever! When did he learn to do that?'

Clare shouldered the door open. There was a little fluttering as she brought the tray in and set it carefully on the grand mahogany sideboard. Mamma rose to unlock the caddy. 'That will do, Clare. Thank you.' The parrot cried 'Tea' again and Mamma clucked indulgently. 'Oh, do be quiet, you silly boy. It is funny, isn't it? He's only taken that word into his head lately. I'm not certain he understands about the drink, he seems to believe it's Clare's name.'

Clare curtsied. Belinda watched her leave with envy. It must be so much more comfortable down in the kitchen with Sawyer.

Crockery chinked and clattered while Mamma served the tea. One of the parakeets began climbing across the bars of its cage, all talons and beak. A single emerald feather drifted slowly to the floor.

Tea-making always used to be Belinda's task, but she resisted the urge to get up and help her mother. At last, Mamma rattled back over to her with an insipidly weak dish. Of course, there was no sugar.

'Oh, I *am* glad to have you here,' Mamma repeated.

Belinda took the saucer and wrapped her palm around the warm porcelain bowl, sensing how fragile it was.

'Your father did not consider, when he left for the West Indies to sort out this dreadful credit business, how alone I would be.' Mamma fetched her own drink and went on, 'Even Luke is in Bristol now, doing something with copper hulls. And I *have* been feeling ever so anxious since your terrible news arrived. Doesn't it make you morbid? I cannot help thinking that Mr Bainbridge was about the same age as my Kipling. When I imagine that in a very few years' time...' She trailed off to take a delicate sip of tea.

Belinda tamped down her irritation. It was typical of Mamma to make this about herself. Her fear of widowhood – her fear of everything. Mamma was only fifty-three, but she had fretted herself much older. While her hair remained wheat-blonde, the skin around her eyes had taken on the texture of crêpe. Lines marked the sides of her mouth and there was an unhealthy sallowness to her complexion. Hardly surprising, given she never left the house. Lack of exercise meant there was no muscle at all on that fidgety frame.

'Wilfred's father *was* of a similar age,' Belinda admitted. She remembered her few glimpses of *the old man*, as Wilfred called him, sitting in a wingchair, nursing his swollen foot and his grudges. He had died in that very chair late at night, having first discharged his pistol into the wall. A strange man, so unlike her own papa with his weather-beaten skin, striding confidently around the City. 'Yet you must see their circumstances are very different? Poor Mr Bainbridge was never active and hearty like Papa is. Gout kept him confined – and he did not have a solicitous wife to oversee his health.'

Mamma swallowed. 'No, no, you are right there. Mr Bainbridge had no wife to care for him. Goodness knows, I do *try* to advise Kipling! But he does not listen to me as he used to do. All these voyages, at his time of life!' She heard one of the birds hop to another perch. 'I wish he would give the mahogany trade up,' Mamma said fervently. 'Many have, now the banks are in trouble. I wish we could forget the whole sordid business.'

But that was never going to happen. Papa was no quitter. The tea bowl grew slippery in Belinda's grasp. She turned it around and took a sip.

'I will be better now *you* are here,' Mamma went on. 'My Bel, my beloved. You always make me better.'

The tea seemed to stick in her throat. She swallowed it down, wincing. 'It's my pleasure to come. And I was keen to take the opportunity, while I still can.' The baby gave a kick, prodding her to say more. She wet her lips. 'You must realise that I won't be able to sit with you like this again for a long time.'

It was only a beat of silence, yet to Belinda it seemed to last an age. Mamma's brow contracted, then cleared. 'Oh, you mean the precious baby! Your confinement, and then that endless wait to be Churched. Of course, I remember it well…' A sigh. 'Yes, the separation will be hard for me to bear. But at least when you return, you will bring a consolation with you.' Mamma smiled benignly at the swell of Belinda's belly. 'Another little light. I cannot wait to meet them! And Freddy will accompany you on *that* visit, of course.'

Belinda's heart thudded in her throat. What if she just… did not say it? Played along and then sent a letter to her mother later, from The Bridge? The temptation was enormous, but she couldn't play such a shabby trick.

'No, Mamma, I meant…' She adjusted her position on the sofa. 'I meant it will not be in my power to come so far. Because we will all be living at… at The Bridge.' She didn't dare to look up. She kept her eyes fixed on the anaemic tea, ripples crossing the surface as her hand trembled.

There was no response from Mamma. The birds chirruped, blithe and oblivious. Belinda waited. The passing seconds became dangerous, each heavier than the last.

Finally, Mamma dropped a single word. 'Why?'

'It's… it's the ancestral estate.' Belinda sounded like a child who had failed to learn her lesson. 'People who own country houses generally do... live in them.' The baby wriggled, as uncomfortable as she felt.

'Nonsense,' Mamma replied harshly. 'The Bridge is an escape for a month or two a year, nothing more. If your husband had ever intended a more permanent residence, he would have moved you there from the start of your marriage.'

Actually the topic had been broached, but Wilfred never liked to play second fiddle. He would have chafed living in his father's household again, his orders undermined at every turn. Besides, Belinda had known how Mamma would take it. Like *this*. They'd agreed to wait.

'Well, I cannot tell what was in Wilfred's mind back then,' she said awkwardly. 'But he intends for us to live at The Bridge now: that is an absolute fact. I received a letter just this morning, instructing me to be ready to leave next week.' Warily, Belinda raised her gaze. Her mother was a statue, even her hands utterly still on the saucer.

'I forbid it,' Mamma decreed.

An old, childish panic flared inside Belinda's chest. She placed the tea down. 'You *cannot* forbid me. Only my husband has the power to do that. I answer to Wilfred now.' Perhaps it was cowardly, blaming everything on him, but it was the best she could do.

Mamma seized her own bowl of tea and threw it against the wall. The birds shrieked as it shattered. She sobbed bitterly.

Belinda curled into herself, protective arms wrapped around the baby. 'Please, Mamma. Don't be upset.'

'Upset!' her mother echoed. 'This will break my heart. I might as well put an end to myself immediately.'

She often threatened this. Sometimes, unforgivably, Belinda wished that she would. One quick, sharp bolt of agony compared to the prolonged pain of her displeasure.

'You must think of Freddy and his future,' she tried. 'This is his chance to become a proper gentleman. Landed gentry! *He* need never go anywhere near ships or trade. That part of his legacy will be erased.'

Mamma's chest was still heaving. 'That's all very well for the years to come. But right now, he is so young! He ought not to be moved. He should be kept where he is *safe*.'

'Will… will he not be safe with his own parents at The Bridge?'

'I do not know!' Mamma cried, driving her fingernails into the arms of her chair. 'I have no acquaintance with that part of the country. Anywhere new, anywhere you do not understand, is *unsafe*.'

'But… But Wilfred knows it. He was bred there. I have visited before – why, Freddy was even born in the house!'

Even as Belinda spoke, a cold finger touched her heart. For Mamma had used a word that described exactly how she'd felt during those first weeks at The Bridge with baby Freddy. *Unsafe*. Hunted, somehow.

But many ladies experienced such feelings just after childbirth. It was nothing out of the common way.

Sunlight slanted through the windows onto the floor, touching the patch of tea soaking into the carpet and the little shards of porcelain that lay in it like broken teeth. Shadows cast lines across the mess. Long, narrow shadows, the bars of the birdcages.

'Children are so fragile,' Mamma protested. 'One false step may scar them for life. Do you not realise how much damage can be done to a child by a bad environment?'

The irony that Mamma should say that here, in the very room where she had kept Belinda her prisoner for nearly twenty years.

'*Nothing* bad will happen,' she blurted out. 'I won't let it. I'd never let harm come to Freddy. And The Bridge is not a bad environment! It is a country estate. Wilfred will be there, and Sawyer will be there... Everything will be under control.'

'You think you know the world now.' Mamma's hands drew together again. She picked at the skin on her index finger, already red and raw. 'But I once spoke as you do. I gave my mother every assurance when I married. I said Kipling was as loyal as a hound and would always keep me safe.' She shook her head. It was more like a spasm, a quiver that ran into her lips. 'Look, Belinda. Look what became of me.'

CHAPTER 2

The Great Hall at The Bridge felt cavernous by night. Although logs were piled high on the fire, heat only crept out a short distance, never reaching the shadowy corners. Overlooked as it was by a gallery above, the room could boast neither comfort nor privacy. So *why* had his father been sitting out here the night that he died?

Wilfred gazed up at the walls. Firelight trembled across the swords fanned out there and the display of old guns. A small space, the size of a pistol, was conspicuously blank. It was baffling. His father must have taken down an ancient shooter and… what? Sat guard against his own death?

Wilfred shook his head. How like the old man. He'd felt the end approaching and simply tried to bully it back. He wasn't always so wizened and crotchety. At the edges of his memory, Wilfred stored a version of his father who had taught him to shoot and ride, a man whose praise had been more precious to him than jewels. But that man had perished long ago. Wilfred had finished mourning for him. Now, with this second death, all he could feel was curiosity and a vague sense of unease. What *had* his father seen to make him fire? A mouse, a shadow? Maybe nothing at all. Old triggers were light. Hands could spasm at the moment of death. The whole episode was probably an accident. And yet...

Wilfred moved his candle closer to the mark, tilted his head to inspect it from a new angle. He'd always considered holes to be dark places, but this crater remained shockingly pale, singed only at the edges. The bullet had burrowed too deep to prise out, right through the dark panelling into the lighter wood at the centre.

There was no debris, no spray of splinters. Knowles must have swept them away. The only mark visible on the flags was a stain that had been there for years, a stain you wouldn't even notice unless you were looking for it. Or unless you remembered, as Wilfred did. He shivered through the thick material of his mourning suit. Of all the places in this huge hall, his father had shot precisely *there*... Coincidence, surely?

Or maybe he was viewing this the wrong way, maybe the target wasn't in the Great Hall at all. Beyond this wall lay the music room. It had barely been used since his mother died some seventeen years ago, but perhaps the old man thought he'd heard an intruder within?

Wilfred pulled the door open. No sconces were lit, but the glow from his candle brushed over the wallpaper inside: pink, like gums. He remembered happy hours spent here, listening to his mother play. Now there was dust on the piano and a smell of pot-pourri. Neither he nor Nathan had learnt to play music. The instruments gathered inside couldn't speak again without a lady's touch. But soon Belinda would come and make this room her own, she would set that harp singing. The Bridge was theirs now, as it was always meant to be. They would make a fresh start.

Shaking off his memories, Wilfred turned, ready to shut the door and lock the past behind him. But he paused. Something lurked in the shadows behind the music stand, poised as if to play a tune. A shape as tall as a man's. For a moment his breath was suspended. He took a step closer, brandishing his candle like a shield. Softly, it illuminated the face that watched him: painted and flat.

'For pity's sake,' he exhaled. Hadn't they agreed when he last visited? All of these wretched antiques were supposed to be rounded up and confined to the attic. With his mother gone, there was no cause to keep them on display – and who would want to? There was no joy to be had from a collection of wooden screens designed to look like people. 'Silent companions.' At best they were absurd. But to a child, to him and Nathan anyway, they'd always appeared sinister.

This one was the very worst of the bunch: a footman with a pair of hooded brown eyes that seemed to move with your every step. Wilfred couldn't deny it was a good likeness, and that only made him hate it more. Those full lips, better suited to a woman, twisted in their habitual smirk. He could not meet its gaze.

Why the devil would the old man suffer *this* to remain in his house?

'Sir?'

He wheeled round. Young John Knowles hovered in the doorway, wearing the same livery that was painted on the wooden figure: a blue coat with yellow facings.

'What do you want?' Wilfred snapped.

The youth shifted awkwardly. 'I'm sorry, sir. I didn't mean to startle you.'

He drew in a breath, ashamed of the way he'd spoken. The boy's father had served The Bridge since time immemorial; this wasn't an insignificant lackey to be sniped at. It was just the shock of confronting that face again...

'I was *not* startled. But please try not to sneak up on people in that fashion.'

'Yes, sir.' John peered with a frown at the music stand and the gloating figure behind it. The same distaste Wilfred nursed for the thing registered on his pimpled face.

'Well?' Wilfred demanded.

John raised his brows. 'They're ready for you, sir.'

For an instant, Wilfred couldn't think what the boy meant. He'd become so lost in his investigation, he'd forgotten why he was waiting down here in his best suit to start with. 'I see. Thank you.'

Puffing out his candle, he walked past John and back into the Great Hall. The temperature must have risen in his absence. The air beneath the high, wood-beamed ceiling felt positively warm compared to that of the music room.

John helped him on with his greatcoat, hat and gloves. Wilfred was certainly dressed for the part: the new master performing his solemn duty. Why, then, did he feel like a sham? He'd thought it would be simple, that he'd been born for this, but it turned out power and status were weapons he must learn the weight of before he could wield them responsibly.

He closed his eyes briefly, saw that awful painted face again.

The door opened on a damp and musical night. Rain pattered on the gravelled drive, plopped into the swelling basin of the fountain and drummed against the roof of the old carriage. Wilfred strode through the drizzle, horribly conscious of the hearse at the front of the procession. The coffin and pall would be drenched.

He took sole possession of the mourning coach. The old man hadn't used his carriage for years, and it showed. There were threadbare patches in the pea-green upholstery. It was just as well that his father hadn't been a popular figure for Wilfred would be ashamed to invite others to ride in this contraption, to squirm uncomfortably on the lumpen squabs and hear the grinding of the wheels as they moved. The whole thing was damnably ill-sprung. It bumped him from side to side like a weaver's shuttle.

At least the journey was not far. On another day, another occasion, he could have walked across the grand stone bridge and taken the road that ran alongside the river, sheltered by chestnut, larch and elm. But it was as well to start as he meant to go on: with dignity. He must show people he was the master now.

Silver needles of rain flashed before the carriage lights. By the time they neared the village of Fayford, it was lashing mercilessly at the trees. Given the weather, he'd not expected to see any tenants watching the coffin pass, but there they were, shadowy figures gathered at the doors to their broken-down cottages. The old man may not have been beloved, yet he'd managed to engender the respect that comes from fear, enforcing the Game Act to its full extent.

Wilfred felt a stab of misgiving. There were so many of them and he was just one man. A sudden, desperate longing for Nathan burnt in his chest. He should have invited his brother to attend the ceremony, or at the very least sought him out and informed him of the death...

The wheels bumped over a rut. Wilfred jolted in his seat, and the motion seemed to shake him out of his panic too. He was being ridiculous. He'd spent his boyhood here, the villagers must *know* he was not cut from the same cloth as the old man, and if they didn't, he'd soon show them. He would show them even now, by his deportment at the service.

All Souls Church was an ancient affair. As they drew closer, he saw the original wooden spire reaching up into patchy moonlight. Little had changed from the days of his youth. The place was slightly more worn, perhaps, but that was only becoming for a venerable building. He'd expected worse after seeing the state of the cottages. Yet whatever his father had skimped on, it clearly wasn't the upkeep of the church.

Knowles opened the door, an umbrella poised. Wilfred climbed out and stood silently beside his manservant. The church's incumbent, Mr Chapman, did not reside in the parish. He'd made the journey down especially for this occasion and stood beneath the dripping lychgate, looking thoroughly disgruntled.

How sad it was that no one truly wanted to be here. The old man had died unloved, scarcely mourned except for show. Relatives had declined to travel down and attend the service. Even the pallbearers unloading the coffin were hired hands, no connection to the dead at all. Wilfred felt a sliver of shame. Could matters have been different? Would the villagers have liked his father any better if it had never happened?

'Are you ready, sir?' Knowles asked kindly. He was a good fellow, had been from the very start. Wilfred couldn't remember The Bridge without old Knowles.

'One is never ready for this,' Wilfred admitted. 'And it doesn't seem right, does it, squirrelling him away under the cover of darkness like this?'

Knowles pressed his lips together. 'It's for the best, sir,' he ventured.

Perhaps he was right.

The coffin was ready for its final journey. Without a word to Wilfred, the vicar set off down the grave-lined path towards his church. More villagers were huddled behind the low walls, watching. Their silence, their very stillness, seemed to pose a threat.

Wilfred let his gaze travel across them, wondering if he would recognise any faces from his youth. He didn't. The night was too dark, too wet, to make out individuals. They were one solid mass, unflinching beneath the rain. He hated how they stood on the fringes, as if they dared not cross the boundary into holy ground.

He'd make the past up to them somehow. He *would*. When his own time came to be interred here, the villagers would truly grieve.

He began the slow shuffle towards the church. For the first time that night, the moon broke wholly free from the clouds, lighting a man who hovered at the edge of the graveyard. Something about him was unpleasantly familiar. Although he'd removed his cap and held it clutched before him in both hands, there was no humility in his expression. It *leered*.

Wilfred's feet stumbled.

'Sir?' Knowles caught his arm, surprisingly strong for his years. 'Careful there. It's slippery in the wet.'

Wilfred righted himself, hoping no one had noticed. 'Yes, yes, thank you, Knowles.'

He searched for the man again but there was only a patch of compressed grass where he'd stood. That face... It had the same full lips, the same heavy-lidded eyes, as Wilfred had just seen, painted on the wooden companion.

CHAPTER 3

'Mamma, look! Sheep! Baby sheep! *Lambs.*' Freddy pressed his nose flat against the window, excited breath misting the glass. 'Baaa!' he bleated.

Belinda laughed. The glee on her son's face made up for two days of arduous travel, stopping only briefly at insanitary staging inns. It was even worth the inconvenience of urinating into a Bourdaloue when the baby bounced on her bladder.

'I see them, sweetheart. Perhaps Sawyer can add some lambs to the picture she is drawing for you?'

'Doing it even as we speak, ma'am.' Rather than gazing out of the window for reference, Sawyer's eye remained fixed on the sun-splashed piece of paper before her, conjuring a landscape from memory and invention. It was a marvel she could keep her hand so steady, with no stray lines or patches where the pencil had pressed too hard. Belinda couldn't even read in the carriage; it made her feel sick.

Instead, she looked up to the powder-blue sky and its fluffy clouds, so reminiscent of Freddy's sheep. Fine weather had blessed their journey: another good omen. Her spirits rose. All her life she'd envied her brothers as they set off for exotic climes with Papa, leaving her behind to mind their mother, and returned with thrilling tales to tell. Next time they met, she may have some stories of her own.

'How far away are we now?' Freddy demanded.

'Close enough,' she said, trying to remember. 'Not far until Torbury St Jude and from there we are on the home stretch.'

Home. It was strange to think of The Bridge by that name. Nowhere she'd lived in her twenty-six years had truly felt like a home. Her father's house had been a penance to escape at every opportunity, whilst Wilfred's establishment was her first testing ground. But she *had* proved herself worthy of his choice, hadn't she? She'd managed that household, provided an heir, and now there was another on the way. Perhaps The Bridge really could be the home she'd pictured when playing with her dolls as a girl.

Freddy fell back from the window and snuggled against her. 'Will we see Papa again soon?'

'Yes, love. I'm sure he has missed you very much.'

These past days could not have been easy for Wilfred, burying a parent and putting the estate into order. At least her arrival would provide him with a helper. She remembered the first time Papa had brought Wilfred home to dinner, dressed in a green velvet suit and formal bag wig. Papa's voice had purred warm against her ear. 'You'd be aligned with an ancient family, my gal, landed gentry through and through. One day that young buck will inherit an estate, and you'd be lady of his manor.'

Now it had come to pass.

But she was under no illusions about the quality of that manor. It would need elbow-grease, as Sawyer would say, to make it liveable. After they passed through the medieval market town of Torbury St Jude with all its bustle and colour, the landscape fell into a state of decline. The fields, bare of any crop, were edged by broken hedgerows. Less livestock grazed. Even the road was derelict, jolting them about as the wheels cast up stone chippings. Freddy giggled as if on a merry-go-round.

Sawyer was forced finally to put her pencil away. 'What an adventure, young master! Come, sit with me and give your mother some space.'

Belinda clenched the strap beside her seat with one hand and tried to keep her belly steady with the other. The last thing she needed was for her waters to break in the carriage. Yet Sawyer was right; it *did* feel like an adventure. There was even beauty in the untamed foliage outside. While the weeds were messy, they were thriving, every shade of green imaginable.

Slowly, they rumbled through Fayford, the little village that served the estate. That, too, was in dire need of work. But once the cottages were rethatched, the bracken cut back and a few of the walls repaired, Belinda saw no reason why it couldn't be a charming place, so close by the river.

Sawyer had not visited before. The sight seemed to strike her differently. She gazed out of the window and frowned. 'Where is everyone?'

'How do you mean?'

'It's a village. Don't you think it strange that there are no carts, no people walking to and fro? If it weren't for the smoke coming out of the chimneys, I'd say this place was deserted.'

Belinda hadn't considered that. Everywhere seemed quiet and subdued to her compared with London. 'Perhaps they are all out working the land?' she suggested. But there had been no obvious signs of cultivation.

Freddy drew their attention away. 'We're going over a bridge now! Look at the big stone lions!' His blue eyes widened. 'I never saw water run so fast, Mamma! If I made a paper boat, would the current carry it all the way out to sea? Like one of Grandpa's ships?'

'Well, perhaps we shall try it.'

'Maybe Papa will teach me how to swim?'

Sawyer spluttered a laugh. 'Not in a current that fast, Master Freddy. I bet the water's cold too. You'd be all goosebumps!' She affected a dramatic shiver and he squealed with glee.

Once they passed over the water, it was a nobler scene, with the old deserted gatehouse and the hills that tumbled down, down towards the manor. No decay or passage of time could mar that Jacobean edifice. It remained impressive, formidable, like a grand old dower who refused to die.

Belinda drew her shoulders back. 'Do you see it, Freddy? That huge house is your home now.' She couldn't keep the pride from her voice. Those born with noble blood would never experience this sense of elevation, of floating a little above the ground.

Sawyer sat straighter in her seat to look. 'Well, I'll be,' she muttered.

A lantern tower drew the eye first; tall and imposing. Beneath that came the gable roof and rows of glittering windows, not a single one boarded over to avoid the tax. The main entrance was a massive, iron-studded door, more suited to a castle keep, flanked by matching wings to either side. Each terminated in an ivy-coated turret. Trees curved beyond, holding the manor in a gently cupped hand, but Belinda was not studying them. Her eyes sought the parterres before the house; shallower soil where she could plant her own roots.

Freddy was beside himself. 'It's giant!' he gasped. 'Big enough for a – a – an elephant! Like we saw at the Tower, Sawyer.'

Sawyer cocked her head. 'Actually, I think it's a good deal bigger than the pen they assigned to that poor elephant in the menagerie.'

'Then maybe he can come and stay here with us instead!'

Belinda let their chatter fade from her ears. She was the artist now, studying her canvas. Her own grounds at last. Where would she start? Nothing too tall should be planted in front of the house, for it would be a pity to spoil that prospect over the hills. Nor did she want to skew the careful symmetry. It would be better to repair the formal hedges and weave patterns using box and cherry laurel. Here could be the edging plants, prim- roses, pinks and London-pride.

Out the side and round the back would be a differ- ent story. The wildflowers would be better suited there, winding in a pretty little wilderness towards the orchard. She'd make herself quick-draining shrubberies for the winter, full of benches and serpentine paths.

Gravel crunched as the wheels began to slow and the carriage arched around the sweep. Dragging her eyes from the gardens, Belinda caught sight of a mullioned window at the very end of the west wing. The same prickles ran over her skin as before, a sensation she'd forgotten in her absence. Had *that* been the room? She thought it was. The very casement she'd spent days lingering by with newborn Freddy in her arms. A ghost of her past self seemed to be gazing down at the very spot where they were now drawing to a halt.

'There's a dog on the fountain!' Freddy cried. 'Can *we* get a dog now we live in the country?'

Belinda turned to face him, put on her best smile. 'A moment ago you wanted an elephant. You must make up your mind which it is to be before you ask Papa.'

Whatever unease she felt, she was determined to leave the carriage as if she belonged here. Hours of deportment lessons and that tedious elocution tutor had all been building to this: the irreversible twining of her merchant blood with the Bainbridge lineage.

Creswell, one of the few servants who had accompanied them, opened the door, let down the steps and handed her out of the vehicle. A light breeze soughed through the ivy and rippled the tinkling water of the fountain. Belinda inhaled. The air here tasted different from London, seasoned with greenery – it was almost herbal. Freddy tumbled out behind her and Sawyer followed him. The maid's eyes skirted around the edges of the house. It was difficult to tell if she was committing its lines to memory in preparation for a sketch, or trying to locate every possible exit.

They had scarcely taken five paces before hinges creaked and the huge main door grated open. Wilfred himself appeared on the threshold and trotted quickly down the steps, ready to catch up Freddy who dashed towards him.

'Ho, there! Look at this boy!' He swung his son into the air. 'Look at the size of him! What's this? A trick? I thought they were bringing my son Fred!'

'It *is* me!' Freddy squealed in delight. 'I'm Freddy.'

Wilfred affected astonishment. 'No! It's not possible. Why, this boy is big enough for breeches. He's big enough for his own horse!'

Freddy threw back his head and shrieked with glee.

Breeching, already? The idea of shearing off those long golden curls, of making Freddy into a tiny man… But she was thinking weakly, smothering him like her own mother had done to her. She must let him grow up.

At last Wilfred set Freddy down. The boy trotted off to dip his fingers in the fountain, while Wilfred took Belinda's hand and kissed it. 'My love, I beg your pardon. I am abominably rude to keep you standing out here while we lark. You must be fatigued.'

In truth she was flagging, but she hoisted up a smile. If she admitted to tiredness, he might hustle her back into that old suite of rooms with its four-poster bed, where she'd languished before. 'On the contrary, I am keen to make a start. I have so much to discuss with Mrs Knowles.'

'In time, in time. Take a moment,' he urged, drawing her arm solicitously under his own. 'Tell me, how was your journey? I fear those roads must have given you a good shake – but they will be set to rights. I promise. I will put everything right.'

'I came to no harm.'

He smiled upon her. His bearing reminded her of their wedding day: pride radiated from every pore. 'That's the spirit. Now come, I want you to savour this special moment. You are about to enter The Bridge for the first time as its rightful mistress. Are you ready?' She nodded. He helped her up the steps into the house, pushing open the huge door and making a flourish with his spare hand as the Great Hall unfolded before them. 'Mrs Bainbridge – welcome to your true home.'

It was far more imposing than Belinda remembered: a scene from Horace Walpole's novel, full of medieval grandeur. Weapons were displayed upon the walls: great fans of gleaming swords that warned, rather than welcomed, a visitor. The stone floor was set with lozenges; the ceiling was high and beamed. A gallery looked down from above.

Freddy, who was too young to recall any of this, turned around and around, his mouth a perfect circle.

The iron grate of the fireplace yawned empty in deference to the mild weather. All the doors leading to other rooms were firmly shut. But three servants hovered in the far corner, beneath the shadow of the staircase. They must be the Knowles family she had heard so much about. Belinda made the calculation in her head. Three Knowleses, Sawyer, the footman Creswell, Wilfred's valet Hurley and the driver-cum-groom Dawkins. Seven live-in staff. It was enough, but male-heavy. She would prefer more maids.

'Ah, yes,' said Wilfred, 'here are the Knowleses, come to pay their respects to you. You must remember them from before. See how young John has grown!'

The youth flushed. He was an awkward, gangly boy with bad skin. Belinda took care to receive his bow kindly and comment on what a fine lad he'd become, but she had little recollection of him or his parents. Had her mind been so badly disordered, following Freddy's birth? It alarmed her to think so.

Knowles Senior was older than she'd remembered – a good deal older than his wife. But his advanced years made him seem reliable, rather than frail, with his bob wig and stalwart figure. Mrs Knowles' only defining feature was her harassed expression – understandable, given the lack of female attendants to help her. She and Belinda had been corresponding already.

'It is good to see you face-to-face,' she said, as Mrs Knowles curtsied. 'We have much to arrange between us.'

'Yes, we do, madam.'

Despite her exhaustion and swollen ankles, Belinda found herself relishing the idea of a challenge. She would not be powerless here, as she'd been in her mother's house, or overawed by a strict housekeeper like Mrs Marsh. The reins were hers to hold.

Mrs Knowles glanced surreptitiously over Belinda's shoulder. She turned and saw Sawyer lingering there. 'Oh – yes. Mrs Knowles, this is my...' She had to stop herself. If she were at liberty to be honest, the words would flow easily enough. *This is Sawyer, my dearest friend. You will respect her as if she were my deputy.* But society muddied the waters, made her draw lines where none should be. 'Sawyer. My – my lady's maid. Although she is helping with Freddy too, at the moment,' Belinda explained haltingly. 'Sawyer performs a variety of roles, she – well, she is invaluable. I mentioned her in my letters. She's served my family for many years. As you have served the Bainbridge family.'

Mrs Knowles nodded calmly, as if Belinda had not embarrassed herself and blushed up to the roots of her hair. 'Pleased to meet you, Miss Sawyer.'

'Likewise, Mrs Knowles.'

'Capital!' Wilfred exclaimed. 'Everyone is acquainted. Mrs Knowles, perhaps you'd be good enough to fetch my wife some refreshments. She is the picture of politeness, but I'm sure she is fit to drop after that journey.'

'Yes, sir. I'll set the tea tray.'

Sawyer stepped forward. 'I'll help. You can show me around the kitchen.'

Belinda wished her maid would stay with her.

'As for me,' Wilfred went on, 'I have a good deal of catching up to do with my son.' He turned and swept Freddy into his arms again. 'What do you say, my boy? Shall we look over the house? This will all be yours one day. What shall I show you first?'

Freddy didn't respond. He was staring fixedly at a point on the far wall.

Belinda followed his gaze. There was nothing much to catch his eye, only a small divot in the panelling. 'I think he's looking at the weapons?' she guessed.

Wilfred adjusted his son in his hold. 'Well, they're antiques, Freddy, every one of them. The swords were always my favourite, when I was your age.'

Rather than answering, the child pointed, making duelling pistols of his fingers. 'Bang,' he said softly. 'Bang, bang.'

Wilfred paled.

Freddy was aiming at the bullet mark on the wall.

*

By the time Belinda retired to her old suite of rooms in the west wing, she was too exhausted to fret over the unpleasant memories they inspired. The baby had been pummelling her insides without mercy. Her head still teemed with the menus and laundry lists she'd discussed with Mrs Knowles. To recline on a chaise-longue – any chaise-longue – would be bliss.

Yet she chose to sit in the little dressing-room, rather than entering the bedroom proper. There was still a reluctance to cross that threshold, even if it offered her a washstand and the chance to lie flat. Foolish, really. There was little difference between the two chambers: both were decorated with pale paper, slightly worn carpets and floral embroidery. If anything, the bedroom offered more space and light. But it had never *felt* light. That was the trouble. Like Mamma's parlour, the air was suffused with invisible weight. As Belinda allowed her head to nod, she could almost feel it, thrumming through the closed door.

There was a scent, too. Something powdery that teased at the edges of her consciousness, something familiar that should be pleasant, but cloyed instead. Roses.

Maybe Mrs Knowles had put out a vase of them to welcome her. A flower to associate with the bedroom furniture, which was all made of rosewood, from the dressing-table to the carved four-poster bed. An expensive timber. Belinda should know. But she didn't appreciate it as she should. It was too dark, too lowering.

Her eyelids had shut without her noticing. She felt herself drifting, unmooring. A scene began to play in her mind, but she couldn't tell if it was a memory or a dream. She was lying upon that bed, her hands pressed over her ears, her body still. But the flowers carved on the posts were beginning to wilt. Petals sagging, releasing a sickly-sweet tang. Vines slithering down towards the floor. Inch by inch, the tester was getting lower. A canopy slowly descending to smother her.

Hiss.

Belinda jerked awake.

'My love? Are you asleep?' There was a tap at the door.

She pulled herself upright. It must have been Wilfred's knocking that woke her. Yet it had sounded like something else…

'Belinda?'

She found her voice. 'Yes, come in.'

He entered softly and, seeing her position, grimaced in sympathy. 'Forgive my intrusion. Have they over-taxed you, dearest? I shall leave you in peace, my news can wait.'

She shook her head. The last thing she wanted was to be left alone, free to drift into more troubling dreams.

'No, do not go. We have not spoken properly in weeks. Sit down. You must wish to tell me how the funeral went.'

'Pfft!' He made a dismissive gesture with his hand. 'Every funeral is the same, Bel. I've no desire to bore you with details of that. Rather, I have a surprise for you.'

'A surprise?'

He grinned like a boy. 'The nursery. I fitted it up, as promised.'

'In so short a time?'

He nodded eagerly. 'I have not taken Freddy up there yet. I thought you might like to see it first.'

'Well... yes. I would love to.'

Wilfred's kindness often took her aback. Her father and brothers never stinted on their gifts, yet they gave her the kind of presents you could buy for any lady, on the assumption that the most expensive item must be the best. Wilfred listened to what she *wanted*. Selected not just specific items to please her, but performed acts of service too. He viewed her in a way only Sawyer had before: as an individual.

Taking Wilfred's offered hand, she squeezed it, hoping to convey the feelings she was never quite able to articulate.

'It's in the east wing, I'm afraid, but we'll go slowly.'

With the help of his hand and the chaise-longue, she managed to climb to her feet. They throbbed with their own pulse. She leant her weight on her husband's arm as they shuffled out of her suite of rooms and into the corridor. The walls here were covered in red flock paper. She watched the repeating pattern, relieved to see it held firm. After Freddy was born, she'd had a notion of these walls running like wax – but as Wilfred said, it would be different this time. *She* was different. Back then she had been so young, married for less than a year, still a conduit for her mother's fears.

They approached the stairs leading down. 'Wilfred,' she started.

He stopped, one hand on the banister. 'Yes?'

'If the nursery is in the east wing... ought I not to be a little closer to it? Maybe we could swap suites of rooms? Then I'd be in easier reach.'

He considered, brows raised to the line of his wig. 'That did not occur to me. I've set myself up in the old man's rooms over these past weeks, but belongings can be moved. Yes, why not? It makes sense, doesn't it? I'll tell Knowles.'

Belinda beamed. Now she would be liberated from that tainted room and all its memories from five years ago. This would be a new start.

They hobbled downstairs together, gradually coming within sight of the gallery overlooking the Great Hall. Faded tapestry sofas were positioned at intervals along the wall where one could sit and admire the splendour below. Sawyer occupied the nearest of these. A few steps further down, their view widened and they could see Freddy pressed against the gallery's handrail, peering down at the drop to the stone floor.

'Good God.'

Belinda stumbled as Wilfred yanked his arm from hers and leapt the remaining stairs. He sped past a startled Sawyer to snatch up his son.

'Ouch! Papa, put me down!'

But Wilfred didn't listen. He was deadly pale. 'What were you thinking?' he snapped at the maid. 'I told you to watch him!'

Sawyer rose warily to her feet. 'Sir... I *was* watching him.'

'I daresay you would sit there and *watch* him dash his brains out! I meant *supervise* him. Don't you know—' The stairs gave a creak as Belinda slowly edged down them. Wilfred stopped to glance at her. He was still clutching Freddy too tightly, but the sight of his wife seemed to steady him. 'No,' he said dully, closing his eyes. 'Of course, you do *not* know. I forgot you are new here.' He cleared his throat. 'Sawyer, these railings are very old. They are not firm. A person once fell from up here.'

Her eyes widened. 'I understand, sir. I will keep Master Freddy away from them, going forward.'

He nodded, regaining his breath. 'Please do.'

Belinda had never seen him so agitated. 'It's all right,' she said softly. 'Freddy has come to no harm. Why not set him down now?'

Swallowing, Wilfred put the child on his feet. 'I'm sorry, my boy. I did not mean to scare you.' He ruffled Freddy's curls. Wilfred's own wig sat slightly askew after the dash. 'But you must be careful up here. I don't want you to hurt yourself.'

Freddy pouted at him. 'It was the *other* side.'

'I beg your pardon?'

The boy ran his little fingers across the balustrades, making hollow music. 'It's fine here. *This* side didn't break.'

Wilfred blinked. 'What do you – how would you...'

Turning from his father, Freddy ran towards Belinda and hid his face in her skirts.

The peculiarities of children. No doubt Freddy spoke at random, making up a story to excuse himself, but she could see from Wilfred's expression that he had hit upon the truth. The fall must have happened on the other side of the gallery.

She patted Freddy on the back. 'There, now. It doesn't matter what happened before. We must do as Papa tells us *today*. You'll be careful to heed him in future, won't you? You won't lean on any rails.'

'But—' Wilfred stuttered. 'Why would he say—'

Belinda didn't know how to answer him. She bent down to her son, keen to change the subject. 'Freddy, Papa just told me that he has a surprise for us both. Can you guess what it is? He's decorated your nursery in the latest fashion and everything is brand spanking new. Would you like to come and see it with us now?'

Freddy peeped out from behind the folds of her bombazine gown. 'Yes.' Then hesitantly, 'May I, Papa?'

Wilfred straightened his wig, adjusted the stock at his neck. He still looked vaguely dazed. 'Certainly. Yes, let's leave this place at once.'

Sawyer followed behind them, her head bowed. Belinda hoped she wasn't smarting from the undeserved reprimand. Wilfred had simply been frightened.

Belinda's written instructions for the nursery had been minimal and to the point, but when Wilfred pushed the door open onto a bright and cheerful room, she saw that he'd considered her taste in every particular. Yellow paper with a cowslip pattern covered the walls. The carpet was thick enough to keep little feet warm on a winter's morning and a folding screen hid the fire from reaching hands. A new bedstead, far larger than the one in London, was made up fresh with an eiderdown coverlet.

But of course Freddy charged, squealing, straight to the rocking horse at the centre of the room.

'Look! Papa really *did* get me my own horse!' The toy was at least twice the size of him, shining with new paint. Real horsehair, white as snow, flowed from the mane and tail. Dapple grey had been chosen for the coat. Every detail, from the large soulful eyes to the snorting nostrils, was surprisingly lifelike.

She smiled. 'Aren't you a lucky boy?'

Freddy hitched up his skirts and tried to climb on. The horse pitched forward, bumping on its green rockers.

'Hold on a moment, little man. Here we are.' Wilfred scooped him up and sat him in the saddle. Pure rapture shone from Freddy's face. 'Let me adjust these stirrups, then I will show you how to hold the reins.'

While they played, Belinda turned her attention to the rest of the room. There was a wardrobe and plenty of space to unpack the toys Freddy had brought with him from London. Over in the corner stood a shortened table and chairs where he could take his meals with the nursemaid, when they hired one. But there was something else she did not expect to see: a crib. It must have cost Wilfred a small fortune.

She moved to take a closer look. The bassinette hung on a walnut frame at about waist-height, exactly the kind of design she liked, all smooth lines and unspoiled grain. Lemon dimity curtains cascaded from a peaked hood. The inside was piled high with lace, silk cushions and new linen, which Belinda picked up to inspect. Starch crackled beneath her fingertips. Perfect.

Wilfred must have remembered how she'd loathed the dark old cradle that had been fetched down from the attic when Freddy was born. How reluctant she'd been to set their baby in the shadow of that high headboard. It felt like interring him in a coffin.

Sawyer touched her shoulder. 'Ma'am?'

Belinda started. 'Oh! I was lost in my thoughts.'

'I asked if I am to sleep in here, for the time being?'

'Yes – I think it would be best for you to stay with Freddy, if you do not object? The applicants Mrs Knowles found for the nursemaid's position do seem promising, but I will not be making any hasty engagements until I've had an opportunity to vet them myself.'

'Oh, I don't mind filling in for a little longer,' Sawyer enthused. 'It's always a pleasure for me to spend time with the young master.' She looked indulgently over to where Freddy was still giggling, rocking back and forth with Wilfred's steadying hand upon his back.

Belinda surveyed the space around them. 'There should be room to set up a truckle bed for you, or...' She trailed off as she saw another door on the far wall. 'Wilfred, what is through there? Is that a closet for the nursemaid?'

He glanced up briefly. 'No, it's my old schoolroom. I'm afraid I haven't set to work in there quite yet. Sit straighter, Freddy. Heels down. There's a boy.'

'May I look?'

'Of course. It might be in a sorry state. I told the fellows decorating in here that they could use it for storage.'

Belinda crossed towards the schoolroom with Freddy's gleeful laughter ringing in her ears. Yet as she passed the rocking horse, her skin prickled. There was gooseflesh on her arms. She stopped.

Sawyer noticed her hesitate. 'Do you need me to get the door for you, ma'am?' Gliding past, she applied herself to the heavy iron ring. The door opened slowly, letting a wave of hot, sickly-sweet air roll out.

Belinda stepped forward to peek inside. She experienced a sudden plunging sensation, like missing a stair. 'Oh!'

The rocking horse bumped to a halt. 'What's the matter?' Wilfred demanded. 'Bel?'

'Nothing – nothing is wrong,' she faltered, still staring in. And it wasn't, precisely. Not *wrong* – only strange.

Light fell in blades across the panelled schoolroom. Once, there must have been a display of ferns hanging in the window but they had long since withered, leaving bare tendrils and brittle leaves upon the floor.

A chalkboard stood to the right. Facing it were four desks. Each one was occupied. Painted figures stared unblinking from where children should sit. Three girls and a boy, all as tall as Freddy, but compressed, like ancient portraits cut free from their frames.

Wilfred arrived behind them with Freddy writhing discontentedly in his arms. 'Oh, Lord, so *that's* where they put the confounded things. I thought we'd agreed on the attic.'

'But... what *are* they?' Belinda asked. Freddy's wriggling forced her to edge forward into the schoolroom to avoid his kicking feet. She had the horrible sensation that four pairs of painted eyes moved to watch her. 'I've never seen anything like them.'

The boy and a girl to the left wore plain working clothes. Their skin, their eyes, their hair and expressions, were all storm-cloud dark. But the other two looked wealthier. One was dressed almost like Freddy, in clouds of muslin and a coloured sash with leading strings hanging from her shoulders.

'Oh, these are the supposed *treasures* of our house,' Wilfred explained dryly. 'Antiques passed down as heirlooms. My mother took a particular fancy to them, she even had some of her own made. What do you think? I never cared for them myself.'

'I cannot comprehend their use. What are they *for*?'

Wilfred shrugged. 'It's all some tomfoolery from Amsterdam. You know how the Dutch love their toys. We'd use them as fire screens now and then, but my mother wanted them as decorations. As... "companions", she said.'

His focus, like Belinda's was drawn to the last girl on the right. There was something about her, even with her plain face and faded paint, some magnetism that could not be put into words. She stood taller than the others, her pile of red-brown hair set elaborately with ribbons and beads, an olive-coloured gown suggesting the fashion of a previous century. She carried a basket of roses. One white bloom was pressed against her breast. But that was not what drew you in. It was the eyes, Belinda realised. Eyes tinted green, like a cat's tracking its prey.

'My mother claimed that their faces cheered her. They do not much cheer *me*,' Wilfred admitted. 'Rather the opposite.'

All at once, the baby began to turn somersaults. As Belinda placed a hand on her belly, the movement was echoed by Freddy, who began to thrash in his father's arms. 'I want to see!'

'Now look here, Fred, this is not how a gentleman behaves.' Wilfred was forced to set him down. Freddy darted off into the schoolroom, coming to an abrupt halt before the painted boy.

'Maybe it's the same as Mrs Kipling keeping birds,' Sawyer suggested. 'Maybe these were Mrs Bainbridge's pets?'

'At least you may whistle to a bird,' Wilfred sighed. 'We once spoke of disposing of these "silent companions" entirely. It seems my father never went through with that plan. Last time I was here he said he'd move them to the attic, but I suppose he grew sentimental towards the end.'

Sawyer swallowed, flexed her hands at her sides. 'I could... carry them away, sir. If you'd like. Put them somewhere else.'

'No, no, Knowles will see to that, it's his role.'

Belinda didn't join in with their conversation. She was too busy watching Freddy as he started to weave his way around the desks, inspecting the figures. Seeing him near them scared her more than his leaning on the fragile rails of the gallery. But why should that be? They were nothing more than large, flat dolls.

Mesmerised, Freddy pressed his palm against the rose on the girl's chest. Almost as if he were feeling for a pulse. 'I want to keep them.'

'You do?' Wilfred raised an eyebrow, unenthused.

The baby's squirming was unbearable. That, combined with the scent of dead leaves and the patina of dust… Nausea rose in Belinda's throat. She needed to get out of this place.

'Come on, dearest,' she called, her voice sounding strange and squeezed. 'Let's leave your schoolroom for now until it is cleaned up.'

Freddy didn't move. He sat cross-legged at the base of the figure. The floorboards there were filthy, he'd ruin his pure white gown.

Sawyer held out a hand, trying to tempt the child. 'Do you want to come and draw with me, Master Freddy?'

No answer.

Wilfred tutted. 'Come on now, old chap, this isn't the thing at all. Do as your mother tells you. You needn't draw if you don't want to. We'll get you back up on that rocking horse, shall we?'

But Freddy only had eyes for the wooden girl, for her provocative smile.

CHAPTER 4

Wilfred strode back towards the library, convinced matters would look more promising now he'd eaten a good dinner and drunk a glass of claret. Surely there had been an oversight; he'd missed a figure or failed to locate all the relevant documents. There was no cause for alarm.

Everything remained just as he'd left it before going down to eat. His pen was still in the inkwell, his papers neatly stacked. Open curtains showed the mass of sticky buds forming on the trees outside. A stiff wind shook them back and forth.

As a child his father's library had seemed like a treasure trove, but now he noticed how shabby it was, so much smaller than his sanctuary in London. There were only half a dozen bookcases, all imprudently set into the wall opposite the windows, where daylight would fade the spines. One battered leather-bound volume had made a bid for freedom and lay splayed like a dead bird on the carpet. He picked it up as he passed, stuffing it haphazardly back on a shelf. There was only one book on his mind at present: the estate ledger. Flicking up the tails of his coat, he sat at his father's desk and scoured the pages once more.

The last few entries were in his own tidy script. Nursery decorations, funeral expenses, the money he'd put behind the bar at the local pub to drink to the memory of the deceased. Pale spring light washed over the figures and made them look stark. Even his father's spidery, crabbed writing was legible – but the numbers themselves defied comprehension. They *must* be wrong. The old man had been wandering in his mind towards the end, shooting at walls, for pity's sake.

Wilfred ran his index finger across the lines. There was a consistent pattern of mildew, blight and rot on The Bridge's crops. Rents had been raised, tenants forced to leave. Several of the farms stood vacant, earning nothing. Plans were underway to enclose all of the common land and grow wheat instead – a measure which would sap any remaining goodwill towards him left in the village. It was akin to taking food off the poorest tables. For most villagers, who held no garden of their own, it was the only area where they could graze livestock or grow a few vegetables, the only place where they could snare a rabbit without being prosecuted. But Wilfred could not see any other way to turn a profit for the estate. To say the recent harvests had been plagued by bad luck would be an understatement.

Thud.

Wilfred glanced up. The book had fallen again. Irritated, he rose and returned the volume to an empty place. Everything here was ramshackle, even the shelves.

Repairs were needed, comprehensive repairs. Yet as he flicked through the ledger, the records indicated that they'd already taken place. He frowned. That simply couldn't be true.

On Lady Day, there was an expense: *To rethatch all cottages in Fayford.* But he'd *seen* the decay there. Had the old man paid in advance? Maybe the work was due to take place soon, in the milder weather? He pulled open the drawers of the desk, searching for a letter that would explain it all.

Someone tapped at the door. The same leather-bound book swooned and plummeted to the carpet, landing with a puff of dust.

'Dash it,' Wilfred muttered. Then, louder, 'Come.'

To his surprise, Belinda appeared on the threshold. He rose to his feet as one should in the presence of a lady. 'Do I disturb you?' she asked.

'Not at all.'

She waddled into the room, one hand on the small of her back. In the other she carried her own book, bound in red Morocco. 'I thought I might sit with you and read awhile. If… if it is agreeable?'

It *was* agreeable. The type of intimacy she did not usually offer. 'Nothing would please me more. Let me find a chair for you and wipe it down.' He moved out from behind the desk. 'It's all so abominably dusty in here.'

She glanced at the shelves. 'I cannot say I'm surprised. It's such a large house with so few staff – and even now, they are mostly men. But Mrs Knowles and I have arranged for chambermaids to come by the day. You will not be forced to suffer these conditions much longer.'

'I was not passing judgement on your housekeeping.' Finding a chair, he placed it beside the window, where she could admire the trees. Belinda stooped down, trying to pick up the fallen book. 'My dear! There's no need for you to do that.' He hastened over. 'You must sit, rest. Allow me.' Snatching up the infernal book, he laid it down flat on top of a similar volume so it could topple no more. 'Come, now. The trees are all budding. You will like to sit and watch them, won't you?'

'Yes. Thank you. I confess, I am fatigued.' Belinda did not look altogether healthy as he settled her in her place – it was that penetrating spring light again, falling through the window and turning her skin to ash. 'I am not sleeping very well.'

'The room in the east wing does not agree with you after all?'

'It's not the room. The baby is restless. Its little legs are going like a prize runner.' She smiled weakly. 'Either it will be a madcap boy or a little hoyden.'

'Never fear. A man called Quigley will be calling upon us soon – I ought to have told you that before now. Fraser, my acquaintance on a neighbouring estate whom I played with as a boy, was able to send me a recommendation. Mr Quigley oversaw the lying-in of both Fraser's heirs. He's well thought of, the best in Torbury St Jude.'

Relief took possession of her features. 'That's wonderful, thank you. I don't suppose anything is amiss – just a lively child. The accoucheur in London said everything was progressing nicely. But I should like to consult someone here.'

'Of course.'

Kissing her forehead, he left her to her reading. Between his gallantry and her polite reserve, they never quite managed a meaningful conversation, but he had hopes she was coming out of her shell. He could be patient. He'd seen all too plainly how a brusque and demanding manner could alienate a husband from his wife's affections. He would not repeat his father's mistakes.

Speaking of which... He sat down at the desk again. The ledger was a testament to the old man's folly. These records of repairs made no sense. He pulled a sheaf of letters out of the bottom drawer, hoping they'd provide

clarification. There was no ribbon to tie them, no ordering system to help. He spread them open on the desk
and glanced over the contents. It took a moment for his
brain to process what he read.

This correspondence came from holy men, leaders of
nearly every faith: a rabbi, an imam, a Roman Catholic
priest, a Methodist preacher, even a pandit. He pushed
one aside, then another, lost for words. Each man wrote
of coming down to The Bridge and meeting his father.
No further details were given. The interviews must
surely have taken place, for the dates mentioned were
a good two years ago. Wilfred sat astonished. Had the
old man really known his death was coming? Was he
seeking absolution?

One of the pages was stained with brandy. His father
must have been drinking as he read it. Careless. Ominous,
too, for something in the shape of those brown splashes
reminded Wilfred of the flags in the Great Hall. His
stomach clenched.

He leafed back through the ledger to the year in question. No doubt these spiritual advisers had all extracted
a fee for their guidance... But he never found out, for his
eyes were arrested by the shortest entry of all. Simply
a name, and a sum large enough to speak volumes.
Roberts: £75.

Cuckoo.

Wilfred flinched. By the window, Belinda lowered her
book.

Cuck-oo.

'Oh, how lovely!' she cried, peering through the panes.
'Do you hear, Wilfred? The herald of summer.' She
strained her eyes but the branches were all in motion,
buffeted to and fro by the breeze. 'I wish I could see
it. How nice to listen to birds in the wild, rather than

in cages.' He must have been scowling, for when she turned to him her manner became contrite. 'My apologies. I have interrupted your train of thought.'

He closed the ledger with a snap. 'You have. But the interruption is welcome. I have taken my fill of numbers for today.' His mind was turning cartwheels. Seventy-five pounds! A huge amount to be paying, this long after the incident. He'd hoped the tempest would have settled by now but clearly that was naïve of him. He scrubbed a hand across his eyes. 'Distract me, Bel. What are you reading?'

A blush tinged his wife's cheeks. At least it put a little colour into her face. 'It is *Émile* by Rousseau.'

'Goodness. And what do you make of it?'

Belinda wet her lips. 'Well... I am only on book two. I have not reached the controversial parts. But what I have read so far rather pleases me. I like the idea Rousseau proposes of a less formal childhood. I am not saying children should be allowed to run wild... But it is – well, it is very different from the manner in which I grew up.'

He nodded, trying to focus on what she was saying. 'Yes, I can imagine.'

'Though it was worse for my brothers. They had the strictest teacher. Poor Luke was always being caned for one thing or another, and my father didn't protest. He said it did a boy good to be whipped on occasion.' She grimaced. 'But what about you? You had the run of the grounds here, did you not, when you were not at school? That must have been extremely pleasant.'

'Indeed it was. We were hardly in the house at all...' *We*. That was how it had been, in those days. There was not a single memory without Nathan or Tiffany attached. He could picture the gardens now, dappled by sunlight as they always seemed to be during his childhood. Crab apples on the trees, too sour to eat. Weeds that stuck, scratched or stung by turn. That winding path to the kitchen garden and the well… He cleared his throat, recommenced. 'My boyhood years were good ones, in the main. But as it turned out, we were allowed a little too *much* freedom in this family. We ought to have been watched more closely.'

This time the flush crept into Belinda's neck too. 'I'm so sorry,' she gabbled. 'I was not thinking, I should not have said—'

He waved a hand. 'Never mind. I know you were not speaking of my sister. My past is complicated. Full of thorns.' He pursed his lips, thinking. 'But Freddy's childhood will be different. What shall we do about a tutor for him? We will be in mourning until the winter at least. Perhaps he could simply spend this summer learning through his playtime adventures, conducting natural experiments like Émile in your book? Heaven knows, we will have enough to do between us, settling in and welcoming the new baby. More formal education can wait.'

Belinda brightened. Shadows from the branches outside waved over her puffy face. 'I might interest him in botany, when I replant the gardens.'

'Yes, why not? Next year will be time enough for employing tutors and launching ourselves into local society. This summer can be for us. Our family.'

Their eyes met. There was a spark, an affinity, something approaching true connection between them. Wilfred felt his lips curving in a smile. Then the book fell from the shelf.

Belinda's gaze ripped away. 'Oh! There it goes again.'

But how? Hadn't he laid it down flat? He was about to rise but Belinda had already climbed to her feet. 'My dear, do not trouble yourself to pick it up, not in your condition.'

'It is no bother. The baby is impatient for me to move. And I did want to take a look at the books your family had collected.' For all Belinda's brave words, she seemed to struggle across the room and could not bend down when she arrived at the shelves. She was forced to brace her legs and squat in a comical fashion before she could reach the fallen tome. Straightening slowly, she flicked through the opening pages. 'This one appears to be quite ancient!'

'It will probably fall apart in your hands.'

'It seems to be... a diary. Owned by Anne Bainbridge. An ancestor of yours, my dear?'

Wilfred baulked. 'Impossible! Our family would not use *that* name again. Is it dated?'

Belinda leafed through the handwritten pages, her head bent. 'Yes, but you will hardly credit it. Sixteen thirty-five! So long ago. The reign of... King Charles I, was it not?'

'Good God.' It was almost a spasm that made him surge from his chair and stride towards her. 'Why would they keep such a thing? Give it to me, Belinda. That should not be in here. The contents can only distress you.'

Puzzlement creased her brow, but she passed the book over.

Now Wilfred knew what it contained, the cover seemed to tingle, alive with contamination. Grimacing, he laid it back on the shelf and piled other volumes on top of it for good measure.

'Wilfred... I do not understand.'

He stopped. Her face was turned up to his, expect-ant, reasonable. It made him feel rather boorish. 'No. Forgive me. I daresay I am overreacting, but Anne

Bainbridge was our most infamous ancestor. We have spent over a hundred years trying to erase her legacy. She is best forgotten.'

'Why? What did she do?'

He hesitated. Right now Belinda seemed so calm, but he could not forget how she had been just after Freddy was born: afraid of her own shadow. She'd locked the door to her rooms and refused to come out until her Churching ceremony. Of course, there had been extenuating circumstances. The child had arrived early and nothing had been ready. Sawyer had not accompanied them, so Belinda was a first-time mother quite alone. It was not her fault. Even a lady with nerves of steel could succumb to melancholy in childbed.

'Anne's tale is hardly fit for a lady,' he explained. 'Let alone one in your condition.'

'Do you think I shall swoon?' She smiled, playful. 'I promise to keep my composure, Wilfred.'

It was hard to resist her. She was bound to find out one way or another; if not from him, then from the servants. Perhaps it was better that he did say something. 'Well... The fact of the matter is, Anne Bainbridge was burnt as a witch.'

Belinda took the news more calmly than he would have supposed. She only frowned. '*Burnt*? It was my understanding that the punishment for witchcraft used to be hanging.'

How did she know that? She never failed to surprise him. 'Anne's case was... peculiar. There were numerous charges,' he said equivocally.

'But surely *you* do not believe in such things, Wilfred? You cannot be afraid of her?'

He spread his hands. 'No. I do not credit Anne Bainbridge with evil powers. That is all faradiddle. But there can be no doubt she was a truly wicked woman. Her trial was not the usual story of a healer taken to task over a neighbourhood feud. The charges against Anne were… substantial. I would not care for you, or anyone I love, to read words written by such a dark mind as hers.'

'Gracious! Would it be prying to ask what, precisely, her crimes were? You are awfully cryptic.'

'Delicate,' he corrected her.

The problem was, this was such an old, old house. There were tales of woe enough from Wilfred's lifetime alone. The stories had seldom bothered him, but Belinda had been kept so damnably close. Fed on a diet of her mother's fears and sailors' yarns. He did not wish to excite her imagination at so fragile a time.

She placed a hand on his arm and squeezed. 'Very well. Keep your dreadful little secrets. But do not forget that I am a Bainbridge too, now. It is my family story as well as yours.'

Through her wrapping gown, he could make out the shape of a tiny foot, pressing underneath his wife's skin. New life, amidst all these records of death and decay. Hope.

'This house has a sad history, Bel, but both you and I know that need not be how it ends. We will change things for the better. Together.' Hesitantly, he gathered her into his arms. 'It will be your work as much as it is mine. *Ours.* The future is ours.'

Belinda relaxed against him. He rested his cheek on her pinner cap and the soft blonde hair beneath. The moment was sweet. It would have been perfect, except for the noise at the edge of his consciousness.

A call – low and insistent, galling in its constancy.

The blasted cuckoo again.

CHAPTER 5

Belinda had dressed the part of a lady-botanist in her green apron and a chip hat with a trailing veil. Viewed from behind lace, the gardens appeared gauzy, as if caught in a cloud of mist. Ivy-clad walls, a derelict well, patches of nettles and dandelion clocks. There would be room for all the specimens she could dream of out here, unlike her cramped London plot.

But first she would need to clear some space. The rectangular flowerbeds were a mess, choked up with thistles, their amethyst florets peeping over spikes of green. Only one bed had escaped contagion; it yawned bare, the soil slightly heaped, like an oversized burial plot.

A door opened and closed. Turning her head, Belinda saw Sawyer, John Knowles and Freddy, who was hurtling towards her from the house. 'Mamma!'

Her son appeared a different child. His long curls were tied back in a queue. He wore his first coat over a frilly, open-necked shirt and pantaloons made of nankeen. 'Look, I'm dressed almost like a gentleman! Papa says I look "all the crack".' He jolted into her legs, threw his arms about her knees.

'Goodness! So you do.' Her heart twanged to see her baby looking so grown up, but it made sense. If Freddy was going to be riding rocking horses and enjoying the outdoors, it was time to leave his infant's skirts behind. 'Well then, my little gentleman. Are you ready to learn about plants?'

He pulled a face. 'I'd rather play with my hoop. May I?'

Belinda sighed. He didn't know his own luck. She would have loved this opportunity as a child: to be out in the air, seeing actual plants instead of staring at illustrations. 'Not just now, dear. It's important you attend to your lessons.'

Sawyer arrived beside them with a clatter of wood. Belinda glanced over and recoiled. 'Why on earth have you brought *that* out here? I thought they were destined for the attic.'

It was one of the companions: the fey girl with her hair piled up and a rose pressed to her chest. Outside in the budding spring, she looked more ancient and drab than ever. Sunlight exposed every crack and peel in the dull paintwork.

'The young master insisted on keeping them,' Sawyer explained. 'He wouldn't even come outside until I agreed to bring this one along.'

Freddy bent down and began plucking at blades of grass. 'She gets cross if I leave her alone. She wants company.'

Belinda met Sawyer's eye. The maid grinned indulgently, and she tried to smile back. Children *did* have these fancies, imaginary friends and so forth. But why did Freddy have to pick such a wretched object? 'Well, we cannot have her getting in the way of the gardening. Where shall we put her?'

'She wants to go by the well,' Freddy declared.

'All right, the well it is.' Sawyer set off. Belinda watched her progress, taking in the nettles at the base of the structure, the rusted chain, the boards nailed over the mouth. Surely that couldn't be *the* well...? Shuddering, she turned away.

John made his way over with a more welcome cargo: spades and dibbers, billhooks and shears. Last of all, he wheeled a small barrow containing her order of young plants from Torbury St Jude. The April earth should be warm enough to plant them. In a few weeks they'd make a carefree riot of colour with tall lupins, delicate iris, bright bursts of Sweet William and spires of mignonette.

'Come and see these, Freddy.' Taking his hand, Belinda pulled him over to the barrow and pointed out some young columbines. As yet, the buds were only dangling berries. 'Do you see the colours emerging?' She teased the leaves apart and found one beginning to unpeel. 'They'll be lovely colours. Violet and blue.'

'Do they grow *down*?' Freddy asked. 'Not up?'

'Yes, the flowers hang. They are called Granny's Bonnet for that reason. But they also have a Latin name. You will learn Latin, when you are older.'

'What's the Latin name?'

'*Aquilegia vulgaris*. Do you think you can say that?' Freddy parroted her with perfect accuracy. 'Well done!'

He prodded at a bud with his index finger. It swung like a tiny bell.

'So many flies!' Sawyer cut in, returning from the well. She batted a hand in front of her face. 'Swarming all over those purple, spiked flowers. What are they – thistles?'

'The creeping thistle,' Belinda told her. 'A weed. They have a thick and complex root system, hard to eradicate. But we must try.'

'They'll need a good clipping before we can get close enough to dig them out,' John piped up. His ready blush reminded her how young he really was. Fourteen at most, still a boy, really. 'At least... that's what I think, madam.'

'You are perfectly right. Clipping is my task for today.' Belinda placed a hand on the swell of her belly. The baby kicked back, still waging its assault against her insides. 'I cannot bend to plant, but I am quite able to prune.'

Sawyer approached the tools, picking out a trowel. 'Master Freddy, you must be careful not to soil your new clothes.'

Belinda glanced down. He'd plucked off a columbine bud and was tearing it apart with his fingernails. 'Don't do that, Freddy! The flowers will never set seed if you pull them off!'

He let the bud drop without saying a word.

They fell to their work. Belinda donned thick gloves and started with the topmost growth: little bulbous heads, like cankers, just starting to bruise purple. The thick stems oozed when she cut them. She wouldn't have expected so many buds to burst this early on in the year. Thistles usually flowered in July – or so she had read.

'Where are the worms?'

'Sorry?' She looked around.

John sat back on his haunches, dirt crumbling from his gloves. 'I thought there'd be beetles and... all sorts, really. But I haven't come across a single one. Is that normal, madam?'

Belinda stared at the earth. He was right. 'You have not dug so very deep,' she reasoned. 'And the weather has been dry. I'm sure you will find worms soon.'

She moved to balance on the edge of the flowerbed where grass gave way to soil. The heat of the day was building, unseasonably warm. As she paused to brush away an ant, the motion turned her back towards the well and that wooden girl. Light stippled through the surrounding trees onto its face. The eyes that watched Belinda were a blend of green, yellow and brown, their expression an enigma. Unsettling.

All at once, Belinda's footing crumbled beneath her.

Instinctively, she threw the billhook wide as she fell. She landed with a crunch amidst the thistles. The pain was like wasp stings; small, sharp pricks up her arms, on her face, across her spine.

'Madam!'

'Mamma!'

Belinda lay stunned. From down here the thistle stems towered over her. Her hat was crushed, the long veil tangled and netting her firmly in place. Panicked voices rang in her ears, but she couldn't make out the words. All she could hear was the drone of flies. Glancing down, she saw one of the spears had snagged on her gown against the baby bump. Stretching its prickly fingers over her child.

Strong hands pulled her up. Her hat left her head with a tearing sound. Still, the thistle clung fast to her belly as she regained her feet. 'What happened, madam? Did you swoon? It's too warm out here. You ought to be inside.'

The world wavered. She could see nothing clearly, did not even know which direction she was facing. 'I... I am not certain what happened. It was my own fault, I daresay. I just... fell.'

Yet it had felt strangely like being pushed.

A flicker, a shudder of images. The world slid back into place. She saw John and Sawyer standing either side of her. Behind them loomed the well and the wooden girl – but Belinda could swear its expression had *changed*. The corners of the painted mouth no longer twitched up in a coy smile. This was a decided grin.

She put a hand to her forehead. 'I think you are right, Sawyer. I had better go inside. I have had too much sun for today.'

※

Fair weather had dried the dirt track but it remained soft, holding imprints of the horseshoes that had trodden here before them. If Wilfred did not know better, he would swear the road had deteriorated in even the short time he'd occupied The Bridge.

No doubt the estate's problems had always existed. He'd just been too young and too distracted by family affairs to see them back in his youth. Living as he did at school for most of the year, with regular trips to London, the dust, tangled weeds and rotten wood of The Bridge had seemed charming. He'd never thought about the costs of rethatching cottages and fixing broken fences.

'How many walls do we have down?' he asked Knowles.

The servant looked up from beneath the brim of his wideawake hat. 'Three on my last inspection, sir, but we must ask around and do a proper survey today.'

'Three! The ledger shows we hired workmen to fix walls at Christmas. Surely they're not the *same* walls?'

'I can't recall, sir,' Knowles admitted, frowning. 'No mortar seems to hold fast enough against the woodland hereabouts. There's always moss and ivy pushing its way in, bringing things down.'

'Then we need to take better care. Someone should be cutting all of that back on a regular basis.'

'Yes, sir.'

'We'll employ someone specially for the job. My father should have done so long before now.'

Attention to detail was never the old man's strong suit, even in his personal life. He didn't notice the cracks appearing until it was too late. But Wilfred would make a better job of it. Show the tenants he was a landlord worthy of their respect. He ought to have started while the old man was still alive, instead of letting everything slip into this state. His father had clearly needed help in his later years – so why had he not sent for Wilfred?

They were approaching the stone bridge which divided the village from the great house. Grass on the riverbank grew knee-high, thick with cow parsley and bittercress. Three women knelt laundering on the other side, snapping their wet linen. They glanced up at Wilfred and Knowles as they crossed.

'Good morning,' Wilfred called.

The women nodded warily, showing no signs of rising to their feet as they should when greeting the landowner. Water burbled into the silence.

The river flowed steadily to the right of Fayford, while the woods crowded in to the left. From this distance, the village looked derelict, nothing but overgrown gardens and ramshackle walls. Only the spire of the church seemed to stand tall.

'Where to first?' he asked Knowles.

The man cleared his throat. 'A chimney has collapsed at the Robertses' house, sir.'

Wilfred couldn't stop the muscles from twitching in his jaw. He was conscious of the women, still within earshot. 'I see. Then we had better look into that right away.'

Why did it have to be the Roberts family? The entry in the ledger flashed before his mind. Seventy-five pounds. That was more money than a servant earnt in an entire year. Sufficient for them to repair their own chimneys. To move away even. But the Robertses were an insolent bunch, always grasping for things that were not theirs.

All Souls' neglected graveyard looked better beneath a bright sky. Long grass lent a luscious fringe to the headstones. There were garlands of wood sorrel and stars of buttercups. But the old man did not sleep amongst them. He was trapped in the dank family crypt beneath. The only trace of him was the notice nailed to the church door, announcing the upcoming enclosure of the common land. Wilfred had no choice but to go through with it now. Perhaps that was the reason why the women had looked at him so sullenly.

'Knowles,' Wilfred began as they passed by.

'Sir?'

He wet his lips. 'I have been meaning to ask you about some correspondence I discovered. Letters to my father from… spiritual men.'

A pause. 'Yes, sir.'

Discretion was one of Knowles' many virtues as a servant. But just this once, Wilfred wished he were a regular gossip, that he would not force him to ask precisely the right question to get an answer.

'Tell me, did they all visit The Bridge, as he asked them to?'

'They did, sir. Interesting gentlemen. Although not very generous with their vails, I must say.'

Wilfred raised a smile at this touch of humour, but he refused to be steered off topic. 'And my father did not confide in you about their visits? He did not give a reason for their coming?'

'No, sir. But I believe it was curiosity.'

'About religion? He never showed an interest beyond the usual before.'

'No, he did not. But a man can take up new notions as he gets older. I speak from personal experience, sir. You begin to realise how much knowledge you have neglected to acquire. Mr Bainbridge had a little flurry of studious activity.'

Wilfred swallowed. He ought not to push this any further, yet still he found himself asking, 'That was all? I find it strange he didn't consult Mr Chapman. Seeking outside opinions was not my father's way. I don't suppose... He was not... troubled in his conscience, was he?'

Wind trailed its fingers lazily through the bracken. A cuckoo called from the trees beyond, followed by the tap of a woodpecker. 'That is not for me to say, sir. But I cannot think of any reason why he ought to have been uneasy.'

'No, of course not,' Wilfred said briskly. 'I'm being foolish. There could be no reason at all.'

Even as he spoke, the creaking branches seemed to echo the terrible sound of the accident. There'd been no scream as the footman fell from the gallery. Just the squeal of wood and then the impact. Insides, exposed. Blood slipping across the flags.

If any other servant had plunged to their doom in that manner, few eyebrows would have been raised. But the old man had good reason to want this one dead.

The Robertses' cottage appeared, a dusty haze hovering over its thatched roof. A magpie was stealing the best of the straw for its nest. As Wilfred placed his hand upon the rough wooden gate that enclosed the small plot of land, the front door of the house swung open. He saw the same smug countenance he'd glimpsed in the churchyard on the night he buried his father. The same features his mother had ordered to be painted onto a silent companion. Only now, Wilfred had the wherewithal to realise who this must be.

'Ross,' he said.

The man grimaced at him, exposing a jagged rockfall of teeth. 'That's *Mr* Roberts to you. *I* ain't your servant.'

Ross had always been insolent, like the rest of the family, but he never used to resemble his uncle so strongly. It took Wilfred's breath away. Yet Ross's over-all presentation was a far cry from the dashing footman who had once served at The Bridge. There was no livery or powdered wig here. Rough stubble speckled his cheeks and the cloth knotted around his neck looked like a dishrag.

'We are come to assist you,' Wilfred said, carefully polite. 'I hear you are having some trouble with your accommodation?'

It was clearly an understatement. Moss grew from every cranny of the cottage. There was no chimney visible at all. A small pile of bricks was stacked amongst the weeds. Evidently they had once been above a fireplace for they were black with soot and crumbling to powder.

'Aye. The whole place is a wreck. Hardly fit for dogs. See here, our chimney fell all to pieces. Inside and out. Now I can't even light a fire to cook without risking the whole place going up in flames.'

'Of course it must be repaired,' Wilfred said reasonably. 'I saw from my records that my father granted you a lump sum about two years ago. Was that not provided to pay for renovations to your cottage?'

Ross folded his arms and leant against the door jamb. 'No,' he said shortly. 'It was not.'

Wilfred had forgotten that goading smile. But he must not let it rattle him, as it did when he was a boy. 'Well, but you might use some of it *now*?'

Ross raised his brows above dark, mocking eyes. 'Use my own tin to fix *your* property? That's hardly fair, is it? Not when my uncle served your mother *so well*.'

Knowles gave a little gasp. Wilfred held his temper firmly in check. 'Seventy-five pounds is a vast deal of money, Ross,' he reasoned. 'What the devil have you done with it all, to be in this state?'

Ross cocked his head. '*That* money was an arrangement of mine with your dad. What I've done with it is my own business. But now he's gone... Perhaps you and I can come to a new agreement. Being *kindred* and all.'

Wilfred's head was starting to pound. He grasped the crooked fence. 'What utter rot. There is no connection between our families, as well you know. I shall pay a man to fix your cottage, but you will get no more cash from me.'

Ross considered him, unperturbed. 'Is that a wise decision on your part?'

'Is that a threat?'

Ross smirked. 'From me? I wouldn't dare. Not with all the "accidents" up at your place. First the girl, then my uncle.' He shook his head. 'Even Mrs Bainbridge wasted away. Such... *convenient* disasters.'

Wilfred opened his lips to retort, but Ross cut him off.

'Oh, he was scared at the end though, wasn't he, Knowles? Old Bainbridge knew what must be coming to him in the next life. Sent all over for someone to tell him he was forgiven.' He spat on the dirt. 'Well, he may have escaped the Hanging Oak, but there's no pardon for murderers.'

Only a sense of what was due to his station stopped Wilfred from vaulting the fence and giving the wretch a black eye. 'You're treading on thin ice, Ross. Need I remind you that you only live here by my sufferance? Any more slandering of the dead and I'll throw your miserable tribe out into the woods without a penny. Women and children too, I swear to God.'

Ross puffed a derisive breath. 'I believe you. You're the old man's son, all right... No matter what your sister was.'

Rage flashed across his vision. He heard the fence creak under his grip. But before Wilfred could say or do anything rash, Ross had turned and slammed the cottage door in his face.

CHAPTER 6

The trouble with physicians, even with this accoucheur Mr Quigley, was that they fancied themselves judge, jury and executioner. Wilfred had never met one who did not give off an air of disapproval along with the fumes of camphor and vinegar. This man was supposed to welcome babes into the world and reassure anxious mothers. But with his black suit and old-fashioned, full-bottom wig, Mr Quigley resembled a fellow mourner.

He apprised Belinda from all angles as she rested on the chaise-longue in her dressing-room, wearing only her shift and powdering-gown. At last, he asked for permission to touch the patient. Asked Wilfred, not Belinda herself.

She flinched as Mr Quigley's fingers pressed on her belly.

'Have you pain?' he asked.

'No, no, I am sorry,' Belinda replied. 'Your hands are chilly, that is all.'

From his position in the corner, Wilfred sought his wife's eye and offered her an encouraging nod. It must be unpleasant to have a stranger paw at her like that. Mr Quigley felt out the shape of the baby, made a few harrumphs.

Guilt surged. Wilfred wished he hadn't been out of the house when this tumble occurred, wasting his time on Ross Roberts of all people. 'Do you think any damage has been done by the fall?'

'No,' Mr Quigley said slowly. 'Nothing seems to be amiss. But really, Mrs Bainbridge should never have been out in the gardens in the first place. It is high time she was confined.'

Wilfred saw the panic constrict Belinda's face. Mr Quigley did not understand his wife. She'd spent most of her life *confined*. Like the flowers she loved, she could never thrive in the dark. She needed her liberty, she needed light and air.

'Surely it is a little soon for that,' he reasoned. 'We might give her another week or two, with this glorious weather?'

'The weather is precisely the problem, Mr Bainbridge.' Mr Quigley left off touching Belinda and straightened up. There was something so dampening, so chastising about his voice. 'Your wife ought to be kept in a shaded room with the shutters closed. If her blood becomes overheated, I shall have to draw some from her.'

'Oh, no,' Belinda bleated. 'I hate to be bled.'

Mr Quigley ignored her. 'You said the last child arrived early, and your lady suffered from vapours?'

Wilfred shifted his feet. He didn't like to talk about Belinda this way, as if she were not present before them in the room. 'Yes, that much is true.'

Mr Quigley pressed his lips together and gave a knowing nod. 'So, you see, this pregnancy ought to be *properly* managed. We must avoid any repetition of such unhealthy tendencies. For the sake of both mother and child.'

'I do not suppose I am to have any say in the matter at all?' Belinda protested.

Mr Quigley sniffed, bent to pick up his leather satchel. 'Your husband has asked for my advice, madam. I have made my recommendations. It is not my responsibility to enforce them.'

Wilfred made a quick motion to Belinda, signalling they would discuss this later. There was no use bandying words with a man like Quigley. He was not likely to cede any ground. 'No, indeed, and we are very grateful for your time.' The main thing was, the baby had come to no harm from its adventure in the thistle patch. 'Do make sure to send me your bill, Mr Quigley.' Stepping forward, he gestured to the door. 'Here, I shall see you out myself.'

Mr Quigley bowed. Belinda averted her gaze and pulled her powdering-gown close around her once more. She looked awfully like Freddy when he felt he had been unjustly scolded.

Wilfred remembered the first time that he'd seen his wife: a slender thing, shivering like a whippet at her father's dinner table. Of course the match had been arranged. Kipling wanted the ancient Bainbridge name to wash his new money clean and was offering a dowry large enough to entice any man. But her fortune wasn't the real reason Wilfred had gone along with the marriage. Nor had it been love – not back then. He'd done it because he wanted to rescue a pretty girl from a place in which she was clearly unhappy. That was what had won him over: Belinda's need of him. And she needed him still.

He escorted the dour accoucheur through the corridors and down the stairs, wondering if he could source an alternative before the baby was born. But these fellows were all

cut from the same cloth. The one in London had recom-
mended some kind of lowering-vegetable diet that sounded
more like a penance than a treatment. And who was Wilfred
to say that they were wrong? Maybe he *was* coddling his
wife, but he would rather spoil than neglect her.

'I trust that you have your nursery in order, sir?' Mr
Quigley asked as they reached the Great Hall.

Wilfred hesitated. 'Almost. Mrs Bainbridge has yet to
select her staff. The move from London has... delayed
matters somewhat.'

'I would urge you to make it your priority. From what
I have seen, the child is almost ready to appear. They will
not wait until you are at leisure, sir.'

'No,' Wilfred returned irritably. 'Of course not.'

Mr Quigley's disapproving gaze stalked over
the displays of ancient weaponry and lingered on
the railed gallery. 'I would not deem this situation *ideal*
for infants. But I am sure you are making adequate
preparations.'

Wilfred's stomach clenched. From the way Mr Quigley
spoke, he had a sneaking suspicion that even this man
had heard of the Roberts incident. The Bainbridge family
must be infamous as far as Torbury St Jude. 'Naturally.
I was raised in this house myself, Mr Quigley. I know
exactly what I am about.' He opened the main entrance
and, as he did so, realised he was debasing himself yet
further, suggesting he did not have reliable servants who
could attend to visitors.

Mr Quigley's horse was still tied to the hitching post
on the gravel sweep, swatting its tail at flies; Dawkins
had not come to take it around to the stables.

'I do apologise—' Wilfred began, but was cut off by
the crunch of gravel and a child's shout.

'Papa!'

Freddy scampered towards them, completely unattended, his hair flying loose from its queue. 'Papa! You must come and see what I've found!'

Under other circumstances the lack of ceremony might have been brushed aside. Now Wilfred felt a blast of shame. Whatever standards a paterfamilias could be judged by, he was falling short in every way before Mr Quigley. 'Freddy, what are you doing here? Where is Sawyer?'

But Freddy was undeterred, already tugging at his sleeve. 'Come and looook!'

Mr Quigley cleared his throat. 'I shall take my leave of you, Mr Bainbridge.' He made a short bow. 'No doubt I shall hear from you soon. One way or another.'

'Yes... goodbye.' Wilfred smarted at the last, ominous words. Had his care really been so slipshod? He'd *seen* a lady made gravely ill by pregnancy, and Belinda was thriving by contrast. Her appetite had remained strong and no nausea held her immobile. But he was not a physician. He ought to have taken warning from the past, not given way to complacency.

Freddy pulled him towards the gardens, past the fountain and its soothing burble. Sunlight touched the emerging water and made it sparkle. The day was far too warm for Wilfred to be wearing black velvet, but he did not have a choice of mourning clothes.

Frustrated with his slow pace, Freddy stopped tugging and sprinted ahead into the long grass. The air was alive with pollen and butterflies. Sawyer sat with her skirts pooled out around her, sketching again when she ought to be watching her charge. It would not do. She was a maid, not a guest, however much Belinda might love her. Sawyer had obviously brought down the silent companions to amuse Freddy and then left him to romp about as he pleased.

Over in the shade of the chestnut trees, John was more usefully employed. His hands were gloved in dirt as he planted seedlings from a barrow into an empty bed. Wilfred watched the youth work for a moment. When he looked back, he saw Freddy standing by the well.

His heart came into his throat.

'Freddy!' he called out. 'Come away from there this instant.'

Sawyer glanced up from her drawing in sudden alarm.

Freddy didn't move. He remained motionless, staring, the shadow of the house falling over his fair curls. Dandelion seeds swarmed around, highlighting his stillness.

Sawyer climbed to her feet. 'Master Freddy—' she began, but Wilfred was already striding past her.

'Freddy! You will listen when I'm speaking to you.' Fear made his voice sound harsh. He fought to regain control of it, to be rational. The well was boarded over now, no longer a real hazard. It had only become an eyesore, burnt with rust and smothered under weeds. He ought to level it. Fill it in and make it into some kind of memorial.

Freddy finally turned and beckoned his father over. 'Keep quiet, Papa, you'll frighten them.'

'Frighten who?'

'Look!' Squatting, Freddy pointed to the nettles at the base of the structure. Something stirred the leaves. All at once, a tiny frog hopped out onto the grass. Freddy grinned broadly. 'I found a whole family of them!'

Frogs. This long walk in the heat all for frogs? Wilfred tried to look suitably impressed. 'I congratulate you, my boy, but this discovery does not excuse your manners. You must pay attention when I speak. I called to you twice and you did not come.'

'Sorry, Papa.'

'I would prefer you to stay away from this well when you're playing. It's covered, but the boards are old.' There was a chunk missing from one. Wilfred averted his eyes. He hated to think what was festering down there: dead birds and vermin. 'It is deep and dangerous.'

Freddy scuffed his feet. 'I know. She told me.'

'Who told you? Sawyer?'

The boy seemed to deliberate. 'Yes,' he said not altogether convincingly.

Well, that was something. Wilfred wondered how much Sawyer knew, what Belinda or the other servants had related to her. He hoped no one had gone into detail. He wanted Freddy to be aware of the danger, not the fact that Tiffany had died here.

Mr Quigley's words took on an added weight. Perhaps The Bridge was *not* altogether safe for children. This was the second place that Wilfred had needed to warn his son away from on pain of death. But other, more ancient estates managed to raise their scions without incident; estates with battlements and lakes and spiral stairs besides. There should not be a problem if Freddy were properly supervised. 'Well, then. You can observe the frogs from a safe distance, can you not?'

'Yes, Papa.'

Sawyer hovered awkwardly behind them. Wilfred turned to her, mollified that she had at least warned Freddy about the well. 'I think Mrs Bainbridge would be glad of your company, Sawyer. The physician has departed. I can mind Freddy for the moment.'

'Sir.' She curtsied and stooped to pick up her sketch-book. The well was miniaturised there, rendered in shades of charcoal and grey.

The crumbling brickwork reminded him of Ross Roberts' chimney. Lord, he still had to sort that out, and a thousand other small village worries. Of course, his family were more important, but it would be wise to appease his tenants as much as possible. Especially in light of the upcoming enclosure. Ross's mention of the old Hanging Oak, where Fayford people used to administer their own rough justice in less civilised times, was surely intentional. A threat. When they no longer had common ground to glean extra food from, the villagers' mood could ripen from resentment to outright hostility.

Sawyer strode away, her shoes crushing wild daisies and her skirts sweeping over the long grass. Freddy had retreated a short distance from the well to stand by one of the companions, the boy with a shepherd's crook.

'Papa,' he piped up, 'Merry says frogs are a bad *omen*. What does that mean?'

Wilfred blinked at him. 'I'm sorry – *who* said that?'

'Merry,' Freddy repeated, impatient. He pointed to each of the three companions in turn. 'Merripen, Keziah and Hetta.'

So he'd given them names. Wilfred bit his lip. He had to remember Freddy was only five years old. The behaviour which had been so disturbing in his own mother, a woman grown, was not so unusual in a young person. Children played.

'Oh, I see.' He had forgotten what Freddy had asked him in the first place. 'Shall we go and look at what John is doing, over there in the shade?'

He set off without waiting for an answer. Freddy trotted obediently at his side. Birdsong filled their ears, interrupted by the occasional chink of a spade. The walled garden was banded by a thick stand of chestnut trees which cast welcome shadows. The temperature was lower where John worked, but when he turned his face up to them it was covered in a sheen of sweat.

'You may take a rest,' Wilfred said. 'You are very diligent, but we do not want you to catch the stroke of the sun.'

The youth cast his spade down and flexed his fingers. 'Thank you, sir. I've been working as hard as I can. I wanted to get it looking nice for my mistress, to cheer her up after her fall.'

'That is most thoughtful.'

The bed now showed neat rows of tender green plants hoping to take root.

Freddy dropped to his knees and began to pluck at stray buttercups on the surrounding grass. 'But you've not gone deep enough,' he said gravely.

'Beg your pardon, Master Freddy?'

They both looked at the boy. He shrugged his thin shoulders. 'You need to dig further down. All these plants are going to die.'

Poor John appeared flummoxed. Wilfred let out a short laugh. 'Upon my word, you give your opinion most decidedly. Where has this expertise come from, my boy? It sounds as if you have been paying close attention to your lessons. Mamma has been teaching you botany, has she?'

Freddy glanced over at one of the companions. The girl that he called Hetta with her green dress and basket of roses.

'Yes,' he said, twirling a flower between his fingertips. 'It was Mamma who said that.'

CHAPTER 7

Once again, Belinda found herself trapped. Forced to lie still and silent like an effigy, as she had done in Mamma's parlour for years upon end. She would have thought herself accustomed to it by now, but after tasting freedom, confinement became unbearable. The dimness, the close air. Mr Quigley's prescription of a strict and shadowy detention.

Now night had fallen like a heaping of cinders, smothering even the precious scraps of light that had managed to find their way through the shutters. She could not sleep. She had been sleeping all day, between writing letters to family in London, Bristol and the West Indies. Her mind was restless and alert.

Placing a hand on her bump, she felt how tight and taut the skin there had become. It itched like the devil. She ran her finger up to her belly button, imagining she could trace a faint scratch even through her nightgown. Impossible, of course. But it was one of those things, like imagining fleas: once you thought of them, your skin would not stop prickling.

She tried to distract herself by listening to the noises of the house. Old buildings settled and creaked in a way that could either be disturbing or comforting as the mood took you. She heard a door close somewhere in the depths, signalling that one of the servants was still about. At least she was not quite alone in her wakefulness. She had been starting to feel that she was the last person left on the face of the earth.

She moved her head on the pillow. Hang Mr Quigley. He and his affected airs, as if women had not been giving birth for centuries without help from the likes of him. Certainly, she had exerted herself beyond her strength that day in the garden. And, yes, she had been alarmed to see what she thought was a changed expression on the face of the silent companion, when a later inspection had revealed nothing of the sort. But shutting her up in a room alone was the very worst treatment for frayed nerves. In boredom, her imagination was more prone to wander and make much of nothing. Like this tickling sensation on her skin. If she had something to occupy her, she would hardly notice it at all.

Drag, thump. That was odd: a noise like someone moving furniture on the floor below. Fumbling about, Belinda lit a candle and inspected her pendant watch. It showed a minute to midnight. Far too late, surely, for a servant to be rearranging rooms?

She waited patiently in the silence, her breath fluttering the candle flame. At last it came again. *Drag, thump.* Something scraping, fingernails against slate. *Drag, thump.* What was going *on* down there?

Belinda swung her legs over the side of the bed and sat up. A stab of pain at the base of her spine made her gasp, but it passed. She listened hard, without and within. No more hauling noises. No more pangs. Still, she was up now. She would stretch her legs.

Using the bedpost, she pulled herself to her feet and made her way towards the door leading to her dressing-room. All lay in gloom beyond. The lace toile stretched over the table resembled a shroud. Her pots and potions were neatly lined up on top. Walking over, Belinda opened the lavender pomade and took a sniff. Usually, the soft scent would relax her but it did nothing tonight.

She amused herself by unwinding her plait, running a comb through her hair and braiding it once more. Deep down, she knew she was waiting for the sound to come again. Finally, it did. A long, slow drag, terminating in something like a hiss.

Curiosity, rather than fear, drove her back to her feet. Suppose she just peeped outside into the hallway to see what was going on? There was no one about to scold her for breaking her confinement. If she happened upon Knowles moving furniture around in the dead of night, they would both be caught in the wrong.

Yes, she would do it. Snatch a glimpse of freedom in the dark. Neither Wilfred nor Mr Quigley would ever know.

Picking up her chamberstick, she ventured to the second door and turned the handle, letting it glide noiselessly over the carpet. The passageway on the other side was dark, but moonlight trickled down from the lantern tower and introduced shades of grey. Belinda shuffled forward. Marble busts watched her from either side. One had its nose chipped off, leaving a rough and unsightly triangle beneath its blank eyes. Belinda glanced quickly away. Old wives' tales said looking upon something deformed could damage an unborn child. Probably nonsense, but she would rather be safe than sorry.

Drag, thump. There, again, scraping along her bones. The sound was definitely coming from below. It might even be in the nursery. Placing her feet very carefully, she crept along to the staircase and started her descent.

Perhaps Freddy had woken up and tried to ride his rocking horse. That might explain the bumping. But when she reached the floor below, she saw that the door to the nursery was open, soft yellow waves rippling out from the oil lamp.

'Freddy?' Belinda started forward.

A whisper, Sawyer's voice. 'Hello?'

'Sawyer, it's me.'

'Ma'am! What are you doing here?' Sawyer sat up on the truckle bed, casting wildly from side to side. The four wooden figures they'd found in the schoolroom were ranged around Freddy's bed, but the mattress itself yawned empty.

Horror kicked in Belinda's chest.

She could almost hear her mother screaming the word *kidnap*. But children *did* get up during the night. Her brothers had once snuck down to the pantry and stolen seedcake, not that they'd shared any of the loot with her. Freddy must be nearby.

'It doesn't matter why I'm here. Where is my son?'

Sawyer rose quickly and picked up the lamp. She pushed the door to the schoolroom wide, swept the light over the cobwebbed corners and underneath the desks. Nothing. 'I don't know... I didn't hear him get up.'

Had she really slept through all that noise?

'Freddy can't have gone far,' Belinda reasoned. But as she ran a mental lap of the house, a feeling of dread coiled about her throat. 'Oh, Lord. The gallery! The swords!'

Sawyer came towards her with the lamp, its flame reflecting in the pupils of her grey eyes. 'Don't worry. We'll find him.'

They left the room arm-in-arm. Shadows retreated before the warm glow of their lights. Sawyer led the way down the next set of stairs, into the gallery. 'If he'd fallen, I would have heard *that*,' Sawyer said. 'So put that notion out of your head. He might not have come this way at all. He could have gone to his father.'

'I must check.' Pinching up her nightgown, Belinda thudded down the steps and called out her son's name. Her voice echoed back at her.

Cold stone met the soles of her feet. She padded to the centre of the Great Hall and turned slowly on the spot, determined to sweep every inch of the room. Metal glinted. Blades of shadow stretched across the floor towards the hem of her nightdress. There was no sign of Freddy.

Sawyer caught her elbow. 'He's not here. Let's try the kitchens.'

Still holding tight to the chamberstick, Belinda let Sawyer drag her away. She was starting to feel ponderous and heavy. Pain shot down the backs of her legs as they passed through the servants' door into a warren of plain passageways. It smelt of starch and cooked meat. Scorch marks on the walls showed where candles had burnt for hours on end.

Hiss.

She flinched. 'What was that?'

Sawyer didn't allow her to stop. 'I heard nothing.'

Belinda's candle juddered and blew out as they rounded a corner and ploughed on into the kitchen. Yesterday's fire had left the ghost of its warmth and the scent of ashes. A large, scarred table stood at the centre of the room. Belinda pulled away from Sawyer and hobbled towards it for support.

'Ma'am, look!'

Sawyer's shadow rose high on the wall behind her, pointing to a doorway leading out onto the stable yard. It stood half-open.

'Yes! He could have gone out to visit the horses,' Belinda breathed. But that was not much reassurance. New fears piled into her catalogue, the pages flicking fast: Freddy flattened beneath heavy hooves, Freddy trying to ride and falling off. Mamma was right: there was danger everywhere.

'I'll go and see.' Still in stockinged feet, Sawyer ventured out into the night. Belinda heard her calling Freddy's name and the low whinny of horses in response.

Panting, she leant heavily against the table. 'Come on, Bel,' she muttered to herself, trying to summon the energy to follow. Her back ached. It felt as though her hips might snap beneath the mass of the baby. At last she found a burst of strength and stumbled out of the house.

The stable block formed a semicircle around her, its clock-tower reaching for the moon. Sawyer appeared from behind the dung heap. 'He's not in with the animals. What about the gardens?'

A horse kicked against its stall and snorted. Two moths fluttered around Sawyer's lamp.

Belinda forced herself to breathe. 'You run ahead and look. I can't walk fast.'

'You should go back to bed. You weren't even meant to leave your room.'

'I cannot possibly return, not until Freddy is found!'

Tutting her disapproval, Sawyer grabbed Belinda's arm again and used her strength to move her along. The gardens were a mass of tangled shadows. Even in the cool of night, Belinda could smell roses. Her pain was turning to a steady pressure.

'I think I see him, up ahead,' Sawyer whispered.

'Oh, thank God!'

Sawyer's eyes were keener than hers. Moments passed before Belinda perceived the small figure grovelling on all fours. Why was he down so low? What was he *doing*?

'Freddy!' she started, but Sawyer pinched her arm.

'Hush! He's night-walking. You mustn't wake him.'

Freddy had never been given to somnambulism before.

He was kneeling beside a flowerbed, his pale night-shirt pooled about his legs. For a terrible instant, the stains on it resembled dried blood. But as they drew closer and the halo of lamplight extended, she saw that it was dirt: claggy, clotted earth that smelt of minerals and ancient spice. Freddy was digging frantically with his bare hands.

Pain clamped the base of Belinda's spine. She couldn't take another step. 'Sawyer... help him.'

The maid paced cautiously forward and bent to the child's level. 'Time for bed,' she crooned. She tried to touch him, but Freddy strained forward, hands still digging. 'This way, Freddy.'

The baby lashed out. Belinda couldn't stop a cry from bursting forth, or the sudden gush of liquid between her legs. Freddy jolted awake. His pupils rolled back, huge and unseeing.

'Oh, it's coming!' Belinda spoke through clenched teeth. 'The baby.'

'The baby,' Freddy repeated, like one in a trance.

*

They'd told her the second time would be easier. Maybe it was; maybe she'd forgotten this merciless grinding in the interval of five years. Perhaps Freddy's birth had felt even worse – although it was hard to imagine. Belinda wished for nothing more than to climb out of her own skin. But the windows were shuttered, the door locked tight again, even the keyhole was blocked. She had no escape.

Turning with a groan, she made her way back towards the birthing stool. Changing position snatched her a moment of relief. She levered herself onto the seat and strained. Still no shift from the baby. Turmoil raged within but she was stoppered shut, a corked bottle.

Mr Quigley inspected his pocket watch. Time had lost all meaning. It felt like years since her waters had broken; the stains on her nightgown were drying in the heat.

'Perhaps it is time we try the bed, Mrs Bainbridge.'

Belinda glanced over at the hulking structure, its elaborately carved posts, and shook her head. She had a premonition that if she lay down there, she'd never get up again.

A hand on her arm made her start. 'Do rest, madam. I've changed the sheets all nice and fresh, see?' Mrs Knowles. The pity in her eyes brought Belinda close to tears. It was a sorry state of affairs, having only a housekeeper for comfort at a time like this. Not even a mother- or sister-in-law. She clutched at Mrs Knowles' hand, felt bones shift beneath her fingers.

'Sorry,' Belinda gasped. 'I'm ever so sorry.'

The rolling was in her head now, as well as her belly. She was tilting to and fro like a ship at sea, like one of Papa's West Indiamen... Yes, that was the way to cope: flee into her mind. Picture a place far, far away.

Without knowing how, she found herself lying upon the mattress. She leant her head back and closed her eyes, saw herself standing at the bow of a ship. Waves crashed against the hull with the same choppy rhythm as her pain.

'Freddy,' she murmured. 'Where is Freddy?'

'Don't you fret, madam. The young master is safe in his nursery now with Miss Sawyer. We've had quite a night of it, haven't we?'

The accoucheur harrumphed. 'No doubt the labour would be less severe if my instructions had been followed. Mrs Bainbridge ought to have been confined to bed, not scampering around the gardens at midnight.'

'Well, sir, there's nothing to be done about it now,' Mrs Knowles reasoned. 'I worked right up to the moment my boy was born. May I ring down for some tea? It's been a long time since my mistress drank.'

Belinda's eyes opened. Her vision had been clear in the dream; here, objects doubled and slid.

Mr Quigley dabbed at his forehead with a handkerchief. 'Only *weak* tea. Small sips. I shall take this opportunity to update Mr Bainbridge on our progress. Call me immediately if there is any alteration in her condition.'

A dull thump of dread. There could be no good news if he was going to Wilfred. Had she really caused this? Harmed her baby because she could not remain still?

When Belinda closed her eyes, she was back on the ship, the deck awash with foam beneath an iron-grey sky. Veins of lightning flashed in the distance. She wasn't holding the course. She wasn't in control. It felt as if she were fighting against something, some*one,* for possession of her baby. The ship heeled to one side; she staggered sideways into the railing and liquid sloshed into her face.

'Careful! Get another pillow behind her, make her sit.' Sawyer's voice. Where had she come from? 'There now, ma'am. Drink it up. You *must* get something inside you. You need your strength.'

Another bolt of lightning and time seemed to have jumped with it. Hazily, Belinda opened her eyes upon dry land. Somehow she was back at The Bridge. Mr Quigley stood at the end of her bed. His sleeves were rolled up, her own legs spread. Rose petals of blood on the sheets.

'Almost there, Mrs Bainbridge.'

Heat and rushing. Something dredged from her very depths. There was a wet sound like a person wading through mud.

'Here! Where is the hot water? Fetch salt... mustard!'

A resounding slap.

Belinda peered up, still woozy. Mr Quigley was striking a small, slimy piece of meat, plunging it into a tub of steaming liquid. Sawyer passed him a handful of salt and he rubbed vigorously with the crystals, as if seasoning a chop to be fried.

'What's happening?' she croaked.

Mrs Knowles appeared at her side and made a hushing sound. 'Your baby's had an ordeal too, madam. They just need to ginger her up a bit.'

Her. A daughter. Wilfred would be so pleased...

There was a cry; the fury of a child dragged into the world. Belinda propped herself up on an elbow. 'My baby...' Her voice was a worn thread.

Mr Quigley delivered the child, squirming, into her arms. She saw her own face in miniature, framed by wisps of Wilfred's Titian hair. The baby's green irises like smeared glass bottles.

'She was not breathing at first,' Mr Quigley said dourly. 'No doubt she was shaken up by your gallivanting abroad. You must take more care of your children, Mrs Bainbridge. The outcome could have been very different, were it not for my skill.'

CHAPTER 8

It was a peculiar kind of torture, to sit at a distance and listen to his wife scream. Panic corroded within him and yet Wilfred was forced to keep calm as he assured Freddy all would be well. What would he do if matters did *not* turn out well? The idea made him so wild that he refused to entertain it.

He sat in the library, elbows on the desk, hands driven into the stubble on his head. Both wig and coat were too hot to bear. He should have a pipe or even a brandy to calm his nerves, but the thought of either made him feel sick. Somehow the second birth was a more fearsome beast. They'd been lucky to have mother and child come through completely unscathed last time. To go through the process all over again felt like tempting fate. Pushing their luck. He tried to concentrate on his firstborn instead.

Shards of light cut into the carpet and Freddy lay on his stomach in one of them, leafing through Sawyer's sketchbook. He stopped occasionally to make his own additions to the drawings in pencil. Right now, he was lingering on a particularly fine rendition of the front of the house. He began to scrawl. Figures appeared behind the windows in his childish hand. A sinister, shadow audience, stickmen with their faces blacked out.

Distantly, Belinda's cries ebbed into sobs.

'Who are the people?' Wilfred asked. 'Are you draw-ing us?'

Freddy shook his fair head. 'No. They're the others.'

'The... *others*?'

'The ones who came before.'

'Oh, our ancestors, do you mean? Like in the portraits on the walls?'

Freddy kept his focus and did not answer. With his red, puffy eyes and a hollow expression, the poor child looked exhausted. Fancy him walking in his sleep! Burrowing like a rabbit. A most unaccountable thing. Sawyer had spent the best part of an hour scrubbing out dirt from beneath his small fingernails.

Wilfred had wet the bed himself as a boy, when matters between his parents were at their worst, but he'd never taken to sleepwalking. He could see no cause why Freddy should be troubled here at The Bridge. Yet children were adept in the art of concealment. He of all people should know that.

'Fred, come and sit here with me for a moment, would you? There's a good chap.' Freddy laid his pencil down and climbed to his feet, wandering over to the desk. Wilfred pulled the boy onto his lap, more to comfort himself than his son. 'There, now. How are you holding up today?'

'I'm sleepy.' Freddy snuggled his head into Wilfred's chest, his cheek against the embroidered waistcoat. 'And I want Mamma.'

'Yes, well, Mamma is occupied at present, I'm afraid. We shall both have to be patient.' He grimaced as Belinda chose that moment to shriek again. He pulled Freddy closer. 'And I'm not surprised to hear that you are tired. It must have been frightening, waking up outside as you did.'

'Yes.'

'Do you know how you came to be out in the gardens in the first place? Were you dreaming?'

He felt Freddy nod. 'A girl was calling me. She sounded like Hetta but she was all... echoey. Like she was far away. Or deep down. In the well.'

Wilfred shuddered and smoothed the child's hair. 'I expect that was your mother or Sawyer,' he reasoned. 'You heard them in your sleep.'

'You said I mustn't go near the well,' Freddy went on. 'So I didn't, Papa. I listened harder. She was... underground. She wanted to come out and meet the baby. Everything smelt like flowers... then I woke up.'

There was a rough logic to the progression of the dream. Part of Freddy's mind must have been dwelling on John's planting, which he'd noticed last week, so his body had taken him to the flowerbed to fix the problem. Belinda and Sawyer had been talking about the onset of her labour, and he'd heard them before he woke up. 'I see. That sounds like a confusing night for you, my boy, but do not fret yourself. It was only a dream after all. We will lock the nursery door at night so you cannot go wandering off again.' Wilfred stroked Freddy's cheek. 'You know, people often sleepwalk when they are upset. *Are* you upset about anything?'

Freddy shrugged.

'I suppose there has been a lot of change for you, in a short time. We are living in our new house, Phoebe has gone, and now you're becoming a big brother. But you must not let it worry you. Papa will always keep you perfectly safe. You know that, don't you?'

Safety seemed a bold claim, while Belinda groaned so pitifully in the background.

Freddy squirmed. 'Yes,' he said slowly. 'But it's not really *our* house, is it?'

'Whatever do you mean by that?'

There was an abrupt hush. Freddy turned his head to watch the door, distracted. Wilfred held his breath. A flurry of voices, then nothing.

Ominous silence reigned. Surely not. Surely life could not be so cruel...

All at once, a baby wailed.

He exhaled in a rush, ruffling Freddy's curls. 'Ho! Do you hear that? That's your new sibling saying hello.' It was a lusty cry, thanks be to God.

Freddy leapt from his lap. 'Why are they making that *horrible* sound?'

Wilfred laughed. He could not stop laughing, he was so overcome with relief. 'Babies cry, Fred. They cannot talk yet, so they cry to tell us what they want.'

The boy wrinkled his nose. 'And they're going to be in *my* nursery, with *me*?'

'I'm afraid so, old chap. But you will get used to it.' Wilfred rose to his feet, tidied himself, donned his wig and coat once more. Foolish as it was, he wanted to make a good first impression on his child.

At last there came a tap at the door.

'Come,' Wilfred said, impressed by how collected he sounded.

The accoucheur entered, unsmiling. He looked so serious that Wilfred reached instinctively for his son. 'A daughter, Mr Bainbridge. Both mother and child are doing well.'

A daughter. For some reason he'd been expecting another boy. There had not been a daughter in this house for such a long time. It felt like a second chance.

A little girl to dance with Freddy, to take shopping for dresses in Torbury St Jude. He could see her whole future unspooling before her like a ribbon. 'And – and I may visit them?'

Mr Quigley inclined his head. 'I can have the child brought to you momentarily.'

'There's no need to separate them. I wish to see my wife.'

'As you please.'

'I'm coming too!' Freddy insisted.

Wilfred held him back. 'You may, but you must not pester your mother, Freddy. She'll be very tired. Just give her a kiss and say hello to your new sister. There's a responsibility for you, little man.' He squeezed the boy's shoulder. 'Protecting your sister must always be your most important task from now on.'

Freddy pulled away from his grip. 'Why must it? I wanted a brother.'

'No, you didn't. A sister is… easier.'

They strode after Mr Quigley, down the maroon-papered corridor, while the baby kept testing her voice. As they entered Belinda's suite of rooms, an unholy blend of odours pressed back against them: acidic, musty and sickeningly sweet. Mrs Knowles and Sawyer were bustling around with linen and bowls of water. After the stillness of the library, it was an assault upon the senses.

They found Belinda in the next room, propped up in her four-poster bed, slick and grey as an oyster. She'd clearly had a rough go of it. Rat's tails of hair straggled over her shoulders. A bundle of linen lay in the crook of her right arm, the baby barely visible through swaddling.

'My love—' Wilfred started but Freddy shot forward.

'Mamma! You were *screaming*.' Before they could stop him, he had hopped up on the bed – the sheets had thankfully been changed since the birth – and was worming his way towards Belinda. 'Did my sister hurt you?'

A tired laugh puffed from his mother's lips. 'She did not mean to, Freddy. We are both quite well now.'

He peered down at the bundle, nonplussed. 'She's not very pretty, is she?'

'And *you* are not very gallant, Fred!' Wilfred chuckled. 'All babies are wrinkled. Her looks will improve in time. We will be fighting off beaux for her before you know it. Now, come along, what did I say? A quick kiss for Mamma and back to the nursery. I daresay Sawyer will take you.'

Dutifully, Freddy pressed his lips to Belinda's wan cheek and squirmed back off the bed. The frilled collar of his shirt was sticking up at all angles. Sawyer came to take him by the hand. 'Goodbye, Lydia,' he tossed over his shoulder.

'Lydia?' Belinda repeated. 'Why do you call her that?'

Freddy blinked, as though it were obvious. 'It's her name.'

Wilfred watched Sawyer lead the boy away in bemusement and shut the door behind them. Finally, Belinda and he were alone. Or almost.

He approached the bed. 'I am sorry, darling. Freddy so wanted to see you, but he's half-drunk on exhaustion. How are you? Quigley said it was quite the ordeal.'

Belinda tried to smile, but it was fragile, quivering, and a tear slipped down her cheek. 'Oh, I am well enough. Truly, I am. It was just all rather a strain.'

He wiped her tear away with his thumb. 'Naturally! You have been excessively brave.'

'I have been excessively stupid,' she countered. 'I never should have left my room. I put her in danger. But, oh, look at her, Wilfred. Freddy has no taste – I think she is perfect.' She passed the baby to him.

Rosebud lips, bright embers of hair. He loved her instantly, desperately. 'What a gift, Bel! You are the cleverest lady in England.' Careful to support the baby's fragile skull, he brought her face close to his. Her myopic gaze struggled to focus. 'How do you do?' he whispered.

'I may have produced a wonderful child, but I have not been clever, Wilfred. I have not been anything like it.' Belinda cuffed away fresh tears. 'You are always so good and indulgent to me, but I really am ashamed of myself. What was I *thinking*? Sawyer should never have had the care of Freddy. She is an excellent maid and she loves him very much, but she is not trained for minding children. If I had not woken her up last night, who knows what could have happened to him out in the gardens? And that precious girl you are holding! Mr Quigley said he was only just able to save her. She came out of me without any breath in her lungs.'

He pulled the child closer, horrified by the thought. 'She did?'

'Yes! And all because I could not give up my gardening or keep myself still in bed. Well, that folly ends now. You must have Sawyer bring me my writing slope. I am going to engage nursery staff at once. Rousseau and Locke are all well and good, but some things must be done the old-fashioned way.'

She was too hard upon herself. He was at fault as much as she. 'I agree that you should hire your staff, but please do not agitate yourself, my love. Recover your strength. We must take care you do not grow nervous like last time.'

'Oh, I am not nervous!' she cried, in a way that made her sound just that. 'Only annoyed with myself. But I will put this energy to good use, I promise you. I will make it up to our daughter, I will use my confinement to plan her a lovely Christening.'

'You want to have a large ceremony?' he asked, surprised.

She bit her lip. 'Yes. I thought so. Or... or is that in poor taste, so soon after your father?'

Wilfred blew out his breath, thinking about the estate. Parading his own status would gall those villagers who were struggling to make ends meet. He had no wish to be dragged out to their infamous Hanging Oak. But when he looked at the sweet child, the sweep of her little eyelashes against her cheek, and Belinda's pain-ravaged face, he wavered.

'I think we shall have to strike a balance. It is difficult for you, I know. In London you would have friends over to drink caudle... here you are lonely. But it is not wise to invite guests beyond family. Perhaps your brother Luke, since he is still in the country? And we can go to the church, rather than have the vicar come here. We will put out some flowers and order a fine repast. What do you think?'

She nodded. 'Yes, yes. Whatever you judge best. I just want our daughter to have something nice of her own. It is not *her* fault she was born into mourning.' Belinda put out her arms. 'May I take her back?'

Reluctantly, he gave the warm bundle over. 'Before she can be baptised, Miss Bainbridge will need a name.'

Belinda rearranged the blanket around the baby's face. 'I had presumed it would be Tiffany.'

A seizure in his chest. Of course, he had been thinking about Tiffany from the moment Mr Quigley announced the birth of a girl. But hearing the name aloud did not conjure memories of the smiling sister who had sung to herself and made daisy chains. He saw only the crumpled body at the bottom of the well, her neck bent at an unnatural angle.

'That is kind of you. Most kind.' He cleared his throat. 'I would have thought so, too. Yet now I see our daughter… It is as you say. She deserves something of her own. Free from the past. The name of a dead aunt is too heavy a burden to put on young shoulders.'

Something kindled in Belinda's tired eyes. A fellow feeling. They understood one another. 'Well, I do not have any objections to the name Lydia…'

His lips curved in a smile. 'It's her name,' he repeated in Freddy's voice and they both laughed. 'He *is* a funny little chap. Where does he come up with these things?'

'I cannot say. But I do like the idea of his naming his sister.'

'Well, Lydia it is, then. A pretty name. Shall I go and write the announcement for the newspapers?' He rose from the edge of the bed, kissed her forehead. It was salted with sweat. 'You will soon be inundated with letters of congratulation.'

'And I need my slope too, Wilfred. Do not forget to tell Sawyer.'

'I will not fail you, my love.'

He looked back fondly over his shoulder at mother and child. Strange to say that Belinda had never appeared in greater beauty to him than she did now: breathless, sweaty and drawn. He was proud of her. She had turned a corner, discovered a new sense of purpose.

Such a contrast to her last confinement. To his own mother during that final pregnancy, which had never reached fruition.

Strange to think that terrible time would be seventeen years ago when summer came around. The grim details were still as fresh in his mind as if they had happened yesterday. Mamma's translucent skin. Her hollow cheeks working over a chamberpot. The sour smell that had haunted the room along with the sound of retching.

He would never forget her last words to him.

'It makes us women sick, Wilfred.' She was gasping, wiping saliva from her chin. 'The thought of bringing an innocent child into this wicked world. It makes us sick to our very souls.'

With a shudder he turned away, closing the door on both Belinda and the memory.

CHAPTER 9

Lydia was born in late April. Five whole weeks must pass before Belinda could be Churched. It would be simpler if they held the Christening at the same time, since a single ceremony meant only one summons to Mr Chapman. He must be a negligent sort of clergyman, to take his tithes from All Souls and yet live elsewhere. Either that or he considered the village of Fayford a lost cause. Belinda couldn't help but wonder if his absence had anything to do with the past and Anne Bainbridge's supposed witchcraft, but she had promised not to dwell on fanciful matters like that. Not for this confinement.

She rarely stirred from the elaborately carved four-poster bed. To her relief, nothing seemed to be warping or melting before her eyes. There was only the strange hissing sound by night. But that noise woke Lydia too, so it could not be imaginary. Yes, Belinda was certainly doing better this time. A different room, a different wing and a different season made all the difference. She would wait and watch the white blossom on the trees outside her window. Observe the petals brown, curl and drop.

'Then,' Belinda whispered down at Lydia as she nursed, 'you and I shall be free.'

She kept her mind occupied, firing off letters like a squadron of artillery. Dawkins rode out to the post

office at Torbury St Jude every day with a pocket full
of her black-sealed correspondence. A detailed description of the baby for Mamma, carefully skirting around
the circumstances of her birth and resuscitation. Shorter
missives to Papa and her brothers. *They* would not much
care what Lydia weighed and how long she slept at a
time. She informed a few friends, asking for any London
gossip they could share in exchange. Then she started on
the task of appointing maids for the nursery.

Sawyer sat with her for a while, reading through the
responses to Mrs Knowles' advertisement, which had
been published in the local newspapers before they
arrived here. Many applications used what could only
be described as inventive spelling, and some were down-
right illegible.

Sawyer finished one closely scrawled page and sighed
as she put it aside. 'I think I'll miss looking after Master
Freddy.'

Belinda felt a twinge of sympathy, but she would not
renege on what she'd said to Wilfred. There could be no
more night-time escapes from the nursery. 'It is back to
your old, troublesome charge, I am afraid,' she teased.
'You cannot get rid of me that easily.'

Sawyer's lips curled, yet the smile did not reach her
eyes. 'Oh, I've no complaints about you, ma'am.'

'Lady's maid is a more prestigious role,' Belinda
reminded her.

'It is. I know I'm being foolish. Only Master Freddy
and I have had such fun together.'

A curious claim for on the few occasions Belinda had
seen her son recently, he didn't appear to be enjoying
himself at all. His face had taken on a more serious,
troubled expression and his eyes were always bloodshot.
What could be keeping him awake? Surely he couldn't

hear the baby crying at her bedside from all the way down in the nursery?

She put the question to him as he stood on tiptoes beside the crib, peering at his little sister. He shrugged and did not answer her. Instead he said, 'Lydia's *our* baby, isn't she, Mamma?'

'Yes, my love. She is part of our family now.'

'And no one else is supposed to have her, are they? Papa said it's my job to protect her. The most important job I have.'

She supposed Wilfred would say that, after poor Tiffany. But it was a bit much to expect vigilance of a five-year-old. 'He meant all of us, darling. We will all look after Lydia together. Including your new nurse-maids when they arrive.'

Freddy dropped back onto the soles of his feet. The spring light made an aureole around his fair curls. 'But no one protected Aunt Tiffany, Mamma. She *died*.'

Belinda scrunched the bedsheets in her hand. 'Did your father tell you that?'

'Merry told me. After I went digging in the garden.'

She frowned, perplexed. '*Merry*? You mean, the wooden boy? Your silent companion? Freddy, he couldn't possibly...' Her son looked so solemn that she did not have the heart to tell him his friend was not real. But she must not listen to this kind of talk. She would not start imagining things again.

Sawyer entered the room with a fresh stack of post and came over to stand by the side of the bed.

'Lydia shouldn't sleep in the nursery,' Freddy went on. 'Not even when the new people come. She's better here with you.'

'Oh, Master Freddy,' Sawyer clucked indulgently. 'We *talked* about this. Don't pay any heed to him, ma'am.

He said the very same thing to Mr Bainbridge: that he doesn't want a crying baby in his nursery. But you and your sister need to learn how to rub along together, Master Freddy. That's how it is with siblings.'

Freddy muttered something darkly to himself and sat cross-legged on the floor beside the cradle.

*

Choosing between the applicants didn't prove difficult. Belinda invited a few for interview, but most had already gained employment elsewhere. Some withdrew their interest entirely, without explanation. Wilfred thought that was Mr Quigley's doing.

'No doubt he's been blackening our name,' he huffed, 'spreading gossip about Freddy's sleepwalking and you breaking your confinement.'

For Freddy, Belinda managed to engage a sensible woman named Rebecca Morris who was thin and neat as a pin, her sharp features relieved by a ready smile. But there was only one available wet-nurse for Lydia.

Belinda was taken aback when Mrs Knowles ushered a young woman scarcely nineteen years old into the dressing-room. 'Amy Whitfield, madam.'

To Belinda's tired eyes, Amy looked little more than a child herself, with a fine bloom upon her plump cheeks. She gazed dumbstruck at the papered walls and silk-upholstered furniture. Belinda had been self-conscious about receiving visitors in only a fresh powdering-gown and slippers, but now she felt it was just as well – she was not too imposing a figure for this poor girl.

According to Amy's reference, she'd served families in Torbury St Jude. They must have been far less wealthy than the Bainbridges.

'Good morning, Amy. Thank you for coming.'

Her thick-soled boots stumbled on the carpet as she curtsied. Perhaps she was a little rough around the edges, but her plain cambric bodice and tidy cap suggested she was not frivolous. What she lacked in experience, she made up for in ruddy good health. Hopefully that would be passed on to Lydia through her milk.

'I can start as soon as next week, madam,' Amy offered. 'I've only to settle my boy with my sister-in-law.'

Belinda smiled back encouragingly. 'Wonderful. And how old is your little one?'

'Thirteen months, madam. All weaned now and thriving.'

She ought to have brought the child with her as a kind of testimony. 'I am glad to hear it. But will he not miss you terribly?'

The question seemed to take Amy aback. 'Oh. I guess he will, madam. But it's not for long when all's said and done, is it? Less than a year. And Thomas likes his auntie.'

Belinda thought of Freddy's strange ways and grave expression. He could certainly do with a distraction. And although Wilfred might demur, she knew from experience that it did not hurt a child's manners to play with someone below their station. 'If it would be more convenient,' she offered, 'you may bring young Thomas along with you. Our nursery is quite capacious. I am sure my son would like a playmate.'

Amy took a step back. Something wary shifted behind her light eyes. 'That's – that's very kind of you, madam. Thank you, but… I don't think…' She shook her head. 'Well, we'll see how it goes, shall we? If Thomas doesn't take to the separation, maybe I will. But for the moment it's best he stays where he is.'

Belinda wondered then if it were true: what Wilfred had said about Mr Quigley dragging their name through the mud. There was a palpable hint of fear in Amy's response.

'Whatever you please. I only thought it might be a pleasant experience for your son.'

Amy put her hands behind her back. 'The truth is, madam, it's a lot grander here than anything he's used to. I know it's pretty, but honestly...' She met Belinda's gaze for a fleeting moment. 'I think my Thomas'd be scared.'

A familiar, dull thump in the pit of her stomach. 'Frightened? Of The Bridge?' Belinda tried to laugh it off but didn't sound convincing. 'What a notion.'

Faintly, through the door separating the two adjoining rooms, Lydia began to cry.

CHAPTER 10

Wilfred spent the weeks of his wife's confinement in the estate office near the stable yard. He sifted through maps, projected crop yields and tried to get his head around land management. He'd never been much of a farmer – the old man was even worse. He'd left Wilfred a legacy of depleted herds and fields fallen to rack and ruin. What they needed was a full land staff: a steward, bailiff, gamekeeper and more besides, but there was not enough capital for that. With Knowles' help, he at least managed to employ enough workers from Fayford to cut the hay. It was as well he did, for when Lydia's Christening finally arrived, the weather turned traitor.

An east wind rattled at the roof tiles and banged at the doors of the church, as they all gathered around the octagonal font at the top of the nave. Everything *looked* perfect, as Belinda had planned. Her hair was powdered once more, her eyebrows darkened. She wore an open black silk gown over panniers, with threads of silver and beads of jet on the stomacher. Black ribbon encircled her neck. She and Sawyer had spent days adjusting the long family christening gown to fit Lydia and embroidering her a cap. But it was all in vain.

There was no cheer in the occasion. Light failed to penetrate through the stained-glass windows. The eagle

lectern and the high-backed family pew where Wilfred
had squirmed as a boy appeared Gothic and ominous.
He could not explain it clearly but there was something
lacking about All Souls, an absence of serenity. This
church resembled a tower under siege: ever-watchful,
on the defensive.

Then there was the wind. Its clatter upset poor Lydia,
who scrunched her face beneath her cap. She cried pier-
cingly, as only a small baby can, the noise bouncing off
stone and echoing up to the rafters. Freddy clamped his
hands over his ears.

'Dearly beloved,' Mr Chapman began, 'for as much as
all men are conceived and born in sin…' His words were
barely audible beneath the baby's squall and the wind
swooping outside.

Wilfred allowed his mind to wander. Memories of
Tiffany's elaborate funeral spun webs across the gloom.
Back then, the whole church had been swathed in pure
white, from the altar cloth to the flowers on the rood
screen. Lord, what a show that was, more fitting for a
wedding than a burial. Those suffocating lilies and the
thick pillar candles surrounding a closed coffin.

It was closed for a reason.

Wilfred had made the mistake of hovering in the doorway to watch his mother prepare Tiffany's broken body
for its final sleep. Now he'd carry those images in perfect
detail to his own grave. Dark locks fanned out across
the pillow, unable to hide the brutal dent in her skull.
Mamma humming monotonous tunes as she covered the
scrapes and bruises in a cream gown. Somehow, seeing
his sister like that was worse than seeing her crumpled at
the bottom of the well. The pretence had sickened him.

The vicar began his gospel reading. Lydia started
to wriggle, her tiny fists clenched. The train of her

Christening gown snagged on the foot of a standing candelabrum. Sawyer bent discreetly, untangled it and straightened.

Still the wind ravened. Behind them the north door, the devil's door in folklore, jumped in its frame.

'Dost thou, in the name of this child, renounce the devil and all his works?'

'I renounce them,' they intoned dully.

'O merciful God, grant that the old Adam in this child may be so buried, that the new man may be raised up…'

He couldn't concentrate. The wind, Lydia's cries, and now the blasted door, like the pounding of approaching hooves, *bang, bang*. It had not been like this for Freddy's baptism. He had a vague recollection of rainbow colours flooding the aisle and broad smiles, even from the old man. But Lydia would not stop crying. It was like a screw twisting deeper and deeper into Wilfred's temple.

'What do you name this child?'

The godmother was supposed to announce that. They were rather at a loss for godparents, since Belinda's brother Luke could not escape from his business in Bristol. Wilfred and Belinda were standing sponsor for their own daughter, with Sawyer representing Mrs Kipling by proxy.

Belinda cleared her throat, strain and disappointment showing in the lines beside her eyes. 'Lydia.' Gently, she removed the cap and bared the baby's head. The wisps of her red hair were a shock against all the white. The vicar took her and began to lower her towards the font. She yowled and thrashed, making the water ripple beneath her. 'Lydia, I baptise thee in the Name of the Father, and of the Son, and of the Holy Ghost. Amen.' The dip was only brief. 'We receive this child into the congregation of Christ's flock and do sign her with the sign of the Cross...'

The north door blew in with a crash. Wind gusted through, catching the train of Lydia's gown until it floated, wraith-like. All of the candles guttered out.

They froze around the font, as if they had been caught in the middle of a crime. Even Lydia stopped her wailing. Now there was only the wind, a ghostly echo of the noise she had made.

'Dear me,' a deep voice said. 'This is rather awkward. I do beg your pardon.'

Wilfred saw a young man on the threshold, closing the north door behind him with difficulty. He wore no wig, only his own leonine hair grown long and tied at the nape. There was a hint of the exotic to him, with his weather-tanned skin and what could only be described as a cavalier beard.

Freddy hid himself behind Wilfred's legs.

'Did you not hear me knocking? I went up to the house, but they told me you were all here.' The man spoke with the assurance of an old friend. His collarless coat was the same piercing blue as his eyes, and the waistcoat beneath a work of art, shot through with golden thread. 'The front door was barred, so I tried my luck up in this part...' He trailed off, noticing his reception was one of shock and not warmth. A rueful smile twisted his lips, and in that moment Wilfred recognised him. The stone floor seemed to tilt under his feet.

'But I am not expected. Or, indeed, invited. You must forgive me, Mrs Bainbridge. I've spent so long abroad that my manners are savage.' The man raised his walking cane and gestured to the font. Those deep blue eyes met his, peeled him to the core. 'What do you say, Wil? Am I too late to stand godfather?'

*

The carriage swayed on its leather straps as the anxious horses battled to make headway against the wind. Belinda was glad of the extended ride home; it gave her time to gather her thoughts.

Sawyer sat on the squabs opposite, astonishment printed on her face. The gentlemen had opted to walk back to the house together – if they were not blown away like kites.

'I have three uncles now,' Freddy chattered as he gazed out of the window at the gusting leaves. 'Uncle Luke, Uncle Paul and Uncle Nathan.'

Belinda settled the sleeping baby on the cushions beside her. 'You always *did* have three uncles. Nathan was always… there.'

But where? Now she reflected, she realised Wilfred had been dreadfully vague. He'd told her of a sister who died young and a brother who lived away. From the manner in which he had spoken, she'd gathered Nathan to be somehow incapacitated, unable to participate in society. One of her cousins was epileptic and required around-the-clock care at a distant facility – Belinda had presumed Nathan's situation was similar. But the man who had intruded upon Lydia's baptism was in the pink of health.

'I thought Mr Bainbridge's brother was ill, ma'am,' Sawyer said, keeping her voice low.

'As did I. Except… Wilfred never said that. Not absolutely.'

'What *did* he say?' Sawyer asked.

It was difficult to recollect. 'He told me Nathan had been sent away when he was still quite young. Those were his words. "Sent away". But maybe it was to start a profession? They take boys into the Navy at an early age, do they not? Eleven or twelve?'

'He mentioned being abroad. And he does *look* as if he's travelled. His face was tanned... Not at all like Mr Kipling's, though.'

She was quite right. Papa's skin was weathered, a touch leathery from high-sea winds. By contrast, Nathan's appeared sun-kissed.

'Perhaps not the Navy, then,' Belinda conceded. 'I cannot say *where* he has been. He did not attend our wedding, or Freddy's baptism, or even his father's funeral. I'll have to ask Wilfred for an explanation. But he looked as startled as we were.'

'Mr Bainbridge looked as if he'd seen a ghost,' Sawyer agreed, leaning forward. 'I don't think he was pleased, ma'am.'

'Uncle Nathan's *not* a ghost!' Freddy pouted.

'No, Master Freddy, that's not what I meant.'

They rumbled along, the wind barrelling at them over the hills as they descended to the house. Baby Lydia's eyes opened briefly. She blew a bubble and Belinda wiped her mouth with a muslin cloth. The Christening may not have gone as she'd hoped, but Nathan's homecoming was something. An excitement, a flash of colour.

She mused over the gentleman she had seen. There was not a strong family resemblance; he wouldn't have struck her as Wilfred's brother at first glance. They shared the same jawline and blue eyes, but while Wilfred's were the pale blue of a spring sky, Nathan's were bright as cobalt. And there was something else. A certain air of charm. Wilfred was a good-looking man, but his brother was positively handsome.

Belinda scolded herself for the disloyal thought.

As they drew round the gravel sweep, another noise made itself known beneath the wind blowing outside: something short, sharp and angry. Lydia awoke and grizzled. The sound came again.

Freddy's ears pricked. 'Is that barking?' he demanded. 'Is that a dog? Is there a *dog* in our house?'

He yanked at the door before the carriage had fully come to a stop. It was all Sawyer could do to keep him from leaping out onto the gravel. As soon as Creswell put down the steps, the boy was scrambling down, falling onto his knees and springing back up again in his haste to be inside.

'Careful, Freddy! Wait!' Belinda called over the wind. Sawyer took the baby while she climbed out. 'Nathan must have brought the animal with him, I suppose. Rather a bold move, to turn up uninvited with a pet in tow.'

Sawyer lowered her eyes. 'He *is* family,' she reasoned. 'You don't mind really, do you, ma'am?'

'No, of course I do not mind. This will set Freddy up for a year.' Belinda's panniers seemed ready to take flight. The boisterous wind was making instruments of all it touched, even blowing spray from the fountain towards her. 'Be careful, Freddy,' she called again. 'Not all dogs are friendly.'

As the four of them drew near to the main door, the barking turned to an excited yip. Claws skittered upon stone. Finally, Mrs Knowles opened up. Her husband stood in the background beside the suit of armour, struggling to hold the collar of a muscular white hound, while his son spoke soothing words from nearby.

'Sorry, madam. We're turned all upside down in here. Do come inside. The creature isn't vicious, just playful.'

Mrs Knowles heaved the door shut behind them. The dog stood on its hind legs and wheeled its front paws in excitement. It was a breed Belinda had never seen before, at least as tall as Freddy even on all fours, with a lithe build, a long, intelligent face and a thin whip of a tail. Blue eyes and a pink nose lent it a curiously human expression.

Lydia didn't like the noise of its whine. Her little face bloomed red as a rose, clashing horribly with her hair as she cried.

'Hush, now.' Belinda jiggled her up and down.

She had expected to find the Great Hall ripe with a canine tang, but this dog brought no odour with it. All she could smell was... roses. Roses even though Mrs Knowles had been cooking all morning. It made no sense.

Freddy was stealing across the flags towards the dog. 'Is it a boy or a girl? What's its name?'

A vein stood out in Knowles' temple as he restrained the dog. 'He's a foreign beast with a foreign name, young master. I didn't quite catch what Mr Nathan said. Sounded almost like David.'

'No, it was Dev,' his son John said. 'But most dogs respond to a whistle and "boy", no matter what. Here, Master Freddy, hold out your hand and let him sniff it.'

Belinda watched anxiously as the pair met. The hound was large enough to knock Freddy clean off his feet but it grew calmer in the presence of the child, as if knowing by instinct to be gentle.

Freddy's fingers caressed the short, pure white coat. 'He's beautiful!' he beamed.

Belinda shook her head, contrasting these with his first words about Lydia.

Footsteps sounded. She turned her head to see the servants' door open and the nursemaids coming to claim the children. But something else caught the corner of her eye. There, piled on the oriental rug in the shadow of the staircase. Trunks.

Did Nathan anticipate a lengthy stay?

That was presumptuous of him, especially considering they had a new baby in the house, but as Sawyer had said, this was his childhood home. And it was not as if they could enjoy any other company for months on end. The laws of mourning prevented them from hosting dinner parties or attending balls until the beginning of winter at the earliest. It might be diverting to have a guest.

She handed Lydia to Amy, sorry that the baby had gleaned no joy from her special day. Freddy was in better luck and went to Rebecca full of news about the dog and his brand-new uncle. Sawyer lingered, looking slightly lost.

'There is to be a special dinner for you all in the servants' hall,' Belinda reminded her.

'Yes, but not for a while yet.'

Of course not. The servants could not eat together until Mrs Knowles had sent up all the food and the men had finished waiting at table. Sawyer was caught between the two worlds. It was horribly awkward.

'Perhaps Mrs Knowles might need your help?' Belinda suggested. She had meant it kindly, as a way for Sawyer to pass the time, but when she heard the words spoken aloud, they sounded like a dismissal.

Sawyer dipped a curtsey, refusing to meet her eye. 'I've gowns of yours to take in at the waist, ma'am. You can tell me all about Mr Nathan when I undress you this evening.' She mounted the stairs. The family staircase, not the servants' one concealed behind a baize door. She looked pitiful and poor in her plain grey gown beside The Bridge's antique grandeur.

Belinda felt close to tears, as she often had in these weeks following the birth. If she'd had her own way, she would have made Sawyer Lydia's godmother in her own right, rather than standing proxy for Mamma. What earthly use was Mamma? Throughout Belinda's childhood it had been *Sawyer* who was the steady fixture: soothing and advising. But maids asked their mistresses to stand godmother to their children; it did not work the other way around. It wasn't proper to bestow honours upon a person in your employ, as if they were your social equal.

The main door opened again. The Bainbridge brothers entered, dishevelled from the wind, carrying their tricorne hats. Upon seeing his master, Dev broke free of Knowles' hold and bounded over the flags.

Nathan smiled broadly. 'Here I am, you silly fellow. What, you can't go an hour without me now? I am sure you have been terrorising the servants and my poor sister-in-law.' He made Belinda an elegant bow. 'I beg your pardon again, Mrs Bainbridge. Heaven knows what you must think of me, darkening your doorstep in this manner. I have thrust my dog and all my worldly goods upon your mercy. I see now I ought to have left them at the port and come up alone by post. That would have been the decent thing to do.'

'Oh! Not at all,' Belinda said. 'We are – happy – to have you. I do hope you will be joining us at table?'

'If I may? That is most gracious of you.'

'Of course you *may*,' Wilfred huffed. Colour grazed the top of his cheeks, as if he had already been speaking in temper. 'We are not in the habit of refusing our flesh and blood hospitality.'

Belinda baulked, embarrassed. Wilfred was usually so urbane. But it was Nathan who smoothed matters over with a smile and a subtle roll of the eyes in her direction. As if Wilfred's whims were a burden they carried together.

Mrs Knowles spoke discreetly in her ear. 'The cold repast is laid out on the sideboard already, madam. John set a third place. I've put wine upon the table. Mr Nathan has given a bottle of Champagne to mark the occasion, I thought I would save that to serve with the fruit.'

'Goodness. How kind of him. Thank you, Mrs Knowles, I thoroughly approve.' Wilfred was watching her. Belinda itched to get him alone and find out precisely what was going on. 'Mrs Knowles says we can eat now, my dear.'

He smoothed his wig, straightened his coat and offered her the crook of his arm. She took it. Nathan followed behind them with the dog. She noted for the first time that he was not in mourning clothes like them; his waistcoat was positively gay, adorned with elaborate picture buttons.

The dining-room was another of The Bridge's ponderous, heavy chambers, burdened by its own luxury. Brocade the colour of tarnished gold hung upon the walls. Curtains swamped the mullioned window, and the air was thick with the smell of furniture polish. It boasted a sideboard, chairs and a grandfather clock made of shining mahogany – but Belinda did not notice them today. Her gaze flew straight to the figure at the head of the table.

'Oh!' She felt Wilfred recoil, just as she did.

A low growl rumbled in the chest of Dev behind them.

It was a companion, but not one of the children Freddy played with. This figure was twice their height. A lady in mustard-coloured silk, brandishing a sword.

'Ah!' Nathan exclaimed. 'You have found my mother's silent companions, then.'

'Yes, but – ' Belinda spluttered ' – not *this* one. This was not here before, was it, Wilfred?'

Dumbly, he shook his head. The thing occupied his place, daring him to fight her for precedence. Most of the companions were lifelike, but this one's face was badly drawn. Her lips were too small, her nose too thin, her cheeks crimson with rouge. The effect was eerily clownish.

But Nathan was not daunted. He waggled his eyebrows playfully at Belinda. 'That is quite common, for them to appear out of nowhere. The companions move by themselves.'

She gaped at him.

'They do no such thing,' Wilfred assured her. 'Nathan is referring to jokes our mother used to play. If she did not like the guests our father had invited for dinner, she would make her footman set the companions up to surprise them.'

'She *didn't*?' Belinda gasped.

'Well,' Wilfred shrugged, 'it is a way to rid oneself of unpleasant company.'

'Why does she carry a *sword*?'

'Oh, I think this figure is meant to represent Justice, or something in that vein. Do you remember, Nathan?'

'No, not I. We never cared for them, did we?'

'No,' Wilfred agreed. 'Here, I will move the wretched thing. Take your seat, Belinda.'

He took the figure away from the table and turned it to face the grandfather clock. It was better to see only the wooden prop and the blank behind, a welcome reminder that the companion was not in fact animate. But how had it got there? She could not imagine one of the Knowleses bringing it in... Unless John shared the same spirit of mischief as Wilfred's mother? She tried to imagine being bold enough, not to mention popular enough, to scare her own guests away.

Belinda settled in the chair at the bottom of the table, which Wilfred had pulled out for her. Tempting dishes were laid out on the sideboard: all manner of salads and cheese, slices of tongue, pickled fish, a pound cake and a pyramid of salmagundi right at the centre. The dog sniffed the air but retreated beneath the tablecloth at an order from Nathan as he took his newly laid place at Belinda's side.

What was she to say to him? She did not want to betray her ignorance about his life. If Nathan realised how little Wilfred had mentioned him, he might be hurt – or worse, he might think Wilfred didn't trust her as part of the family.

Thankfully, the arrival of Creswell with the soup tureen gave her a little time to plan her words. She waited until the bowls were filled and then began, 'I hope, Mr Bainbridge, that you had a pleasant journey?' That was surely vague enough.

'I had a lengthy journey,' Nathan specified. 'I always find a voyage is a mixture of heaven and hell, don't you? Have you travelled much, sister?'

She shook her head. 'No, I am afraid not. Apart from here and London, I have been absolutely nowhere!'

'You are forgetting our honeymoon to the Lakes,' Wilfred put in.

'Oh, yes. That was a beautiful part of the country.' She stirred her soup.

An awkward silence fell.

'As it happens, this is something of a detour for me,' Nathan recommenced. 'I had originally planned to set sail for America.'

'Oh?'

'Now I am glad that I did not. The news from there grows disturbing. There is trouble brewing – if you will excuse the pun.'

The grandfather clock in the corner chimed. She felt the dog under the table nudge her foot.

'Oh – because of the tea at Boston! *Brewing*. Yes.' She released a polite giggle, but it was the silliest noise she'd ever made. She wished it back at once. She glanced at Wilfred, silently spooning his soup like an automaton. If he was not going to help her, she would just ask outright. 'And… where was it you were coming from, Mr Bainbridge?'

He dabbed his lips with a napkin, smoothed his fine pointed moustache. 'Please, you must call me Nathan. We are brother and sister.'

'Nathan, then.'

Wilfred cleared his throat.

'I was on the other side of the argument entirely,' Nathan told her, 'working for the East India Company – the ones with too much tea to sell. I was on one of their ships at the Cape of Good Hope when I received the letter from my father's lawyer, informing me that he had died.'

Her stomach lurched. Had Wilfred really put such a personal matter in the hands of lawyers? It seemed unlike him. 'Yes, I am – I am very sorry for your loss,' she fumbled. 'I had forgotten to say that.'

Nathan inclined his head in thanks. 'I appreciate your sentiment. We were never close. I did not expect any kind of remembrance from my father, and he did not leave me one. Not exactly. But he did ask for a final missive to be delivered to me. A parting blessing in his own hand.' He glanced ruefully at Wilfred. 'Or what amounted to one, from the old man. It gave me a sentimental hankering for home.'

Wilfred picked up his wine glass and took a long swig. Belinda returned to the soup – it was expensive mock turtle, but she could taste nothing. Heaven knew she had endured many awkward meals with Mamma, but her mother was a known entity. Between this new Wilfred and his brother, she was not certain where it was safe to tread.

'Have you worked for the East India Company a long time, Nathan?'

He nodded. His natural hair was tawny, almost autumnal. 'Many years. If you remember the prisoners being rescued from the Black Hole of Calcutta – well, that is about the time I was thrown into the black hole of the Company.' He grimaced. 'But I ought not to gripe about it. India is a remarkable country to have lived in. Still, I...' He hesitated, reached for his wine glass. 'I do not know how to explain it. You may accuse me of being unpatriotic, but I have grown weary of our interference there. Seen such abuses of power as I refuse to speak of, in front of a lady.' He took a deep draught of wine, suddenly resembling his brother. 'My time there has come to an end. I will not be a part of it any longer.'

Fellow feeling stirred in Belinda's chest. 'I quite understand,' she said eagerly. 'My father has timber interests in the West Indies. He and my elder brother are there now and have been ever since this banking crisis began. I am – well, I am ashamed of the connection. My mother and I conceived a real horror of the trade, in all its forms, some years ago. She will not even sweeten her tea now. But mahogany plantations are no better than the ones that grow sugarcane! Quite aside from the terrible human cost, there is the damage to the natural land, the beautiful forests that have been felled! It is sickening, to be reliant on such an industry.' She realised she had spoken a little too warmly for politeness and glanced down at her soup. 'So, yes – I can comprehend why you might wish to leave such a situation.'

Nathan smiled. 'Well, brother, I must congratulate you. You have managed to find a pretty wife with sensibility and morals – a rare commodity in these days.' Belinda felt herself blush. 'I only pray I will be half as fortunate in my turn.'

Wilfred was in the process of raising a spoonful, but at this he returned it to his bowl. 'Is that your design then, in coming to England? You are seeking a wife?'

'I do not know about *design*, but yes, marriage is certainly an object for me now. It has taken some thirty years, but I am finally coming to appreciate the appeal of domestic ties.'

Ties was the right word, Belinda thought. At least when it came to Mamma.

'In the end,' Nathan went on, raising his glass, turning hopefully from Wilfred to Belinda and back again, 'family is all that matters. Is it not?'

CHAPTER 11

Wilfred stood reduced to childhood in his nightshirt and cap, watching Knowles and his son move Nathan's trunks into Wilfred's own room in the west wing. He had offered his chambers up, yet it still felt like being supplanted.

'Really, this is too kind,' Nathan remonstrated. He stood at the foot of the bed, looking more like the elder brother in his stylish suit. 'One of the old guest rooms would have done for me. You know I'm not particular, Wil.'

Wilfred did not know that. He recalled the vagaries of a boy named Nathan; he knew next to nothing about the man his brother had become. 'The guest rooms are in a devil of a state. Not one of them has been aired since we came down five years ago, and Mrs Knowles says moths have been in the linen up there.'

'Well, in that case,' Nathan said, glancing around appreciatively. There, below the pretentious beard: just a flicker of the boy he once was. Wilfred could not decide which unnerved him more: past Nathan or present Nathan. 'It's all grander than I remember! A bit of a change from our days in the old nursery, hey?'

'Actually, I've done the place up for Freddy,' Wilfred told him. 'I will show you. Sometime tomorrow, perhaps.'

'I would like that.'

Nathan smiled warmly, open and trusting. The unconscious tribute paid to an elder sibling. Wilfred had even seen it in Lydia; the way she tried to keep Freddy always in her sight, as if he were the most interesting object in the room. Needles of guilt pricked at his skin.

'I will bid you goodnight, then. My man Hurley will do for your toilette.'

'Capital. Goodnight then, brother. And thank you again.'

Bowing felt too formal, but there had to be some acknowledgement. Wilfred dipped his head awkwardly and turned, taking his candlestick with him. Knowles followed a few paces behind, bringing all the articles he might need to Belinda's rooms.

Wilfred watched the candle's fitful light play over the maroon walls as he walked. How much larger the house felt tonight. A beast grown beyond his control. He did not seem to be striding through it like the master but as a youth again, wondering how he might tame it for his own. The past trod closer than ever, right on his heels.

He supposed there *was* no such thing as a secret in a house like this. Events could be concealed, but they bled into the walls, a record held in time. The stains on the flags. The boarded up well. The spliced handrail and the newer balusters in the gallery, which did not quite match the others.

'A bit of a turn-up for the books,' he said, as lightly as he could. 'What do you make of Nathan coming back, Knowles?'

'It is not something I ever expected to see, sir. He did not even return home when the late Mrs Bainbridge passed. I thought Mr Nathan had put The Bridge behind him.'

But Wilfred knew that was the wrong way round. If they were being honest, it was *they* who had rejected *him*. 'I was going to send my brother a banker's draft. I was going to tell him about our father, of course.' He sounded defensive. 'But there has not been an opportune moment. I did not feel any need to hurry – I knew Nathan would not want to attend the funeral, given the way they parted.'

'He has spared you the trouble of international mail, sir,' Knowles replied, tactfully bland. It did not assuage Wilfred's guilt.

'Knowles... Only you and I were here before. Tell me, what does your wife know about Nathan's departure?'

Knowles was quiet for so long that Wilfred glanced over his shoulder to check he was still following. 'Very little, sir. Mrs Knowles understands that Mr Nathan was at loggerheads with the late master.'

'And this letter Nathan speaks of? Had you any knowledge of that?'

Knowles shook his head. 'No, sir. Mr Bainbridge must have left it with the solicitor personally. My late master kept to himself a great deal near to his death. But you once asked me about the holy men who visited, sir. Perhaps it was their advice that he should make peace with all his kindred as the end drew nigh?'

That did make sense. Whatever his faults, the old man was not a monster. Now Wilfred had children of his own, he could see how impossible it would be to leave the world on bad terms with one of them. He was a blockhead for not anticipating as much before now.

'Nathan never *was* as bad as people make out,' he conceded. 'A little wild, sometimes, but no black sheep.'

'No, sir. As boys I always considered you to be... much the same.'

The candle wavered in Wilfred's hand.

They were approaching Belinda's rooms. The marble busts seemed to float in the dimness. He could hear excited chatter between his wife and her maid through the closed door.

'And what did it taste like?'

'Sharp! Look, I saved this piece for you.'

'For me, ma'am? That was kind – oh, but isn't it strange? I'm not sure I can put that in my mouth!'

A screech of laughter. It made Wilfred feel curiously alone.

He tapped on the door. There was the sound of a stool moving and giggles subsiding.

'Come in, Wilfred,' Belinda called.

He entered to the scent of orange blossom and pomade. Belinda still sat at the dressing-table. Sawyer curtsied to him, her face puckered.

Wilfred raised his eyebrows at her. 'Ah. I see you have let Sawyer sample Nathan's pineapple.'

Belinda beamed. 'Yes! I am not certain it is quite to her taste.'

At least not everyone was bowled over by his brother's worldly glamour. 'It was a princely gift,' Wilfred admitted. 'A pineapple would cost a fortune here, though I think there is still something to be said for plain old English strawberries. Don't you agree, Sawyer?'

She curtsied again. 'I am grateful for the opportunity to try it, sir.'

It was a day of being thrust back into old intimacies. He hadn't shared a bed with Belinda since Lydia had started to show, but now they would have to sleep side by side to accommodate their guest. After dismissing the servants, he climbed beneath the embroidered sheets and tested the strange pillow. Belinda slipped in beside him.

'I have been longing to be alone with you,' she whispered, turning herself to face him.

He sighed. There were no amorous sensations in his body tonight. This was the old man's room. The old man's mattress. Not even Belinda's bright eyes and sweet scent could counter that. Wilfred longed for nothing more than the opportunity to puff out his candle and disappear in sleep.

'We have so much to discuss,' Belinda clarified.

That prospect held even less appeal. He wished ardently that he was the type of man who could roll over and ignore his wife. But that would only be delaying the inevitable. He must tell her something. Where on earth to start?

He remained on his back staring up at the canopy above them. 'What is it you would like to know, Bel?'

She drew in a breath, began confusedly. 'Well... You did not tell me that... I did not realise Nathan...' She exhaled. He felt the warmth of it on his cheek. 'I do not understand what has happened today, Wilfred. Somehow I'd taken up the notion that your brother was too ill to move in society.'

'You did,' he agreed. 'And I allowed you to go on believing that because it was simpler than the truth.'

'Which is?'

Wilfred closed his eyes. Of all the places to say the words aloud, he wished it were not here. At The Bridge, the scene of it all. He did not believe in hauntings, precisely. But it did feel as though the players in this drama were still in the house and would hear every syllable he spoke. 'I never intended to lie to you, Belinda. The matter is... delicate.'

'Like the family witch?' Spoken with a hint of pique.

'No, not like that,' he sighed. 'I am not trying to protect your feelings this time. I am attempting to guard my own.'

Her hand reached out, caressed his face. He took it, held it. 'I am your wife, Wilfred. You must talk to me.'

That was the foundation of a successful marriage, wasn't it? Honesty. Trust. Wilfred had never seen it in action. Quite the opposite.

'I will try, but it is painful to me. I must say things which dishonour the memory of my parents. Impinge upon their reputation. And whatever their faults, I loved them.'

'I shall not breathe a word, Wilfred. Not even to Sawyer. I swear it. They are my family too.'

At last he opened his eyes, turned his head on the pillow to face her. Candlelight gilded the soft down on her cheek and picked out golden threads in her braided hair. 'I suppose I must start with Tiffany. I told you that we lost my sister at a tender age?' She nodded. 'What I did not tell you was that I had good reason to believe she was only... half of my blood.'

She tried to disguise it, but he saw her pupils flare in surprise, maybe even shock. 'Oh.'

'My mother had a favourite footman. Roberts.' The name stuck in his throat.

'The one who moved her companions around for her.'

He snorted. 'Amongst other things, yes. She even had a silent companion made to resemble him. But that was... after.'

'After what, Wilfred?' she asked gently.

Here was the crux of it. Worse than adultery, worse than scandal. 'My father acknowledged the child. This I *will* say for him: he never blamed Tiffany for the sins of her parents. He loved her, I believe. But then, of course, she died.'

'She fell down the well.'

'And not long afterwards, the gallery snapped to pieces. I told you that someone had plummeted to their doom from there. That person was Roberts.'

He wished she would say something. Anything. The silence seemed to curdle and thicken. At last she parted her lips. 'An accident?' Perhaps she was not conscious of the way she inflected the end of the sentence and turned it into a question.

'I was downstairs when it happened.' He swallowed. 'I saw the aftermath. But my father and Nathan were up there with him at the time he fell. Only they know the full circumstances.' He was painfully aware of his heart racing and the blood thudding past his ears. 'Nathan was sent away, almost immediately. Either he saw something he shouldn't or else *did* something he should not have.'

Belinda's eyes were wide. She didn't even blink. 'Which do you think it was?'

How could he possibly answer that? He squeezed her hand. 'People in the village believed that my father pushed Roberts. Then used his own son as a scapegoat, to save face. And, of course, he was the local magistrate. There was no investigation. He ruled it an accident and banished Nathan to a distant cousin in Calcutta. A tacit admission of his guilt.'

'But *you*, Wilfred,' she persisted. 'You must have known your brother best. Do you really believe he murdered a man? Or that your father could have done?'

He could not meet her earnest gaze. 'I believe Nathan was wronged. And even if he *were* guilty, I honestly could not condemn him. Roberts was a scoundrel. We both of us hated the man. And we were little more than children ourselves. Nathan was only twelve... Our emotions were addled, we were still in mourning for our sister. It is quite possible Nathan did not mean to – did not fully comprehend the gravity of his actions.'

Her eyes glazed over and he saw her taking this in, weighing it all up. 'Did you speak up for him, at the time?'

Bile rose at the back of his throat. She had put her finger on the wound. 'I had a choice: either stand by my father or defend my brother. And, God forgive me, it was easier to stick with the old man. He held my future in his hands. It shames me to admit this, Bel, but there it is. I was fifteen and craven. I cut all ties with Nathan because I was told to – not through any conviction of his wickedness. Please understand that I would never allow him into our home, with our children, if I truly believed him to be a danger.'

Belinda frowned. 'But you do not seem to like him, Wilfred. You are not very cordial.'

'Am I not? I shall try – I *will* try to do better. The fact of the matter is... I am ashamed.' His voice wavered. 'Ashamed I did not seize upon the opportunity of the old man's death to bring Nathan back into the fold at once. I *could* have written to him, in all these years, without my father being aware of it. I did not. Only when our mother died, a year after he left. And now he has turned up, full of gifts and goodwill, keen to escape the life the old man thrust him into. Nathan has imagined me to be here, all this time, secretly wishing him well. And I wasn't, Bel! I did not consider him at all. I wanted to forget he had ever been and close the door on that chapter of my life entirely.'

Her form had grown hazy before him. It was not the candlelight affecting his eyes but the blur of unshed tears.

'I understand, Wilfred. Truly, I do.'

'You do not think me an abominable coward?'

'Not at all! You are not the only person who has struggled to stare the truth in the eye. Often it is easier to pretend. Or ignore it entirely. I do that myself.' She returned the pressure of his hand. 'But now you have an opportunity to put it right. You can be kind to Nathan. We will make him welcome here. You can have a brother again.'

A brother. Closer, in some ways, than a wife. Truly blood of his blood. It used to be Nathan, curled up in bed beside him. Nathan, whispering secrets in the dark. He was there first.

But there was no way of turning back the clock. Those halcyon days in the nursery were long gone. Whatever Belinda might say, the boy from his memories was as lost to him as Tiffany, broken at the bottom of the well. And Wilfred had a terrible suspicion that it was all his own fault.

CHAPTER 12

The wind was still up, but more playful than violent today. It blew the clouds merrily along as they took the path towards the gardens: Belinda and Wilfred arm-in-arm, the children attached to their nursemaids and Nathan, bringing up the rear with his dog.

'Say it again,' Freddy wheedled. 'I want to remember.'

She half-expected Nathan to protest, but his patience with the boy was inexhaustible. 'Dev is a Rajapalayam hound,' he repeated distinctly. 'I'd wager you won't find another like him in England. It's all mastiffs and blood-hounds in these parts, is it not? Ugly brutes.'

'Dev the Rajapalayam hound.' Belinda smiled to hear Freddy pronounce the words as accurately as he had said '*aquilegia vulgaris*' that day she fell into the thistle patch. He had a good ear. Evidently he was thinking of their planting lessons too, for he went on, 'Do dogs have Latin names as well, like flowers do, Uncle Nathan?'

'Latin, you say? I haven't the faintest idea. I don't suppose Dev would answer to that. Let's see, shall we? *Veni, canem!*' Nathan called. The dog trotted on without glancing back at him. 'No, I'm afraid he doesn't speak a word of Latin.'

An indifferent jest, but Freddy hooted as if it were the best he had ever heard. She felt Wilfred's arm grow rigid beneath her palm. He was jealous, she realised. He wanted to be the hero in Freddy's eyes.

'Does he play fetch?'

'He has been known to.'

'There are some huge sticks in the orchard! I saw them the other day. Papa, Papa! May I take Dev and Rebecca to the apple trees and play?'

There were no firm paths in the orchard. It was well enough for a romping child, but not suitable for Belinda's satin slippers or Nathan's red-heeled shoes.

Wilfred groaned. 'Yes, if your uncle does not object to your borrowing his dog. I *had* rather hoped to take a nice sedate walk as a family.'

Freddy whooped, ignoring everything except the affirmative. He sped towards the orchard gate, calling Dev after him. The dog glanced at Nathan for approval. He nodded, and the hound took off at an elegant lope.

'Do not worry,' Nathan told Rebecca as she began to follow them. 'He'll do whatever the boy tells him. He's a biddable cur.'

'Thank you, sir.'

'Bring Lydia too!' Freddy called, dangling himself from the rungs of the gate. 'It's my job to keep her safe, isn't it, Papa?'

'She'll be safe enough with us, Fred,' Wilfred said.

Freddy shook his fair head until his queue whipped. 'Not in the garden. Mamma fell over there. It's better in the orchard. I want Lydia to come.'

Wilfred made a weary gesture of assent to the wet-nurse. Smiling and shrugging her shoulders, Amy set off with Lydia, leaving the three of them alone.

Nathan came around to Belinda's left side and slipped his arm confidingly through hers. 'There we are. We may proceed more comfortably now, all together.' He smiled. His beard framed his lips perfectly. 'You are a rose between two thorns.'

'Oh!' She felt like one of the fast girls at Vauxhall Gardens, with a beau on each arm. It was strange to have another man so near; let alone a man who may have used this very arm to push a servant to his death. 'You flatter me. But I fear you will be left wishing for roses, or flowers of any sort, in our gardens. I am ashamed to take you there, Nathan. We barely made a start on planting before Lydia came along.'

'Please, do not apologise on my account. You forget I am used to seeing it in a natural state – our parents never went in for pleasure grounds, did they, Wil?'

Wilfred gave a shake of the head. 'Or pleasure at all, I suppose.'

'Ha!'

Belinda half-smiled, unsure if she was supposed to laugh along or not. The strange thing was, she could still smell roses on the air; the sweetness of petals warmed by the sun, as if they were about to enter a garden full of blooms instead of thistles. John had planted some flowers for her, but none of them had been roses. She was starting to think there was something wrong with her nose.

'An English garden is a special treat for me,' Nathan went on. 'I have been longing to see one in any form.' He raised his chin to the branches beckoning over the wall and inhaled. 'Even glimpsing the woodland has done me a world of good. Sturdy chestnut. Steadfast oak. Old friends.'

'Did you not care for the gardens in India?' she asked, curious. 'I was rather hoping to quiz you about them. I have heard there are some glorious flowers there.'

'Oh, indeed there are, sister! Do not mistake me.' His face took on a wistful expression. 'The luscious *champak*, the vibrant *palash*, such courtyards and greenery as would take your breath away. But to me they are not familiar. They are not *home*.' He dragged his cane along the grass at their side, thoughtful, almost like a caress upon the land. 'An Indian summer is bright and vivid, whereas here it is… softer. Something in the quality of the light… I cannot fully explain. An English garden feels gentler.' He grinned across her at Wilfred. 'A carroty-pate like my brother would burn to a crisp in the Indian sun.'

'No doubt about it,' Wilfred agreed. 'I am hot enough today as it is.'

He truly looked it. Pink and mottled beside Nathan's nut-brown. The contrast between the brothers was stark, one of them bewigged and dressed in sombre black, the other wearing pale stockings and light breeches. Summer and winter, walking either side of her.

Despite Nathan's assurance, she felt a drop of dismay as they came within sight of the wild tangle at the back of the house. The lawns were almost knee-high now, strewn with buttercups and daisies. The thistle patch ran rampant, overspilling its bounds. Ivy had stretched its web down another section of the walls.

'You see,' she said hopelessly, 'what I am attempting to tame!'

Nathan whistled. 'My, it is perfectly feral! I must say, I rather like it myself. Those romantic, Gothic land-scapes always appeal to me. But this is not a fit garden for ladies and children.' He disengaged his arm from hers, took a few paces forward to inspect the grounds. 'This is certainly what I would call a *project*. And not just the gardens.' He turned to Wilfred, the breeze play-ing with a few bronze strands of his hair. 'I confess, I was surprised to learn you'd taken it all on when the old man passed.'

Wilfred frowned. 'Why should you be surprised?'

'Well, you were all set up in London, weren't you? A fashionable address and society for your wife. The company is rustic out here.' He winced. 'Do you remember how the Torbury St Jude assemblies used to bore our mother to tears?'

'You have not had the pleasure of knowing Belinda for long,' Wilfred said, a thread of warning in his voice. 'Her tastes are markedly different from our mother's.'

Nathan shrugged. 'To be sure. But staying at home for the evening brings few comforts in such an old pile as this. It's so formal, even when you are at your ease. As if the house… disapproves.'

Something inside Belinda quickened. Yes, that was exactly how it felt. The suits of armour, the heavy carvings, even the wall around the gardens: everything here seemed designed to oppress.

But Wilfred snorted. 'Bosh.'

'Well, you are old and stuffy too,' Nathan teased. 'I meant to ask you: are there mice in the skirtings? There was an odd kind of ruckus last night—'

'Really?' Belinda found herself leaning forward, eager for more. 'What sort of noise did you hear, Nathan?'

He considered. 'It's hard to say really. A sort of rasp? Or hiss? It put me in mind of a saw.'

Wilfred stiffened.

But Belinda's relief spilled onto her lips. 'Yes! That is precisely it.' She had not imagined anything; she was not alone in this. 'Oh, I am so glad someone else has noticed that sound! I thought I was running mad. And the dragging? Did you hear that too, Nathan? Like furniture being moved?'

He opened his mouth to reply but Wilfred cut across him. 'Really, listen to the pair of you! It is an old house.

It is never quiet. You've been away for too long, Nathan. You forget, we heard these bumps in the night from our very cradles.'

Nathan raised his brows, caught Belinda's eye with a twinkle. Again she felt that shared understanding; the sense that they both loved Wilfred and so must tolerate his foibles together. 'Well, we shall see if Dev brings me any trophies tonight. He's quite a ratter. He'll sniff them out.' Movement from the house distracted Nathan. He turned his head to look, and Belinda followed his gaze. She just caught sight of Sawyer's face at an upper window before the curtain swished across.

Her spirits sank. Poor Sawyer. If they had not hired the nursemaids, she would be out here with them, watching Freddy or carrying Lydia. Enjoying the day. Now she was left indoors to tidy Belinda's rooms and manage her wardrobe.

'I believe I saw that young woman at the Christening,' Nathan said softly, still looking up. 'Pray, what is her name?'

'Miss Sawyer. She is my lady's maid, Nathan. A very dear servant. We were much together as girls. She was presented to me almost like a gift.'

'Ah!' He nodded. 'That explains it. I was about to observe that she has a remarkably genteel air.'

Belinda rewarded him with a warm smile. 'She is an excellent creature.'

'We are fond of Sawyer,' Wilfred agreed. 'Which is as well, considering she spends more time drawing than doing her actual work.'

Belinda narrowed her eyes as they walked on. Had Wilfred always been this morose? Surely not. It was Nathan's arrival, it had put him out of sorts. But the explanation he had given her last night did not seem to justify the strength of his reaction. *This* was not a murderer! Perhaps Nathan's beard was a little roguish, but the expression beneath it was open, honest and manly. Far easier to imagine that Wilfred's surly father had pushed the servant who cuckolded him, then banished his younger son as the only witness to the crime.

They were approaching the rectangular flowerbeds beneath the chestnut trees. All the thistles Belinda had pruned were revived, deep purple and speckled with ants. To the left was the bed John had planted and promised to water during her confinement. She'd hoped to see new green shoots pushing up through the soil, flower buds plump with promise. There was nothing. No growth, no colour.

A patch of uneven earth showed the hole Freddy had dug with his bare hands. Beside it, the columbines were dead. Not etiolated but thoroughly withered from the roots up. As if the essence had been sucked out of them.

'Oh, no!' She stopped, pulled Wilfred up short. 'I do not understand. What could have happened? Did John not water these as I asked?'

'On the contrary, he appeared most diligent.' A shadow passed across Wilfred's face. 'But... Freddy did say the plants would all die.'

'*Freddy*? How would he know?'

'They were not planted deep enough?' Wilfred queried. 'Or something of the sort. He told me you had taught him that...'

Shaking her head, she went up to the edge of the bed and squatted down. 'I said nothing. John's work all seems to be in order. He did no wrong. But for the flowers to shrivel like that...'

Nathan stooped beside her. He touched the soil and put it to his lips. 'Salt,' he declared.

'I beg your pardon?'

'The soil is salty.' He held out two grubby fingers to Belinda with a grin. 'Taste it.'

'Nathan!' Wilfred objected.

'No, I believe you. But why would that be?' Belinda stared at the mounded soil, still innocent of any worms. Now that made sense. 'I have salted against slugs before, but only a little. And you said your parents did not garden themselves?'

Nathan shrugged, straightened up. 'I cannot say *why* it is salted. I can only tell you that nothing will grow in salt earth. You will have to dig this all up and refill the bed with something loamy. I would be happy to lend you my assistance, sister. Your manservant will need a hand, it is a large task for him.'

Wilfred placed a hand upon her shoulder. 'Do not fret, my dear. There's no need for John or Nathan to wade about in the dirt. Remember, I have the Torbury parish labour gang at my disposal next week. They can get this done for you in half the time.'

'The labour gang?' Nathan cried. 'What the deuce have you hired them for?'

Wilfred stepped back, stood facing his brother across Belinda once more. 'Enclosing the common land,' he said heavily.

The leaves soughed above them, their shadows running like ink across the flowerbed. 'Upon my word,' Nathan breathed, 'the villagers won't like that.'

'I don't *like* it,' Wilfred flared. 'The old man set everything in motion before he died. There's been too much expense and legislation to turn back now. But to be honest, I do not see what else he could have done. The estate needs the capital a regular wheat crop would bring.'

Quietly, Belinda rose to her feet. There was something deeper playing out here, something she did not perfectly understand. She only hoped interposing herself between them would lessen the tension.

It did, for a moment. Stepping back, Nathan reached into his pocket and withdrew a gleaming snuffbox, worked in swirling agate and edged with gold. There was a certain suavity to the way he flipped the lid open with his thumbnail. As he took a pinch of the powder inside, Belinda detected a hint of its sour spice. When he spoke again, his tone held less emotion. 'Wilfred, it's a waste of your time. You must see that. You will be angering the cottagers for nothing. You might as well plant your wheat in this salted earth – you'll get no crop from the common.'

'What makes you say that? Livestock are grazing out there, acorns are dropping for the pigs. It's not a barren landscape.'

'But there's a curse,' Nathan replied, reasonable, matter-of-fact. He closed the snuffbox with a click. 'On the old Hanging Oak. Don't you remember? You'd have to chop it down before you planted the common, and the villagers are dreadfully pagan about that tree. They see it as their protector, killing off their criminals for them and guarding their common land from... well, from us. Come, you *must* remember. Tiffany used to play in that tree all the time. She said whoever cut it down would be cursed.'

Wilfred's crack of laughter was sharp. 'What utter rot. She never told such a tale in all her life. And *you* certainly do not believe in curses!'

'All the same... It's safer not to touch it, don't you think?' Nathan was struggling to hold something back. It did not seem to be anger. It was more like fear. 'It's bad luck, old chap. The worst luck. You may laugh at me, but these things are best left well alone.'

Wilfred appraised his brother curiously, as if he did not know what to make of him. 'You've spent too much time abroad, Nathan. Taken on foreign ideas. A tree is a tree. Common land is just land. I've seen the estate figures and, believe me, The Bridge needs this.'

Nathan bit his lower lip. 'Well, it is your land, Wil. You know it best. But the people of Fayford revere their oak. If you do this… do not be surprised if things take an unfortunate turn.'

*

Wilfred had grown out of the habit of riding in London. It was so easy to take a chair or go by water while Belinda used their carriage for her morning calls. They had never been the sort to parade up and down Rotten Row, showing off their clothes and their horsemanship to the rest of the quality. But riding out here, on his own land, was different.

Everything seemed shifting and magical in the fluid light of the trees. The woods followed their own patterns. Gnats hovered in clouds by the bracken. He could hear the hooves of Knowles' horse falling behind him, and the usual forest sounds: crunches, rustling, distant wings.

His heart lay heavy within his chest. Who was he, to curb nature? He did not want the enclosure and so-called 'progress' any more than Nathan did. But as the eldest, he held a responsibility, not just towards his own family and the tenants, but towards the generations who would come after. Better to convert the land now than be forced to mortgage it later.

They emerged from the chestnut coppice into June sunshine. From there it was only a few strides until they were passing by the cornfield. Stalks rippled with a husky whisper. From up high, Wilfred could see the neat rows planted while the old man had still been alive. The crop had been sold at the same time, a price arranged and agreed upon before it was even standing in the field: a risky measure Wilfred would never instigate himself.

Like enclosing the common for wheat. But both choices had been taken out of his hands.

He could not erase the image of Nathan's face at breakfast. His brother had not offered any words of reproach, but his countenance had been pale and queasy, as if he were watching someone making a grave mistake. If he'd pleaded for the tenants, for their poverty, Wilfred would have understood. But the objections Nathan had made out in the gardens, his claims of a curse, were astonishing. Where could he have heard such tales? It was true that the village of Fayford had been here long before the house. Long enough for there to be records of rough justice administered on the common land: miscreants hung from the boughs of the oak and buried by its roots, where the acorns dropped. But all this talk of the tree protecting villagers from the Bainbridge family and a curse upon it, were new to Wilfred. While Tiffany had certainly climbed the tree, she'd never said a word to him about the rest of it.

Did these superstitions play some part, he wondered, in his father's decision to enclose the land and cut the oak down? Did he think such a macabre landmark was better gone? As Nathan had said, the whole thing smacked of paganism. They needed to prepare the village for the future and a more enlightened era.

His mare Gimcrack tossed her head. He turned in the saddle to look at Knowles and saw that his mount, too, seemed a touch uneasy. These were carriage horses, unaccustomed to the saddle.

'I'll have to get myself a steady hack,' he told Knowles. 'A cobby sort suited to farmland. And Freddy will need a starter pony too.'

Knowles kept his eyes on the nodding head of his horse. 'I will ask around, sir, but I imagine it will be expensive.'

'No doubt. Good horseflesh does not come cheap. But I don't see how else we are to manage. Horses are not a luxury in the countryside but a necessity.'

'And hopefully our new wheat crop will help offset the cost. I confess, I'm not knowledgeable about the grain markets these days. Perhaps Mr Nathan or Mr Kipling will be able to advise you on how best to dispose of your harvest when the time comes. I imagine it will fetch a higher price in London than Torbury St Jude?'

That was a given. But Wilfred doubted he had enough steel within his heart to go through with such a measure. He wanted to be liked. He always had. Sending grain away from the local villages and raising the price of the loaf would make him even more of a pariah with his tenants. He'd avoid *that* betrayal if he possibly could.

Beyond the corn, the land rolled wide in an ocean of heath and heather. A rabbit darted across their path and disappeared with a flash of its white tail. Shapes floated on the horizon: small bushes, stunted clusters of oaks and the rocks beside the river. One great, grizzled tree stretched its claws towards the sky. Unmistakably the infamous Hanging Oak. Underneath it, the labourers had gathered ready for their day's work. Piles of fences were stacked beside them, slats criss-crossed like prison bars. There were mallets, axes and a sturdy horse traced to a plough. Wilfred saw at once that he would not be able to spare any members of the gang for Belinda's garden plans. The task before them was colossal, given the time frame.

A few of the villagers lingered, gathering their live-stock and driving them away. They watched him with baleful stares. He could not blame them. Where would they keep these animals now, and how would they afford fodder? There would be goats sleeping in with the children for want of space, cows butchered because they'd stopped producing milk. It ought never to have reached this pass.

He saw Ross Roberts claiming a fat-bellied sow, but he did not draw near Wilfred. It was an elderly woman with her cow who approached him. She was missing teeth and wore her shawl crossed over her body, tied at her lower back. 'We never thought you'd do this. The old one, maybe. But they all said you'd put a stop to it.'

He recognised her now as Goodwife Griffin. Time had not treated her well. He remembered her as a dairymaid up at the house, when they'd still kept a dairy. It was awkward, peering down at her from his lofty height. He was uncomfortably conscious of the shine of his boots, the proximity of his riding crop. 'I'm afraid it is out of my control, Goody. Petitions have been through Parliament, commissioners have visited. And the harvests have been so bad.'

'It seems to have happened awful quick after the other one came home,' she muttered.

So they knew about Nathan's return. Of course they did; he had come striding into Fayford on the day of the Christening, banged on the church doors. And it sounded as if this villager was blaming him. The Prodigal Son, accessory to murder, come to strip her of her common land.

It was grossly unfair. He took a breath to tell her how his brother had spoken up in protest at the scheme, but released it again. What did it matter? Nothing would stop the deed being done. 'At least, Goodwife Griffin, we are in time to plant some winter wheat. That will mean you can afford more bread over the cold months, will it not? And there will be harvesting work for the people of Fayford too.'

The cow stretched its neck and began to crop at the grass. Goodwife Griffin watched him, a challenge in her wrinkled face, to see if he would force her to stop. Of course he didn't. He was not so petty. 'I'm not certain I believe you, sir,' she said baldly. 'There's plenty of work for Fayford lads here today, but you've called the work-house in for cheaper labour.'

'The common is a different matter entirely. It would be beyond the pale to ask the villagers to enclose it themselves. I could not expect them to do something so utterly against their...' He was about to say 'inter-ests' but caught himself in time. 'Their beliefs,' he said instead.

'How considerate of you, sir.'

He ignored her sarcasm. Ignored everything except the one ragged labourer who picked up an axe and tested its weight in his hands. The world seemed to narrow to that single point. Goodwife Griffin was speaking rubbish. No matter how desperate for coin the Fayford villagers became, he knew they would never consent to do this.

He heard the collective intake of breath as the man swung his axe, landing it with a dull *thunk* in the torso of the Hanging Oak. With difficulty, he dislodged the axe-head from the trunk and tried again, sending out a fine spray of wood. Splinters pale as flesh.

Wilfred winced. Below the steady chop, he heard the goodwife muttering a prayer.

Or perhaps it was a curse of her own.

CHAPTER 13

Belinda had spent a morning scouring the pleasure grounds for signs of roses. Wild dog roses, a bush hidden under the brambles, anything. When that proved fruitless, she took the housekeeping keys from Mrs Knowles and went through all the presses and medicine cabinets but found nothing, not so much as a bowl of pot-pourri. There was rosemary and lavender to ward off moths; chamomile, feverfew, mugwort and wormwood for physic. No roses. Although she smelt them nearly every day, the only traces she could find were an old rosewater pomade at the back of a drawer in her dressing-table and the blooms painted on Freddy's silent companion.

It was baffling, disturbing, and Belinda knew that if she continued to dwell upon it, she would run mad. Walls would start to melt again, bedposts to wilt. She had to distract herself. With Wilfred out for another day supervising the enclosure of the common and Lydia sleeping soundly, she decided it was time to resume her own projects.

'Do you want to plant some more flowers with me, Freddy?' she asked.

He was sprawled on the rug beside Lydia's cot, lining his toy soldiers up in formation. The silent companions had been relegated to the schoolroom for the time being

– an example of children's fickle loyalty. And in the same way, Freddy, who had once been so interested in the plants, now shook his head. 'No, thank you.'

'We'll ask Uncle Nathan if you can bring the dog. Dogs like to dig.'

He did not look up from his task. He was moving the little cannons now, a full range of artillery. 'No. I won't do it. She tricked me into digging before.'

Belinda exchanged a bemused glance with Rebecca. 'Nobody tricked you, my love. You were digging in your sleep. Whatever you saw or heard was just a dream.'

'I want to stay in here with Lydia,' he insisted.

Belinda supposed she ought to be grateful for his filial affection. So many elder siblings reacted to a new arrival with nothing but jealousy. Her friend Mrs Jones in London had endured tears and tantrums for months after her third son was born. Leaving Freddy to his miniature regiment, Belinda took Sawyer outside with her instead.

It was another fine day, the sky cornflower blue and lightly gauzed with clouds. Warm, too, for a shimmer of heat seemed to rise as they entered the stable yard to borrow a wheelbarrow and gather the tools.

Dawkins eyed them, perturbed. 'You're going to dig up the flowerbed yourself, Mrs Bainbridge? Just the two of you?'

'Yes,' Belinda replied stoutly. 'Why should we not?'

Of course he could not answer that.

She noticed Sawyer biting back a smile as the maid grabbed the handles of the barrow and began to steer it around the water trough, back towards the gardens. Once they were out of earshot, she said, 'You know he's right, ma'am. We don't have the strength to change all that soil on our own. Certainly not in one day.'

'Well,' said Belinda archly, 'maybe *you* do not.' And they both laughed, for it was obvious that Sawyer was the stronger of the pair by far.

It felt good to laugh again, after all the tension Belinda had felt lately. With Sawyer, she could speak without worrying about setting an example to Freddy or losing respect amongst the other servants. More than anything she wanted to be *doing* something. Working her muscles, getting the blood flowing. The memory of her confinement was still close enough to give her a horror of sitting still.

'Where is Mr Nathan today?' Sawyer asked as they made their way slowly across uneven grass. 'Is he helping Mr Bainbridge with the enclosure?'

'No, I do not think he would do that. He disagrees with it. I ought to have asked Nathan his plans at breakfast. I suppose that makes me a sorry hostess.'

'Well, it seems he feels at home here, ma'am, and does not need you to entertain him.'

Belinda batted at one of the thistles as they passed. 'I still do not know what to make of him. He is not like my own brothers. He's more playful, more gallant.'

'He is a very... elegant gentleman,' Sawyer offered.

'Yes.' Belinda yearned to say more, to share what Wilfred had told her about the cause of Nathan's being sent away, but it was not her secret to tell. She could not betray her husband's confidence.

The wheelbarrow made a valley through the long grass. Sawyer set it down beside the blighted flowerbed and mopped her brow. 'It's a shame about all those plants. Poor John worked so hard.'

Belinda selected a spade with a long shaft and a sturdy blade. 'Yes. I did not have the heart to ask him to come out here and dig it all up again.' She planted the blade in the earth and stood on its shoulder, relishing the crunch it made as it sank.

Of course, Sawyer had been correct. The novelty of digging soon wore off as the heat of the day built. Sun pressed down upon Belinda's shoulders like a weight. The sliver of exposed skin between the neck of her gown and the brim of her hat felt like it was starting to burn. She stood for a moment, resting a hand on her hip. The barrow was only a quarter full and her arms had already begun to ache.

'Go and sit beneath the parasol for a while,' Sawyer advised, pushing her own spade deeper. 'There's a bottle of Mrs Knowles' lemonade unopened.'

Earlier, the maid had set up a little camp with pillows and some shade, as if predicting this would happen. Belinda obeyed her instructions, feeling like a weakling. Though in fairness, it was not so *very* long since Lydia's birth. She was still recovering. She reclined and sipped at the sweet, sticky liquid. Bees were droning softly nearby. Belinda watched Sawyer with pride and even a touch of envy. How effortlessly she moved, scooping up the crumbling soil and stringy roots without raising a sweat. Belinda did not doubt she was the more fortunate of the two, being a lady, but there must be satisfaction in relying on your own body and trusting in its resilience as Sawyer could.

'I say, sister! This is rather bad form.' She looked around, startled to see Nathan striding across the lawn towards them. Although he spoke reproachfully, he was smiling and his tone merry. He was as finely turned out as ever. The braid on his hat, the fob of his watch and the buckles on his shoes all sparkled in the sun. A pale blue silk waistcoat fell to his hips like a cascade of cool water. 'I offered to help you with this task and there you are, at your ease, while this lovely creature labours in my stead.'

Neither heat nor work had tinted Sawyer's cheeks, but at these words she blushed red as a poppy.

Belinda forced a laugh, hoping to divert his attention. 'You have caught me out. I am a cruel mistress.' She made to regain her feet and he held out a hand to help her. 'I did not wish to trouble you, Nathan. You are my guest. You should not be running my errands.'

'There is no workhouse gang at your disposal then?'

'Not for me. Wilfred cannot spare them. And to tell the truth, I am glad. However harsh I may look, watching my poor Sawyer toil, I would not be comfortable asking unfortunate people to tend my pleasure grounds. It would be frivolous. Tasteless.'

'I quite agree.'

Seeing that Sawyer had recovered her composure, Belinda carried over some lemonade for her while Nathan stripped off his coat and draped it over the thistle bush. Then he began to unbutton his cuffs and roll back his sleeves.

'You are not going to dig in those beautiful clothes!' Belinda protested.

'I am,' he countered with a grin. 'Do you think me a dandy?'

'No, I think you will drive poor Mrs Knowles to distraction trying to scrub the dirt out of your fine silk.'

Nathan laughed at the justice of this. 'Nevertheless, I am determined. But before we begin, I require a little restorative.' He pulled the snuffbox out of his waistcoat pocket.

Belinda saw it clearly today. The piece was quite exquisite. Chestnut agate gave a marbled effect to the sides, while the lid was overlaid with gold filigree.

He opened the box, offered it to her. 'Care to try?'

'Me?' she said, surprised. 'Why...' Stupidly, she found herself looking to Sawyer as if for her permission. 'I do not know. I never took snuff before!'

'There is a first time for everything. It is easy. Watch.' Expertly, he took a pinch between his thumb and index finger. He sniffed gently and it disappeared as if by magic. 'Ah! That's better.'

Belinda hesitated. The powder looked like finely ground soil. A tiny crumb of it still lingered in Nathan's moustache. 'What is *in* snuff?'

'This is rappee. A dark tobacco. I add attar of roses. Come, now. It will not hurt you to *try* a little.'

She took some, held it to her nose. Roses, again. She snorted a little too hard. Her right nostril ignited. Her very brain seemed to tingle in her skull. Belinda spluttered and sneezed.

Nathan laughed.

'Ugh! It's ghastly. How do you bear it?'

Rather than answering, he nodded across the flower-bed. 'Miss Sawyer? You are very welcome to sample it too, if you have the courage.'

Sawyer's cheeks pinked again; with pleasure this time, instead of embarrassment. She seemed glad to be included. Belinda had rarely seen her look so girlish, so young. 'Thank you, sir.' She bobbed a curtsey and laid down her shovel. 'I will certainly try.'

She stepped hesitantly around to their side of the flowerbed, not quite looking Nathan in the eye. She took a larger pinch than Belinda had dared to. Belinda grimaced, anticipating her pain. Sawyer inhaled. Her pupils expanded and she looked a little stunned, but there was no choking.

'Well?' Nathan asked, watching her intently. 'What is your verdict?'

'I... I like it, sir,' she declared.

'Excellent!' He snapped the box shut and tucked it away. 'I shall make a convert of you yet. I see you are made of sterner stuff than my sister.'

Sawyer ducked her head.

Belinda gasped, feigning offence. 'Well, for *that*, you can start digging at once. Pass him your shovel, Sawyer.' She grinned impishly. 'I *would* help you, Nathan, but clearly I am too weak to bear it.'

'Touché. I am quite ready to start.'

She liked the way Nathan had adopted her as part of his family so readily, teasing her as easily as he did Wilfred. Her brother Paul would never do so, nor would he involve himself with 'feminine' concerns such as gardens. Luke might, but out of duty, not pleasure. She felt a pang for Nathan, stuck out in India all those years without people to call his own. He was clearly a social creature.

He fell to work with gusto. She had seen soldiers drill their weapons with less show than he wielded that shovel. After a while, Sawyer joined in again.

Belinda tried to think of something else witty or amusing to say. But instead, the question that had been bubbling for days sprang to her lips. 'Did you mean what you said the last time we were here, Nathan? About the common land and the tree being cursed? Do you truly believe something bad will happen after the enclosure?'

He tossed a shovelful of earth into the barrow. It pattered like rain. 'Yes, something bad *will* happen,' he said frankly, 'and it is that the people of Fayford will turn against Wilfred. He is taking away their footpaths, their stream, their grazing and their place to lay snares for rabbits. As for the rest...' He sighed, drove his shovel into the earth and leant against it. 'No. Rationally, I doubt that vengeful ghosts will rise up from the stump of the Hanging Oak. And yet I still do not want it cut down. It's hard to explain. A superstition. I associate that tree with our sister. With Tiffany... She liked to play there.' His gaze drifted towards the well.

Belinda swallowed. She knew she should not probe, but her curiosity was like a loose tooth; she could not leave it alone. 'Wilfred does not like to speak of her much.'

'No, I suppose he wouldn't. He's always been very... practical.'

She regarded the crumbling structure. How deep did it go? The dead girl could only have been a few years older than her Freddy. 'The loss must have been very difficult for you both,' she said with sympathy. 'Were you... there, when she fell?'

Nathan jerked to attention. 'Fell?' he repeated. 'My dear Belinda, Tiffany jumped.'

Sawyer stopped digging.

They both stared at him. The chestnut leaves waved gently above.

'She jumped down the well?' Belinda repeated, incredulous. 'Why would she do that?'

Nathan sighed. He drew out a handkerchief and dabbed at his damp brow. 'I'm sorry. Perhaps I should not have told you.'

'No – I – it is *I* who must apologise.' Belinda could not believe she had been so insensitive. 'I did not mean to distress you. It is only that Wilfred has said so little about her and I... I am trying my best to understand.'

'You have said nothing wrong, Belinda.' After folding the handkerchief back into his pocket, Nathan resorted to his snuffbox again. His fingers trembled this time as he took a pinch. 'You are part of the family. You deserve to know the truth, as painful as it is.' He took a snort of the powder. Exhaled. 'Tiffany was... What can I say? "Set apart"? I have spent too much time abroad, I do not know how to convey things in the English fashion. "Touched"? Her wits were not the quickest, but she had a *perception* others do not.'

Belinda's mouth seemed suddenly dry again. 'What do you mean?'

'She saw things, "knew" things she could not possibly know. She claimed she spoke with spirits.' He gave a wry smile. 'I see you doubt me, but second sight does run in our family. Every few generations it pops up. This... gift, I suppose. Has Wilfred told you about the witch?'

'Anne Bainbridge?' Belinda felt like Eve, tempted by forbidden fruit. 'Only that she was burnt at the stake. Which I thought strange, because I understood witches were typically hanged.'

She saw Sawyer, dappled with patches of light, watching them in astonishment. Wilfred would not want the maid to know any of this... but she was not actually *telling* Sawyer. It was not her fault if a servant overheard a family conversation.

'You are quite right,' Nathan admitted. 'Anne's punishment reflected the nature and volume of her crimes. She is the reason the villagers looked to a tree to protect them from Bainbridge influence. The plain truth is that our ancestor was both a traitor and a murderess.'

Her head was spinning. Another murder. Just how many people in this family had been accused of the blackest crime?

But Nathan spoke without a hint of self-consciousness. Surely he would not be able to look so grave and disapproving if he really had killed a man himself?

'Those are very serious charges. Just who did Anne...?'

Nathan lowered his chin. 'I'm afraid that's the worst part. The witch preyed upon those closest to her. One day, when her husband was returning from his duties as a magistrate, he found her wandering these very gardens covered in earth and… well, blood.' Nathan chewed his lower lip. 'Everyone else in the house was dead. Anne had poisoned the servants in his absence. And the young daughter of the house was missing. They never found her, but… the house was in such a state that they could not doubt what had befallen the poor girl.'

'Anne murdered her own daughter?' Belinda breathed.

'Yes, we must assume so.' He suddenly seemed to recollect himself. 'But I have been speaking like a brute. You are distressed and Miss Sawyer looks very pale. You must both sit down for a moment.'

Belinda waved him away. She could not sit, her mind was alight. So many people had been killed in *her* house! Why had Wilfred not told her? Well, she knew why. It was because of that nervousness she had felt before. That she was feeling now. And she had been *right* to feel it.

Sawyer let Nathan take her hand and deposit her on one of the cushions beneath the parasol. He apologised profusely, and bestowed such an elegant bow on her that she might have been a lady born. But Sawyer was no milk-and-water miss. Belinda could see plainly she was not distressed; she'd merely seized upon the opportunity to be made much of by a gentleman. At another time it would have been amusing.

'But… what does this have to do with Tiffany?' she pursued. 'Do you believe your sister inherited this *sight* from Anne Bainbridge?'

Folding his hands behind his back, Nathan returned to where she stood. He lowered his voice, as if he did not wish further to offend Sawyer's delicacy. 'Do not mistake me – my sister was nothing like Anne. She could be a little minx at times but she was not a witch and she was certainly no killer. Yet she used to say…' He hesitated, pained.

'You can tell me, Nathan. I do wish that you would. Wilfred never will speak of it.'

'My brother is more discreet than I,' he acknowledged with a grimace. 'But he does not know the half of it. Tiffany never confided in him. She used to tell *me* that she saw ghosts. And she claimed that she spoke with this murdered daughter of Anne's – Henrietta Maria, her name was. They were friends, of a sort.' Nathan exhaled heavily, ran a hand through his mane of hair. 'Tiffany used to tell me that Henrietta Maria was calling to her. Calling her from deep in the earth.'

'Good God.' Belinda shivered, despite the heat of the day. It was too terrible, too lurid. A murdered girl, calling another to jump to her death? 'You must promise me you are not inventing this, Nathan? This is not some manner of joke?'

His face stiffened. He looked offended. 'I only wish that it were. I saw it happen.'

All this time, Belinda had thought that *she* was the one with the dubious bloodline. But like their lineage, the secrets of the Bainbridge family reached far into the past. Nathan's arrival had opened Pandora's Box and now all these revelations were spilling out. So *many* dark mysteries. The adulterous footman and his unexplained death; the eeriness and abrupt end of poor Tiffany; the witch who killed her own kin. And so much of it had happened right here. In the garden where she let her little boy play.

Belinda felt nauseous. This must be what she had sensed five years ago. She had understood without truly knowing.

But one thought troubled her more than the idea of a haunted house. If Wilfred had concealed all of this from her... could he be hiding something still worse?

CHAPTER 14

The ivory ball rolled smoothly, striking its target on the rightmost curve with a click. Wilfred's ball conceded the ground. Nathan's hovered on the edge of the pocket for a breathless moment before finally dropping into the net.

'Twelve!' he cried, triumphant. 'Good game, brother.' He swapped his cue into his left hand and held the right one out for Wilfred to shake. A sportsmanlike gesture on the face of it, though after being thrashed so badly, it felt like condescension.

'Well done,' Wilfred said, grasping his brother's hand and dropping it swiftly. 'You find me out of practice with billiards.'

'You have employed your time more wisely.' Nathan grinned. 'And you are not used to playing for losing hazards. Whereas the younger son must become a master of the losing game.'

Wilfred went to the end of the table and retrieved Nathan's ball from its tasselled net. 'I shall tell you what *does* feel like a losing game at the moment: estate management. I am starting to understand why the old man grew such a devil of a temper.' He took both balls back to their marquetry box.

'Don't lock them away yet! Let's play another game. Winning hazards, if you prefer. You need the practice, you just said so yourself.' The eagerness in Nathan's voice was slightly pathetic.

Wilfred took the balls back out. 'I appreciate you giving me a chance to redeem myself, but I'm sure it will end exactly the same way. String for the first shot?'

They lined the balls up on the foot string. Both were ivory, but Nathan's had a large black dot at the centre, which made it resemble an eye.

Bending down, Nathan aimed his cue. The ball rolled and came to rest against the head cushion. 'Too hard,' he commented, before turning back to Wilfred. 'Sorry, what was it you were saying about the land? I take it the villagers responded poorly to the enclosure? Yet here you are, still in one piece. I half-expected them to drag you from your horse and string you up from the old oak itself, like they did to the Royalists during the Civil War.'

'They were surly, but nowhere near as bad as you anticipated. I think my promise of winter work and bread appeased them.' Wilfred made a bridge of his hand and rested the cue upon it. His strike was firm, but the green wool baize had rucked at his side of the table and slowed the ball down. It stopped neatly beside the cushion, not quite touching it. Perfect.

'See?' Nathan said. 'Your luck is changing. You shoot for points first.' He waited for Wilfred to take his shot before speaking again. 'When will you employ a steward? You cannot possibly take on all the estate business alone. Knowles is helpful, of course, but he's getting on in years. When his time comes, you'll be utterly confounded.'

Wilfred stood back from the table and held his cue in both hands. 'You're right, of course. But it's the expense.

Nothing here has been managed properly in recent years. With my family growing and all the repairs... I think I'll have to wait until the wheat makes us a profit.'

Nathan frowned. Despite the way he bemoaned being the younger son, he didn't look like someone who comprehended financial hardship. Gold buttons on his waistcoat, lace ruffles on his sleeves. For all Wilfred knew, his brother might be as rich as the nabobs he'd worked with.

'I don't suppose...' Nathan trailed off and bent to the table to take his shot. His ball smacked into his brother's and both fell into the pocket. 'Damn.' He went to retrieve them. He weighed Wilfred's ivory ball in his palm, apparently admiring its smoothness. 'I think I could help you, Wil. Why not let me be your man, until you have the tin to employ someone? I know the land, I know the village. Keep it in the family. If the estate is in the hands of someone you trust, it will free you up to focus on the house.'

Dear God, no. Wilfred hoped his alarm wasn't written all over his face. Didn't Nathan realise how they spoke of him in Fayford? He really seemed to think he could stroll back into his old life with the scandal forgotten. But if the villagers were a threat to Wilfred, they would tear Nathan limb from limb. 'It's beneath you,' he said shortly. 'I won't use my own brother like a lackey. Besides, the wheat will take until winter to grow. I doubt you mean to stay with us that long.'

Nathan let the ball drop with a thud and roll across the baize. 'I might,' he said, provokingly. 'Your wife's little maid smiles at me so prettily. Where else have I to go?'

The whole world. Anywhere. 'I thought you said America?'

'America is a bust for me now. It will just be more of the same: oppression, resentment, conflict. I've had enough of that in India.' He stroked his beard. 'I was hoping to stay here until your mourning is over and then move on to London for the winter.'

Months: he meant to loiter around here for *months*. Oblivious to the fact that they had a new baby. Wilfred needed to be blunt. 'Old whispers are arising,' he admitted. 'Ross Roberts is still in the village. He was drawing some kind of stipend from the old man and I've stopped it. He hardly had much to blackmail me with, before you came back. But now...'

Nathan swallowed. His throat worked beneath the tight stock. 'I see. You begrudge me even a few months to find my bearings.'

'Not begrudge—' Wilfred started, although it was true.

'I took the fall for you, Wil, and I never complained. I never told the old man you had a hand in it.' Nathan gripped the edge of the table. 'He died without knowing you had weakened that balustrade. All he saw was me giving Roberts that little shove in the right direction. Just as my big brother told me to do.'

'For heaven's sake, lower your voice!'

Nathan turned blazing blue eyes upon him. His face was crumpled not with anger, but with hurt. 'I knew my place, even then. It was more important for the heir to keep his hands clean. To let both parents blame only me. But I always thought you'd look after me, Wil, when you came into your own.'

Wilfred scrubbed a hand over his face. The truth was, he'd started to believe his own fiction. With Nathan out of sight, it had been easy to pretend he had never been an angry little boy who had wanted his mother back, his father happy and Roberts dead. The boy who sat up late at night plotting with Nathan until they saw a way to make it happen. 'Can't you see, I *am* looking to your best interests? You would be safer away from here, where no one will accuse you. I cannot let you wander around Fayford at the mercy of Ross Roberts and his like. They hated the old man and they hate you. I know it's unjust, but they do. Goodwife Griffin even blamed *you* for the enclosure – she thought you'd persuaded me to do it.'

Nathan smiled nastily. 'And I'll wager you let her go on believing it was my fault, didn't you? You never tell the truth. Not even to your own wife. Belinda knows nothing about Roberts, does she? She did not even realise Tiffany had jumped down the well.'

Wilfred turned cold. 'Good God, what did you say to her?'

'Nothing of note. You needn't kick up a dust. I explained how Tiffany was, and that she'd gone down the well on purpose, thinking to find her friend. Belinda was quite able to bear the truth. You ought to be more honest with her. But I suppose lying is second nature to you now.'

Wilfred cast his cue upon the table, all pretence at continuing their game at an end. 'So that is what you mean to do? Blackmail me, just as Ross Roberts did our father? Threaten to tell Belinda my part in the plot if I do not let you stay here?'

Nathan made a sound of exasperation. 'Blackmail!' he repeated scornfully. 'When you cannot even afford a steward? How stupid do you think me, Wilfred? I am your brother. I am not seeking material goods. All I want is for you to treat me as I did you: with kindness. And I don't think it is too much to ask, to spend a few months in the house I was driven from for your sake.'

That hit home. Wilfred felt very young again, very raw. The intervening years had formed a kind of protective armour around him, but now it slipped away as easily as a piece of dead skin.

'You are right,' he said thickly. 'You are quite right. I'm sorry, Nathan. Of course you may stay.'

Even with that beard and the fine head of hair, the face that turned towards him was boyish in its hope. 'Do you mean that?'

'Yes. I do. And I appreciate what you did for me – for us. Even if I never said it, I felt it.'

They faced each other across the billiards table, so changed and yet precisely the same. 'You were a child,' Nathan said quietly. 'As was I. And let us be honest. Roberts... well. He was not a *great* loss.'

Wilfred remembered that twinkle in his brother's eye. Despite himself, he guffawed. 'You are incorrigible.'

'I am honest.' Nathan shrugged.

It was such a relief to speak of it, to say the words aloud. They had killed Roberts. They had killed him together. And the crime bound them tighter than their blood.

A metallic sound rippled through the air. Wilfred flinched, but it was just the gong, telling them it was time to go to their rooms and change for dinner.

Packing away their equipment, the brothers left the billiards room and emerged uncomfortably close to the gallery where the terrible deed they were discussing had taken place. To Wilfred the air seemed to hum, as if what had once happened there had permanently changed the pressure. If he turned his head, would he see it all happening again? See himself creeping at dead of night to saw partway through the handrail and a few of the balusters beneath? Little Nathan waiting until

Roberts was in just the right spot, then springing from his crouched position to push at a pair of silk-stockinged legs? The whole episode could only have taken a few seconds. Such a short time to change and end lives.

They climbed the stairs and were about to separate to go to their respective rooms and dress when they saw Belinda standing by the portraits, as still and pale as a marble statue. Lydia was clutched to the *buffon* neckerchief at the front of her mother's gown, gurgling in protest.

'My dear—' Wilfred started, but Nathan pushed past him.

'Oh, I wish you hadn't changed that picture! Did you not like my great-aunt Caroline? I was very fond of her. I will take the portrait from you, if it is not to your taste.'

Belinda swivelled to face them. 'That's just it. I never asked – I did not give orders for the pictures to be changed. Did you, Wilfred? You *must* have.'

'No, why would I?'

He would not even have noticed the alteration unless they had pointed it out. He walked past these portraits every day and never truly observed them. Nathan was right: Great-aunt Caroline's cheerful face was gone, but the painting that replaced it was beautiful enough, illuminated as if from within. Careful attention had been paid to the details of a birdcage and the sparrow perched inside. A plump lady was reaching out as if to tempt the bird onto her hand while a doll-like girl clutched at her skirts, peering up into her face.

'It's an interesting piece…' Nathan started then froze. When he spoke again, his voice was tight. 'Oh. Oh, heavens. I had no idea such a picture even existed.'

Why were they both so rattled? Wilfred glanced at the bottom of the frame to read the sitter's name.

Anne Bainbridge with her daughter Henrietta Maria.
His stomach turned. Who would have guessed the woman in this portrait capable of the terrible deeds she had committed? This was no pimpled witch or raven-locked murderess. Anne Bainbridge had kind, tired eyes, blonde curls set with ribbons and a dress the colour of sunshine.

'The child,' Belinda murmured. 'Wilfred, have you seen?'

He leant closer, inspected the fey little creature with tortoiseshell hair piled upon her head. There was a horrible jolt of recognition.

'It looks like the companion,' he said. 'The girl with the basket of roses.'

'All this time, Freddy has been playing with the likeness of... of a slaughtered child!' Belinda shivered, making Lydia squirm.

'There's a companion?' Nathan demanded. 'A companion of Henrietta Maria? I never saw that! I was always told that the figures came from Amsterdam—'

Wilfred held up a hand. 'Please, calm yourselves. No doubt it's a coincidence.' He didn't like the resemblance any more than they did, but many children in early portraiture looked similar: puppet-like adults reduced to miniature proportions. 'And the figures *did* come from Amsterdam, Nathan. The girl with roses was probably modelled on a Dutch child.'

'But, Wilfred,' Belinda frowned, 'you told me that your mother had her own companions made. Is it not conceivable that past generations did the same thing?'

'Perhaps the grieving father...' Nathan suggested. He looked vaguely nauseous. Was he also remembering their mother in the first throes of her loss? How she replaced Tiffany with that silly board and spoke to it as if it were real?

'It does not really signify if the companion *is* supposed to be this Henrietta Maria,' he reasoned. 'It's horrible, yes. But the subjects of *all* those silent companions, if they *were* based on real people, are long dead.'

'But not murdered!' Belinda protested. 'That makes a difference.'

It was strange. The picture gave the impression of a close bond between mother and child. Nothing to suggest this woman would turn on and kill the daughter twined about her. But paintings were not an accurate record. They were altered to flatter and appease.

'Give me Lydia,' Wilfred said. 'You are upsetting her. You are upsetting yourself.' He put the child on his shoulder and rubbed her back soothingly. 'I daresay Knowles is simply cleaning the frame around Great-aunt Caroline's portrait, and just put anything up here in the meantime. I will speak to him at dinner. It will be removed. And the companion will be removed too if you wish it... though it seems rather cruel to take it from Fred when he is so attached to it.'

The baby gave a sudden yell and kicked at his stomach.

'Wilfred,' Nathan said, 'Belinda is not making a fuss over nothing. Do you really not remember?'

'Remember what?' he snapped, wrangling the fractious Lydia.

'Of all Tiffany's imaginary friends, it was Henrietta Maria she mentioned the most. If there really is a companion of that girl, in this house, I... I don't know what to think.'

Why would he say such things in front of Belinda? 'You're mistaken, old chap. She never said that name to me. Tiffany's fancy was an active one, but I never heard her talk to, or about, the silent companions. She just sang her songs.'

They were both staring at him as if he were the one deluding himself. He had an overpowering urge to get Lydia away from their grave and haunted expressions. Because now he was remembering how that damned diary of Anne Bainbridge's had fallen repeatedly from the shelf in the library. How Freddy spoke of 'the ones who came before'. Notions he could not, would not, entertain.

'I will ring for Knowles straight away,' he said. 'Now go and dress yourselves for dinner. We are going to be late.'

*

It was one of those airless summer nights when the weight of a sheet was torment. Yet Belinda kept her body covered and lay still, her eyes firmly closed against anyone, or anything, which might choose to walk by night.

She was grateful for Wilfred in the bed beside her, the rhythmic sound of his breathing. During the day, it was easy to keep her composure. But when darkness fell, anything seemed possible. She became her mother's daughter.

The worst of it was, she could not even reason herself out of fear. All the evidence only seemed to vindicate her. Day by day, there had been little signs that Henrietta Maria Bainbridge remained in this house. And it made sense. If any wronged spirit were going to linger, surely it would be this one: a girl cut off in the bloom of her youth by the person who was supposed to love her the most.

She thought of Freddy, claiming the companions wanted company. The basket of painted roses and the scent of them, hovering restless around the house. Her heart pounded, felt loud enough to wake Wilfred from his sleep. She must get a hold of herself. Wilfred and Nathan had survived their childhoods here. So had countless others. Even if there *was* a ghost, it did not follow that she meant them any harm.

Suddenly a cry split the night. Belinda opened her eyes. The panelling of the tester stretched above her, grainy and indistinct in the gloom. The wail came again, a baby's lament, but it wasn't in the nursery below where Lydia slept. This was close at hand. In her very room.

'Wilfred?' she whispered.

His breathing continued without interruption, in and out like the tide.

Belinda pulled herself up against the pillows. The door remained closed, but the curtains and shutters were open, flooding the room with moonlight.

A mewling arose from the end of the bed. With dread crushing her chest, Belinda leant slowly forward and peered over the footboard. In a pool of silvery light stood the old cradle from Freddy's birth. Ebony wood, high-backed, shaped like a casket. She could not see over the high sides. But as she watched, the cradle began to rock, pulled by invisible strings.

Belinda recoiled, clutching the sheets to her chest.

The crying intensified, sharpened its pitch. The cradle creaked as it rocked.

'Wilfred, wake up!' she hissed. He did not even move when she shook him. Terror tightened its grip.

Someone would come. Any moment now, another person would hear the cry and investigate. They must.

But nothing changed. Belinda was caught alone in a bell jar with the noise, the heat and the smell of roses. There was no escape.

Breathing fast, she forced herself to climb from the safety of the bed. She crept forward, her long nightgown brushing her ankles. Chalky light washed through the windows and made her a ghost herself.

Still the cradle rocked. She didn't want to watch, but she couldn't rip her gaze away. The movement was unnatural. Jerky. Whatever lay interred within was not just sad; it was furious.

She swallowed. Persuaded her bare feet to take another step. Inch by inch, she crept forward until she was close enough to feel the thump as the rockers hit the floor.

She tried her voice. 'Hush.' Weak, but still there. 'Hush, now.'

She couldn't glimpse a profile or a head upon the pillow, there seemed to be nothing inside the crib...

Abruptly, the rocking stopped. The stillness was harder to bear than the movement. Belinda took the last pace forward and screamed.

Lying flat against the base of the cot was a silent companion: baby-sized and baby-shaped. She would know that face anywhere. Lydia, rendered lifeless in paint.

'Belinda!'

The world collapsed around her. She was falling, thrashing, sightless, until she landed with a jerk upon the mattress.

Wilfred was there, peering down at her as she had peered into the crib, his face haloed by candlelight.

'Belinda, my love! It is a bad dream. Nothing more. Calm yourself.'

'Oh, Wilfred!' There were tears on her cheeks. 'Thank God! I could not wake you...'

Concern creased his face. He looked older in the shadows. 'You *did* wake me. You were calling out for Lydia.'

'It was so... real,' she panted.

Wilfred set the candle down on the side table. He stroked her hair. 'But it was not real, Bel, only a nightmare. I am here, and you are quite safe.'

'Don't blow out the light!'

'I won't.' He wrapped himself protectively around her back. He smelt of starch and pepper. Regular, sensible things. 'No one can harm you now,' he murmured into her hair.

She held on tight to his arm. She wanted to believe it. But when she closed her eyes the terrible sight was still there: her child, reduced to wood and paint. The essence of Lydia sucked clean out, like a flower pressed between the pages of a book.

CHAPTER 15

Midsummer was supposed to be the longest day of the year and yet the sun had abandoned its post already. A shelf of grey cloud covered the sky. The birds called begrudgingly. It was the very dregs of a morning; nature seemed as tired as Wilfred felt himself.

He tried to focus on the rent roll before him. Midsummer was also quarter day, when the bailiff was sent out to collect rents. Here at The Bridge, Knowles had to act as bailiff, steward and butler all in one; an unfair division of labour, for his wage. He was already dressed for his task, a large money satchel slung across his riding coat as he stood before the library desk.

'Everything in order, sir?'

After the enclosure, Wilfred felt as if he was sending a sheep out amongst the wolves. Asking for money after he had already taken so many resources away from the villagers was sure to goad them further, but he had no choice. He rolled the records and passed them over. 'Yes. But are you sure you ought to go alone? I cannot gauge the present mood of the village.'

'Forgive my bluntness, sir, but whatever their mood is, they would only be more hostile if you came along with me. They see me as closer to them in station.'

'You should take my pistol with you, in case any trouble arises.'

Knowles shook his frosty head. 'Do not fret yourself, sir. The villagers have never threatened me before.'

But there was a first time for everything. Midsummer madness might take hold. Although the villagers had lost their Hanging Oak, there were plenty of other ways for them to administer mob justice. Wilfred parted his lips to say so when Freddy screamed.

In a heartbeat Wilfred was up and speeding from the room. He'd only heard his son shriek with glee or frustration. This cry was utterly chilling. The pitch felt high enough to crack glass.

A glimpse of the portraits as he descended the stairs showed Great-aunt Caroline back in her rightful place, her benign smile at odds with the charged atmosphere.

Lydia started to cry, her lament carrying up to the lantern tower.

Wilfred had just reached the bottom of the stairs when he saw his son hurtling towards him at breakneck speed. One of his shoes had flown off. He stretched out both short arms for Wilfred. 'Papa! You have to stop it!'

Wilfred dropped to one knee as Freddy collided into his embrace. His little face was drenched in tears. 'Good God, Fred, what is the matter?'

'You... you...' Freddy gasped. The poor child was beside himself.

'You want me to stop something?' Wilfred offered. 'Someone?'

He nodded vehemently. 'Mamma,' he managed. 'Stop Mamma.'

His blood chilled. Of all the possible names, he'd least expected to hear that one. 'Why? What is she doing?'

A fresh burst of tears. Wilfred had never felt as furious with Belinda as he did at this moment. What could possibly be worth upsetting their son this much?

He put his hands on Freddy's bony shoulders and nodded encouragingly. 'Tell me.'

'She – she wants to – to take Hetta to the – the attic,' Freddy stuttered through his sobs. 'She *can't.*'

So Belinda was really going through with it. He would not have thought his wife capable of such hard-heartedness. 'She's taking away a toy you want to play with?'

Poor Freddy looked as if a trapdoor had been opened from under him. 'I don't want to *play* with her! Not any more. Merry told me…' He shook his head as if it did not matter. 'But she'll be so angry! She hates to be shut away.'

Wilfred stroked his son's hair, unsure how to respond. Freddy had a vivid imagination, but that would have to stop at some point. 'You know,' he said kindly, 'Hetta can seem very real. But she is only a piece of wood. She cannot really *feel* emotions.' He paused. 'Are you sure it is not actually *you* who will be angry if she is put away?'

'No, I'll be *scared!*' Freddy cried. 'I'll be so, so scared.'

Creaks on the landing. 'Hey-day, what's all this? I thought I heard a little fellow screaming fire.' Wilfred glanced up as Nathan padded into view, the dog welded to side. 'Is everything all right?'

Freddy did not turn, he kept his entreating eyes fixed upon his father.

'We've had a bit of an upset,' Wilfred said vaguely.

He did not want to raise the topic of the silent companion with Nathan, who would probably take Belinda's side. It was Nathan's fault that she even *knew* there was a girl murdered at The Bridge in the first place. It only proved how right Wilfred had been to take Anne

Bainbridge's diary out of her hands. He did not have to look far to see where their son got his lurid fancies from.

The dog came snuffling up and licked at the tears on Freddy's cheeks, but he pushed it away.

'Oh, dear! This won't do at all, Freddy,' Nathan sympathised, his voice light and sing-song for the child. 'Can I make things any better? I was about to go on a long walk in the woods with Dev. Perhaps you would like to join us? That might cheer you up. You can see how fast he runs to catch rabbits!'

It was a testament to Freddy's distress that he did not leap at the opportunity. His pale brows just knit together.

Wilfred patted him gently on the back. 'Actually, I think that's a capital idea, Fred. Get yourself out of the house with Uncle Nathan and leave me to speak to your mother.'

'She doesn't understand,' Freddy breathed, low enough so that only Wilfred could hear. 'Hetta wants to be near Lydia. And bad things happen when Hetta doesn't get what she wants.'

Wilfred nodded and rose to his feet. This was reminding him rather painfully of Tiffany. But Freddy's inventions, or dreams – whatever you called the phantoms that flitted through the minds of children – were more structured than hers had ever been. Freddy felt his stories viscerally, whereas Tiffany had always retained that dreamy expression, singing and giggling and whispering to herself. He still could not remember her mentioning a Henrietta Maria, or even a Hetta, as Freddy called her, but then he had never paid much heed to what she said. His little sister had been almost ten years his junior – more of a pet than a peer.

Freddy slunk reluctantly towards Nathan. He wrapped an arm around the boy. 'Let's find that missing shoe, shall we? Oh, look, Dev's already got it in his mouth! Bring it here, there's a clever dog.'

Freddy puffed out a tiny laugh to see the dog fetching his shoe as tamely as if it were a dead grouse. He slipped it back on, dried his eyes. 'Can I hold his leash?'

'Of course you can!'

Wilfred waited until they had passed from his sight, their footsteps and the pitter-patter of the dog's paws fading out. He took a breath, composed himself. If there was one thing he had learned from the whole Roberts fiasco, it was that he should never act when he was in a temper. Showing Belinda his anger now would achieve very little.

The scene he found inside the nursery softened him. His wife stood mopping her eyes with a handkerchief – evidently, she had been crying, too. The door to the schoolroom stood ajar. He could hear the nursemaids in there with Lydia while Mrs Knowles knelt before the silent companion with its basket of roses, carefully disassembling the prop that stood it upright. The painting of Anne Bainbridge and Henrietta Maria was leaning against the wall.

'Oh, Wilfred,' Belinda said, 'I am sorry for all the racket. We have disturbed you.'

'*Disturbed* is a fitting word. I *am* disturbed to see poor Freddy sobbing his heart out.' He gestured at Mrs Knowles. 'Come, is all of this really necessary, Bel?'

She raised her handkerchief to catch a new tear. 'I did not mean to upset him! It breaks my heart... But, yes, I'm afraid it really must be done. I am his mother, I know what is best for him.'

Wilfred frowned. 'My dear, I think you mean what is best for *you*.'

She flinched, bunching her handkerchief in her hand. Her eyes remained on Mrs Knowles, who was

LAURA PURCELL 169

studiously performing her task and saying nothing. The silent companion creaked as it leant backwards. Such a thin, flimsy piece of wood to cause all this fuss.

'My dream seemed like a warning,' Belinda admitted. 'And besides... it *is* in poor taste for Freddy to play with a memorial to a dead child.'

'You are a sailor's daughter at heart. But on dry land dreams are not premonitions. You were simply thinking about the family history because you saw that portrait, and then you dreamt of it.'

'But it *is* strange,' Belinda persisted. 'Mrs Knowles does not even know where the painting came from, do you?'

'No, madam.' The housekeeper was standing now, the silent companion tucked lengthways under one arm. Only the pile of hair and the sharp green eyes glared out. He could see why Freddy might imagine the girl was angry. There was certainly something unpleasant simmering in that gaze. 'My husband doesn't remember putting it up either... But he *is* getting on in years. It wouldn't be the first thing he forgot.'

Wilfred realised he'd left poor Knowles standing in the library. He inspected his pocket watch. 'I am meant to be sorting out the rents with him right now... But I must put this right first. By all means get rid of the portrait, Bel, but Freddy is dead set against having that companion removed. The poor boy practically begged me to stop you. Are you really going to go through with it?'

Her delicate jaw set. 'I am afraid I have no choice. Take it away, Mrs Knowles.' The housekeeper glanced at Wilfred as if for confirmation, but Belinda was resolute. 'Take both the painting and the companion and place them in the attic.'

Wilfred did not attempt to conceal his sigh as Mrs Knowles obeyed her orders. Despite his best efforts, it seemed to be happening again. How long before Belinda grew afraid of her own shadow and locked herself up with Lydia, as she had with Freddy all those years ago?

When the nursery door closed, Belinda sagged against the iron bedstead in relief. 'I am sorry,' she repeated. 'I *know* it appears extreme. But at least I will not have any more nightmares.'

'What about Freddy?' he objected. 'Our priority should be to stop our son suffering from bad dreams – as he certainly will now.'

'Oh, do not plague me, Wilfred, I feel guilty enough. Maybe it *is* silly, but I need to do this for my own peace of mind. I am doing everything I can to prevent myself from growing nervous again. To me it has felt like there is a, a – ' she lowered her voice ' – a *ghost* in the house. The ghost of that girl. She has been everywhere I go. Hopefully now it will stop.'

Wilfred bit his lip. What he truly wanted to say to Belinda, he could never share. That he knew for a fact ghosts did not come back seeking vengeance. For if they did, he and Nathan would be tormented by Roberts. Yet there had never been any hint that the footman remained in the house.

Belinda was not waiting for his response. She was looking beyond him, frowning at the rocking horse Freddy had ridden with such glee. 'How long has it been like that?'

'Whatever is the matter now?' he asked wearily.

She pushed herself off the bedstead and walked past him to the toy. Placing a hand on the saddle, she bent down to inspect the underside of the horse. 'Look at this, Wilfred.'

He bent to where she was pointing. The wood bore thick, white scratches, scoured with something sharp, veining all the way down to the top of the horse's legs.

He cursed under his breath. That damned dog of Nathan's got into everything. It was just as well he had arranged for Freddy to have a real horse before long; riding this one would give him splinters. 'Dev must have been pawing at it. This cost me a pretty penny – I've a mind to bill Nathan for a replacement.'

Belinda pushed the rocking horse. It squeaked as it swung back and forth, back and forth. 'Something is not right, Wilfred. Don't you feel it? A kind of... pressure. Like the air before a storm.'

She could not comprehend the amount of *pressure* he was under. If she did, she would not be wasting his time with trifles like this. 'Well, the barometer was low today. Maybe rain is coming,' he offered blandly.

She nodded, still watching the horse. 'Yes. I suppose that must be it.'

*

Bonfires burnt off towards the village, even though the sun had not fully set. Freddy sat on the window seat in the card room, watching columns of smoke rise on the horizon.

Belinda's attempts to teach him whist and faro had failed. He refused to be distracted, remaining as fractious as he'd been that morning. Even the dog was curled up beside her feet, under the games table, knowing any advances would be rebuffed.

It was all her doing. Was she a terrible mother, for taking her son's toy away?

Belinda piled the cards back into a deck and began to lay them out for solitaire. The rhythmic turning, the very pattern of the game, took her back to her mother's parlour. Prickles ran up the back of her neck. Had she acted in the same way as Mamma? Upset her child, just to quell her own fears? But she did not see what else she could have done.

'Why are they burning fires?' Freddy demanded.

'People often do, dearest, because it is not St John's Eve, but St John's day. It is a holy day in the church calendar.'

'*We* should light a fire,' he said savagely. 'A big one.'

Belinda placed another card down. A traditional St John's fire was kindled not only with wood, but bones. She shuddered at the thought. 'No, it's too warm tonight, darling. Anyway, Rebecca will be coming to fetch you to bed in a moment.'

'I don't *want* to go to bed!' The inside of Freddy's lower lip showed wet and pink as he pouted. Behind him, the sky was bruising darker, the divide between dusk and the smoke on the hills beginning to blur.

'Why not?'

'Because *you* put Hetta in the attic!' he sparked back. 'She'll be moving up there all night. I'll hear her!'

Belinda's blood ran cold. She paused, the three of diamonds in her hand. 'Are you *sure* her name is Hetta? Could it not be… Henrietta Maria?' He stared at her. 'Or perhaps Hetta is short for that?' What was she doing, what was she saying? Wilfred had been right to scold her. She ought to be comforting Freddy, not encouraging his fears. But she could not stop herself. 'Freddy, tell me, what does it sound like when Hetta moves?'

He screwed up his face. 'A scrape. A big, dragging scrape.'

The card shook in her fingers. She laid it flat. Hadn't she heard that noise the night Freddy walked in his sleep? Just before she'd seen the companions, ranged about his empty bed?

The companions move by themselves. Did Nathan really mean it?

Rebecca knocked on the open door. Belinda nearly leapt from her chair. 'Sorry, madam! I did not mean to startle you. Shall I take Master Freddy to bed now?'

Freddy slumped dramatically from the window seat and lay down upon the carpet. 'Noooo!'

Belinda grimaced. 'He is none too eager, as you can see. Let us give him a moment to collect himself. Perhaps you can close the shutters and light the candles now? It is getting rather dismal in here.'

'Yes, madam.'

The maid stepped neatly over Freddy and began to pull the shutters. Belinda could not overlook his tantrum so easily. She was responsible for it. She had made her son afraid to go to bed and she needed to put that right.

Her eyes rested upon the open door, showing a slice of the powder-pink music room beyond. Tunes had often soothed Mamma in querulous moments.

'Freddy, shall I play you a song? Something to make you sleepy?'

He peeped up at her from his position on the floor, curls spilling over his flushed face. She could practically see the cogs turning inside his young mind. Any excuse, any delay. 'Yes.'

She pushed back her chair and stood. Dev rose with her, giving a yawn and a stretch. 'Come along, then. The instruments are all next door.'

She'd had little leisure to spend in the music room until now. Since her marriage, Belinda had viewed playing as a winter pursuit, something to amuse herself when the weather prevented excursions. And there was something rather sickly about this chamber with its pink paper and the scalloped ceiling, like a sugar-paste cake that made your teeth ache.

Dev slunk into the room and settled under the piano-forte. It was furred with dust, the ivory keys discoloured. A harp of satinwood and brass stood in the corner. Belinda leant in favour of playing that. The tension in the strings looked adequate, they might not take much tuning.

'Go and sit on the piano stool and I will play the harp for you. I wonder what Dev will make of it. Do you suppose he's heard music before?'

'He won't mind music.' Freddy dragged himself up onto the stool and let his short legs dangle over the edge. He pressed a single key. Dev's ears twitched. 'See? He's done everything. He's a big brave dog. He crossed the ocean on a ship with Uncle Nathan. He helps me protect Lydia.'

Belinda moved over to the harp and settled it against her shoulder. She wished Lydia were here too, her little face opening in astonishment to the new sound. But it was too late in the evening to fetch her; Lydia would be fast asleep.

Pushing up the half-sleeves of her gown, Belinda strummed the strings. The air shimmered with a bright, silvery sound.

In the card room, Rebecca turned her head in the direction of the music.

'That's pretty,' Freddy said. 'Do a tune.'

Belinda closed her eyes and plucked the strings by memory, playing Haydn's 'Rustic Dance'. The melody bore her away from the witches and murdered children of The Bridge, back to ballrooms and ostrich feathers, fluttering fans and ratafia. She never thought she'd miss the crush of a London Season, but she did. When she was there, she had longed for open space and green fields, but no one had warned her that her country estate would come with a ghost.

Snap.

Belinda flinched as the broken string nearly twanged into her face. Her fingers stung.

'Madam! Are you hurt?' Rebecca was there, taking the harp from her grasp.

'I... no.' Shaken, she checked the tips of her fingers, ran a hand over her cheek. The snapping string had sounded like an explosion in her ear. 'No, I don't think so. It was just a nasty shock.'

'It nearly hit you!' Freddy squealed.

'It was silly of me to play on old strings. I ought to have inspected them first. Don't worry, darling, there is no harm—' She stopped, frowned. Dev rose and sniffed his way over to the door on the far wall, which led into the drawing-room. 'Did someone just knock?'

'No, madam.'

'I thought...' Even as she spoke, Dev let out a dissatisfied 'whuff' and began nosing at the base of the door.

Freddy swivelled on his stool. 'Maybe it's Papa? Come in, Papa!'

The door did not move.

'There was no knock, madam,' Rebecca assured her, returning to trimming the candle-wicks. 'There's no one out there.'

But Belinda knew what she had heard.

The door taunted her with its stillness. It was like the feeling she'd had in her suite and outside the schoolroom. A presence, waiting. Dev lifted his tail and his

head. A growl rolled in his chest. 'There *must* be someone,' she reasoned. 'Why else would the dog do that?'

Rebecca pressed her thin lips together. 'Very well,
madam, there is only one way to find out.' Abandoning her
task, she moved to the far wall and chivvied Dev out of the
way. 'I do not imagine anyone would stand about waiting
for us to—' Her voice caught as she pulled the door open.

The silent companion of Henrietta Maria stood on the
threshold.

For a moment they all stared. Dev's growl rumbled
low, like a distant storm. Then Freddy started to scream.

In a flash he was up, pushing past Rebecca and
barrelling out of the open door. His shoulder hit the
companion and sent it swooning. Rebecca gave chase.
Shakily, Belinda followed, unable to understand what
had happened. Every inch of her skin tingled as she
stepped over the felled companion. She would not look
at its sly face, would not acknowledge that it brought the
perfume of roses swirling back with it.

There came a noise from the Great Hall, like the clash
of sabres or a mob in the streets. A woman yelled. Dev
started to bark.

Belinda dashed out and instinctively recoiled.

The sky was falling: that was her first confused
impression. Flashing light, motion, a deafening roar.
Then something rattled at her feet, close enough for her
to feel the vibrations through the stone flags. Tarnished
silver. A naval cutlass.

The display of antique swords was dropping from the
wall.

'Freddy!' she screamed.

She could only see Nathan, descending the stairs. He
pulled back, astonished, as a sword pierced the tread
below him.

Everything happened so quickly. Light ricocheted and metal clattered as each and every sword fell. There was no path for Belinda through the deadly rain. She could scarcely distinguish one blade from the other, until she saw the giant claymore begin to move. It descended with a nightmare slowness, straight as an arrow, and as her eyes followed its course, she finally saw her son. He was frozen in terror amidst the chaos, directly on the spot where the claymore would land.

'Freddy!'

Nathan did not hesitate. He hurdled the banister rail, threw himself bodily upon the child. The blade planted itself in the soft flesh of Nathan's rump. Blood began to flow and he made an unearthly moan.

Giddy, Belinda managed to stagger forward, but before she could reach Nathan, Rebecca seized her arm in a slick, hot grasp. She was missing a finger, dyeing the lace at Belinda's cuffs with gore as she babbled hysterically. Belinda couldn't understand a word.

She was not aware of the others pounding down the stairs or emerging from the depths of the kitchens; they were just suddenly there, gathered horror-stricken beside the fireplace. She turned to look.

A crimson rug spread out across the flags. At its centre knelt Mrs Knowles. The broadsword had entered through the back of her neck, between the shoulder blades. Blood spurted from her mouth and cascaded down her sleeves. For a moment she twitched horribly. Then she toppled forward, landing with a crack and spatter as the red flow sought channels between the flags.

CHAPTER 16

Now that disaster had come, Belinda found herself strangely calm. Part of her detached itself to move between rooms, carrying lint bandages and burning camphor to purify the air. She could almost watch herself doing it. Maybe all of that energy inside of her had been waiting for this release.

Of course, Knowles and his son could not possibly help. The physician had given them something to make them sleep, but she doubted even the most potent drug would erase that sight from their minds. Poor Mrs Knowles. It was a hideous way to go. Someone would have to wash and lay out the body before long and Belinda prayed the task would not fall upon her. There were limits to her bravery.

A cup of heated wine steamed in her hand as she carried it towards the nursery. Lydia had caught the general air of panic and was crying without intermission. The sound increased as Belinda pushed open the door. Amy was rocking the baby. Rebecca sat by the fire, draped in a blanket, her narrow face bleached of colour. Despite the heat of the season and the flames, she was still trembling. Belinda crossed the room and wrapped the nursemaid's good hand around the warm cup. 'Drink this,' she said. 'It will help.'

It was only as she looked down that she realised how closely the wine resembled Mrs Knowles' dark red blood.

'Mamma!' Freddy called out from the bed. Belinda sat on the edge of the mattress and took him in her arms. Thank God for the warmth of him, the weight of him, the perfect little body still intact. If Nathan had not been there at precisely the right moment, her world would have ended this night.

But although Freddy was physically unharmed, he bore other wounds. His big blue eyes were glassy. Hectic colour grazed his cheeks. She stroked his hair, felt his gentle quaking against her chest. The lace at her elbow was brown like molasses. She frowned at it, confused, before she remembered.

'I knew she'd be angry,' Freddy whispered into her bosom. 'I *knew*.'

The face reared up in her mind: flat, painted and smug. The companion. Hetta. All the other horrors had eclipsed her reappearance.

'You must try and sleep, my love,' Belinda murmured, rocking Freddy. 'This has all been a shock. A terrible, terrible shock.'

How many awful images had his innocent eyes viewed? He'd seen Nathan's wound, there was no avoiding that. But she could not recall who had carried him up the stairs and whether they had shielded him from seeing the gore flowing out of poor Mrs Knowles. She fervently hoped so. Mamma's words came creeping back. *Children are so fragile. One false step may scar them for life.*

And Mamma knew, didn't she? She had witnessed something very like this: a bullet to the head, brains sprayed over brocade squabs. Horror enough to stop her from leaving the house, even though she was a woman grown.

'I can't sleep. I mustn't,' Freddy moaned. 'It's my job to protect Lydia.'

A fissure ran through her heart. 'No, darling. Mamma, Amy and Rebecca are here. We will all keep your little sister safe.'

But the promise sounded hollow, even to her own ears. Belinda hadn't managed to guard anyone. She'd stood there, paralysed, while Nathan leapt to the rescue.

Once she'd persuaded Freddy to lay his head upon the pillow, he could not prevent his eyelids from drooping shut. Terror had sapped his strength. Sleep claimed him and Belinda hoped it would be dreamless. She rose and held out her arms for Lydia. 'Let me give you a break, Amy. She might settle for me.'

The wet-nurse was only too glad to relinquish her squalling charge. Shock had laid its hand upon Amy too; you could see it from the blankness of her expression. She went to sit by Rebecca.

Belinda could not bear to have her baby bound and stiff, as she had seen her in her dreams. She loosened Lydia's swaddling to let her kick.

'It was an accident,' she murmured into Lydia's cap. 'An accident in an old house.' But the timing suggested otherwise. Three omens in quick succession: the string snapping, the companion's appearance and then the falling swords. She closed her eyes against the image of Mrs Knowles, skewered. Mrs Knowles, who had taken the silent companion to the attic that very morning on Belinda's orders.

At last, Lydia calmed enough to be placed down in the crib. Belinda left the nursery and plunged into the darkness of the corridor. Naturally no servants had been doing their evening rounds to light the sconces.

She groped her way upstairs. Thunder rumbled in the distance. Midsummer Day was truly over, the heat and the light utterly gone. She followed a candle burning at the end of the corridor, outside what was now Nathan's room. The surgeon's voice carried towards her.

'It may be somewhat embarrassing, but Mr Bainbridge was fortunate to sustain the injury where he did. No arteries have been damaged. Providing we can keep the wound free from infection, the worst he will suffer is a permanent limp.'

Thank God for that. Belinda quickened her step.

'The dressing will need to be changed regularly and the wound cleaned. I can recommend a nurse if there is no one suitable here.'

Wilfred glanced briefly at Belinda as she reached the pool of candlelight. He was not wearing a wig or a jacket. Even by the dancing flame, she could see his shirt was flecked with blood. 'Yes, perhaps that would be best. Our maid cannot be expected to – I would not ask her to – it is somewhat delicate,' he finished awkwardly.

'Nathan is going to be all right?' she clarified. 'May I see him?'

Wilfred exhaled. 'We have reason to hope, Bel. Sawyer is in there with him now. He may be sleeping. How is Freddy?'

'As well as can be expected.'

Her husband nodded. 'Good. Good.' He was not himself. His words were stilted, as if there was hardly space for language inside his mind. 'And – and you will check the nursemaid again before you leave, sir? Her finger?'

'If you wish it, Mr Bainbridge,' the surgeon said.

They took the candle with them and darkness folded around Belinda once more. She reached for the handle to enter the suite of rooms she used to dread. She must see Nathan, if only for a moment. Words could not express the debt she owed to him.

She found the chamber swimming with shadows. Now it truly conveyed the fears she had felt when Freddy was born: dark shapes that crept and stretched across the walls. The air smelt metallic, like blood leavened with herbs. Sawyer stood at the washstand, presumably rinsing cloths. In the gloom, the four-poster bed resembled an altar with Nathan offered up for sacrifice. He lay on his stomach, face turned towards her on the pillow. There was a greyish tint to the once tanned skin. Lines of pain creased the sides of his eyes which were usually so merry.

'Belinda,' he croaked.

She came forward and knelt by the side of the bed. 'How are you?'

A sheen of sweat sat upon his forehead. His hair was loose from its tie and tangled behind him. 'I will not tell a lie,' he gasped with an effort at his normal levity. 'I have certainly been better.'

She caught his hand and squeezed it. The palm felt rough, compared to Wilfred's. 'The surgeon is hopeful. Take courage. You will not be lamed.'

'And Freddy? How is my nephew?'

'He is well. All thanks to you.' Her eyes filled. 'Nathan, how can I ever begin—'

'No, no, none of that. Any man would have done the same.' Sawyer approached with a damp cloth for his forehead. Belinda moved aside for her. 'You see,' Nathan went on, as the maid mopped his brow, 'I am not to be pitied when I have such an angel to tend upon me.'

Even by candlelight, she could see Sawyer's faint flush. 'I reckon Mr Nathan has taken a fever, ma'am,' she jested. 'He speaks such nonsense to me.'

Belinda smiled. 'No, he is quite right. You are a fine nurse. I never would have made it through the whooping cough without you, dear Sawyer. But you need not keep your watch for long. The surgeon said something about bringing in a nurse from Torbury St Jude.'

'There's no need for that,' she said quickly and moved back to the washstand, hiding her expression. 'I can do it.'

'But the wound...' Belinda paused tactfully. 'You know, being where it is.'

Sawyer tucked down her chin, focused on the basin of water. 'Oh, I don't pay any mind to that. I am trying to save you some money. All of the nurses I ever met were old and soused. You can't trust them.'

Nathan groaned from the bed. 'Pray do not take Miss Sawyer from me. It will be mortifying enough to have the dressing changed by anyone, but I would rather not be exposed to a total stranger.'

It made Belinda hot and uncomfortable to imagine: Sawyer, touching his bare skin. Yet how could she object? This man had just saved her son. 'It must be your decision, Nathan, you are the patient.' He dragged in a breath. She saw how much it cost him to focus on anything except the pain. 'I will leave you to rest. I only wanted to say, God bless you.'

The hand she had dropped caught upon her skirts. 'No. Please. I must speak with you, Belinda. And it is probably best if I do so alone.'

His blue eyes glowed, feverish in the shadows. She had wanted to consult with him too, more than anything, but now the moment came, she was afraid.

'Yes,' she said through numb lips. 'Yes. Sawyer – could you go and light the sconces for me? The corridors are all pitch black. We ought to have some illumination. I doubt anyone will be sleeping tonight.'

Sawyer gave a tight nod. Shaking her hands free from water, she wiped them on her apron and took a taper from the fire. From her short, sharp movements, Belinda gathered that she wanted to keep Nathan to herself. But surely she knew better than to cherish a secret tenderness for a gentleman? The maid shut the door with a click behind her.

Nathan began at once. 'I have not been entirely truthful with you, sister.'

Thunder pealed outside. As Belinda stood staring at him, breathing hard, a single spot of rain hit the window. 'What do you mean?'

'I was trying to view matters as Wilfred does. He is my elder brother, after all. I am used to being guided by him.'

She knelt down once more so she could see his face clearly. His dark beard made him look solemn, a ghost from another age. '*Which* matters, Nathan?'

'The… the matters of the house.' His hot breath smelt of laudanum. 'Tonight's events are more than simple bad luck, or punishment for felling the Hanging Oak. Do you remember what I told you about Tiffany, about Henrietta Maria calling to her?' She nodded. How could she possibly forget? 'Seeing that portrait of the girl made me uneasy, so this evening I went to the library and found Anne's diaries for myself. I wanted to know for certain what had happened to my sister… And now I believe I do. It is dangerous here, Belinda. Your children are not safe at The Bridge.'

A thrill of horror ran through their connected hands. The words held more weight, coming from this travelled man, than they did from her anxious mother. 'Because it is falling apart?'

'You *know* it is not that. We don't have much time before Miss Sawyer returns. There is a letter. It's in the pocket of my burgundy coat, the first one hanging in the wardrobe. I want you to read it, Belinda. Go and read it now, so you know this is not delirium brought on by pain.'

Trembling slightly, she regained her feet and moved to the heavy rosewood wardrobe. The inside was scented with tobacco and rosemary. Velvet brushed her fingertips as she found the coat and pulled out Nathan's letter. The paper felt flimsy, almost crumbling away. She took it to read by the fire.

The rain was falling steadily now, hissing softly as it dropped into the hearth. Whoever had written used a cramped and shaky hand. She squinted. The words danced beneath the hectic light of the flames.

Nathan,

I forfeited all right to address you as my son long ago, so I will not take that liberty now. But I beg, for the sake of the tie which cannot ever be dissolved, that you read this letter. I shall not trouble you with a lengthy account, and it will be the last time I obtrude upon your notice in this life.

Once, I reproached you for not owning up to your faults and apologising for them as a gentleman ought to do. If nothing else, I am resolved to die free from hypocrisy. So let me plainly confess that I was wrong to treat you as I did, and I regret it most bitterly.

I have come to believe that the sin was never truly yours. No more than poor Tiffany was at fault for ending her own life. There is an evil in this house, Nathan, which defiles everything within its touch. Even your mother cannot be blamed for her conduct. She was seduced not by a man, but by the dark wiles of the Enemy.

Tiffany used to speak of spirits, did she not? I, too, consider myself haunted. Knowles assures me that such megrims come to all with age, but there have been too many incidents I cannot explain. Even men of faith have sensed a malign presence dwelling here. Neither their prayers nor mine have prevailed.

I believe the answers must lie with Anne Bainbridge, our accused witch, and the dark master she served. There were rumours that she kept a journal, which I will make it the work of my final days to seek out. Perhaps she will explain the spell she cast. Perhaps the evil may be purged at last. In the meantime, I must take steps to cleanse the place of superstition and devilry. Rid the villagers of their pagan Hanging Oak and get them back into the church. I wish Mr Chapman would champion my cause, but the Reverend keeps his distance from this parish. No doubt he feels the evil too. Flees from it, as perhaps I should.

You will think I have lost my wits, writing to you after so long a silence, and on such topics. I did begin this letter merely to say that I consider you innocent and to bless you. But now part of me rejoices in the awful circumstances which carried you far away from The Bridge. It was ultimately better for you. You are safe.

Yet what of Wilfred? He will inherit a cesspool of darkness when I go. He will bring my poor grandchildren here. I must find a way to speak with him again, face-to-face, and make him understand. It will not be an easy task. No. I do not think she will allow me to do it.

Nathan, I feel my time running short. I feel this darkness closing in like a pack of wolves and I do not know how long I can hold it back. My health will not permit me to travel. The lawyers are coming here, they will put this letter aside for you, but I do not know if I will be able to see your brother again before it is too late. A letter will not convince him. He will explain it all away. He will lie to himself, as I did for decades.

Watch over him, Nathan, when I cannot. I know it is audacious to ask anything of you. Consider this the plea of a dying man. You were ever loyal. I doubt very much that aspect of your character has changed. Even your crime, I think, was born from a sense of faithfulness to the family name. A virtue this place saw fit to twist for its own diabolical means.

I must bid you adieu. I have no strength to continue. Only know, Nathan, that my love for you never did expire, despite the wicked efforts of this house.

Yours in regret,
William Bainbridge

*

Belinda left the room at a quick trot, afraid she might lose her nerve. She crossed the landing without speaking a word to Sawyer. By the time she arrived at the library door, she could hear the rain drumming on the roof and ricocheting off the lantern tower. Her breath came so hard that it threatened to tear the candle flame loose of its wick.

She must know. She could not dangle suspended for a moment longer, no matter how terrible the truth turned out to be.

Wilfred kept the room unlocked. She let herself in, her candle pushing the darkness back. Light glinted upon tooled spines, tasselled curtains, the desk... She froze. A figure stood in the alcove there: a lady of two dimensions. Small, imploring eyes above plump cheeks and curls set in coral ribbons. A companion.

'Anne.'

Just like the portrait. Not the hideous witch described in Mr Bainbridge's letter, but a woman desperate to speak. Or was that a trick? Some glamour of Anne's, to appear innocent and lure people in?

Two bound volumes lay upon the carpet. Belinda prodded one with her foot and stooped to pick it up. The leather felt soft and smelt of mildew. It seemed to thrum in her hands, speaking of old knowledge. The diaries Wilfred had reacted to with such disgust.

The companion's face flickered and shuddered in the shadows. 'You *want* me to read them, don't you?' Belinda whispered. 'You kept pushing your diaries off the shelf.'

Of course, there was no audible answer.

It felt like every moment since she'd first arrived at The Bridge had been leading to this. Belinda stared down at the books, worrying that she might be walking straight into a trap. Looks were deceiving. Anne's pretty face and kind eyes could easily hide darkness within.

But trusting her now seemed the only choice. There was no other door to the past and the answers that Nathan swore lay hidden in the year 1635. Weakness prevented him from recounting what he'd read tonight. He needed to rest. So if Belinda wanted to know the truth at once, she would have to fly in the face of her husband's orders and consult these pages herself.

Taking a deep breath, she creaked open the first volume and began.

CHAPTER 17

Now there were two stains on the flags of the Great Hall.

Wilfred watched from the gallery as the day maids scrubbed in stunned silence, red frothing from their brushes. They would not return after today's work. Not when the mood of the village was already so firmly against the house. He couldn't begin to deal with the news Knowles had brought back from Fayford: that the people had smashed his enclosure fences that night. Piled up the wood ready for their Midsummer bonfires. They had as good as burnt his money.

But vandalism faded into insignificance besides the accident. He could easily have lost his son and his brother in one fell swoop. Wilfred's gaze travelled over the few remaining swords on the wall as he tried to understand what had happened. Was it possible one of the angry villagers had stolen into the house and tampered with the display too? Or could it have been one of the women below him now, labouring on their calloused hands and knees? No. This was no plot, nor was it the threatened consequence of felling the Hanging Oak. The most likely explanation was that it had been an accident just waiting to happen, because neither he nor the old man had kept the hangings in good order.

Ultimately, it was Wilfred who had tarnished these smooth stones.

He could not look at the fatal spot any longer. Turning, he made his way towards the staircase. The light today was as dull as stone. Rain fell relentless, blearing the windows and running from the eaves in torrents. Nothing about the house was in its usual order. Nobody was themselves. As he gained the head of the stairs, he saw Sawyer approaching with Nathan's snuff-box in hand.

'How fares the patient?' he asked. 'Do not tell me he is still managing to snort that horrible powder in his current state?'

'He says snuff helps him with the pain, sir. I'm going to the kitchen to grind up some more now. Mr Nathan has given me the ingredients from his bag.' A guilty smile played about her lips. 'I must confess, I've taken a little of it myself. It keeps me awake.'

He noticed the purple marks beneath her eyes and the speckles of dried blood on her apron. She had not changed her clothes or gone to bed since it happened. 'Thank you for caring for my brother, Sawyer. It is above and beyond your role. We are truly grateful.'

She dipped an awkward curtsey. 'It's my pleasure, sir. He saved Master Freddy. He's a hero. I would render him any service I could.'

Did childhood rivalry never fade? Even now, even though he agreed with all his heart, Wilfred felt a twinge of jealousy. Or something more than that. Emasculation. He ought to be able to protect his *own* family.

'Well, I'll let you get along, Sawyer. Perhaps, while you are down there, you might make some tea? No one has broken their fast yet.'

All trace of a smile dropped from her face. 'Of course, sir. It was Mrs Knowles who used to cook for us.'

A flash of her, run through like a pig on a spit. Wilfred walked, forcing his mind down a different path. How would they ever replace Mrs Knowles? No housekeeper in their right mind would consent to work here after learning how her predecessor vacated the position. Perhaps Knowles and young John would leave as well. The memories might prove too painful for them to endure.

At the end of the corridor, far from the windows, it was as grey as dusk. He tapped on Nathan's door, hoping his brother hadn't drifted into a drugged sleep. He needed to say aloud how painfully this all reminded him of the day that Roberts died. How the guilt, the horror – and yes, the exhilaration – had never truly gone away.

No answer came from within. He creaked the door open, expecting to find the shutters drawn and Nathan comatose. But what he saw was quite different.

The chamber resembled one of Sawyer's pencil sketches, layered in shades of grey. The curtains of both the bed and the window were thrown back. Raindrops slipped fast down the glass. Nathan was lying prone as he had left him. Pillows supported his head to turn it to one side. Dev was curled up on the mattress and there, kneeling with her skirts pooled out on the floor, her face as close to Nathan's as a lover's, was Belinda. She seemed to be in a state of high excitement. Two spots of vivid colour on her cheeks, glittering eyes. When she snapped her head towards the sound of his entrance, he saw that her hair was falling over her shoulders like a young girl's, held back with only a ribbon.

'I must tell him,' she whispered.

Wilfred stopped on the threshold. 'Tell me what?'

Nathan shot her a warning look. 'Come in, Wil. I did not want to trouble anyone else until we had more definite answers, but Belinda is right. I cannot ask your own wife to keep secrets from you.'

He felt wrong-footed, cheated somehow. All he'd wanted was a few moments' quiet counsel with his brother. 'Secrets?' he queried, still not quite entering the room.

Downstairs there was movement, an exchange of voices.

'Not precisely *secrets*, Wilfred.' Belinda sat back on her heels. 'This is information that may concern us all. We are trying to establish exactly what occurred last night.'

'It was an accident,' he said dully. 'A terrible accident. And I am the one at fault. I've been remiss in checking everything is structurally sound. I mean to ride to Torbury St Jude this very day. I will hire an architect, and someone to take down the rest of the weapons. They're just another vanity like the silent companions: antiques, so-called rarities that no longer bring any joy. One has to break with tradition at some point.'

Footsteps sounded on the stairs behind him.

'The truth is,' Belinda began hesitantly, 'that the swords falling was not the only strange occurrence that day. There were other things... Even your father thought— Tell him, Nathan, about your father.'

Wilfred could feel the weight of unspoken words ready to descend. He'd been itching to ask his brother about that letter the lawyer had sent him, but now the time had come he couldn't bear another burden. Mrs Knowles' death was heavy enough.

'Sir?' The voice came from the corridor behind him.

Wilfred whipped around. Dawkins the groom stood there, his oilskin coat dripping. Who had let him inside the house? He'd trodden muddy boot prints into the carpet. 'What are you doing here, Dawkins?'

'I'm sorry, sir.' He had the grace to look sheepish. 'I'd usually send a message up to you with young John, but obviously he's not about.'

'Can it not wait?'

'No, sir. Sorry, sir. The horses have come and there's a man says he needs to be paid.'

The horses. They had completely slipped his mind. Freddy's first pony and a nice steady hack of his own for riding about the estate. He never would have bespoken them if he'd known what would happen to the enclosure. He was going to have to foot the bill for Mrs Knowles' funeral too, it was the only decent course of action. Expense after expense.

'Of course. I shall come straight away.' Wilfred glanced back to the interior of the bedchamber. 'Belinda, Nathan, you must excuse me. We will discuss this later.'

Belinda opened her mouth to object, but Nathan cleared his throat.

'Later, then, Wil.'

He was not completely sorry to close the door upon the pair of them. Whatever trouble they were brewing, it could wait.

*

After a little coaxing, the umbrella opened its petals. Raindrops played percussion upon waxed canvas. 'Come along, Freddy. This will keep us dry enough.'

The child hovered on the doorstep, peering out. Wilfred and Dawkins had collected him from the nursery on their way downstairs. Hopefully, this surprise would eclipse all the horror the poor boy had witnessed last night.

'The air tastes like metal,' he said.

'So it does. Quickly, now.' Wilfred held out his hand and Freddy followed at last. He gave a shout as his shoes slapped the wet ground, splashing his ankles.

'Will I get in trouble for dirty stockings?'

'No, Fred. I don't think Rebecca will care two figs about your stockings today.'

They started towards the stables. The clouds above them were as dark as pistol smoke. The gardens had become a mass of bouncing droplets, seething with a life of their own.

'Are we going to see the horses?' Freddy asked Dawkins.

'Yes, young master. The rain can make them skittish, so take care to be extra quiet with them today.'

'I won't scare them,' Freddy promised solemnly. 'I know how horrible it is to be scared.'

A twist in Wilfred's chest. He wanted to say something fatherly, wise and comforting, but knew not how.

Steam rose from the dung heap. Rain diluted its usual pungency. Everything in the yard seemed full of movement; the raindrops shining like thread. Gimcrack whinnied and kicked at her stall door. A man stood beside her, under the narrow shelter of the eaves, water cascading from the three corners of his hat.

'Who is that?' Freddy demanded rudely.

'Someone for Papa to do business with.' Wilfred had paid half the money for the horses upfront. He felt in his inside pocket for the remaining banknotes, thankfully still dry. He nodded to the stall at the base of the stable building. The half-door had been lowered a few inches at the top and was shining with new green paint. 'Suppose you and Dawkins go look in there until I'm finished?'

'In *there*? But there's nothing kept in that stable.'

'Let us see, Master Freddy. Something might have changed.' Dawkins opened his coat wide and took the boy underneath it.

Wilfred kept the pair in the corner of his eye as he settled his account. When they had reached the awning, Freddy emerged from the coat and raised his chin to peer inside the stall. 'There's… something *in* there.' He sounded afraid. Movement stirred, a shifting in the shadows. All at once, nostrils appeared, flaring above the half-door. Freddy cringed. Then he saw.

It was the nose of a skewbald pony, tilted up to see into the yard. The door was still a little too high for him, but the eyes were just visible beneath a shock of straw-like mane.

Freddy stared agog. 'It's… a new horse. A *small* horse.'

'He's a Shetland pony,' Dawkins explained. 'Fifteen years of age with a nice, steady temperament.'

Freddy stared back at him, amazement and disbelief warring for supremacy. 'He's mine? For me to ride? *My* horse?'

The reaction was everything Wilfred had hoped for. He passed over the banknotes to the waiting man with a smile. 'I do apologise. I would normally send you to the kitchen for refreshments before you leave, but we have suffered a bereavement. Nothing is in order.'

The man sucked his teeth. 'Much obliged to you, sir, I'm sure, but I'd rather not anyhow.' He cast a deprecating eye towards the house. 'I've heard strange tales of this place.'

There was simply no need for that. Wilfred turned away, judging the fellow did not deserve the courtesy of a response.

Dawkins was showing Freddy how to feed the pony a slice of sugar: flat on his palm with his thumb tucked underneath. The boy squealed in delight as the velvety lips brushed over his hand. 'Good boy, Sebastian!'

So he had named the gelding already. Wilfred was hardly surprised. Freddy seemed to have a stock of names inside his head ready to bestow; heaven only knew where he'd heard them. 'How are we getting on over here? Did you find something in the stable after all?'

Freddy turned a beaming face back towards him. 'It's a horse for me, Papa. *My* horse. Dawkins, you must take extra good care of him because he's mine.'

The groom smiled indulgently. 'I will do, sir.'

'Is he even better than your uncle's dog?' asked Wilfred.

The gelding snorted. Freddy laughed. 'That's Sebastian saying "yes".' Suddenly, he flung his arms around Wilfred's waist. 'I was so sad and frightened, Papa, but now I feel better.'

Wilfred hugged him back, tight. It was worth the money. He would have paid three times as much to hear that. 'Good. I know last night was terrible, but you never need to be afraid, little chap. Papa will always protect you.' He'd said it time and again. Only now did he realise it was a promise he could not possibly keep.

Seeing there were no more treats, Sebastian turned back into his stall. Dawkins moved off to tend to the other horses. Wilfred stood holding his son's damp head against his stomach. It was then that he noticed.

Two eyes watched him from far back inside the stable. One of the silent companions stood beside the rack as Sebastian quested for hay. A female figure, holding a broom. She wore a dull green dress, her apron and sleeves covered for work. Lace ruffles encircled her neck and made her head look strangely high. She smiled a Mona Lisa smile: cryptic, unsettling.

Dear God, the silent companions were like an infestation. How many of the damned things were there in total? Ten? Twenty? They ought to have kept some kind of catalogue. One day soon he would round the wretched pieces up and sell them. But how could Dawkins have filled the hay net and altered the door without even noticing this one?

Freddy stood to attention, suddenly alert. 'Something's wrong,' he said.

'No! Nothing's wrong,' Wilfred lied. He was grateful that Freddy was not tall enough to see fully over the door. After all that upset about the companion Belinda had had taken away, it would probably rattle him to glimpse another one now. 'Sebastian's just a bit tired after his journey, that's all. We should leave him to settle in.' He steered Freddy away, beneath the umbrella. 'When the weather cheers up, we'll teach you how to ride.'

But the frown remained on Freddy's lips. 'I wasn't talking about Sebastian. Something else is wrong. I can hear… hissing.'

Wilfred looked at the running gutters, the bubbling puddles. 'It's the rain, Fred.'

As they entered the gardens, a fork of lighting shot across the granite sky. Wilfred did not hear any thunder, but Freddy clamped his hands over his ears. The leaves of the chestnut trees dripped steadily upon the umbrella. Diamonds of water speckled the thistle patch. Beside them, the muddy pit Belinda had dug was boiling like a caldron.

Freddy stopped dead.

'What is it, son?'

'Over there.'

'The flowerbed?'

He nodded. That was where Freddy had dug, the night he walked in his sleep. 'It's deep enough now,' he whispered.

Freddy took off across the grass, heedless of the downpour. His hair and the bottoms of his pantaloons were instantly soaked. Wilfred followed, calling his name. The ground was waterlogged, hard to keep traction upon.

A smell emanated from the earth, not the mineral tang Wilfred had come to expect. This was like incense, spice kept in a jar.

'There!' Freddy pointed at the flowerbed. Something white and sharp as a splinter of chalk pushed up from the soil. 'She's coming back!'

Wilfred couldn't understand. Everything seemed to ripple and move in the rain. It was as if the earth was shifting, giving birth to something long retained.

A shape began to emerge, long and curved. A rib bone.

He fought against panic. It could be an animal bone. The deer were on this land long before the house... But it was too short.

Freddy attached himself to Wilfred's side like a leech. 'Stop her, Papa,' he begged. 'She's mean. I don't want to play with her any more.'

But Wilfred could not stop the sludge from melting away. A dome emerged, rising up through the soil like some ghoulish bulb. It was the colour of dirty teeth. As the brown water ran away, a skull grinned up at him from the earth. Not a deer skull. This was human. Small.

The skull of a child buried in an unhallowed grave.

*

The drawing-room was dim even on the brightest of days, with dark wooden panelling to shoulder-height and drab blue wallpaper above it. This afternoon, the place felt positively dismal. Marble had made its way into this part of the house. Not in the shape of busts as in the corridor upstairs but urns and small sculptures, brought back from the Continent by a Bainbridge scion on his Grand Tour. Aptly funereal for this morbid discussion.

Wilfred leant against the mantelpiece. He could not bring himself to sit. The coroner and the parish constable had been coming to inspect Mrs Knowles anyhow; now he was arming them with even more gossip to spread about The Bridge.

'Of course it will be difficult to establish the cause of death this late on,' the coroner was saying. 'Or the identity of the unfortunate child.'

On the sofa opposite, Belinda picked at her fingernails, a habit brought on by stress. 'But there was a daughter of this house who went missing, wasn't there, Wilfred? A long time ago.'

He frowned, remembering her reaction to the portrait. 'Yes,' he said slowly. 'I imagine you gentlemen are aware of the legends. Back in the last century, Anne Bainbridge murdered her daughter and many other victims, whose remains were left in this house. But the body of the little girl was never located. They found Anne wandering in the gardens after the killings… I suppose the story does tally with what we discovered. Anne must have buried her child on the grounds.'

'But a legend is hearsay, not evidence,' the constable pointed out. 'I shall have to go through my reports of local missing female children.'

The coroner inspected his notes. 'We are looking for a child between the ages of seven and ten, I would say. And obviously this would not be a recent disappearance. The body would have taken, at the very least, a year to decompose to this level.'

'Please!' Wilfred objected. 'My wife is present.'

The constable scribbled something in his pocketbook.

Belinda adjusted her position, making the sofa creak. 'The earth was salted,' she said. 'Long ago, they used to salt the earth to ward off evil...'

Wilfred stared at her and she fell silent. 'As you say, my good fellow, this *must* be a burial of some age, for no gardeners have been employed here for decades. Mark my words, it's Anne's daughter. This is the answer to a long-standing family mystery. The correct place for those remains are the Bainbridge family crypt.'

Belinda had picked the side of one thumbnail red raw. She appeared *more* disturbed by the idea that this was Henrietta Maria than if it had been a complete stranger.

The constable wrinkled his nose. 'I don't disagree with you, sir. But I must look into all avenues of possibility.'

'Naturally, naturally,' Wilfred sighed.

'No one in the village will answer our questions. They seem to be afraid we are intending to prosecute them for some kind of vandalism – is that correct?'

Belinda looked at her husband, a question upon her face. He had almost forgotten. 'Oh. Yes. That is true enough. Fences were damaged. I *could* claim redress. But prosecution is the last thing on my mind at this moment, I assure you.'

'All the same, the villagers are keeping their lips sealed,' the constable said. 'We shall have to make do with what your staff can tell us for the time being.'

'They have had their own tragedies to contend with. They are in a state of distress. It cannot be necessary to bother them today?'

'Actually, sir, it is best to speak to them while events are fresh in their memory. Please understand, Mr Bainbridge, that you are not being called into question about this skeleton. If anything untoward did take place, it would not have been during your tenure.'

He drove his fingernails into his palm. The inference was clear. If they suspected anyone of murder right now, it was the old man. Because of what had happened before. Because of Roberts. Because of Mamma. She had died of acute morning sickness, but there were inevitably whispers of poison.

How long would it take before their suspicion fell upon Nathan, too? Appearances were stacked heavily against his brother. They might begin to draw links between the old skeleton in the garden and his banishment, years ago.

Belinda rose. The men scrambled to do the same. 'I will go and fetch Sawyer. She should be calm enough to discuss the events of Midsummer. But I think Mr Knowles and John will need a little more time to prepare themselves.'

She shot Wilfred a look he could not interpret. He was still ignorant of what she and Nathan had been whispering about earlier. He felt a chasm was opening up between them, but there was simply no time to put it right. The duties of the house, of the family, were pulling them in opposite directions.

'Excuse me then, gentlemen.' Belinda opened the door to the Great Hall. Freddy toppled across the threshold from where he had been listening with his ear pressed up against the panels. 'Freddy!' she cried, catching him. 'Where are your nurses?'

'They're with Lydia.'

'This is a discussion for the adults, little chap,' Wilfred said, starting forward. 'You should be in the nursery.'

'I don't *want* to be in the nursery!' Before they could stop him, he pushed past his mother to face the two men. 'What will happen to her?' he demanded.

They looked at one another, bemused. 'What will happen to whom, young sir?'

'You *know*.' Freddy's voice quivered. 'Hetta.'

Belinda raised a hand to her mouth.

'What will happen to her bones?' Freddy repeated stubbornly.

Mortified, Wilfred stepped in and scooped the boy up. 'It's all right, Freddy. This has been too much for you. Once the formalities are over with, the skeleton will have a proper burial. In the family crypt. Where Grandpapa is.' He thought for a moment about Belinda's talk of ghosts. He would nip that in the bud right now. 'She will be perfectly at peace, with all that's due to her. There's nothing for you to fret about.'

Freddy shook his head. 'She won't be at peace. She's trying to get out. You ought to put her back.'

Wilfred shared an uncertain smile with the coroner. 'Put her back? We can't do that, my boy. People need to be buried decently in a church. It's the done thing.'

Freddy's eyes flooded with tears. 'Put her back in the salt earth,' he said fiercely. 'That's where she belongs.'

CHAPTER 18

Belinda dreamt of Henrietta Maria that night – or Hetta, as her family had called her. A girl born of potions and herbs, of incantations whispered under a full moon. So the diary claimed. Anne Bainbridge believed herself to be a white witch, blessed with the power to help others – until she helped herself to the daughter they said she would never bear. Then everything went terribly wrong.

Or did it?

This part Belinda could not untangle, it was twined as tight as ivy about a tree. For behind her closed eyelids she saw the girl, not as a flat and sinister companion, but as her doting mother had described her. *Hair blushing every shade of autumn. Upturned lips and soft dimples. Watering the rosemary with her tears.* An uncanny child, yes. Unable to speak, sharing an affinity with plants. But she danced, light-footed through Belinda's dreams, spreading the perfume of a summer meadow.

From what Belinda had read, it was only when the silent companions arrived from a mysterious shop in Torbury St Jude that the horrors at The Bridge began. Hetta slaughtered a horse in the stables and let a young groom called Merripen, a boy who was supposed to be her friend, hang for her crime. She poisoned the servants with bitter greens. Last of all, she used vines to strangle her faithful nurse. *I saw my oldest friend, the woman I had loved like a mother, with the life throttled from her body, and standing over her, the goblin I had once called daughter. There was no apology in her face – only a loathsome, gloating triumph.*

Belinda saw it all in vivid colours. Saw Anne stalking across the schoolroom with a knife in her hand. No wonder that place had always made her shudder.

Anne *had* killed Hetta: that much of the legend was true. She killed her daughter to stop the reign of terror, and the girl's blood had flowed to the feet of the silent companions.

But where did the wickedness come from? What was the root of the evil Wilfred's father had sensed in this house? Either a child spawned of darkness had died and possessed the figures – or it was the other way around. Cursed objects fixing upon a vulnerable girl and stealing over her like night creeps across the sky.

Either way, Anne had buried her daughter in salt earth to try and prevent the evil from coming back.

The Hetta in Belinda's dream was bathed in sunlight. Her face was fresh as the dew upon the grass. She beckoned Belinda closer, stood on tiptoes, pressed her rosebud lips against her ear. *Hissssss.* It crackled through Belinda, scraped across her bones. *Hisss.* The warm moisture of a tongue, questing.

She started awake.

The room was black as pitch. She reached out a hand for Wilfred.

Something squeezed back.

'Oh!'

'It's me, Bel. You were dreaming again.' His voice sounded weary, resigned. She doubted he had slept.

His fingers threaded through hers, soft and comforting. She could feel the little hairs on the back of his hand. 'Wilfred,' she said, unable to stop herself, 'we must leave this place.'

'Leave?' he repeated softly.

'Yes.' It was easier to speak in the dark, without his sceptical gaze, the confused quirk of his auburn eyebrows. 'It's what Nathan and I were trying to tell you before. We should go as soon as possible.'

'But Nathan *cannot* leave,' he pointed out. 'He cannot even stand.'

Obvious though it was, Belinda hadn't considered that.

'There must be a way to move him. We can ask the physician, people have travelled in frailer states—'

'Belinda.' There was a world of sadness in the way he spoke her name. 'Believe me, I understand your wanting to flee after all that has happened in the past few days. But you must be sensible. Consider. Mrs Knowles is not yet laid to rest. Human remains have just been discovered on our land. What impression would it give if we all stole away now like thieves in the night?'

She swallowed. 'I don't care. I do not give a straw what people think of us. I just want to go back to London.'

'My love... we cannot. It is not only a matter of our reputation. Lack of money prevents us.' Gently, he withdrew his hand from her grasp. Hers felt very cold without it. 'I have not had an opportunity to tell you about those damaged fences the constable mentioned. On Midsummer, the villagers broke down my enclosure and trampled the new wheat. That is the winter crop gone. But my father also took payment for a harvest of corn before it was fully grown. Today I rode out and found blight upon the ears.' He gave a short, mirthless laugh. 'Was there ever such a run of ill luck as ours? I shall have to pay back the money, of course. We must give up the lease on the London house to do so. We are overcommitted, Bel.'

The darkness seemed to be closing around her, walling her in. Cursed land. Of course. Hetta could make plants grow or die as she pleased. 'My father?' she suggested wildly. Papa may not have been generous with his time or his affection, but he had never begrudged her material things. She could force herself to swallow her pride and borrow his ill-gotten gains if it meant saving her children. 'My father could advance us some money if we asked him.'

'I very much doubt that. You are forgetting the crisis which took him overseas in the first place.'

It could not be possible. Was something as simple as money really going to hold them captive in a house of horror? She'd never been in want of funds before, never been forced to value the contents of her pocketbook above her own safety. But Wilfred did not understand the severity of the situation. He had not read about Hetta and the warping of a sweet child into something utterly deplorable. It was worth taking on any debt, surrendering any comforts, to protect Freddy and Lydia from a similar fate.

'*Your* father knew that there was something very wrong at The Bridge, Wilfred. He wrote to Nathan about it. You call me nervous, but have you ever seen me so flustered outside this house?'

'My father was a foolish old man. And you are not founding your fears in reason, my love. All you have said is that Anne Bainbridge was a wicked woman, and I knew that already.'

'I – I read Anne Bainbridge's diaries,' she admitted, adding in a hurry, 'I *know* you told me not to, but I am *glad* that I did. They explain so much. About the companions, about—'

'You do not trust me.' Hurt thickened his voice. 'You do not trust me to protect our family. And now you tell me that you deliberately went against my wishes?'

She could feel his tension through the sheets, the resentment radiating from his body. 'A servant died, Wilfred. Our son and your brother could have died too. I do not think I have acted unreasonably in trying to find an answer.'

'And *have* you found one? Or are you just filling the gap with Nathan's stories about curses and ghosts?'

Frustration was welling up, threatening to overspill. Why could he not listen to what she was saying? 'You are mocking me. But the truth is you concealed some very important information. Until Nathan arrived, I did not even know that your sister had jumped down the well! Or that she sensed things, as Freddy does.' *As Anne did*, she wanted to add, but stopped herself in time. 'You cannot have it both ways, Wilfred. You cannot lie to me and then scold me for not trusting you.'

He turned over, away from her. The mattress gave an unpleasant jolt. 'Dash it, I'm too tired for this. I've spent my day caring for our bereaved servants and trying to build a future for our children. *You* have wasted *yours* on tales of terror.' Her eyes filled with foolish tears. 'Try not to wake me if you give yourself another nightmare,' he added coldly. 'Some of us require our sleep.'

*

Once again, she was seeking out the chamber she'd been so desperate to swap with Wilfred. Perhaps it had been a premonition, five years ago, that something momentous was going to occur there. This time she could not simply scoop up her children, lock the door and wait out the storm. No part of the house, even the overgrown gardens, was secure.

But at least she was not alone. Providence had sent her an ally.

She found Nathan asleep, frowning and muttering against the pillow. Dev lifted his head at her entrance but laid it down again, unconcerned. Outside, a shimmer of rain was falling. It seemed to be easing. Small islands of blue floated in the grey sky, promising to expand.

Sawyer sat beside the window in a Chippendale chair. A snuffbox lay open on her lap – not Nathan's agate square but an oval made of enamel and painted with butterflies. Where had it come from? She inhaled sharply as Belinda entered, then dusted off her fingertips.

'You look dreadful,' Belinda whispered, and she did; her skin drained of colour, her eyes as dull as the clouds outside. 'Have you not slept?'

Sawyer shook her head, gently shut the snuffbox. 'I must not. I slept too deeply when I was watching Master Freddy and he got out into the gardens. What if Mr Nathan should take a turn, and I just snored right through it?'

Dearest Sawyer. While Belinda had fancied herself tired by nightmares, her maid had been sitting here alone battling utter exhaustion. 'But you will fall ill yourself if you get no rest! Go and lie down for an hour or two now. I shall sit with Nathan.'

Sawyer glanced towards the bed, reluctant. 'You will fetch me if I'm needed, ma'am?'

'Of course.'

'I – I don't really like to go to my room,' she admitted. 'Mrs Knowles is still laid out upstairs and the sound of her poor menfolk weeping for her...'

Belinda shivered, guilty to her core. She still felt responsible for the housekeeper's dreadful fate. *She* had ignored Freddy's warnings and ordered Mrs Knowles to put the Hetta companion away in the attic. And as Freddy said, bad things happened when Hetta was angry.

'Use the chaise-longue in my dressing-room,' she advised Sawyer. 'It is comfortable.'

Pocketing the snuffbox, the maid rose unsteadily to her feet. She was half-drunk on tiredness. 'Thank you, ma'am.' She cast one last wistful look over her shoulder at Nathan before she quitted the room.

Spreading her skirts, Belinda sat herself in the Chippendale chair and watched the rain. She was impatient for Nathan to wake. The laudanum must be keeping him under for she did not see how else he could possibly rest, knowing what he did. Dev came to sit upon her feet, reassuring her with his warmth.

Sawyer's sketchbook rested on the windowsill, a pencil tucked inside a page to keep her place. She must have been occupying herself to stave off sleep. Idly, Belinda picked it up and began to flick through. But what she saw sharpened her focus. These were pictures of death.

A boy hanging from a scaffold. A girl drowning in a river. Another child, skirts over her head, bent and broken at the bottom of a dark pit. Then came a study of the Great Hall: a fireplace, crossed blades upon the wall and a gallery above. An old man sat in a chair, holding a gun. He aimed at a shadowy figure. Two more watched him from the gallery.

Real events. Two deaths from Anne's diary, Tiffany in the well, Wilfred's father.

Last of all, drawn with thick lines impressed deep into the paper, was a picture of a girl who resembled Henrietta Maria. She stood in a garden of thistles with a baby in her arms.

Belinda choked. Lydia? Was this Lydia?

'What's the matter? Who's there?' Nathan's voice came groggily from the bed. With difficulty, he turned his head in her direction, wincing at the light. 'Sister? Is that you?'

Dev rose and padded back to his master's side.

'Yes, Nathan, it's me.' It was a struggle to control her voice, but she must let him come to before she launched into an outburst. He was hurt, in pain. 'Can I fetch you anything?'

He blinked at her, the film of sleep gradually dissipating from his blue eyes. 'No. Do not worry about *me*. What has happened? Has something dreadful brought you here?'

She shook her head. 'Nothing else. Not yet.'

He relaxed back against the pillow. 'Thank God. I dreamt such dreams. And when I saw you there instead of Miss Sawyer, I thought some harm must have befallen her.'

'No, no, she is quite safe. Except...' Belinda considered the book in her hands. 'Did you tell her about Anne's diary? Does she know about the deaths of poor Merripen and his sister... in detail?'

Nathan's wits were still befuddled. He looked as if he were trying to calculate a sum. 'I... do not know. Perhaps the laudanum made me speak in my sleep... But I thought we had agreed to explain it together?'

Guilt squirmed within her. 'Yes. We did. But I... may have tried to speak to Wilfred. Alone. I gave him no particulars, I only said I had read the diaries, but...

he does not believe we are in any danger.' She waited a moment, considering her husband's response. 'No. That is not quite true. He knows something is wrong but he does not *want* to believe me. He wants so badly to love The Bridge and make it a happy home.'

Nathan sighed. 'He always did. He always believed he could make everything right again. Poor Wil. He has a compulsion to fix things. Even those that cannot be mended.'

'He says we *cannot* leave, Nathan. We do not have the funds. The villagers tore up the enclosure. And now Sawyer is sketching horrible things, events from the diary and deaths in your family.'

'My father did write that the darkness here touched everything. Everyone.'

She felt a twinge of remorse for disliking the old man now. No wonder he was dour and surly, facing this horror alone for so many years. 'But what *is* it, Nathan? This evil? Is it Hetta or the companions themselves?'

He closed his eyes briefly, fair lashes fluttering against his cheeks. 'My money would be on Hetta. I told you that Tiffany used to hear her calling, didn't I?'

Calling from below the ground where she was buried. But in life Hetta could not speak. How could she call out? 'You did say that.'

'It makes a kind of sense to me, to imagine a little girl trapped within this house. After all, what does a bored child do? They torment others, they play tricks. Only this child's tantrums end in murder.'

Belinda shuddered. Could Hetta hear them, even now? Did their fear amuse her? 'A child can be appeased,' she said. 'She must *want* something from us. Perhaps she has spent all these years trying to be heard. If we give her what she seeks… she might leave us alone.'

'A hundred and forty years in the same place,' Nathan sighed. 'Personally, I would seek a way out, wouldn't you? And maybe we are on the point of granting Hetta just that. Once the bones have been examined and buried... if they *are* her remains... she might find peace at last.'

Belinda rubbed her forehead. She could not gamble her children's safety on a *maybe*; she had to be sure. But what could she do? Gather up the silent companions and destroy them? After what had happened with Mrs Knowles, she dare not. It might make matters worse. Apparently, the companions could unlock doors. Dislodge weapons. Who knew what else they could do?

Perhaps she ought not to be asking Nathan. She ought to ask her own son. He *knew* the companion with the basket of roses was Hetta from the start, and he sensed things, just like Tiffany did. All the strange things Freddy had said and done since they arrived at The Bridge came roaring back to her.

Digging in his nightshirt where the skeleton was buried. Bringing the Hetta companion to the gardens because she wanted company. But Freddy was too quick-witted to trust her. Hetta could not hope to use him as Nathan said she had used Tiffany. *He* would never jump down a well because she told him to. No. He'd got wise to her, hadn't he, and stopped playing with her soon after Lydia was born. Because he had figured out what he truly desired.

Freedom from this place. It was what he'd said to the coroner. *She's trying to get out.*

She remembered Freddy's dogged insistence that he must protect Lydia. That thistle, snagged across her own belly. Freddy lining up the soldiers around the crib.

It all seemed to hang hand in hand with the vile drawing Sawyer had made.

Belinda stifled a gasp. 'Dear God.'

'What is it?' Nathan demanded.

Hetta wanted to get out of the soil, out of the companions. Into something else.

Belinda turned to her brother-in-law, sick to her very core. 'Nathan... I think Hetta is trying to get inside my baby.'

CHAPTER 19

Sawyer was reading aloud. Wilfred could always tell for her voice changed in performance; her diction improved and the volume increased, as if she had found a different version of herself inside the book. He ought not to begrudge Nathan amusement on his sickbed, but he did.

Through the door, he made out enough words to recognise the novel as *The Expedition of Humphry Clinker*. Sawyer tittered at something she read and Nathan responded with a bright laugh. Their merriment grated. How could his brother be so blithe, so oblivious to the havoc he'd wrecked?

He entered without warning. Sawyer rose hurriedly to her feet and closed the book. A breeze flicked at the strands of dark hair escaping her cap. The window stood ajar, letting some of the mustiness of the sickroom escape.

Nathan was just about sitting up in bed with cushions supporting him. His untrimmed beard gave him a lopsided appearance. 'Ah, Wil! Just the fellow I've been longing to speak with.'

Wilfred did not return his smile. He was fighting an urge to throttle his brother where he sat. But Nathan had always been overeager, like a puppy. Even after Roberts died, he hadn't been able to understand why Wilfred wasn't delighted with his work. 'Will you excuse us, Sawyer?'

She nodded and trotted off. At least she had been reading from Tobias Smollett and not Anne Bainbridge's diary. She was generally a rational woman, he could not imagine her encouraging these ghost stories, but he couldn't be sure. Divided as her loyalties were between Belinda and Nathan at present, and with staying awake for long hours at night, her good sense might succumb. He would have to take her aside at some point and establish her views.

He sat down heavily in the chair beside Nathan's bed. 'You need to stop.'

Nathan frowned, startled. 'I beg your pardon?'

'You know precisely what I mean, Nathan. I need you to stop feeding Belinda this nonsense about ghouls. The poor girl is afraid of her own shadow! You cannot comprehend the damage you are doing to her nerves. She thinks every little thing that happens in this house bears some link to the witch's diaries. You are making her unwell. Please stop.'

Nathan parted his dry lips as if to defend himself. Then he closed them again, lowering his eyes to the bedclothes. 'Upon my word, I'm sorry, Wil. The last thing I want to do is harm Belinda. But I have not lied to her. You seem to think I'm weaving stories for my own amusement. I assure you that is not the case.'

'You believe The Bridge to be haunted?' He raised his brows sceptically. 'Have you laudanum dreams?'

'Damn it, Wil, why can't you open your mind? Even the old man was convinced there was something odd here. He wrote practically begging me to come home and save you from the evil spirits!'

Wilfred stared at him. Those letters from the holy men: they had not been prompted by religious curiosity as Knowles had suggested. 'You did not tell me that.'

'I was going to, before this happened.' Nathan gestured, frustrated, at his propped-up leg. 'But, like you, I was sceptical. It was those swords falling that finally convinced me. The old man said this wasn't a safe house for your children, and he was right. Imagine if I hadn't been coming down those stairs, right at that moment!'

Wilfred could not bring himself to imagine. Even the thought was agony. 'And I'm more grateful to you than I can ever say. But Nathan…' He searched his brother's face. 'How can you believe a *ghost* brought those swords down from the wall? It was simple wear and tear!'

'Or a curse at work, after your decision to cut down the Hanging Oak.'

'Bosh! You must not set any store by what our father wrote, the poor fellow was a dotard by the end. And The Bridge is an old lady. Her skin is sagging upon her bones, and she requires much tending, but she is not swimming with malevolent entities.'

Nathan returned his gaze levelly, undaunted. 'Tiffany would beg to differ. Now that I think back on all she used to say—'

'You know I loved Tiffany,' Wilfred interrupted. 'I would never wish to speak harshly of her, but…' He steepled his fingers, sighed. 'She *was* simple, Nathan. We must admit that fact. You could not take her prattling to heart.'

Nathan's jaw set. '*You* never did. You didn't listen to our sister, you could not even remember the name of her imaginary friend. And you are not listening to your wife now. How many people have to say this house is haunted before you truly hear it?'

'I *am* listening. I am simply declining to agree.'

Nathan screwed up the sheets in his hands. 'But… you *know*, better than anyone, why our family deserves to be punished from beyond the grave. We killed him, Wil,' he whispered, anguished. 'Aside from all the rest – the house's history, the witch and the silent companions – there is that. We killed Roberts. You cannot deny it. Aren't… aren't you ever afraid?'

Wilfred was *always* afraid of divine judgement. That was why he worked so hard to make everything perfect and everyone happy. But Nathan did not want to hear about his moral struggles. He wanted reassurance from his big brother. 'No. Nothing that has happened here has pointed to Roberts,' Wilfred said honestly. 'I will admit there are unpleasant reminders around the place of the girl Henrietta Maria, but *he* – he is certainly gone.'

Nathan turned his face towards the window, closed his eyes against the touch of the sun upon his skin. After a moment of silence, he said, 'Listen, if Belinda really is ill, you ought to take her away for a spell. The children too. Poor Freddy has suffered a shock. Get them down to the sea before the weather turns again. Or I hear Bath is lovely this time of year?'

Wilfred groaned. 'I wish it were in my power. You forget about the harvest – if there *is* much of a harvest to oversee, this year. The villagers are fractious, they need to be kept in line. And there are other obligations…'

'You are too conscientious. Leave me as your deputy,' Nathan urged. 'You *say* the villagers hate me, but it is *you* they've acted against in destroying your fences. Maybe they'd welcome a change of management. I do not even have to deal with them directly, do I? I can keep an eye on things from afar. Just for a week or two.'

Wilfred's eyes slid away from his brother's. Even if the thing were possible, he wouldn't be able to bring himself to do it. The mere concept of handing the reins to someone else filled him with panic. It felt like passing Lydia over to the care of a schoolgirl. Especially now Knowles was not fully up to scratch.

'That's kind of you, dear chap, but I can't spare the blunt for a holiday. I really can't. I bought Freddy his own pony before all this mess began. And then there's the expense of the funeral for Mrs Knowles, repairing the Great Hall...'

Nathan shook his head. 'It's a pity. A damned pity. A change of scenery would do you all the world of good.'

'We have only been *here* for a few months. We are not travellers like you, The Bridge is still novel enough for us.' Wilfred shot him a sly smile. 'Besides, what kind of man would I be to leave my brother all alone in a haunted house?'

Nathan did not catch at the jest as he expected but looked pained. 'I am always haunted by what I have done,' he replied sadly. 'What can ghosts possibly do to me?'

*

The lamp shook in Belinda's hand as she walked, showing confused flashes of red flock wallpaper. Sweat slicked her nightgown to her skin. Wilfred had said not to wake him, so she didn't. But she could not go back to sleep.

The dream had come with vivid colour and clarity, more real than this moonlit corridor seemed to be. She could swear she had *seen* Lydia lying on her back in the thistle patch, kicking her tiny legs. Every detail had been correct, from the bright wisps of her hair to her upturned nose and the delicate blue web of veins at her temple. Belinda had smelt her baby scent, felt the sun upon her own skin and heard sparrows cheeping. It had almost been pleasant. Until it happened.

A cloud had moved across the sky and dimmed the light. The chill followed instantly. A shadow spread like frost across her child. A shadow in the shape of the Hetta companion.

Lydia had grizzled but Belinda could not reach her, could not brush off the ants that began to swarm over her plump flesh. Only they weren't insects. Not on closer inspection. What marched like a row of ants was *underneath* the baby's skin.

Splinters.

Belinda refused to close her eyes again until she'd established it wasn't true. Only when she'd inspected every inch of her daughter would her heart slow down. The nursemaids might think her hysterical and Wilfred would certainly be appalled, but she did not care. They had not *seen* it.

Reality didn't feel much safer than the dream. Nothing but love for her children would send Belinda through this house in the dark now. The atmosphere was always unsettled, but at night the air felt too thin, not heavy enough to bear the weight of what pushed back from the other side.

As she stumbled down the staircase, she heard a soft tread. The whisper of fabric below. Her throat closed. Could it be Nathan's dog, wandering around? No; there was a light shuddering in the darkness. Behind it loomed something tall, thin and pale.

'Mrs Bainbridge?' She flinched at the voice, so loud in the quiet house. Rebecca. She had not recognised Freddy's nursemaid in a nightgown and cap. Both of them resembled phantoms. 'I was just coming to fetch you, madam.'

Belinda drew closer, her lamp gilding Rebecca's narrow face. The perplexity and alarm she read there made her stomach plummet. 'I *knew* something was wrong! Oh, God, is it Lydia? Is she sick?'

'No, madam. No one is ill. It's…' She paused, not so much nervous as confused. 'It's Master Freddy. He… well, I think it's best if you come and see.'

Sick with dread, Belinda followed her into the nursery where the nightlights shone, holding the darkness back. The first thing she saw was the bassinette, swaying gently back and forth, although there was no hand to push it. The yellow curtains cast an aureole over Lydia's sleeping face. Safe. Relief washed through her.

But Freddy was sitting cross-legged on his bed. His eyes were squeezed shut and he had a finger pressed against his lips. Amy knelt beside him on the floor, murmuring earnestly in a low voice.

It was then that Belinda noticed the golden curls spread over the pillow. Freddy's hair had been cut and not cut well. It looked as if someone had picked up great hanks of it and sliced at random.

'What on earth happened?' she cried.

Amy raised troubled eyes to hers. 'I don't know, madam. He won't talk to me. He was like this when I woke up to feed the baby.'

'I have told him he's not in trouble,' Rebecca added. 'No one is angry with him. But I don't understand how he'd do it, without me hearing! Or where he would find scissors in the first place? There aren't any sharp objects about the nursery, madam, and the door was locked – I've locked it each night since you told me he walked in his sleep.'

Amy rose and moved away to make room for Belinda.

'Darling!' she cried, sitting beside her son. 'Darling, what happened? You can tell Mamma. Did you... did you do this yourself?' Slowly, he shook his cropped head. It certainly *looked* as though a child had done it. But the execution was too intricate. Freddy could not possibly unlock a door, find a pair of scissors, use them, put them away and then lock the door again, all in his sleep. 'Then who did?' she whispered.

Freddy's chest hitched. 'I just... I was just trying to protect Lydia,' he wept. 'I wanted to keep her safe, and then *she*...' He broke down in sobs.

Belinda gathered the boy in her arms, tried not to let him feel how hard she was shaking. Lines from Anne Bainbridge's diary came bursting into her head. A description of Hetta in the garden with her pruning scissors. *By her side I heard the little scissors going* snip, snip. *Cutting nothing. Cutting air.*

Such things should not be possible. But what other explanation did she have?

She shot an anxious look towards Lydia's crib. Saw the change. There was no air left in the room.

'Who in God's name put that there?' she demanded. The nursemaids turned, baffled. 'That was not there when I entered the room!'

It seemed to have disappeared in the commotion of the falling swords, but now the Hetta companion was back, propped against the yellow wall, its shadow looming large and triumphant across Belinda's sleeping baby.

Just like in the dream.

CHAPTER 20

'He *could* have done it himself,' Sawyer argued. 'He's nifty in his sleep. He managed to get past me, all through the house and out into the gardens, didn't he? Any other child would have fallen down the stairs, but not Master Freddy.' She took a pinch of snuff. 'And if an adult had cut his hair, they would have done it... better.' A small giggle erupted from her lips. She bit it back, mortified. 'I'm sorry. I know it's not funny.'

Belinda stared at her. The maid was not quite herself this morning; she was twitchy, verging on hysterical. That seemed to happen to everyone when Belinda spoke of unnerving events. At the prospect of the supernatural, everyone's character warped and rippled, unsteady as a reflection in a pond.

They were closeted together in Nathan's room. He was still confined to the bed with its elaborately carved posts, while Belinda perched on the edge of a chair, Lydia sleeping in her arms. Sawyer hovered about like a restless spirit, folding a sheet here, dusting a surface there and doing a thousand other little things that did not really need to be done.

Belinda turned to Nathan. 'But *you* believe me, don't you? This incident cannot simply be brushed aside.'

'I am forbidden from saying a word about it,' he protested. 'Wilfred has accused me of unsettling you. He thinks the idea of a haunting only entered your head because I put it there.'

'Wilfred is not here,' she pointed out. He had taken Freddy into Torbury St Jude to get a proper barbering. 'He will never know. And besides, he is wrong. Wilfully wrong. He *saw* Mrs Knowles take the Hetta companion to the attic. Yet when I showed him it was back in the nursery, all he could say was that it must be one of a pair.'

Nathan rolled his shoulders. 'Well, he is not being *entirely* unreasonable in that. Some of the companions *do* come in pairs, one for either side of the fire.'

She felt as if she was losing her mind. Now she had what felt like irrefutable proof, fewer people than ever agreed with her. She had not *wanted* to believe it. But Nathan had shown her the diary and now he was drawing back, leaving her alone and isolated in her fear.

'You must admit, ma'am, it is a little *too* absurd, to propose a wooden board could cut Master Freddy's hair?' Another hectic laugh began but Sawyer raised a hand to her mouth and smothered it, moving away rapidly to the chest of drawers.

Belinda was hurt. 'I am not pulling this out of thin air.' She struggled to keep her voice low, so as not to wake Lydia. 'A child's skeleton was found in our very garden. And you have read the diaries now, Sawyer.'

'I *did* read them, ma'am,' she admitted, opening a drawer and refolding the contents. 'They were dreadful things, and no one's denying horrible events took place in this house. But they were only one lady's reflections, ma'am. Maybe it was all true for her, but it doesn't mean it was *the* truth.'

'Miss Sawyer is of the opinion,' Nathan explained, 'that perhaps Anne Bainbridge is not what they would call a reliable witness.'

Belinda was incredulous. 'Do you think she was insane?'

'From the way she writes, I'd say Anne Bainbridge was as mad as a box of frogs!' Sawyer burst out. The words seemed to have said themselves. All at once her face was panicked, contrite. 'I'm – I'm sorry, ma'am. I am out of sorts today. I'll – I'll go and make us all some tea, shall I?'

Without waiting for a response, she hurried from the room, her cheeks flaming with embarrassment.

Belinda gaped at Nathan. 'Whatever is the matter with her today? Did something happen, earlier?'

He frowned, his expression grave. 'I do not think it is only you and the children who could do with a break from The Bridge. The house is having an odd effect upon her. She says nothing, but like you, she is experiencing strange dreams. I hear her talking in her sleep when she is on the couch in the dressing-room.'

'Then why did you not say so when she was here? Why—' She did not finish her sentence for Lydia stirred. Belinda sat her up, cooed soothing words.

Nathan winced as he adjusted his position in the bed. 'I am trying to be diplomatic. Miss Sawyer is clearly not ready to believe what we do – although I must say, she is a little more open-minded than Wilfred.' He hesitated. 'I would like you to tell me more about Miss Sawyer.'

'What do you mean?'

'Well… she is not just a maid, is she?'

A warning note thrummed through Belinda. She did not look up. She gave Lydia her thumb to grasp. 'I consider Sawyer a friend. I did *tell* you we were much together as girls.'

'You did,' he replied softly. 'And *she* told me that the staff found her on the back steps of your father's house, as a baby. That she was taken in out of charity and raised up to work there. But I do not believe it. *She* does not truly believe it, I can tell.'

Belinda's heart was beating fast, as if she were about to be caught in a crime. She remembered a nasty chill she had taken as a child. The maids had covered her chest in a burning mustard plaster that stung like a fury, but when the time came for it to be removed, she had begged them to leave it in place. Instinctively, she had known that air on the sore skin would be worse than anything else.

'I have been told the same story, Nathan. I do not have any more information to give you.'

He sighed. 'Come, sister. You are too wise to swallow that. Only a green girl would believe such a tale.'

'Well, we have already established that I believe things the rest of you do not.'

'I *do* believe the house is haunted. But I am trying to honour the wishes of my brother, and I am trying to think how I can help. My plans may come to involve Miss Sawyer, as someone so close to you.' He took a breath. 'Belinda, you know I am not as delicate as Wilfred. I am not adept at bandying words. But you also know that my family was not always… conventional, and I will not stand in judgement upon your own.'

She turned Lydia, held her close against her shoulder for comfort.

'I have noticed that you and Miss Sawyer have nearly the same eyes,' he went on. 'Different colours, yes, but the shape is precisely similar.'

Those eyes were struggling to see straight. Black patches encroached on Nathan's features. Deep down, of course, Belinda had known. She had observed the similarity herself and tried to ignore it, along with a thousand other signs.

'My father's eyes.' She had not really meant to speak, but the words were out now, expanding to fill the room. Only the thump of Lydia's little heart against her chest felt real.

Nathan bowed his head. 'I see. And her mother? I do not suppose you know—?'

'They all think I was too young to remember what happened. But I *do* remember.' Her numb lips kept moving, as if they had been waiting to speak these words for a long time. 'I remember how my mother cried when the woman arrived at our house. Papa said she was to work for us, and that her baby was to sleep in our nursery. I may not have understood at the time, yet I certainly do now.'

He looked grave. 'I am so sorry. That must have been humiliating for your poor mother. I can sympathise, you know. The old man's rage at being cuckolded... well, I recall it as if it were yesterday.' He knitted his fingers together, swallowed. 'But it seems your father did not behave in the same way as ours. He made no acknowledgement of the child, there was no talk of giving her his name?'

'Oh, no. Not he. The irony was, Mamma ended up being kinder to both of them than Papa ever was. I cannot know for certain, of course, but it seemed to me that she and Sawyer's mother became allies in the end. My mother was different, back then. She used to move in society...' A tear she had not known was hovering spilled down Belinda's cheek. 'But gossip turned nasty.

Others mocked her – as I'm sure they did your father. She stayed at home more and more. Then, of course, there was the robbery.'

'Robbery?' he asked gently.

Lydia wriggled in protest as Belinda's tears fell onto her cap. 'They went out in the carriage. Across Hampstead Heath. A highwayman held them up. Mamma came back hysterical and covered in blood. She would not leave the house again. And Sawyer's mother… never came back at all.'

'Good God.'

'Sawyer was very small at the time. As far as I can tell, she doesn't even remember that she had a mother. I can't imagine the older servants would have told her… it could only hurt her to learn the truth.' Belinda moved the baby and scrubbed at her eyes. 'I do not wish to speak of this. What good can it possibly do? Sawyer's history has no bearing on the events in this house.'

'It might, one day,' he countered. 'Here, take my handkerchief. I truly am sorry for making you recall unpleasant memories. But in a situation like this, it pays to have as much information as possible. To under-stand the people you are living with. Their strengths and weaknesses.' He considered. 'It sounds as though Miss Sawyer has been forced into practicality most of her life. Taking things at face value and not asking ques-tions. That would explain her reaction to the haunting, wouldn't it? But she is affectionate and kind. I think she will come around in time.'

'I do not *have* time!' Belinda protested. 'Hetta is after my baby *now*. I cannot wait for Sawyer to change her mind. I do not see what good it would do to have her believe me, anyhow. Her opinion will carry no weight with Wilfred.'

Nathan rubbed his brow. 'Perhaps not. I have tried to get him to take you all on a short holiday but... I cannot solve this problem for you, Belinda,' he confessed sadly. 'I will keep trying my best to help, but in the end it is a decision to be made between you and your husband.'

Belinda took a deep breath. Nathan was right: it was always going to come to this. She had to stop relying on him or even Sawyer to fight her battles. She was a mother now, Freddy and this tiny baby in her arms were both relying upon her.

'It is not my decision though, is it? Not legally. It's only Wilfred's. Unless I were to... abscond.' She felt dizzy just imagining the scandal and her husband's hurt. And what good would it really do? Wilfred would be within his rights to pursue them and bring them straight back here.

Nathan frowned. 'Oh, no, it need not be as dramatic as that, my brother is not the kind of man you need to flee from. Could you not propose a short family visit with the children and then just keep... extending it? I am sure he would take the hint. But where would you go? I think you mentioned a brother in Bristol?'

'Yes, Luke is there, but he does not live in the city, he is merely visiting on business, refitting one of Papa's ships. I do not know where he is staying or if he could even accommodate us...' She trailed off, imagining her brother's reaction if she turned up on the dockside. His kindly fluster, his ready sympathy. But it would mean nothing. He'd book her on the next stagecoach back to The Bridge, with a helpless shrug. She shook her head. 'The truth is, my family have never been very willing to put themselves out for my sake.'

Nathan's face darkened. 'I understand the sentiment. Truly, I do. All I can propose is renting a house of my own somewhere nearby – like Torbury St Jude. At least then the children could come and stay with their uncle for a few weeks at a time. It would be a refuge close by. But not a permanent solution.'

'I must find a way to convince Wilfred. I must present him with evidence that even he cannot deny. I only wish I knew how.'

She pulled the baby closer. *Her* baby, not Hetta's.

There was but one thing Belinda had in common with that darkling girl: they were both of them desperate to find a way out of The Bridge.

*

Three days later, Belinda still did not have a solution. She would have thought the diary, the accident and Freddy's haircut would have sufficed to persuade Wilfred of the danger they were in, but evidently not. Nor would he accept her argument that the villagers might attack the house next, following their destruction of the enclosure.

She'd never seen a woman successfully exert her own will against her husband's. As she'd explained to Nathan, her own mother hadn't been able to object even when a rival and an illegitimate child were foisted into her home.

Freddy was doing nothing to assist her cause. He would not tell them who had cut his hair. He just kept insisting that she keep Lydia out of the nursery. Belinda asked if he wanted to sleep in their room too, but he shook his shorn head. 'I need to keep my eye on her. She's up to no good.'

He clearly meant the Hetta companion, who was back in the schoolroom with the other boards, smiling as if nothing had happened. Someone *did* need to watch her. But what could little Freddy do to hold back a vengeful spirit? Belinda wanted him far from the line of fire. Who else could she enlist to help? There was only Sawyer.

Tonight Sawyer stood behind her at the dressing-table, her warmth pressing against Belinda's back. After the talk with Nathan, she could not quite bring herself to look her maid in the eyes. Instead she averted her gaze from the mirrors, focusing on the whorl of the wood, the scattered hairpins and ribbons.

She ought to say something. Acknowledge the truth. But how would she possibly begin?

Sawyer's hands were methodical. Each section of hair swept through, her fingers deftly unpicking the knots before the brush could stick on them. Belinda allowed her eyelids to drift shut. Throughout her girlhood, Sawyer's touch had always been as soothing as a cold compress upon a wound. But who had combed out Sawyer's hair? Who had comforted her when she had a bad dream? Belinda had never thought to ask.

It must have been lonely, infuriating, even, waiting upon her own relatives. If Belinda resented the time trapped with Mamma, how must Sawyer feel?

If only they'd been raised naturally as true sisters. Taking it in turns to braid one another's hair for the night, sharing dresses and gossip, petty rivalries and quarrels.

Her heart ached.

And suddenly her head did too. The brush strokes were growing increasingly rough. Wincing, Belinda opened her eyes in time to see Sawyer fumble and drop the silver-backed brush onto the carpet.

'I'm sorry, ma'am. I'm sorry. I must be tired.'

She stooped down to retrieve the brush. Placing it briefly on the table, she pulled out her snuffbox and administered a pinch to her nostril.

'No harm done. Are you well, Sawyer?'

'Yes. Thank you, ma'am.'

Belinda glanced at the adjoining door to the bedroom. It stood wide open so that Lydia would not be out of sight. All appeared to be tranquil within, no companion lurking beside the crib.

When she looked back, Sawyer was pulling hair from the bristles of the brush. Her hands were shaking.

Belinda swivelled round on the stool. She remembered Nathan's words of concern about her maid's health. 'I think you *must* be ill.'

'No, no. I'm... anxious.'

'Anxious?'

Now it was Sawyer's turn to avoid her eye. What could have happened?

Anticipation flared. This would be the moment, Belinda thought. Sawyer was finally about to acknowledge the ghosts. She'd relate an event so momentous that it would convince Wilfred outright.

Belinda's eyes moved expectantly to the outer door as the clock chimed. He ought to be here. He ought to hear this for himself.

'Wilfred is late tonight. I wonder where he could be?'

'That's just it, ma'am.' Sawyer had removed strands of Belinda's fine hair from the brush and began to wind them around her own index finger. Too tight. 'He's speaking to Mr – to Nathan.'

'About what?'

'About ... About the offer of marriage his brother has made to me.'

Belinda nearly fell off her stool. '*Marriage*?' So *that* was why Nathan had been asking questions about Sawyer. Why he'd desired to keep her as his nurse. But he was a gentleman's son! Such a vault over the class divide... 'Nathan really proposed?' Surely he couldn't. Surely Wilfred would never allow the unequal match? Sawyer could bring him no dowry or alliance. 'And what answer did you give?'

Sawyer finished her winding. 'I accepted him, of course.'

Of course. She would have to be a fool to turn down the opportunity of a lifetime. 'But do you...' Belinda stopped. She had been about to ask if Sawyer loved him. There was no need. Hadn't she already seen evidence of an attachment between them? Besides, Belinda had felt nothing more than a liking for Wilfred before their marriage. The sentiment had blossomed afterwards. 'You barely know one another,' she tried instead.

Carefully, deliberately, Sawyer set the brush and roll of hair on the table. 'It's true that we've only been acquainted for two months. But we've been thrown much together, ma'am. I believe I've spent more time in Nathan's company than many young ladies can boast of their fiancés. They only dance with a gentleman two or three times at the assemblies before they marry him, don't they? And as for Nathan's background, his family... well, I already know it's impeccable.'

Impeccable was not the word Belinda would use to describe the Bainbridges now. Not after the Roberts affair and what she had read in the diaries.

Sawyer watched her closely, anxiously. But Belinda was unable to give her the reassurance she craved. The whole plan struck her as foolhardy.

'I cannot understand why Nathan would even *consider* marriage at a time like this! With all the danger and the uncertainty. He said that he was planning...' She trailed off as the realisation hit her. Indirectly, Nathan had told her exactly what he meant to do. He'd spoken of taking a house in Torbury St Jude and now he wanted a wife to manage it for him.

She could hardly breathe. He was not just abandoning her, he was taking her closest friend away with him.

'Dear God, *that* is his solution?' She put a hand to her aching forehead. 'To marry my maid, run away and leave me to cope with all of this alone!'

Sawyer drew herself up. 'With respect, ma'am, none of this is about *you*. It's about us having a home of our own. Children of our own, should we be blessed. No one is *leaving* you, but I'll admit...' She wet her lips, preparing them for the words. 'It will be nice to have days when I'm not waiting upon someone else. Even people I care about.'

Belinda's hand dropped. She scolded herself for being churlish. Mere moments ago, she'd considered how hard life must have been for Sawyer, yet now her maid had the chance to better herself and Belinda was reacting as if it were a personal insult.

It was the timing again – the worst possible timing. As if Nathan had decided to cut his losses now and get out of the house while he still could.

She opened her mouth to speak, but the door opened and Wilfred entered the dressing-room. She saw his pale face reflected in the triple mirrors. He glanced from one woman to the other.

Sawyer ducked her chin and folded her hands in front of her like a child in trouble.

'Sawyer,' he said, his voice strange and false. He paused, as if realising he would need to address her differently from now on. 'My brother is waiting to speak with you.'

The maid curtsied and slipped from the room, her soft shoes barely making a sound on the carpet. The door shut.

Belinda and Wilfred stared at one another in the mirror, stunned. 'I had no warning,' she confessed. 'What do *you* make of this?'

Wilfred expelled his breath and cast himself on the chaise-longue. He looked completely deflated. 'Naturally, I thought my brother would marry higher. But perhaps, with the damage to his reputation...' He shook his head, the tail of his wig bobbing before he pulled it off and cast it aside. 'It must be a love match. She can bring him nothing. And in terms of character, I could raise no objections. It is not as if he has selected some Billingsgate fishwife. I have a high regard for Sawyer. For... what is her Christian name?'

'Daphne.' It tasted strange upon Belinda's tongue.

'Daphne,' he repeated. 'See, it is even a genteel name. Despite her station, I don't think she will embarrass us.'

Belinda turned all the way around to face him. 'Have you given them your permission, Wilfred?'

He shrugged. 'I have. Not that they need it. They are both of age. But have I done the right thing, Bel? A maid like that is not easy for you to replace. And I'm sure your family will have... opinions.'

She closed her eyes. Wilfred must know. Of course he did, if Nathan had been able to spot the connection between her and Sawyer in only two months. 'My misgivings are not related to rank. With all that's happened in this house – not to mention the death of your father! – it seems odd. Indecorous, even. Why did Nathan not wait to declare himself? It's not as if Sawyer is a debutante inundated with other offers.'

Wilfred spread his hands. 'His brush with death must have put the wind up him. He wants the banns read straight away. But holding a celebration in Fayford right now would be something akin to madness. They'd do better to obtain a special licence.'

Belinda's stomach plunged. 'He won't wait? He'll go to the altar injured, when he should be in mourning for your father?'

'Nathan never did anything by halves,' Wilfred said wryly. 'And he has never lost anything for want of asking. He's requested the loan of our carriage, too. He thinks a honeymoon in Bath, drinking the waters, will speed his recovery.'

For a time she sat speechless, picturing both of her allies and her only escape vehicle trundling uphill and over the stone bridge, out of sight. But she was overreacting, wasn't she? Nathan had promised to provide a refuge where she and her children could stay. She tried to see this as a means to that end – not as rats leaving a sinking ship.

She checked the door to the bedroom again; Lydia's crib was still untroubled.

'We'll all go,' she tried. 'The waters would do wonders for my nerves.'

Wilfred climbed wearily to his feet, making the chaise-longue creak. 'I *told* you that I am not flush at the moment, Bel. And I do not want the villagers thinking they've managed to frighten me away. Perhaps next year.'

'Just for a short time!' she begged. 'Nathan would pay for our accommodation in return for the carriage ride, I'm sure!'

'No.' There was a note of finality to Wilfred's voice. 'No, as a matter of fact, I think this little absence of Nathan's will be ideally timed.' He ran a hand over his short, bright hair. 'A separation between the pair of you will prove more effective than any thermal spa.'

CHAPTER 21

These were the dog days of summer. Late July. A haze of dust hung over the town of Torbury St Jude, stirred up by hooves, feet and wheels. Vendors bawled from the market cross, but Wilfred could not see them through the grime on the carriage window. Despite being rank with sweat, he dare not put down the glass for a breath of fresh air. He was more likely to receive a mouthful of grit.

They turned into a cobbled street lined with Tudor buildings. Nathan winced at the bumps. The contents of the polished walnut box on the squabs beside Wilfred rattled and he placed a hand on top to steady it. Horrible how the vibrations travelled from those bones into his.

Unsurprisingly, the coroner had not been able to identify the garden skeleton or do anything but estimate how long it had been in the soil. There was no conclusive proof. He'd agreed to let Wilfred inter the remains on the condition they could be easily accessed if needed. So instead of resting beneath the sod like poor Mrs Knowles', these bones would go into the family crypt.

The place was still fresh in Wilfred's memory from the old man's funeral. The cobwebs, the mice and the brown stains on the floor, treacle-thick. Slabs and rocky shelves housed his ancestors in coffins of all varieties. The older, softwood ones had splintered open at the edges to show glimpses of decay. Still, Belinda would not know the dismal reality and nor would Freddy. Wilfred could bring back a report of laying the murdered girl's remains peacefully to rest and then, *then* perhaps all this chaos would end.

The carriage drew to a halt outside the solicitor's office. Nathan reached for his cane. He was able to limp about now with assistance and seemed to be nicely on the mend. The acceptance of his proposal seemed to have spurred him into action.

'Are you certain you want to go through with this?' Wilfred asked.

'Ah, there it is.' Nathan wagged a finger at him. 'The Bainbridge pride. You are thinking of what the old man would say, if he knew I was marrying a servant.'

To some extent, yes. He had expected his brother to seek out an heiress like any other gentleman of their class. But if this was what Nathan really wanted, he would give his blessing. Nathan had sacrificed enough for the family name already. He ought to have the wife of his choice, even if it brought disapproval from others. As maids went, he certainly could have chosen a rougher specimen. Daphne Sawyer would polish up.

'The old man would say you are selling yourself short, and he'd be right, but *I* merely ask if you can afford to marry.'

'For all its faults, the East India Company *did* pay me. It may be a morally questionable source of wealth... but I have more than enough of it to take a wife.' His brother's smile faded into solemnity. 'You know, Wil, I could make *you* a loan if you really needed it. I understand things are tight at present, what with the enclosure and the corn. I don't suppose any of the villagers actually paid their Midsummer rents, did they? Ease off them a bit. Mortgage a cursed field or two to me. You needn't pay *me* interest like a bank.'

Wilfred deliberated. It was tempting, but he shied from being indebted to a younger brother. Or rather, *more* indebted. For he had enlisted Nathan's well-meaning help once before, hadn't he? Fired the boy up until he could not understand that Wilfred had changed his mind, that it had all been a spleenful, childish scheme, that he did not really want anyone *dead*.

'I will bear it in mind,' he said. A shadow of disappointment passed over Nathan's face. He did love to be of use. Wilfred put out a hand to open the door and stopped. 'But there *is* something you can do for me, if you are inclined.'

'What's that?'

'It is not just the marriage contract we are drawing up today. I'm amending my will to include Lydia.' He wet his lips. His heart so wanted to throw Nathan a bone, but his good sense always demurred. That was the problem, he supposed, with knowing someone since they were in leading strings: part of you always viewed them as a tiny, incapable sibling who needed to be cared for. He shook off his reservations and plunged on. 'I thought it might be time to review the appointed guardians for the children, should anything befall me before Freddy's majority. Pray God, it will never be necessary. But since you have already proved yourself Freddy's defender in the most literal sense…'

Nathan was taken aback. 'Me? You want to make *me* their guardian?'

'One of the guardians,' he specified. 'You would share the role with Belinda's eldest brother, Paul, who is already on the paperwork.' He had not expected to see that expression of panic on his brother's face. Maybe he had overstepped, assumed too much. 'But perhaps you do not plan to stay in England for long. I know it is a serious undertaking—'

'Yes – yes, it is.' Nathan nodded eagerly. 'And an honour, too. I'm touched, Wil. I really don't know what to say.'

'Well, consider the matter. We need not formalise everything today, if you would like time to think…' He reached for the door again.

'I don't feel worthy of such trust,' Nathan admitted, stopping his hand. 'That is why I hesitated. But that is ridiculous, because here I am, taking a wife! God willing, I could be a father myself this time next year. I shall have to rise to the responsibility sooner rather than later. And as you say, it will not really be *needed*. It is just an insurance against the worst.'

'Yes, that's right. I meant it as… as a token of my esteem.' He could not say, as an atonement, as a guilt offering, but Nathan seemed to read what he meant.

'I'm sensible of that. Thank you.'

'Thank *you*, for saving my boy.' Wilfred regarded Nathan, washed in light, and felt a lump in his throat. Tiffany may be gone forever, but his brother was coming back, taking on solid dimensions once more. A life saved for a life taken. Surely it was enough to put things right?

Maybe this wedding was exactly what they all needed, even if it wasn't quite considered decent so soon after the old man's death. Maybe this was how it ought to have been from the start: Sawyer known as Daphne, Belinda's sister, not forced to drag the chains of her illegitimate birth; and Nathan, happy, carefree, never tempted into sin by his reckless brother. They had both suffered misfortune without really being at fault.

This union would be a reclamation. The family, born anew, exorcised of its misery.

Surely, once its occupants were finally at peace, The Bridge would be too?

*

There must truly be witchcraft at The Bridge, Belinda thought, some kind of spell or enchantment spread like a net across the roof. For now both Mrs Knowles and the garden bones had been formally laid to rest, everyone seemed simply to… forget.

Of course, Knowles and his son still wore their black armbands. Rebecca dressed Freddy with one bandaged hand. But as Belinda sat in the summer parlour with Sawyer – no, *Daphne*, as she must think of her now – it felt as if she had torn apart the fabric of her own world and stepped into another. A land where none of it had ever taken place.

Freddy was content to be out in the stables every day with Wilfred, Dawkins and his new horse. The villagers went back to using the common land again and no one moved to stop them. Even the weather had regained its vigour, the sun shining through the window with a glare that erased all else. Lydia squinted up from the pile of cushions Belinda had placed her upon. Save from trips to the wet-nurse, she was not letting the baby out of her sight. *She* had not forgotten the grinning skull rising from the soil or the triumphant look on Hetta's face before the blades came raining down.

Sawyer – Daphne – sat upon the sofa with her back to the window, haloed in light. Whatever horrors she had drawn in her sketchbook did not seem to trouble her now. She had turned over a fresh leaf and was copying a fashion plate out of *The Lady's Magazine*. But she was pressing too hard. Her usual delicate pencil strokes had been replaced by a kind of frenzy that hissed against the page as she drew.

'I thought something like this, for the ceremony?' she said brightly, without looking up. 'Only not so fine, of course. Not for me. The polonaise skirts to be sure. I want – no. Perhaps like this, in dove grey over black?' She did not pause to actually show Belinda her drawing. 'I know Nathan has not kept to mourning but it wouldn't be decent for me to wed in light colours, would it? I wouldn't feel comfortable with that, only six months after his father's death. Am I right, ma'am?' She had barely taken a breath.

Belinda was not in the mood for discussions of etiquette. If they wanted to talk about what was *proper*, what was socially acceptable, none of this would be taking place.

'Is there actually time for you to order something new?' she asked. 'You could always wear one of my gowns. I'd be happy to give it to you as a gift.'

'No!' Daphne's brows drew together in hurt, but then she seemed to recover herself. 'I mean, no, thank you. This will be something that is mine alone.'

Lydia fussed, the sun in her eyes. Belinda rose to scoop her up as Daphne's pencil muttered across the page. She set Lydia on her hip and paced up and down, jiggling the baby as she went. She knew she ought to be delighted. Hadn't she always longed to acknowledge how much Sawyer meant to her? Were they not, by habit and inclination, sisters already?

But a sister was free to leave. There was the rub. And now Belinda was starting to understand the dismay that had gripped Mamma when her own marriage was arranged. This was how it felt to be abandoned to your own ghosts. She pulled Lydia closer.

'I must write to my mother soon. I do not know what to tell her about all of this. She will scarcely believe it.'

Daphne paused in her drawing at last. 'I cannot advise you on the contents of your letter. But you may send Mrs Kipling my best wishes, ma'am – Belinda.'

It was not long ago that Sawyer had offered to take on the burden of telling Mamma about the move to The Bridge. The balance of power was shifting – as it should, perhaps. Officially, on paper, Mamma had not been Daphne Sawyer's problem since she left her employ some seven years ago.

Belinda buried her nose in Lydia's wispy hair, inhaled her sweet and milky scent. This marriage was digging up feelings that had long laid dormant, like Hetta's skeleton. Things she knew in her heart but would not even dare to whisper aloud.

Daphne set down her pencil and pulled out her snuffbox. Nathan had given it to her, she said, on the night of the accident. He had told her she was like the butterfly on top, waiting to emerge from its chrysalis. She had become an expert at taking it now, administering a pinch with all of his deftness.

Why had Belinda never noticed before how pretty she was? That clear complexion, smoky eyes and hair like a sweep of ink from a quill nib. She had never seen Daphne placed so fully in the light like this, free from her servant's apron and cap. No wonder Nathan had fallen in love.

'Are you feeling better now? The other day, you were a little… off.'

'Yes, I am remarkably well,' Daphne returned, dabbing at her nostrils with a handkerchief. 'I have never felt better.'

Maybe the little oddities Belinda had noticed were just the flurries of romance. Naturally Daphne was excited to be raised up out of her station, it was like a fairy tale. Who would *not* be twitchy and a little nervous under the circumstances? She certainly seemed happy. But Belinda could not let it go. She had known Sawyer for a long time, and something felt wrong.

'I saw the drawings you did,' she pressed, nodding at the sketchbook. 'Before. The scenes from the diary. You must admit, those were not the sketches of a mind at peace. Tell me... did you hear strange things on the nights you spent awake nursing Nathan? Did you see anything... odd?'

'I spent a long time without sleep,' Daphne answered, guarded. 'And Nathan was telling me stories about his family. Those sketches were not meant for anyone else's eyes. I wish you had respected my privacy and not looked.'

She had never wanted privacy from Belinda before. 'But *why* did you draw them? You must have been upset or disturbed in some way.'

A muscle twitched beside Daphne's lips. 'Ma'am – I mean, Belinda. We have all been through some frightening experiences. I'm not surprised if you are still unsettled. But I *could* wish that you'd pay a little more attention to the here and now, and stop dwelling on events we can't possibly change. This is the most significant thing that will ever happen to me. Your comments are – well, they're casting a cloud across it.'

Indignation bristled. Could Daphne not see she was tempting fate? Anne Bainbridge had planned a celebration inside this house too, but Hetta had smashed her hopes by butchering a horse. Belinda dared not think how Hetta might set about destroying Daphne's happy day. 'I am sorry if my fears are *inconvenient*. I am not kicking up a dust over nothing. We are all in real danger. Evil will not pause to enjoy your wedding day.'

She would have preferred Daphne to flare back. But she only gave a sorrowful shake of her head. 'I appreciate my marriage puts you in an awkward position. But I had hoped you would be happy for me.'

'I *am* happy!' Belinda cried in a tone that seemed to belie her. 'I only want what is best for you. I am asking all of this out of concern for your welfare. You know the history of this house as well as I. All I want is for everyone to be *safe*.'

Something in Daphne seemed to snap, to break free of its bounds. 'You know who you sound like, don't you?'

Belinda could not have felt the reproach more keenly had she reached out and slapped her face.

CHAPTER 22

St Jude's was a world apart from the church of All Souls in Fayford. The outer walls were made of mellow limestone and warmed in the late-August sun. A square tower, rather than a steeple, rose above the uneven rooftops of the town. As the rickety old carriage shuddered to a stop in front of the lychgate, Belinda noted with a jealous eye how neat and orderly the grass of the graveyard was kept.

'Can we get out now?' Freddy whined. 'It's so smelly in here!'

There had not been enough room for them all in the family coach, but Belinda had refused to leave the children behind while she was out of the house. Consequently, she'd packed them and their nursemaids into this decrepit vehicle, which once belonged to Wilfred's father, and had it pulled by just two horses with a hired driver. The smell Freddy referred to was probably the moth-eaten upholstery, but the rattling journey had made Lydia sick too.

'Let Rebecca climb out first. Be careful!'

She could see the wedding party under the arched porch of the church, making final adjustments to their dress. It had been a wise precaution to solemnise the marriage in Torbury St Jude rather than Fayford. No sinister audience gathered around the churchyard; the only looks came from passers-by, who smiled to see the bouquet and the buttonhole, knowing what they foretold.

In the absence of a footman, Rebecca clambered out to put down the steps and then held out her hands to help Freddy. Her missing finger was prominent. Belinda averted her eyes and watched her son instead, thinking his short hair made him look older than his years, yet somehow more fragile with it.

She disembarked and took the baby from Amy's arms, so that the wet-nurse could climb out unimpeded. Amy was only staying with them for the ceremony; she had been given leave to visit her family in town afterwards.

For Belinda too this felt like a holiday; like the old days of escaping from her mother's house. Hours and hours free from The Bridge, with some private rooms taken at the local inn for the wedding breakfast. She was almost giddy with relief. Nathan and Daphne may have pooh-poohed her claims that something terrible would happen if they celebrated at the house, but they were here, weren't they? They had arranged for it all to take place in Torbury St Jude. On some level, they must have listened.

She handed Lydia back to her nurse and bustled up the path to where the others waited. She'd helped Daphne get ready, but it was still a surprise to see her again, transformed into gentry. The grey and black gown of her sketch four weeks ago was tasteful and elegant, its panniers giving her a waist and hipline she had never seemed to possess as a servant. Hair and face powder lent her a new brightness. And something glittered at her neckline that had not been there before. Light caught on the gems, cast stars upon Daphne's face.

Belinda stopped and stared. 'Are those the Bainbridge diamonds?'

She had worn them for her own wedding. Every inch of the chain was iced with small, round stones, leading to a bow design that hung at the centre, dripping with three more diamonds. Daphne stooped slightly under the weight of them, clearly uncomfortable.

'I loaned them to the bride. I did not think you would mind,' Wilfred said, a warning note in his voice.

She did not *mind* – or at least, not in the way he thought. His tone seemed to imply her objection was on the grounds of snobbery, as if she were not a mere merchant's daughter herself. But since reading the diaries, she knew who the original owner of these diamonds was: the witch, Anne Bainbridge. On a day full of superstitions, this didn't feel like a good omen.

She glanced at Nathan, surprised he would allow it. He was clad in black with a silver waistcoat and leaning upon his finest cane, ebony topped with a tiger's head. 'A diamond is a protective stone, sister. Full of good energy.'

They had certainly not protected Anne. But Belinda would have to let this go. The others were already frustrated enough at her delay and insistence on the second carriage. She had to admit that nothing bad had befallen *her* when she wore the necklace to marry Wilfred.

Giving a short nod, she clipped up the steps and kissed Daphne gently on the cheek. 'Are we all ready, then?'

The church doors gave a satisfying creak as they opened. Inside, the walls had been washed white, the lancet windows glazed with plain glass. Nathan and Daphne's footsteps echoed off chessboard flooring as they proceeded, arm-in-arm, up the aisle. Belinda winced. Something in the way Nathan pulled his injured leg behind him reminded her horribly of the *drag, thump* she had heard the night her daughter was born.

She and Wilfred followed behind the happy couple, careful not to step on Daphne's train as it whispered along, while the nursemaids and children brought up the rear. There were no guests, yet the church didn't feel forlorn or empty. It felt calm. Everything was bright, clean and shining. Even the pews gleamed.

'Now I'll have two aunties,' Freddy whispered behind her.

'Will you?' Wilfred asked, shooting a quizzical look at Belinda. 'How? Neither your Uncle Paul nor Uncle Luke is married.'

She thought for a moment. Realised that to Freddy, there was very little dividing the past from the present. 'That's… not what he meant.' Better she step in now than let the misunderstanding continue. She lowered her voice. 'He knows about Tiffany.'

Wilfred paled and did not say anything else.

Rays of sun poured through the windows as they reached the altar. It seemed to be a benediction upon the couple. Belinda dared to hope.

Maybe it *would* be as everyone said. Hetta's bones *were* entombed on holy ground now. Maybe the ghosts were finally appeased. Nothing strange had occurred since the night Freddy's hair was cut…

She still had her jaw clenched. One of her hands was balled into a fist. She forced them both to relax, took a deep breath. She would not ruin Daphne's wedding. She would not be like her own mother who sat far away, shackled by fear and unable to attend any special occasion.

Today – just for today – Belinda would let her guard down.

＊

It was the perfume that reached out to him and teased him from his sleep: floral yet dusty. Roses pressed between the pages of a book, withered petals and brittle leaves falling with every chapter. Behind Wilfred's eyelids, the burgeoning light bloomed pink. It was morning already.

The smell thickened into a stale taste. Grimacing, he swallowed, but that only made matters worse. It was a dead scent, he realised. Funereal.

He opened his eyes to see flecks upon his pillow. It looked as if he had dribbled blood in his sleep. Reaching up, he touched one. It was dry and soft, like wrinkled skin. Roses. Decaying rose petals.

As he lowered his hand he saw them scattered everywhere, all over the sleeping form of Belinda on the other side of the bed. She resembled a princess in a tale, reclining on a couch of blooms. Her hair had come loose of its plait, free from its nightcap. Crimson droplets were strewn throughout the tresses.

He reached out and shook her shoulder. He had to rouse her, rouse himself from this spell. She frowned in her sleep. Her lashes fluttered and slowly opened to reveal the bluish-green of her irises. But she did not see Wilfred. Her focus was fixed beyond him.

She jerked upright with a scream.

'Belinda?' He flipped over to see what had startled her. Another pair of eyes met his, blue as his own. He cried out and scuttled backwards into his wife.

These were not living eyes. They were dull and showed strokes of paint. Yet somehow, they held a threat that was palpable in the waking room. He could not breathe.

Belinda was climbing out of bed, wilted petals cascading as she moved. She stared in bewilderment. The flowers clung stubbornly to her nightdress and she began to swat at them as though they were flies.

Wilfred wanted to get up too, to comfort her, but he seemed to have frozen in place. The silent companion had been standing over him and watching him sleep.

'What *is* this?' Belinda cried.

'I don't know,' he snapped. 'How the devil should I know?'

She kept brushing at her nightdress, running her fingers through her hair with sounds of disgust. 'Roses… Hetta's roses. But *that's* not Hetta.'

At last his body agreed to move. He shuffled out of Belinda's side of the bed and gathered her in his arms. She was shaking violently. So was he. Together they stared across the rumpled sheets at the companion. Its flat face differed from the one Wilfred remembered. Furtive eyes, pointed features. Distinctly unfriendly, where it used to carry warmth.

'Do you believe me now?' she whimpered into his chest.

He was starting to. A person *could* have set all of this up… But that thought brought no comfort. Acid rose in his mouth as he imagined someone sneaking around their room in the dark, sprinkling confetti on their vulnerable forms, lingering over his sleeping wife.

How had neither of them awoken? It must have been all that wine at the wedding breakfast.

'Could Freddy… could he still be walking in his sleep?' It was a forlorn hope.

Belinda groaned. 'Rebecca *told* you she locks the nursery door. And there are no roses in this house! Where did they come from, Wilfred, if not from Hetta?'

She pulled away from him. 'I'm going to find Nathan, he will—'

'No!' He caught at her wrist, held her back. 'No, Bel, please don't tell Nathan.' It was a plea, not a command. She stared confusedly into his face. 'Not when he is so happy. This would upset him beyond measure.'

'But why?'

He released his grip on her. 'Because this is not just any silent companion.' He gritted his teeth, steeled himself to say the words. 'This is one our mother had made. It's our dead sister. It's Tiffany.'

Belinda's hand rose to her mouth. 'Lydia. I must check Lydia.'

She flew to the adjoining dressing-room where she'd insisted on keeping the crib ever since Freddy's hair was cut. But Wilfred could not move; he was caught in the companion's thrall. This was another mockery of his sister, as false as the tiny bride-like figure he'd seen lying in her coffin. Tiffany used to pick daisies, not roses. She used to smile.

Belinda choked back a cry. The baby started to wail.

Finally ripping his eyes away from Tiffany, he followed his wife into the dressing-room. The crib was in disarray. Coverlets lay on the floor along with wilted roses. Belinda had torn off the swaddling and was clutching their baby tight.

'What's wrong with her? Is she hurt?'

'Look, Wilfred.' Lydia wriggled, but Belinda drew back the baby's gown and presented her chubby arm. All down the bicep. Dark lines like dashes, neat as a row of stitches. Splinters.

He stroked the child's velvet skin with his index finger. Lydia sobbed. These were real, fully embedded, they were not drawn on.

His stomach turned. 'Who would do this to her? To an innocent baby?'

'Not who. *What.*' His wife's eyes held his. 'The same thing that called to your sister and told her to jump down the well.'

CHAPTER 23

He had no explanation left to give, no crutch of reason to lean upon. This was something he could not mend. At least, not yet. There must be a solution, there was *always* a solution, even if it meant something as terrible as pushing Roberts from the gallery. But for now he would have to swallow the bitter pill of acknowledging he could not guard his own family.

Lydia's screams followed him as he slunk downstairs to breakfast. Belinda would eat with the children in the nursery – if she *could* eat, after what had happened. For his own part he felt sick to his stomach. The aroma of roasted coffee and toasted bread could not drive that horrible floral decay from his nostrils.

He found Nathan and Daphne already at table, bright-eyed and smiling. Their plates were half-empty.

Nathan glanced at the grandfather clock. 'What time do you call this, Wil? We're supposed to be the newly-weds, late to everything.'

Daphne laughed and blushed as she buttered her toast.

Wilfred felt the uncharitable urge to shake them both. 'Something has happened.'

He sat heavily in the nearest chair. Creswell stood to attention by the sideboard, and although his expression was bland, he was probably listening keenly.

'Nothing serious, I hope?' Nathan asked, frowning as he stirred his coffee. 'Belinda is not unwell?'

Daphne put her knife down and took a bite of toast. She would usually show concern, but Wilfred registered frustration instead. That would make what he had to say even more unpleasant.

'No – not precisely. But Lydia is…' He trailed off, ran a hand over his face. There was no explaining this in front of the footman, and he was not certain he wanted to speak the words aloud anyhow. 'I am sorry to be the bearer of bad news, but I came to tell you I will not be able to lend you the carriage for your honeymoon after all. Could you take the Mail Coach to Bath instead?'

'Why?' Daphne demanded, through a mouthful. She glanced down quickly, evidently ashamed by her outburst.

On any other day, he would have been appalled that his brother's new wife could act so uncouthly. Now it barely registered.

'It is needed to take Belinda and the children back to London. They are going to stay with Mrs Kipling for a time. We will send the letter ahead by express today.'

They both stared at him. Nathan tapped his spoon thoughtfully against the side of his cup. 'Something *has* happened,' he said darkly.

Wilfred's fingers strayed to the napkin on his untouched plate. 'If it is not an imposition, Nathan, I should like to read the letter our father sent you before you depart.'

'I see.' Understanding dawned in Nathan's face and, with it, a hint of smugness. The 'I told you so' of old. After taking a slow sip of his drink, he said, 'Of course you may read it, Wil. And don't worry about the carriage. Bath can wait, we can postpone our trip—'

'No!' Daphne cried, jangling the crockery in her vehemence. When Nathan glared at her she ducked her chin. 'Forgive me. I am just disappointed. It's our wedding journey, my dear. Can we not take the Mail Coach as Mr Bainbridge says?'

Creswell shifted by the sideboard. Of course they had offered no opinion, but Wilfred gathered the servants were not impressed by Sawyer's meteoric rise to favour. Knowles in particular had looked pained, as if the honour of the family he served had endured a mortal wound. But then again, Wilfred had not seen Knowles smile once since his wife had died.

Died at the hands of... what? He still could not bring himself to answer that.

'Sawyer – I mean, Daphne – is right,' Wilfred cut in. 'You deserve your honeymoon. But it is imperative that the carriage takes my family to Mrs Kipling as soon as possible.'

He did not much like the idea of his family stuck in that parlour full of birds, bored half to death, but at least boredom was safety. Freddy would not see any ghosts. As for Belinda, her mother was the lesser of two evils.

Nathan was still frowning. 'You ought to go with them, Wil.'

'I cannot. You know I cannot.'

'Because of the harvest? Don't be such a martyr to the estate. Do you think the old man bothered to oversee it in detail? Even if the villagers cheat you a little, you'll be no worse off than you have been for years.'

Perhaps he had a point. Perhaps Wilfred needed to learn to let go. But he wasn't ready. After all that had happened here during their youth, all they had suffered, all they had *done*... it could not be for nothing. He might yet find a way to put things right, while they were all gone.

He was the master of this house.

'No. I am staying here. I can fix this, Nathan.'

*

Lydia thrashed and shrieked in Amy's grip.

'Hold her still.'

'I'm *trying*, madam.'

Belinda pinched the hot needle in one hand and a pair of tweezers in the other. Her fingertips were slippery, either from nerves or the heat of the fire. Tentatively, she prodded one of the splinters with the points of the tweezers. Lydia jerked her arm away.

'They are deeply embedded.' She swallowed the bile in her mouth. 'I'll never grab onto the end of one and pull it out. I shall have to… to push aside the skin.'

But doing so would be an operation more precise than any needlework she had ever sewn. Keeping her hands steady was effort enough; never mind Lydia's squirming and the hectic light of the flames. As Belinda steeled herself to try again, she saw a flickering that had nothing to do with the fire. The splinters seemed to be moving like slugs beneath the skin.

Dear God.

Belinda shushed and whispered endearments as Amy took Lydia's arm in a vice-like grip. The baby screamed louder than ever but Belinda's world was narrowing, focusing on the sharp point of her sterilised needle. With great care, she pierced the topmost layer of the skin and nudged it aside. It crumpled easily, thin as a wisp of crêpe. The tip of the splinter jutted up. A weapon, Belinda thought. Like one of the blades in the Great Hall.

Closing an eye, she aimed her tweezers. It took three attempts before she could grasp the end firmly between the pincers. She tugged. Nothing. Pulled again, harder.

The splinter refused to budge.

'She's going to scream herself into a fit, madam!'

Gritting her teeth, Belinda yanked as hard as she could. At last, the sliver of wood slid out. A tiny bead of blood welled on Lydia's arm.

'Give her a rest,' Belinda gasped. 'Then we'll do another.' She threw the splinter into the fire, where it quickly dissolved to ash.

Amy clutched Lydia to her chest and rocked her. 'Her poor, raw little arm!'

'I will put honey and bandages over it afterwards. Syrup of snails should help with the inflammation.'

Amy stared at her in bewilderment. 'Can't you just leave them, madam? They'll work their way out eventually.'

'No.'

She was not about to try and explain to Amy; she could not even explain this fully to herself. But ever since she'd seen Sawyer's drawing of Hetta with the baby, an idea had taken root in her head and planted itself as firmly as one of those splinters.

Belinda had never been able to tell from the diary whether wickedness had flowed into Hetta from the companions or the other way around. But either way, it *had* passed between wood and flesh. Slipped beneath the skin. And now it was trying to do so again.

She flexed her hands, wiped her sweating palms against her skirts. Evil was a coward at heart. It chose the easiest person in the house to overpower, a tiny baby. Maybe it thought it could play the cuckoo, plant itself like one of Hetta's poison flowers inside poor Lydia, but Belinda would be damned before that happened on her watch.

'Again,' she said.

'Give her a moment more, madam, for pity's sake,' Amy demurred.

Sighing, she set the implements down and held out her arms to take Lydia. The baby fought her, confused and infuriated. Belinda endured her thumps, knowing she deserved them. 'Please use this time to pack our things, then,' she said to Amy. 'I mean to be away tomorrow morning.'

'And… are you coming back, madam? Or should I look for another place?'

'I do not know,' she said honestly. 'But Mr Bainbridge will not leave you out of pocket and I will of course be willing to provide a reference.' Seeing the wet-nurse's truculent expression, she added, 'It is for the best, Amy. You must see that, after all that has happened.'

Amy said nothing. Well, it did not matter if a wet-nurse was on her side. At least Wilfred believed her now, and his help was not fickle like Nathan's.

She sang to Lydia, managing to soothe her just a little. Amy was right; her poor arm was red. She wished she could make her daughter understand.

'Not long to go now,' she murmured. 'We'll get all those nasty splinters out and then no one will *ever* hurt you again.' She was almost looking forward to stepping back inside her mother's stifling parlour. Anything seemed easy to bear beside this. She would be more patient with Mamma, this time around. She would strive to remember how it felt to be afraid and have no one listening to you.

As she paced up and down, gently bouncing the baby, she passed the rocking horse. John had sanded down the scratches and tidied it up so Freddy could ride without injury. But now she saw something else, something she had not noticed in all the commotion of the last few days: the horse's mane and tail were no longer even. They had suffered the same rough scissoring as Freddy's golden curls.

Anne's voice spoke in her ear. *There was a dead horse in the stalls. Not just dead – mutilated. Its tail was cropped and nailed outside the door, its mane attacked with a frenzy of scissors. The ostler found a score of lacerations scratched in the skin, like a tally you might carve upon a tree.*

'Amy,' Belinda said. 'Come back. We need to remove these splinters *now*.'

CHAPTER 24

Wilfred rubbed his eyes, chasing the sleep away. A dying fire touched his surroundings with orange streaks. He was not cold, but there was something reassuring in the crackle of flames, something that made him feel less alone while he kept watch.

Ghosts were supposed to visit by night, weren't they? Why was that? Did they envy the peaceful rest of the living?

He did, tonight. Belinda and Lydia slept soundly together on the bed. Occasionally, he heard the baby murmur and shift. Belinda would not trust her to the crib now, would barely let her out of her sight, and he could no longer blame her. He *felt* danger simmering just beneath the surface of all he beheld. If only he could stop the hands of the carriage clock and turn them back, unwinding time with every revolution. It had been so much easier when he did not believe.

He sat in the wingchair and inhaled deeply through his nose, tasting smoke. All the events in his life were reframing themselves under his new and terrible knowledge. The home he had craved, the house that was always meant to be his legacy, had proved as traitorous as any unfaithful spouse.

On first reading the old man's letter, he'd retained a healthy pinch of scepticism. It was too much, he thought, to blame everyone's faults on a nameless evil, as if they exercised no free will of their own. But now he had finished Anne's diaries too, he was beginning to wonder. His mother *did* spend an awful lot of time with those companions. As much time as Hetta herself. And she had died, malnourished and sick to her stomach as something tried to grow inside her.

Only a couple of flames remained in the grate. He could not rouse himself to rise and stir them up. He was thinking of the Roberts companion he'd found in the music room, behind the wall his father had shot at on the night that he died. What was that – one last taunt at the poor old man? Perhaps his father had even tried to get rid of the companions, as they'd discussed, only to have them return to him that night. Wilfred would never know for sure how much he had suffered.

The question was: what to do now?

Could he sell up? Despite all the horror he'd read about, it would hurt him to lose The Bridge. But what was worse, he'd have to let the whole place go for a song. Who would want unruly tenants, skeletons in the garden and a house where repeated accidents befell the servants? Even the land had little value since it was not producing a good yield. Renting the manor out carried the same difficulties. And then there came the matter of conscience. However many generations removed he was from Anne and Hetta, this curse had been brought about by the actions of a Bainbridge. Could he trick other families, with other small children, to *pay* him for the privilege of occupying a haunted house?

No. He wanted Belinda and the children out and safe: that was non-negotiable. But The Bridge was his responsibility. It had been since the day of his birth. If there were demons here, *he* must be the one to vanquish them.

Drag, thump. Wilfred started. The fire was nothing but embers now. He must have dozed in the chair, for when he consulted his pocket watch, it was two in the morning. But that was not the only change. Dead leaves were strewn between his feet and the hearth.

He stared, confounded. The low red light of the fire showed clumps of withered thistles. Rising, he crunched through the leaves to the mantelpiece and picked up a chamberstick. He lit the candle quickly in the smouldering remains of his fire. Turned. His exhalation blew the flame straight out again.

She was by the bed, directly behind where he'd been sitting. Not Hetta. Not even Tiffany, whose appearance had chilled him to the core. This was a companion that should not exist. Could not.

Wilfred's mother stared at him with vacant, unloving eyes.

She was dressed as if for a ball: pearls in her hair, a lace choker at her neck. Side hoops made her imposing, even to his adult self. A face painted lead white showed black velvet patches on the cheek and at the corner of one eye. A closed fan pointed coquettishly at her lips, red as a wound.

He couldn't think. Fear and grief were crashing inside him, turning everything to rubble.

Belinda sighed in her sleep. It gave him the impetus he needed. Striding forward, he gripped the rough edge of the thing and dragged it across the carpet. It emitted a low hiss against the pile. He tried to pull down the shutters over his senses, avoiding those familiar eyes, ignoring the way it somehow *smelt* of the sickness that had killed her. All that mattered was that he got it out of the room, away from his wife and daughter.

They did not wake as he clattered the board out through the dressing-room and into the hallway. He propped it against one of the marble busts, while he closed the door and locked it firmly behind him. Out here, all was in shadow.

He fumbled in his pocket for a tinderbox. After several tries, he managed to relight the candle. But when he turned back, there was only the row of marble heads glowing eerily in the darkness. The silent companion had gone.

Drag, thump. The flame of his candle shivered and distended. *Drag, thump.* Cautiously, he took a few steps down the hallway, towards the staircase.

'Mamma?' he whispered. He sounded like a child.

Screwing up his courage, he made his way down the staircase, following the noise. It might be going towards the nursery, towards Freddy. As he reached the last few steps, he thought he heard a door click, but the candle-light didn't reach far enough to show him anything of note. Only a sea of black lay straight ahead.

He would not give in to fear. This was *his* house. Whatever stalked these corridors always has, and it had never chosen to hurt him before. He heard a creaking, a juddering, like a ship straining in the wind; or perhaps it was footfalls on the old wooden stairs leading to the Great Hall.

He moved quickly to the gallery, where he could command a bird's eye view, keeping one hand firmly upon the wall. But as he searched outwards, towards the rail, his blood ran cold. The Roberts companion was there, standing in the very place he had fallen from all those years ago.

Wilfred opened his mouth. No sound emerged. They *had* come back. The footman and the mother who had loved him. They wanted their revenge.

The flame of his candle guttered. Hinges whined as a breeze fluttered in. Wilfred forced himself to look away from Roberts and peer further over the rail into the Great Hall. The main door had been cracked open and left slightly ajar. Moonlight spilled onto the flags.

He started down the creaking staircase, his jacket flapping at his knees. The candle flame dwindled into a scroll of smoke, but he didn't need it now. The moon rode high in the sky as he burst outside, illuminating his way. The scent of the country air seemed intensified by the night, full of pollen and herbs. Sounds were amplified, too. Each crunch of his boot against gravel came like a gunshot.

Whoever had been there could not have run far... He cast about to the fountain. Silver ripples crossed the water and the stone dogs glowed impossibly white.

'Hello?' he called.

There was no one. Nothing. The hills rose dark and silent on the horizon.

Then the door slammed shut behind him.

Startled, Wilfred turned to see the iron studs gleaming in the moonlight. Impossible. There was no wind to push such a heavy door closed. He tried the handle, made the whole thing rattle, but it would not open. He'd been expelled from his own house.

He swore. This could not be an accident. He was being lured away, prevented from protecting his family. At least Belinda and Lydia were locked inside their room. Freddy was with the nurses. They all ought to be safe...

There was a door around the other side of the house, leading from the stable yard into the kitchen. Maybe it was not bolted at night. He'd try it first before rousing the servants to let him in.

He was glad now that he hadn't undressed or removed his shoes. The gravel cracked beneath them as he rounded the parterres and came into the gardens. Everything was ashen by moonlight. No beams touched the patch where the skeleton had emerged; where Hetta had grown her poison over a century ago. It was dark as a slick of oil.

His breath rasped. He pinched his eyes shut, steeling himself for what he might see in stables or kitchen. The old man had been right: the house played tricks. This all felt horribly familiar. He half-remembered, now, waiting up for his mother to come home from an assembly and stealing out from the nursery to her rooms. Following the whisper of her train, the clip of her heels and the trail of her scent she left behind. Watching through a crack in the door, he had seen what no child ought to see. Not a tired and fond mother ready to tell him of her evening as she undressed. A lover, taken by a servant.

Wilfred opened his eyes. Even darkness was better than that memory.

A lamp burnt up ahead in the stable yard. He couldn't think why it should be there. Dawkins slept in the loft above the stalls and would only wake if one of the horses were ill.

Just as he reached the hunched outline of the well, he heard the scream.

Wilfred hurried forward. It came again; eerie, unearthly, followed by a snort and a bang. Surely it was too deep, too guttural, to be human.

He found all the horses in a state of agitation, their heads swinging wildly over the doors of their stalls. Gimcrack's eyes rolled white, her ears flat. He did not even attempt to soothe her. Grunts and scuffles were coming from the box at the base of the horseshoe arrangement, the stall holding Freddy's little Sebastian. One lamp hung outside and another was flickering hectically within.

Wilfred dashed to peer over the half-door, his hands gripping the rough edge.

It was not what he'd expected.

There *was* a companion propped against the far wall: the lady with the sword who had taken his place at the dinner table. Bright spots of blood mottled her dull surface. But she was not alone. Dawkins knelt in the straw, his mouth gagged and hands bound behind his back. Restraining him was Ross Roberts.

On the other side of the box, poor Sebastian kicked and tried to rear but he could not shake himself free of the halter securing him to the iron ring on the wall. Two deep slashes ran across his flank. Blood dribbled down his brown and white coat.

A man stood hunched beneath the swinging lamp. His face was a confusion of light and shadow, peaks and hollows, but Wilfred could clearly see the gore-tipped sabre gleaming in one hand. The other was braced upon a cane.

Nathan paused, sword held aloft, to face him over the stall door. There was no panic, no guilt. The expression in his eyes was one of disappointment. 'Oh, Wilfred. I wish you had not seen this.'

He did not have time to absorb the gravity of the scene before him. Instinct overpowered anger. There were two of them, one of him. And Nathan held a sword.

He turned, bolting for the shadowy house. If he could hammer at the door and rouse the servants, if he could just get inside, he could fetch help. Witnesses, at least. A knife from the kitchen if all else failed.

Had it been only Nathan in pursuit, with his injury Wilfred might have made it. But Ross Roberts was upon him before he even left the yard, tackling him onto the cobbles. Winded, he kicked and swung for all he was worth. His coat ripped, yet Roberts remained an iron clamp upon him. For all his advantages, Wilfred would never be a physical match for a working man.

Through the scuffling and the terrified whinnies came the steady click of Nathan's cane approaching.

'Careful,' he said, and for a second Wilfred thought his brother would save him. 'We have to do this right. It complicates everything.'

With a final blow to his jaw, Roberts dragged Wilfred up onto his knees and began to bind his hands behind his back, as he had done with Dawkins. The stable yard swam. 'What—' Wilfred tried to say. 'Nathan, why—'

His brother stood blocking the light, his shadow stretching to where Wilfred knelt. 'Damn it, Wil. It was never supposed to go like this. I gave you so many chances! Why couldn't you just *leave*?'

His head was spinning. Everything hurt. He groped uselessly for words.

'Or at least let me be part of it. But you never saw me as your equal, did you?' Something more dangerous crept into his brother's tone. 'I think maybe you knew, all along.'

'Knew...?' Wilfred started, but Nathan gestured to one side, and before Wilfred could understand what he meant, Roberts was hauling him towards the water trough.

He was forced down, his head breaking the stagnant surface of the water. Cold and bitter fluid forced its way up his nostrils, down his throat, bubbled in his ears. This was it, he thought. This was how he died: on his knees beside the dung heap.

Suddenly, he was up. He gasped for breath as water cascaded everywhere. God, it was cold. It hadn't been this cold earlier. He swung back his head, trying to butt Roberts behind him, but all he got was a blow on the base of the skull.

'You didn't even write to me,' Nathan spat. It sounded as though he was still underwater. 'But Ross did. He never learnt his letters, yet he got his sister to seek me out and send me a message in India. Imagine the effort! And *you* couldn't lift a pen more than once in eighteen years.'

Wilfred's face crashed into the water before he could close his mouth. His lungs burnt as a taste of mildew and rotting leaves flooded in. Just as he thought he was about to pass out, there was air. He coughed, vomited. He could only see in bleared streaks, like a watercolour painting.

'Can you guess what Ross told me, Wilfred?'

He couldn't. He could barely grip onto consciousness or follow what Nathan was saying.

'There were letters to prove it. Our stupid bitch of a mother never had an ounce of discretion, did she? She damned herself over and over in her own hand. It wasn't Tiffany, Wil. She wasn't the one. Roberts sired *me*.'

Wilfred just had time to draw in a shocked breath before he was plunged back into the bubbling darkness. Images from the past seemed to twist around him in the water. Tiffany, his mother, Roberts' provoking smile. Was it possible? Had he got it all so terribly wrong?

The night air cut like a knife as he came wheezing up, cold water flowing down the back of his shirt.

'You made me kill him! You made me a patricide, forever cursed. And even though I tried to patch it up, you just wouldn't let me in.' His brother's voice caught. 'Now you're forcing me to do this, Wil. You've brought it all on yourself.'

He had a last, smeared glimpse of Nathan's impassioned face before water overtook his senses once more. It did not bubble in his ears now. It hissed.

He didn't have the strength left to fight. Everything was so heavy. The edge of the trough cut into his chest as his head went lower and lower. There seemed to be no bottom.

All he could see was Freddy, rippling in the water. Those wide blue eyes that had already beheld too much sorrow.

Don't show him, he prayed. *Whatever strange visions Freddy has, don't show the poor boy this.*

Then everything went black.

⁕

A scream tore Belinda from her sleep. Rough and low-pitched, more like a bellow. Dev barked a warning from the other wing of the house.

Her eyes flew open and she gave another start to see Lydia lying next to her, mere inches from her face, silently observing. Her daughter's stillness disturbed her almost as much as the scream. The room was striped with slats of morning light and Lydia had not been fed since ten o'clock last night. Usually *she* would be the one wailing at this time, demanding milk.

But the noise seemed to be coming from outside.

Scooping the baby up and minding her injured arm, Belinda moved to the window, only to find it still shuttered. She didn't have the patience to open everything up. Striding to the dressing-room door, she noticed Wilfred's empty chair. Her skin chilled. Had it been him, crying out? He *must* have left the house and come back again at some point during the night, for skeletal leaves were strewn about and trodden into powder on the carpet. Strange. It was the kind of detritus to be expected in the height of autumn – not the end of summer.

Around her, The Bridge was awakening. The thick walls prevented her from hearing any more from outside. The dog barked again. Feet thumped on the floorboards.

Her fingers reached for the door handle.

It was locked.

She tried again, sure it must be a mistake. But no. She could not budge it an inch. They were trapped.

Belinda whipped around, certain she would see silent companions emerging from out of the woodwork to take her baby. But it was only the same empty rooms, with pale paper and heavy furniture. She took a steadying breath. Placing her back to the door, she kept watch. Her head was starting to pound. Nothing. No threat, no sign of what had locked her in. But the longer she watched, the more agitated she grew.

She banged on the door. 'Let me out!'

Lydia grumbled, her face creasing.

'I said "let me out!" Who is there? Why is this door locked?'

Belinda slapped her open palm against the wood and Lydia started to cry in earnest. Her distress only made Belinda hit harder. 'Hello? Help! We are stuck in here!'

There was a grate, a click, and the door swung open, revealing a bleary-eyed Daphne in nightgown and cap. 'How did you...' she started, confused. 'Who locked the door?'

'It must have been Wilfred.' Belinda pushed past her into the hallway. 'Have you seen him?'

Daphne shook her head and rubbed at her face. 'We've only just woken up. There's something going on down-stairs... and then I heard you shouting.'

The marble busts watched them gravely as if they already knew something she did not. Belinda thrust the weeping baby into Daphne's arms.

'Take Lydia. I must go and see.'

Daphne made a protest, but Belinda did not hear the exact words. She was already fleeing, trying to outrun this feeling of impending doom.

Of course it could be anything. Dawkins kicked by one of the horses. Wild deer got into the garden. A burnt pot in the kitchen, a bird half-eaten by a fox and left turned inside-out. But workaday incidents like that didn't seem to happen in this house. Here everything was amplified.

Nathan was thumping slowly downstairs with his cane, a banyan thrown over his nightshirt. She leant over the balustrade and called to him.

'What has happened?'

He raised a grey, exhausted face to hers. 'Really, I don't know, Belinda, I'm just going to find out.' He took another step. 'Where's Wil?'

'He did not come to bed last night. He was in the chair but now... he's not.'

Nathan yawned. 'Well, he is probably sorting out the servants as we speak. But still, I'll go and see if he needs any help.'

She could not wait for him to plod his way outside and back again. The anticipation would drive her mad.

Why had no one come up with a message? If Wilfred had not sent a servant to tell her what was going on, he must be trying to conceal something. She pinched up her nightgown and trotted downstairs, speeding past Nathan as he called after her. Her feet thumped on the treads in time with her pulse.

She reached the Great Hall at the same time that John stumbled through the servants' door. The boy's face was drained of blood, but his hands were bathed in it.

'John!' she cried, starting forward and grabbing at him, searching for an injury. 'John, are you hurt? What is going on outside?'

He blinked up at her, no longer a servant but a horrified child. His lips moved without words.

She ought to comfort him. Take him in her arms like the mother he had lost. But the blood was not coming from him, which meant it was coming from someone still outside. She pulled away, the marks of his damp red grip all over her.

The kitchen was deserted and the fire unlit. The door to the stable yard stood open in the breeze. Belinda stepped out into milky morning light, the cobbles chill under her feet. For a second, the late-August air was refreshing. But as she inhaled, she caught a scent thick enough to be a taste. Not the dung heap. Metal. Rot.

Old Knowles was kneeling with a hand to his chest, his bald head coated in a sheen of sweat. It looked as if he was suffering a paroxysm of the heart. Creswell was by his side trying to help.

Usually, she'd fly to their aid. But she had caught sight of what had shocked the old servant: a flow of blood, trickling beneath the stable door and winding through the cobbles.

The scratches on the rocking horse, the cutting of its mane. The words of Anne Bainbridge in her ear. *I looked at that animal and I cannot believe this is the work of human hands.*

It was happening again.

Steeling herself, she tottered over, jumping like a child across the cracks to avoid the blood. But it was futile. Soon her stockings were damp and sickeningly warm about her feet.

She could *hear* a horse kicking, snorting and emitting miserable little sounds. It was still alive.

With her ears starting to roar, she peered inside the stall.

Choked.

Slashes ran across Sebastian's flank in the rough shape of an H, dribbling with fresh blood as he moved. More of it had crusted dry on his legs.

But as his hooves slipped on the wet floor, she realised the gore flowing out was not all from him. Dawkins was slumped beside the hay net, a razor in his limp hand. A wide red grin had been cut into his throat.

The companion from the dinner table, the clownish woman with her raised sword, grinned from the shadows.

Belinda stumbled backwards, turned to vomit.

But throwing up did not stop the sick feeling at her core.

She straightened up, panting and wiping her mouth. Time seemed to slow. Hetta stood by the water trough and she was not alone. Someone knelt on the opposite side, almost as if they were paying her homage.

'No.'

Belinda had believed so much so readily, but she could never reconcile herself to this. It could not be true. There was a mistake, some terrible error.

Without knowing how, she ran to the trough and hauled the body out of the water. It was so heavy. She fell as she let it down, landing on top of it, coming face to bloated face.

She screamed.

It was a monster with overripe, marbled skin. But as she pushed herself up, she recognised his clothing, the close crop of his red hair.

'No, no, no!'

He'd said he would never leave her.

He'd promised.

But now Wilfred lay dripping on the cobbles, his beloved face concealed beneath the mask of a drowned man.

CHAPTER 25

Belinda was underwater too. Sound muffled, vision rippled. It hurt to breathe. Everything had happened so quickly, and then it had slowed to this wading pace, where even her thoughts must struggle against the tide. Many sank before they formed, but one bobbed as flotsam on the surface: the children. They made it so much easier and so much harder to bear. Forced her to carry on and yet, witnessing Freddy's grief broke her heart all over again.

He knelt on the rug beside the bed where Wilfred's body was laid out. A plain white handkerchief had been spread over the water-damaged face. Not even childish curiosity prompted Freddy to try and lift it. It was as though he already knew what lurked beneath.

If he would bawl or sob, Belinda could comfort him, but his sorrow was dry-eyed, painfully mature. She thought of the little boy she'd brought to The Bridge, all white skirts and curls. Now he wore his own mourning suit. His hair was short. He looked like a miniature gentleman and Belinda had no idea how to guide him through a world that she hadn't fully inhabited herself.

'Papa can never leave The Bridge,' he said, forlorn.

'No.' She was supposed to be travelling herself. Mamma would be expecting them, fretting. But their driver had been bled out in the stable yard like an animal. For the present there was only this room. The dull light and the faintly rotten smell.

'He's stuck here,' Freddy went on. 'All the people who die here are trapped in the house forever. Like Aunt Tiffany.'

Another piece of her heart shattered. It could not be true. He spoke as if the sky was made of iron and someone had shut up the way to heaven.

'Hetta wants their company. Until she can get out.'

She wet her lips to ask, but could not bring herself to say the words. *Can you see him, Freddy? Is he here with us?*

She knew that Wilfred's essence, his kindness and his dry sense of humour, were not in that waterlogged corpse. Why, then, could she not bring herself to let it out of her sight? Why did she linger here, day and night, as if her husband might suddenly awake? Perhaps it was cowardice. In his stillness and his silence, Wilfred was easier to endure than the people outside.

Soon she would have to act. She sensed herself on the precipice, teetering one way and then the other. She understood now exactly how her mamma had been felled by tragedy. But Belinda was not going to let the same fate befall her. She would rest, she would regroup, and then somehow she would rally.

Just... not quite yet.

Lydia did not shed tears. She lay quiet and sluggish in Belinda's arms, only occasionally plucking at her bandaged arm. Would she remember Wilfred? Her father had spent his last night on earth protecting her from harm, but she would not even have a portrait of him to kiss.

Nathan's cane rapped somewhere nearby. Belinda did not want to speak to him, to anyone. She waited in dread for the thump to draw closer, but before it did the door opened and Daphne entered, bearing a tray of tea that rattled in her hands.

'Here,' she said with quiet authority as she laid it down beside the lilies on the dresser. 'You must drink something.'

Tea had been the only thing Belinda could face. She received it gratefully, exchanging Lydia for a cup of strong bohea. Freddy sneaked over to grab crumbs from the sugar loaf.

'You are not supposed to be waiting on me any more,' Belinda pointed out.

'It's only tea. I don't mind.' Daphne came and laid one hand on Belinda's shoulder, cradling Lydia with her other arm.

At least matters between the two of them felt easier now. Death had a way of stripping back pettiness and trifles. If on some level Daphne mourned the cancellation of her wedding journey to Bath, she did not let it show.

Nathan stumped into the room a moment later. Now he was dressed in black, honouring Wilfred's death in a way he had not done for his father. Belinda saw how the sight of the body pained him. He quickly averted his eyes, turning fully towards her.

'How are you, sister?'

She could not answer that. She was relieved to see Dev creep through the door and go straight to Freddy for caresses. The little commotion saved her from needing to reply.

'My pony got hurt, Dev,' Freddy whispered as he rested his head against the dog. 'I'm glad Hetta didn't hurt you too.'

Belinda felt her lower lip quiver. At least Sebastian would survive his injuries.

Daphne squeezed her shoulder. 'Nathan's been up to his eyes in business,' she said softly. 'Did you know that Wilfred made him executor and guardian of the children?'

She shook her head.

'He did it when we drew up the marriage contract,' Nathan sighed. 'I thank God for his foresight. The other guardian is Mr Paul Kipling, but he cannot be of any use to you until his ship gets in, which could be months yet. At least I am on the spot to help.'

'Thank you,' Belinda said numbly.

It occurred to her now that Nathan and Daphne must have done everything since Wilfred's death. Borne numerous burdens on her behalf while she sat here in her bubble of grief.

'Why don't I take the children to the nursery?' Daphne said. 'Let's go and draw some pictures, shall we, Freddy?'

The boy rose reluctantly to his feet, looking towards the faceless figure stretched out upon the bed. 'All right.'

'I'll watch them closely, don't worry,' she assured Belinda. 'It's just for a little while.'

Belinda lowered her eyes to the dregs of her tea. She had to stop herself from begging them to stay. The children were the last bits of Wilfred she had left, and she wanted to cling to them with all her might. But like Daphne said, it was only for a short time. She needed to get a hold of herself.

The door closed. She heard Daphne's voice murmuring to Freddy as they walked away.

Nathan leant on his cane and sighed. 'Why would he not listen to us?'

'He did! In the end. It was just... too late.'

'This is my fault.' His voice came pinched. 'You were right all along. I ought not to have distracted myself with a wedding. I just thought, once we were all family, he might... well, it does not matter what I thought. I made the wrong choice.'

Tears were dripping into her teacup. She put it aside and wiped her face. 'The silent companions got to him, Nathan. It's no one's fault.'

'It is Hetta's, I suppose.' He shifted his weight. 'I want you to know, Belinda, that you have nothing to worry about for the future. I am already seeking a driver who will take you back to London as soon as the funeral is over. We will get you out of here, we will get you all safe.' She looked up thankfully into his face, his eyes so blue above his black clothes. Was there a whisper of Wilfred lurking there somewhere? She found herself staring, seeking it hungrily. She could not believe she had once thought him more handsome than her husband. 'Money should not be a problem,' he went on. 'There is not much capital, but there are investments that can be sold, land that can be mortgaged if required. You shall have enough to live modestly. And if there should be any difficulty with Freddy's schooling or Lydia's dowry, you only have to ask. I would not leave you destitute.'

'Thank you, Nathan. Thank God, you came back from India when you did! I do not know what I would have done without you. And I am so glad you and Wilfred had a chance to make up your differences before...'

Nathan cleared his throat. It was a moment before he could speak. 'There is something else, Belinda. Something unpleasant, but I would rather you hear it from me than anyone else.'

'I can bear it,' she said instantly. 'Anything is easy to bear beside this.'

He stumped a little further into the room. 'You and I know what truly happened. We know about Hetta. But, of course, no one from Torbury St Jude is prepared to accept a verdict of supernatural murder.'

She swallowed. 'No... I suppose they wouldn't be.'

'They could write off Mrs Knowles' death as a rare accident. And, of course, the doctor was here when poor Mr Knowles finally succumbed to his ailing heart. But when it comes to this...' He nodded towards the bed. 'I'm afraid they are blaming Dawkins.'

'Dawkins?' she repeated, shocked. 'But—'

'I know. The constable asked around the village because they knew about the enclosure being destroyed and the general ill-will towards the big house. But the prevailing theory is that this was the work of a disgruntled member of staff. Someone has told them that Dawkins was angry about being the only groom here and looking after all the horses on a single wage. They think he attacked Freddy's pony in a fit of revenge. That Wilfred caught Dawkins in the act, so the groom chased him down, drowned him to silence him... And then, realising the enormity of what he had done, Dawkins slit his own throat.'

'It's stuff and nonsense!' she cried. 'How could they reach such a conclusion?'

Nathan shrugged his shoulders, his black velvet coat murmuring. 'Dawkins *was* holding a razor. And there are cuts on Wilfred's hands. You saw them. As if he was holding them up to shield himself from a blade.'

She rubbed at her forehead, unable to imagine what could have truly happened that night to place the bodies in those positions. But whatever Dawkins was holding when he died, she knew he would never have hurt Wilfred, let alone one of his beloved horses.

'I must confess,' Nathan sighed, 'I *allowed* them to make their assumptions. I think, really it is the best we can do. Investigations will go no further now unless we push them. There is no one to prosecute on behalf of Dawkins.'

'But it is unjust!'

'It does poor Dawkins a dishonour indeed, yet... what choice do we have? He *is* dead. The law cannot pursue him now. Better he take the blame than some other innocent be sent to hang for Hetta's crime, just like in the diary.'

She thought of John Knowles running inside with his hands stained in blood. Maybe Nathan was right. If only it were not such an insult to the poor groom's memory. 'They won't bury Dawkins now then, will they? They'll hang him in a gibbet as a murderer or use his body to teach anatomy students.'

'I can't help that, Belinda! You are not considering the alternative. You are not thinking who will fall under suspicion if we do not let Dawkins take the blame.' He turned pleading eyes upon her. The cane trembled in his hand. 'Did Wilfred not tell you why I was sent away before? What terrible, false things were whispered about me?'

Suddenly, the odour of the lilies was overpowering. Worse than the roses had ever been. She imagined Wilfred's brother, Daphne's husband, strung up on the gallows before the mob. No doubt that was exactly what Hetta wanted: to destroy her family completely.

'I forgot,' she confessed. 'Forgive me, Nathan.'

'You have nothing to apologise for,' he said sadly. 'I do not like it any more than you do. But there are only a few days to go until the funeral. Let us ride this through, and you will be back in London before you know it.' He gestured to the room around them. 'The Bridge will feel like a bad dream.'

But real-life tragedy did not work like that. You did not wake up from dreams to find yourself bereaved. Nightmares did not traumatise your children or drive splinters into your baby. There were marks on them that would always remain.

She kept hearing Freddy. *Papa can never leave.*

Whatever the future held for her family, Belinda knew that a tiny part of her would forever be trapped here, too.

CHAPTER 26

Bumping drew her to the nursery, the rhythmic creak and thump she had come to dread. With one hand, she opened the door – to see Freddy swaying back and forth on his rocking horse, the jagged tail swishing.

Once, he had giggled with glee at this. Now he sat poker-straight, eyes fixed on the fireplace. The folding screen that should stand there had been replaced by two silent companions: Hetta and Tiffany.

'Freddy!' Her shout woke Lydia, cradled in her other arm. Freddy made a shushing sound that was eerily like a hiss. 'Freddy, get down from there! Where—' She scanned the space from the wardrobe to the table and chairs, to the open door leading into the schoolroom. 'Where are your nurses?'

He did not turn towards her. 'Hush! I'm listening.'

With horror she observed his fierce concentration, the invisible thread that seemed to connect his large blue eyes with Hetta's sly, feline stare. Something was passing between them without words. Or, at least, not words Belinda could hear.

'Stop!' She placed a palm on the horse's rump and jammed a foot against the rockers to stop their motion. 'The companions *killed* your father, Freddy. Don't listen to anything they have to say.' Lydia sobbed. Belinda glanced down. The baby's arm was bleeding again, tiny roses blooming through the white bandage. Hetta was still trying to get in. 'Good God. Get off that horse, Freddy. I don't want either of you anywhere near the companions, do you hear me?'

As she helped him scramble down, she noticed Hetta's pupils had moved. They were trained on Lydia. Giddy with fear, Belinda pulled her children out into the corridor and kicked the door shut behind them.

Lydia moaned. Freddy reached up to comfort her and she calmed slightly at his touch. That poor arm… The splinter wounds had healed, scabbed over. But simply being in the presence of Hetta had opened them in a moment.

'You are never to be alone with the companions, Freddy,' Belinda insisted. 'I want you right by my side until the moment we leave this place. It cannot come quickly enough.'

'Hetta says she didn't do it.'

'What?'

Freddy shrugged. His face puckered as it did when he tried to spell a difficult word. 'Hetta has been after Lydia all along. But she says she never touched Papa.'

'She *would* tell you that. She's a murderer. You cannot trust her.'

Before he could reply, a creak sounded on the stairs and Daphne was crossing the landing towards them. She looked as dazed as Freddy. She did not even ask why they were cowering beside the closed nursery door.

'Nathan's asking for you, ma'am. Downstairs.' Belinda noted a crust of snuff on her nostrils. Seeing her staring, Daphne wiped it away with the back of her hand. 'It's… well. He didn't consult me. I *would* have said something. But maybe it's still not my place.'

'What are you talking about, Daphne? I can't understand you.'

'I don't really understand either!' she cried. 'Perhaps he'll explain it better to us both.' She held out a hand for Freddy to take. 'Shall we go down and ask him together?'

'But I need to change Lydia's bandages. Where is Amy? Where is Rebecca? Have you seen them? Freddy was all alone.'

Daphne grimaced. 'That's just it. They're... Well, come downstairs. If Nathan chooses to do the thing, *he* should be the one to explain it to you.' She pulled Freddy along, not giving Belinda time to object.

She would not have supposed herself capable of rising and following, yet she did. Placing Lydia against her shoulder, she stroked the back of the baby's soft head. How fragile it felt beneath her palm. Gossamer hair, a papier-mâché skull. The weakest of defences.

Voices echoed up from the Great Hall. She frowned to hear their raucous note and a bray of laughter. Masculine tones she did not recognise, conversing easily in a house of mourning.

When they reached the gallery, Freddy stopped dead. Belinda stared down with him. Amy knelt on the oriental rug below with a crawling infant whose round, pink cheeks mirrored her own. Two common men in homespun and gaiters lounged by the fireplace. One rested an elbow upon the mantelpiece while the other had his back to the flames, the tails of his coat raised to warm his buttocks.

Nathan stood to one side, leaning on his cane. He always appeared refined, but next to these two he looked positively kingly. He wore black velvet, a black ribbon in his hair and, inexplicably, a smile upon his face. He limped to the bottom of the staircase to greet them.

'Ah! There you are. Come, come, this will only take a moment of your time, Belinda.' Freddy went rigid, staring at the man leaning on the mantelpiece. Daphne tried to drag him along. 'Quick march, Freddy. Don't you want to see Dev?'

He gave a whistle. The dog came trotting in from the drawing-room but seemed to have second thoughts when he saw the strangers. With a low growl, he retreated again.

Belinda felt the same way. Only politeness compelled her to do as she was asked. She overtook Freddy and coaxed him down. He came reluctantly, still refusing to look away from the man by the mantelpiece.

'Give the children to Amy now,' Nathan advised. 'I have some introductions to make.'

Belinda frowned and kept Lydia firmly in her grip. 'But where is Rebecca?'

'Gone,' Nathan said in the same easy manner. 'There was no reason to retain her when you will be leaving so soon. I sent away Hurley, Creswell and John too. It was all unnecessary expense, eating into Freddy's inheritance.'

Belinda looked to Daphne, who refused to meet her eye. Clearly, this was why she'd been so vague and embarrassed upstairs. The men at the fireplace were staring openly, something hostile and demeaning in their gaze. Belinda fought to conceal her discomposure.

'I would have appreciated some warning, Nathan. They were my staff. And young John! What has been done for him? The poor boy is left an orphan.'

'Yes, to be sure, I took care of all that.' A hint of annoyance crept into Nathan's voice. 'John will do handsomely, do not fret for him. I *thought* you would be pleased that I had arranged it all without troubling

you. I know how much you have on your mind at the
moment.' His blue eyes slid towards Daphne. 'My wife
is vexed too, but I'm hanged if I can see the cause for it.'

'Overeager'. Wasn't that how Wilfred had described
his brother? Burdened with a desire to help that bordered
on the officious. She understood now what he'd meant.

'Perhaps we might discuss this in private? Without
our... guests?' They were still peering at her, unabashed.
Their gaze prickled on her skin, like the silent companions' did.

'No, they are the whole reason I sent for you! See,
here are Amy's family come from Torbury St Jude, her
boy Thomas and her husband Mr Whitfield.' Nathan
stepped back to indicate the taller of the men, who
nodded by way of greeting. 'And this is her brother. He
has been living in the village of Fayford since Wilfred
and I were boys. Mr Ross Roberts.'

The second man did not even incline his head. He
raised one eyebrow, a provocation, and bared a set of
awful teeth. Freddy shrank against Daphne's leg.

'*Roberts*,' Belinda repeated in disbelief. 'No relation
to your erstwhile footman?'

'His nephew, in fact.'

She could not contain herself any longer. Turning
on her heel, she carried Lydia off to the drawing-room
where the dog had retreated. Everything was too rough,
too bright and too loud.

Dev lay curled into himself on one of the cornflower
sofas. She sat beside him, her thoughts spinning. This
was the exact place she had sat when they spoke to the
coroner about Hetta's bones. Now another skeleton
was coming out of the Bainbridge closet, one she would
never have guessed. All this time, Amy had been one of
the Roberts family! How had that escaped their notice?

Why would she even apply to work here? Marriage may have changed her name, but surely not her resentment towards the Bainbridges. Belinda remembered with a chill that, in fact, Amy had been the only remaining applicant for the position of wet-nurse. It was as if she, or someone close to her, had managed to scare all the competition away.

Had Nathan known about this relationship from the start? *How* would he know? Perhaps Amy confronted him when he first arrived, blamed him face-to-face for her uncle's death, but why would he not *say* so? It smacked of secrecy and underhand dealing.

Daphne entered the room, flurried, pushing Freddy before her. 'I didn't know,' she repeated. 'He never told me he was going to do any of this.'

'I suppose he *can*,' Belinda realised. 'They are not my staff now. The house is Freddy's and Nathan is Freddy's guardian. Along with Paul.' It occurred to her that she had not received any answers to her letters announcing Wilfred's death. She'd hardly expected anything to reach her father and Paul, but surely Mamma would have written? Surely Luke was coming to the funeral?

She had a terrible sinking feeling in the pit of her stomach. A dread that had nothing to do with the companions. But there must be some mistake.

Freddy remained curiously silent. He petted the dog without saying a word.

Nathan clipped into the room. 'Really, I do apologise if I have caused offence. I could not have predicted you would take it so badly – but of course, it is a difficult time. Wilfred was always warning me about your nerves…'

'Nathan!' Daphne cried.

He rounded on her. 'And I do not see why *you* should object. All three of them have been perfectly civil towards you.'

'But *why* are they here, Nathan?' Belinda demanded. 'The Robertses, of all people? They are the last family I would expect you to associate with.'

'On the contrary, it is my duty to see to their welfare. Do you not consider what our family owes theirs? My father paid them some hush money at the time of Roberts' death. Ross used that to get his sister trained up for service and then married. But as we well know, cash is no replacement for a lost family member. I wanted to do more, so I arranged for them all to live here together and look after the place while you are gone. Is it not an elegant solution? *Someone* must ensure Freddy's land is managed fairly.'

'But you *hated* your footman Roberts!'

'I did,' Nathan acknowledged. 'But these people are not *him*.'

'And – and this house—'

'Will struggle to find any other caretakers,' he finished before she could, matter-of-fact. 'We ought to be grateful that Amy, Ross and Whitfield are prepared to over-look recent events and stay on. And really,' he leant both hands on his cane, pulled a contrite expression, 'is this not just? A kind of reparation? The establishment of peace between two feuding families.'

She could not believe what she was hearing. Even in her tangled state of mind, she could see the contra-dictions in his arguments. Either The Bridge was a death-trap to be fled at all costs, or living here was a reward to a long-suffering family; it could not be both. And she had just *seen* Hetta, threatening her baby. How did Nathan think cosying up to the Roberts family was going to appease *her*?

Unless he did not believe in her. Had never truly believed in the danger she posed. She put a hand to her forehead. That could not be the case.

'I am struggling to follow your logic, Nathan. And I do not see how a family who loathed Wilfred, and probably despise Freddy too, will manage the property in his interest. They will cheat him at every turn.'

Nathan sighed. 'Well, I *can* stay and supervise them, if you wish it.'

'What?' Daphne burst out.

He tilted his head. 'If Belinda is concerned, my love, then it is my duty to act. Indeed, if I must send the Roberts family away, I see no alternative but for the two of us to remain here on Freddy's behalf. The place will fall to rack and ruin otherwise.'

The women gaped at him.

'I – I do not want to stay here,' Daphne said. There was a plea in her voice. 'Not now, after all the deaths.'

Nathan pursed his lips. 'I made a promise to my brother. I must honour it. And as my wife, I expect your support.' He clicked slowly towards the sofa. 'Do think on it a little, Belinda.' He gave her an indulgent – no, a *condescending* – look. 'There is no need to make rash decisions when you are upset. I am sure, once you consider things properly, you will see what needs to be done for the best.'

*

'I don't know what's got into him. It's like all of his plans and feelings have changed completely since Mr Bainbridge passed.' Daphne inhaled her snuff. 'Could that be the reason? He's grieving for his brother and not thinking straight?' She formed another pinch.

'You have taken an awful lot of that,' Belinda said, nodding at the enamel box.

'I know.' She snorted more powder. 'It usually gingers me up a bit, but it's not working today.'

They were in Belinda's suite, packing trunks while Lydia lay kicking on the bed. The room was in chaos: stockings hanging over the back of chairs, drawers open and hatboxes without their lids. Wilfred's clothes still hung in the wardrobe but Belinda could not bring herself to look at them, let alone pack them all up and take them home without the man who once wore them.

She picked up another shift and began to fold it. 'I understand why Nathan would feel some guilt towards the Roberts family, but not on this level. Did he ever tell you exactly what happened with that footman?'

Daphne put her snuffbox away. Her skin looked slightly moist, like a petal beaded with dew. 'Yes, he said that there was an accident and he was blamed for the man's death. That was why they sent him to India. He was furious about it.'

'He did not say whether he really was responsible?'

Daphne gasped. 'Of course he wasn't! You cannot believe—'

'I meant no offence.' Belinda placed the shift in the trunk. 'He was only a child at the time it happened… And genuine remorse is the only motive I can find to explain his current actions.'

'Well, if that is the case, he *cannot* mean what he said about our staying here. He would be miserable.' Daphne placed one hand on her stomach, wincing. She did not look altogether healthy. 'I am sure he blames himself for Roberts, even if it was not really his fault. Children take accusations like that to heart. No wonder the poor man is seeing ghosts.'

'You *still* do not believe the house is haunted, do you?'

Daphne shook her head. 'No, I do not believe in ghosts.'

Belinda narrowed her eyes. 'So what do you think happened with Wilfred? Honestly? Do you believe that Dawkins would…' She could not say the words.

'No! I – I cannot say for sure.' Daphne hesitated. 'My first thought was of the hostile villagers. They burnt the enclosure fencing, didn't they? Maybe they – maybe…' Her voice dwindled away as she slumped forward.

'Daphne! What's wrong, are you ill?'

She grabbed onto a bedpost for support, the carving pressing into her palm. 'I – I have a cramping in my belly.' She gestured towards the bed and Belinda understood she wanted the chamberpot beneath. She reached down and produced it. Instantly, Daphne voided the contents of her stomach.

'You must lie down. Here.'

Belinda moved Lydia to one side of the bed. She settled Daphne on the other pillow. Wilfred's pillow.

Surely this was not morning sickness already? The wedding was less than a fortnight ago. She felt Daphne's forehead. It was hot to the touch. Her grey eyes looked odd, the pupils too small.

'Perhaps you have eaten something that disagrees with you?' Belinda went to ring the bell, only to realise no one would answer it. 'I'll fetch you some ginger,' she said. 'And some cold water. The physic cabinet is down in the kitchen, I'll – I'll just be a moment.'

She flew from the room. Another commotion was taking place below. She heard Amy's voice, pleading, then the air split by the cracking of a whip.

'Stop!' Nathan choked.

Good God, what was happening? Was it Freddy? Belinda flew downstairs, taking the last steps at a jump.

Her son stood on the landing outside the nursery, wielding his riding crop. The other hand gripped tight to Dev's collar as he cried in utter fury: 'You – killed – my – papa!', slashing at Nathan between each word.

All the breath left Belinda's lungs. Her feet were rooted to the floor. Why would Freddy say that? Why would he think...

Amy tried to reach for the boy and stop him, but Dev growled at her. Nathan tried in vain to edge away.

'You – killed – him!'

'Freddy, stop! Stop!' Nathan begged. The boy had him backed against a wall and not even Nathan's own dog seemed to object. 'Freddy!' She saw Nathan's panicked mind working behind a mask of shock, saw him consider using the heavy-ended cane in his hand ...

'Enough!' she shouted. 'Young man, what do you think you are doing?'

Freddy only briefly turned his head. 'He killed him, Mamma!'

Nathan looked helplessly at her. 'I don't know why he would say that! He's taken leave of his senses.'

It certainly appeared that way. 'I'm sorry,' she said, coming forward. 'He is so upset. Come here, darling.'

Freddy gave one last slash. 'I hate you!' he yelled at Nathan.

'My dear boy...' She had never seen her brother-in-law so shaken. He looked as if the carpet had been pulled out from under him. As if he were reliving the last time someone had made such a grave accusation against him.

Gently, she coaxed the riding crop from Freddy's fingers. 'It's all right, darling. Mamma's here. Let's all calm down now.' She managed to pull him backwards a little. The dog came with him.

'For the life of me, I cannot imagine where he got this idea from,' Nathan breathed, incredulous.

'Maybe Hetta said it?' She remembered Freddy insisting that the companion had not committed Wilfred's murder, but he was wrong about the culprit surely. It was not *Nathan*. He had slept beside Daphne that night; Belinda had even overtaken him, going down the stairs in the morning…

'You were with me on the night your father died, Master Freddy,' Amy reminded him. 'Remember? We were all in the nursery and the door was locked. You didn't see it happen. You must have had a bad dream.'

'No!' He pouted. 'And *you're* a liar. You cut my hair off!'

Amy gasped, but her cheeks flushed bright red. 'I never!' she said to Belinda. 'He's imagining it—'

Nathan straightened up, tried to smooth his jacket. He seemed suddenly all flash and puff, a tinsel picture of a man. 'Amy's right, little chap. You must be having nightmares.'

Freddy looked as if he might reach for the whip again. Belinda grabbed his hand before he could. 'Are you hurt, Nathan? I'm going to the physic cabinet for Daphne. She's dreadfully indisposed. May I fetch you anything?'

'No… No harm has been done.' He glowered at his nephew, rubbing his sore leg. 'Just give Freddy something to… calm him down. He cannot say things like that to me, Belinda, even if he is upset.'

She nodded. 'I understand. Come along, my love.' She pulled the boy after her, who in turn pulled Dev.

'I *saw* it,' Freddy muttered. 'She showed me.'

Belinda did not know what to think, what to say. All she knew was that she needed to get her boy away from that dark and resentful look in Nathan's eyes.

And it wasn't just Nathan she mistrusted. Had Amy really cut Freddy's hair while he slept? Why would she do such a terrible thing? What had she been hoping to achieve? *I need to keep my eye on her*, Freddy had said at the time. *She's up to no good.* Maybe, for once, he hadn't been talking about Hetta.

It was only when they were halfway to the Great Hall that Belinda realised: Nathan had not even asked what the matter was with his wife.

CHAPTER 27

Watching the coffin descend was the worst part. Worse even than coming face to face with her husband's waterlogged corpse, for this was the substance of her nightmares come to pass: someone she loved reduced to an inanimate, wooden shape. Contained forever in a walnut box.

'This is all wrong,' she murmured to Freddy. She knew she was gripping his hand too tightly, for he was trying to pull away, but she could not help herself. 'Your Uncle Luke ought to be here.'

They stood together in the gallery, watching the pall-bearers carefully convey their burden down the staircase into the Great Hall. Not one of the men was known to her. She'd received no response from her family or friends, no letters of condolence at all. Her correspondence must never have been sent. Who collected letters from the postbag now? Ross Roberts and Whitfield: two men she did not know or trust.

They were not helping to carry the coffin. They stood to one side in the Great Hall, watching unmoved as it passed. They did not even bow their heads in respect.

Belinda could feel her anger building, pushing at the barriers of everything she wanted to believe. If Freddy was right…

He could not be. He was five years old, for heaven's sake, deranged with grief. And yet... Where were Wilfred's friends from London? And the gentleman he sometimes spoke of at a nearby estate – Fraser, was it? Nathan had not invited any of them. She did not even know if he'd announced the death in the newspapers. She had trusted him to arrange everything.

But didn't she trust her own son more?

She could not deny what was before her. Nathan was quietly tucking Wilfred out of sight. And she could not believe it was only to appease the unruly villagers in their anger about an oak tree.

A steady thump beside them. Nathan arrived, flustered and red-cheeked but immaculately turned out in black satin. 'I am late. Forgive me.'

Freddy twisted his hand free and scuttled to the other side of Belinda's hooped skirt, as far away from his uncle as he could get.

'Where is Daphne?' Belinda demanded.

'Still in our bed. She is rather worse, I'm afraid.' He shook his head. 'Feverish. She cannot possibly rise and dress.'

Another ally taken from her. Suspiciously timed, just when Belinda needed her the most. 'That sounds serious. Have you sent for a physician?'

He shook his head. 'I have been too occupied.'

'But you cannot just *leave* her. What if she takes a turn for the worse?'

He cast his eyes to heaven. 'I did not *intend* to leave her. I thought that *you* would watch over her, while Freddy and I were at the funeral. But since you *insist* on being present, quite against custom, my only choice is to commit my wife to Amy's care. It will suffice. The ceremony will not be very long.'

Belinda didn't trust the wet-nurse after Freddy's start-ling accusation about his hair. 'But one servant cannot nurse a patient and a baby at the same time.'

Nathan leant on his cane, exasperated. 'Well, what am I supposed to do? Stay behind yourself, if you are so concerned, but I think you are blowing this illness out of all proportion. It is just a trifling cold.'

Freddy poked his head out from behind Belinda's pannier. 'What have you done to my Aunt Sawyer?' he cried. 'Did you make her sick?'

His childish accusation bounced around the rafters, too loud. The pallbearers could not turn around, but one at the rear faltered in his step.

Nathan's cheeks deepened a shade. 'I cannot have this, Belinda. I cannot have him making such outlandish statements at the funeral, in front of everyone.'

'In front of whom? From what I can see, we will be the only ones in attendance.'

He turned a glare on her. Blue ice. For the first time in their acquaintance, she could imagine him doing it. She could see him pushing a footman to his death.

'You are making this more difficult than it needs to be.'

'I don't *want* to go the stupid funeral anyway!' Freddy announced, stamping his foot. 'Papa isn't in that box! He isn't! He's still here.'

'Fred—' she began, but he did not remain to listen. He ran pell-mell to the other side of the gallery and disappeared down the corridor leading to the nursery, his light, rapid footsteps echoing in his wake.

Belinda started after him. Nathan grabbed her wrist, painfully tight. 'Let him go. There's no time for this nonsense. He is too young for a funeral anyhow. Why not stay here with him? Ladies are not generally expected to attend. The ceremony will only agitate your nerves.'

He had a point. She did not wish to leave a distressed son, an injured baby and a sick sister all in the care of a woman who'd deceived her. Yet how could she abandon Wilfred? It was bad enough he was being carried by strangers and attended by so few mourners.

'No. I am determined to see my husband laid to rest.'

'Well then, you had better not be late.' He released her wrist, offered the crook of his arm instead. His mask slipped instantly back into place. 'Shall we, sister?'

Belinda looked at the dark sheen of his jacket, the smile that revealed even white teeth. His cavalier beard seemed to place him in another era. Hetta's era. Did he have more in common with those dark Bainbridge ancestors than she'd ever supposed?

She placed her hand purposefully on the banister, picked up her skirts in the other and descended the staircase alone.

*

The coach had been brand new on the occasion of their marriage. Embroidered hammercloths, Morocco leather squabs and the Bainbridge coat-of-arms painted on the side. Wilfred had spared no expense. He said this was a vehicle to proclaim their quality. To last a rising family for years to come. But now they had left him behind in the shadowy crypt. He would never ride opposite her again.

She'd heard the villagers whispering as she drifted from the carriage to the church. They thought Wilfred had brought disaster on himself by cutting down that old oak tree. To them this was all inevitable. Justice. It was what happened when you tried to stake a claim to land that could not be tamed.

She thought of all his plans for the village. Their designs for the house, the gardens she'd imagined. So many dreams and yet they were leaving The Bridge exactly as they had found it: under a curse, like a fairytale castle.

They had arrived in March, and it was September already. The landscape was showing signs of succumbing to autumn. More lace swags of cloud crossed the sky and there was a jaundiced tint to the grass. Trees crisped at the top as birds arrowed overhead.

Nathan turned the cane in his hand again and again. The silver tiger on top glinted and hurt her sore eyes. Of course, she had cried during the funeral service but she had never seen a man weep the way Nathan had; with angry, jagged sobs and tears he had swatted irritably away. His grief was deep. Complex. Exactly like that of a man who had done something terribly wrong.

Still, she fought to explain his behaviour. 'Are you anxious for Daphne?' she tried.

He shrugged. 'No, not overly. She is certain to recover. We just need to stay at The Bridge a little longer, that's all.'

He was so keen to stay now. As keen as he had been for her to leave. She could not hold back her resentment. 'Staying with your new *friends*?' She raised her chin to indicate the driver's box where Ross Roberts sat, whipping their fine horses to an indecorous pace.

'Please, Belinda. I *know* you do not approve of the Robertses but let us at least be civil, today of all days.'

'You must take me for an absolute fool! Do you think I cannot see that you wished to scare me away from this house, so that you could move your associates in? And I know it is not a coincidence that no friends came to the funeral. You did not want anyone there asking you awkward questions.'

The cane fell still in his hands. He continued to gaze out of the window. 'I *thought* you would appreciate some privacy. A murder case will always cause gossip. I did not want people gawking at my brother's coffin and whispering about how Dawkins had killed him. It would have been unbecoming. And as for the house, you are speaking nonsense. I invented nothing; you have read its history for yourself.'

She had. And she had seen Hetta standing by the trough over Wilfred's lifeless body. But she had been so preoccupied with the threat posed by the silent companions that she had not seriously considered other possibilities. Anyone could have trespassed onto the grounds that night. What about Ross Roberts, who had always despised Wilfred? What about Amy's husband from Torbury St Jude, of whom Belinda knew so little?

Nathan had been eager to blame Dawkins. That was his first concern after Wilfred died: that he might fall under suspicion once more. How had she failed to notice?

She needed to get away from this place, from these people. It did not signify in the end if she was cheated out of her dues. Let Nathan have his precious house, let the Robertses keep their rent money and common land. So long as she and her children were safely away.

But Daphne…

The carriage jolted as they approached the gatehouse too fast. Belinda hit her shoulder against the window. Roberts swerved and checked the horses just short of the massive iron gates. She heard him swear as he jumped off the box.

The gates had always been left open before. Now they closed off the drive downhill. A forbidding 'B' cast in iron split apart at Roberts' touch.

But there was a figure standing to the side of the road. Tall, slender, all elbows and knees. He held his hat respectfully to his chest.

'John!' she cried. 'It is John Knowles, come to pay his respects.'

Nathan groaned. 'He would do better to leave us in peace.'

'I must put down the window and say a word.'

'No, don't encourage him, Belinda.'

He reached out to stop her but she was too quick.

'John! John!' she called.

The youth approached them with deference, bowing his head. He looked so strange out of livery. 'I came to offer my sympathy, Mrs Bainbridge,' he said awkwardly. Nathan was glaring at him through the window. The boy swallowed, Adam's apple bobbing, but ploughed on. 'And to say I'm in the village of Fayford now, should you need anything.'

'She needs nothing from the likes of you,' said a voice from in front of the carriage. Ross Roberts slashed the air with his whip, forcing John to jump back. 'Be gone.'

Belinda watched with silent fury as Roberts climbed back on the box where he did not belong. He whipped the horses to a breakneck pace. They lurched through the open gates, rattling downhill. She gripped the leather passenger strap.

'John is only a boy. It was kind of him to come.'

'Do not be naïve, Belinda. He is begging when I have already paid him handsomely.'

She wanted to scream. Her life felt like this carriage, commandeered and surging at a pace she did not choose. Tomorrow she could leave. Tomorrow, tomorrow. Surely her father and her brothers would help her get justice for Wilfred?

Gravel skidded as they rounded the sweep at such an angle that Belinda thought she would vomit from the motion. At last, they jerked to a halt.

Ross Roberts did not deign to open the carriage door or put down the steps. She let herself out. The air felt blessedly cool against her hot, wet cheeks.

'Give me your hand, then,' she sighed, extending a palm to Nathan. In spite of everything, she was not about to leave a man with a cane helpless and stranded. She would not become as heartless as them.

She saw that he did not expect it. He clambered awkwardly down and landed with a spray of gravel. 'Thank you.'

The main entrance creaked open, pushed by an unseen hand. Turning on her heel, Belinda marched up the steps and entered the Great Hall, eager to check on her children and Daphne.

There was no trace of anyone within. All she could hear was the ticking of the clock. Presumably everyone was upstairs, but the door to the drawing-room stood open. If Daphne was feeling better, she might have come down to sit there and wait for them. Belinda would check inside first before climbing the staircase.

She was nearly at the door to the room when one foot slipped from under her. She wheeled her arms, desperately trying to regain her balance.

'Careful!' Nathan's voice. He was just coming in through the main entrance as she managed to right herself by gripping the door frame.

Shaken, she glanced down to see what she had slid in. Viscous. Claret. Blood. Her shoe had smeared it into a fan shape.

Horror held her mute. The children. Daphne.

Nathan struggled to her side and cursed. 'Where the devil is *that* coming from?' He gazed frantically from side to side. 'What is going on here?'

He limped into the drawing-room and she followed, steeling herself for she knew not what. Red was streaked everywhere, as if someone had dragged a paintbrush along the floor and up the skirting board. Dabs of it were spread across one of the blue sofas. There was a splatter on the far wall.

She heard a high-pitched whine.

Dev emerged from underneath a sofa, his white coat spotted with dark marks. He came slinking up to Nathan for comfort.

'Good God, you poor old rascal! Give me your shawl, Belinda, quickly!'

She flinched as the dog wagged his tail and scattered drops of blood towards her. Someone had tried to dock him. They did it as a matter of course to some breeds – cut their tails short as puppies – but this was clumsy and uncalled for. She thought of Hetta's scissors.

Her shawl was too big. Belinda drew out her handkerchief instead and knotted it tightly around the wound. 'There, there. You'll be all right, boy.' She winced to find the heat of blood on her palms again, had a flash of Rebecca's severed finger. 'I'll fetch the medicine chest,' she said to Nathan as he cradled Dev's head. 'Try not to worry, it looks worse than it is.'

'But how the devil did it happen? He hasn't caught it on anything, that's a proper slice, it's…' A storm cloud crossed his face. 'Freddy. Freddy has done this to get back at me.'

'*Freddy*?' Her voice came out so high it made Dev's ears twitch. 'Do not be absurd. He worships that dog. He would never hurt any animal.'

'But he would whip his own uncle,' Nathan spat, white-lipped with anger. 'There is a violent streak in him. You saw it yourself. Good God. I hoped all this nonsense with him would pass, but clearly it's getting worse.'

'How can you say such things? You *know* what this is: it's Hetta's work. The evil in the house. The silent companions.'

He said nothing. Just kept fondling the sad dog and glaring at the stump of a tail.

Belinda turned to leave and fetch some bandages but Nathan's voice arrested her at the door.

'I cannot let him go, Belinda. He cannot possibly return to London, speaking such slander against me. And now this... I am responsible for Freddy. For his conduct. A violent boy needs careful watching.'

A high-pitched ringing started in her ears. 'Freddy is leaving with me tomorrow.'

'No, he is not. Not now. I will oversee his education here. He clearly requires a strict tutor to keep him in line.'

'That is not your choice!' she cried. 'You are not his parent!'

'No, I am his legal guardian.' He raised his eyes from the dog. 'I have more rights over him than you do.'

It knocked the breath from her. He could not mean it. He could not propose to separate her from her son. 'I will not stir a foot without him. If Freddy remains, so do Lydia and I.'

'As you wish it.'

Her bloody hands balled into fists. She could feel her fingernails, driving into her palms. 'You are willing to stay here. So you do *not* believe this house is haunted.

You never thought it was dangerous. Every word you ever spoke to me was a lie.'

He did not flinch from her gaze. 'Or maybe I am just starting to notice that every incident with the silent companions also involves your son. That maybe we ought to be looking to a living child, not a dead one, to find the cause of the mischief. We said he was touched like Tiffany, but what if he isn't? What if it is plain madness?'

No. Nathan would not do this; she would not let him turn it around. He'd played these sophisticated tricks on her before. First he had been eager to get rid of them and now... Now Freddy had caught him out. And her son was all that stood between Nathan and being master of The Bridge.

'You *cannot* do this,' she asserted. 'Whatever it is you are planning, my brother Paul will never agree to it. He is Freddy's guardian too. He will not let you keep his nephew prisoner here or have him declared unfit to inherit.'

One corner of Nathan's mouth lifted in a smirk. 'Mr Paul Kipling is in the middle of the Atlantic Ocean. What influence can he have in the matter from there?'

CHAPTER 28

There was a bite to the night breeze as it floated through the open window to stir the curtains. No fire had been lit but still Daphne tossed on the bed, throwing off her sheets with a moan. Sweat shone upon her skin. The past few hours had been a cycle of cramps and vomiting.

Belinda paced up and down the room, unsure what else she could do. Nothing seemed to give Daphne any relief. Maybe there was another remedy to try, but she could not call it to mind. She was wrung out, exhausted, sick at heart.

Not once had Nathan come to enquire after her patient. He'd abandoned both these rooms in the west wing and his sick wife to spend time with his vile new friends. Just when Belinda had thought he couldn't sink any lower in her esteem. Had even his regard for Daphne been utterly false from the start?

But perhaps it should not shock her. Not when Nathan had already proven himself heartless, ordering Amy to keep two children away from their own mother.

He would not let Belinda set foot inside the nursery. She expected to find the same thing if she tried the outer doors of the house: locks turned, bolts drawn, chains on the iron gates. The Bridge closing in on itself and hiding its darkest secrets.

Now that Freddy had revealed the truth, Nathan would never let them go.

How could she have allowed this to happen? She kept expecting to wake from another bad dream to find Wilfred beside her in bed. She had been so blind, she had truly believed...

The air stroked her face. It smelt of leaf mulch and still, roses. Her mind seemed to shudder, images flickering unsteadily. *Some* of the haunting must have been real? Her fear of the companions partially justified? The events of the last few months could not *all* have been Nathan's doing.

She ran through it as she paced, trying to separate fact from fiction. Between them, the Roberts cohort could have done much. Changed the portrait of Great-aunt Caroline to the painting of Anne and Hetta. Cut Freddy's hair and scratched the rocking horse. Crept into the bedroom to sprinkle petals. One of them could even have buried bones in the garden. It was Nathan himself, wasn't it, who had encouraged her to dig up the flowerbed?

All these cruel tricks – just because Wilfred had not spoken up for his brother as a child. No. There *must* be more to it than that. Nathan had leapt to Freddy's defence when the weapons fell, sustained an injury to save him. Why would he do that if he'd always meant to take his inheritance? But at that time, Freddy had been serving his uncle's purpose, hadn't he? Speaking of ghosts and moving companions. Now he was accusing his uncle of murder, it was a different matter.

Maybe Nathan's original plan had not been so extreme. Maybe he'd thought Wilfred could be persuaded to entrust him with care of the estate – especially once he was married to Daphne – and would move back to London. But his plot had been discovered, first by Wilfred and now by Freddy. And after that there was only one way to ensure their silence.

Her temples throbbed. She pulled the pins out of her hair and shook it loose. Daphne's groans echoed what Belinda felt inside. Uncertainty. Indecision. Like being torn in two.

Because the threat from the companions could *not* all be a ruse. Anne Bainbridge's diaries were real enough. And the only reason Freddy had suspected Nathan in the first place was because he'd talked to a dead girl who accused his uncle. The swords, the splinters and Dev's docked tail all struck her as Hetta's spiteful work.

There was not space to hold all this inside her brain. Could it be that both things were true at once? Elements of worldly reason and the supernatural blended together until you could not distinguish one from the other?

Just like Hetta and the silent companions.

Soot dropped in the chimney. She realised she was cold. How long had she been pacing by candlelight with the window open and the fire unlit? On the bed, Daphne began to shiver as violently as she'd previously sweated, ice and fire all at once. Belinda hurried to pull the sheets back over her.

'Water,' Daphne gasped. 'My mouth is so dry.'

Belinda tipped the glass gently against her lips, but Daphne grabbed the bottom and tilted it up. She swallowed greedily, liquid running down her chin. Belinda had to look away. It made her think of Wilfred.

Once the glass was empty, Daphne's teeth started to chatter.

'You need a fire,' Belinda murmured. To her shame, she realised she'd never lit one herself. A few pieces of wood were piled beside the hearth and a tinderbox sat behind the vase on the mantelpiece. She would have to try. The Robertses were unlikely to come if she rang the bell and she had no idea where Nathan even was.

Kneeling, she began to lay out the wood, packing some kindling paper in between as she'd seen others do. More soot drifted down to patter over her work. There must be a bird up on the chimney top or else stuck in the flue. She glanced up into the dark funnel – she didn't want to set some unfortunate creature alight. That was when she noticed the loose brick.

It was tucked away from the reach of the flames, blackened at the edges but still relatively clean. Someone had removed and replaced it in haste so that it jutted out like a baby's first uneven tooth. Awkwardly, Belinda reached in and pulled at the crumbling mortar. The brick came away, rough and heavy in her hand. She set it down with the wood.

Her palm was covered in soot. She wiped it against her skirts, which were the black of mourning already. Something pale was stuffed within the gap behind the brick. A paper-wrapped packet.

Daphne mumbled from the bed. Belinda knew she ought to prioritise her sister's comfort, but she could not stop now. She pulled the little parcel out. It was singed at the edges. Along with smoke, it smelt of other things: a sweet, nutty, slightly floral aroma. Hastily, she unwrapped the paper. There were letters inside and some kind of sticky brown cake or tablet. She took the whole bundle over to the candle sconce and knelt below it for a better look.

The correspondence had already been opened. For a moment, she thought to find her own unsent letters notifying her family of Wilfred's death, but these were older, the folds worn. Belinda opened them up, knowing she would not have the time to read everything in detail before she tended to Daphne. She scanned only the tops and the bottoms. All were addressed to Nathan in a small, careful hand. Some were signed Amy Roberts, others Amy Whitfield. But they had the same valediction: *Your humble kinswoman.*

Lightning forked across her mind. It was the missing piece of the puzzle. The only explanation for why the Robertses would agree to team up with a man accused of killing a member of their family. The adultery of Wilfred's mother and the footman stretched further into the past than her husband had imagined.

Nathan was a Roberts all along.

Belinda knelt there, gaping, the writing swimming before her eyes. As she let the letters drop, her attention returned to the fragrant cake. Could it be molasses? Plum pudding? No. Though it reminded her of baked goods, it was like none she'd ever seen. Her fingers worked to remove a bead of viscous, sticky gum. There were chunks of something like honeycomb within. And then she remembered.

If she had not come from a family of merchants, she never would have known. But there had been endless days of her life spent indoors studying cargo lists, asking her brothers questions about the trading routes and the goods exchanged. She'd never seen it raw before, yet she was almost certain: this luxury was shipped expensively from India. Here in England, it was refined and dissolved in wine to kill pain, bringing dreams and elation, sometimes an element of confusion. Taking it away too fast always made the user ill. Hadn't Mamma been just like Daphne was, when she tried to give up laudanum?

But this – this was much more potent than a tincture such as laudanum. The substance adhering to her hand was a cake of pure opium.

*

Belinda waited. Once or twice, she became aware of holding her breath and released it in a judder. She knew the effect of the drug would not be instantaneous. What she did not know was whether she'd used too much or too little on her sister. How did Nathan administer the dose? Not in crumbs through the mouth as she just had. Opium could be smoked, taken in lozenge form, dissolved in liquid – perhaps even crushed to powder and mixed into snuff? She was not sure. But she *was* sure that Daphne's behaviour had changed when she took up the habit.

The night drained slowly away. She managed to get the fire going at last but dawn was pushing at the horizon before Daphne's delirium started to abate. Daylight found its way into the room and seemed to wake her from a spell.

'Ma'am?' She squinted up at Belinda. 'Is that you?'

'It's me. I am here.'

'But… where are we?'

Belinda was able to prop Daphne up against the bolster and get more water into her but she did not have any food to hand. It seemed a vain hope that one of the Robertses would bring up a breakfast tray.

Daphne was still sick and disorientated, but she was coming to herself again. 'I feel better,' she insisted. 'I feel so much better. It's… oh, it feels like a miracle!'

Belinda clasped her own filthy hands together and picked at her nails. It was too soon to tell Daphne what had really happened.

She watched a flock of crows lift from the gardens outside. They reminded her of cinders rising up the chimney flue. She was the one with the fever now, burning with all she had to tell. Still the exact words eluded her.

Did she start with Freddy's accusation against Nathan or the secretive funeral? Could she even be certain Daphne would take her side over her husband's? Belinda closed her eyes and rubbed the lids. It felt as if someone had thrown sand into them. She had not slept a wink.

'Where is Nathan? And what's that on your face? Is it a shadow? Is it real? I still can't...'

As Belinda lowered her hand, she saw Daphne staring at her in confusion. Of course. Without thinking, she'd smeared soot and opium onto her skin.

She took a deep breath. And then it all came spilling out.

Perhaps she was fortunate that Daphne was still weak. She listened without many of the reactions and interruptions she might otherwise have made. But as Belinda drew to a close, her sister grew increasingly agitated, fidgeting in the bed and shaking her tangle of dark hair.

'No. No, that is not right. You're mistaken.' Wearily, Belinda went to pass the incriminating letters over, but Daphne raised her hands as if warding off a weapon. 'I don't need to see them! From what you've said, they prove nothing. You just – you can't bear—' Her voice rose, broke, and finally dissolved into tears.

It took half an hour of gentle persuasion, but Daphne was no fool. As her wits began to clear, her defence of Nathan crumbled. Belinda watched her drawn, stricken face with more sympathy than she could ever express. Losing Wilfred had been the hardest trial of her life and yet she had never been forced to forfeit her good opinion of him. She got to preserve a pure memory. The man Daphne had loved was worse than dead – he had never existed.

'I've been so stupid.' She turned her wedding ring round and round on her finger. 'I ought to have known... I *did* know it was too good to be true. For a gentleman to take to me so suddenly like that. I just – I wanted to believe it. I wanted...' She could not finish.

'You wanted to be in your proper place,' Belinda said. Daphne glanced up, her mouth ajar, and Belinda saw that she *had* known. Probably not about the mother who had died in the highway robbery, but she had figured out she was a Kipling by blood. Of course she had. Daphne had never been slow-witted. 'You wanted to be cherished and truly part of our family,' Belinda went on sadly. 'All the things you *should* have been from the start.'

Daphne wiped her nose. 'But I'm not in a better position, am I? I'm just one bastard child married to another. Nathan must have thought I was like him. Resentful. That I'd turn on you in the end. But I swear he never told me any of this, I knew nothing!' She shook her head, her eyes filming over again, but not with fever. She was replaying the past. 'I did notice that he spoke differently of the house to you. With me, the ghosts were always a bit of a jest. He didn't want *me* to be afraid of living here. He just wanted to scare you away. But I told him I didn't want to stay here, didn't I? Not with all the Robertses and the bad memories. That must be why he stopped giving me the opium: so I'd be sick and forced to remain here.'

'I think he may be taking opium himself,' replied Belinda. 'All his actions seem so impulsive. His methods have been wheedling and harsh by turns. All I can say for certain is that he never recovered from being sent away from The Bridge. Now he will do anything to make it his own. And the people he has on his side want nothing more than revenge on the Bainbridge family.'

'Yes,' Daphne said slowly, 'whatever his original intentions were, he is certainly dangerous now. The power he has over you and the children... We must get you away.' She reached for Belinda's dirty hands. 'If you could get those letters to Mr Luke, he might know what to do with them. They'd be enough to raise questions, wouldn't they? If your brother could convince a lawyer that Nathan isn't of Bainbridge blood, he'd have no right to The Bridge. He wouldn't stand next in line after Freddy, and so he'd have no reason to wish your little boy ill.'

'Except that Freddy is accusing him of murder.'

'But that can't be proved. I do not believe...' Daphne frowned, considering. 'It's possible that Nathan *ordered* the killing, but as I said, he was with me when I awoke that morning. And his injury! He couldn't do all that to Wilfred and the horse in the stables by himself. No court of law would take Freddy's accusations seriously.'

'Nathan *is* taking them seriously, though. Freddy is locked in that nursery, unable to see me, and I know – I just *know* – that Amy is going to come running to me with news of some accident or childhood malady that has smothered him in his sleep! If they would drug you, if they would kill Wilfred, there's no saying what they might do to my children.' She gave a sob. 'How do we get out of here, Daphne? How do we get away? Young John Knowles is in Fayford, I'm sure he would help us if we could only reach him.'

Daphne's jaw set. She looked exhausted, purple pouches beneath her eyes, but determined. '*You* will reach him. You and the children. But I must stay.'

'I'm not going to leave you!'

'You have no choice. I married the man – I must suffer the consequences. He has a claim on me. But once you are with your brother, you'll be safe. And who knows? Maybe Mr Luke can think of a way to help me, too.'

'But—'

'They won't be watching me closely,' Daphne went on, warming to her idea. 'They all think I'm sick. And I can keep *acting* the part while I take enough of that opium to stay well. I know where it's hidden now. We'll plan your escape for the full moon, when the light is good. The date will be in my almanac. I can distract Nathan that night, keep him with me.'

'But I can't get to the children! All the doors are locked and those awful men—'

Daphne was already shaking her head. '*Men* never pay attention to housekeeping, do they? What do you think happened after Mrs Knowles died? I took her keys. And even when Nathan told me to give them to Amy, I didn't hand over any I didn't have a copy of. He under-estimated me. There, in my pockets.' Belinda grabbed at the little bags on the waist-strap, hanging over one of the chairs. They tinkled like coins, like chains falling away. 'I can open the nursery and the gates. I can lock Mr Whitfield and Ross in their rooms. We will get you out of here, Belinda.' Daphne offered a grim smile. 'Let's show my husband that I can surprise him, too.'

CHAPTER 29

Belinda had done this so many times before. More than half of her life had been spent pretending, concealing from others what she truly felt. The stakes had never been this high, but she was curiously placid as she descended into the Great Hall, dressed for dinner, her dark train sweeping the stairs. Her outfit, too, was a kind of sham. There had not been a real dinner here for weeks, only the simple fare scraped together by cottagers – certainly nothing she needed to change her clothes for. She'd be eating elbow to elbow with the Robertses. Still, her gown gave the impression she needed to uphold: that of a pale, slender lady, delicately bred. The very last person you would suspect of planning a daring escape.

Nathan had covered his intentions with polish and charm, but Belinda and Daphne were mistresses of a deeper, more subtle art. They had always been required to perform up close in domestic quarters. To fade into the background as a mere daughter or servant. For nearly two weeks now, they'd kept up a show of obedience and the 20th of September had finally arrived. The full moon would rise tonight. By the time it set, Belinda and the children should be free.

Upstairs with her husband in the room that they shared, Daphne would be convincing Nathan – wavering, doubting, implying that she was warming to his point of view – and Belinda knew that she would succeed. Daphne had spent her life waiting on her own blood relatives, calling them 'ma'am' and 'sir' as if she had no idea what she was due. This charade was barely an inconvenience by comparison.

Amy was in the dining-room, her whole face red and flushed as she clattered around with plates. Belinda winced at the force with which she slammed down the best china. Bread, cheese, some ham and a little hasty pudding were laid out upon the table.

'You need a cook to help you,' Belinda observed, watching from the doorway. 'I'd hire one, if I was allowed to.'

The girl glanced up, clearly flustered. Perhaps she had not considered, as the only female involved in the plot to take over The Bridge, that her elevation to greatness would still include laundry, cooking and childcare. 'I've cousins coming. And Ross will marry soon. It's only for a time.'

'Goodness. An invasion of Robertses.'

Amy was not, Belinda thought, quite as bold as the others. She'd been in the house long enough to actually become acquainted with the family and she was a mother herself. She must have realised how their plans would terrify the children. *That* was why she'd been so keen to leave her own son in Torbury St Jude until now. No, Amy could speak as roughly as the rest of them, but there was something fleeting in her expression, something that looked like a hint of conscience.

'We're doing nothing wrong,' she asserted, slamming down another dish. 'How do you think the Bainbridges got this land in the first place? Force. They took it from others. That's all ownership is. Fight after fight.'

Belinda could not really disagree. It wasn't the land she was interested in anyhow. 'How are my children?' she demanded. 'How is Lydia's arm?'

'Recovering,' Amy tossed out. 'They're much better off with me. The baby's a good deal happier now you're not prodding at her with needles.'

Belinda gritted her teeth. Amy had a nerve, after all she had done. 'Just don't go cutting her hair, will you?'

Amy flinched.

A slow thumping came from the stairs behind. Belinda looked over her shoulder to see Nathan and Daphne, arm-in-arm, carefully making their way down. Nathan still used his cane and Daphne gripped the banister rail, trembling lightly. An act or real weakness?

'You see my wife is improved,' Nathan announced. 'She will be joining us at table.'

Their procession had a sick, decayed sort of grandeur to it. This was what it was, Belinda thought, to be master of The Bridge. A throne of rotten fruit and ashes.

'Do not overtax yourself, Daphne,' she warned. 'But of course we'd be very glad of your company.'

Ross Roberts slunk in from the kitchens. Presumably Whitfield was watching the children until his wife fetched their food upstairs. She bristled to think of Freddy, of tiny Lydia, in such rough care.

Belinda took her seat at the bottom of the table. There was no gentleman to pull it out for her now. Little by little, the others followed her example. Amy plonked herself down with a weary sigh; Ross sat with his legs apart as if he were riding the chair, not sitting on it. Nathan settled Daphne at Belinda's left elbow. Lastly, he claimed the seat by the grandfather clock, at the head of the table. Wilfred's place.

She remembered the companion with the sword, which Nathan must have put there on the very day of his arrival, before coming to find them at church. His first action, while Mr and Mrs Knowles dealt with his luggage and dog: to sit a companion supposed to represent Justice in his brother's place. He had planted his seeds right away, hadn't he, by telling Belinda that the companions moved by themselves?

It did not seem so very long ago. They'd all sat here together for the first time and she had chosen her words to Nathan with great care. She would have to do so again now.

There was no ceremony to the meal. Everyone reached for their own food at once. She noticed Daphne hang back and press her lips together, as if the thought of eating made her queasy. Again, Belinda could not tell if it was real or not.

'It's a pleasure to see you up and about, sister. I was worried about you. I hope you are feeling better?'

'A little – a little better,' Daphne answered breathlessly. 'But I think Nathan is right. We must stay here for the time being. I'm not in a fit state to travel.' Belinda poured her a glass of barley water and said nothing. 'I'm sorry. I know you're disappointed.'

She was playing her part well. Looked truly contrite. It made it easier for Belinda to respond in kind. 'I have no objection to *you* remaining. If you choose to risk a haunted house, that is your decision to make. But your sickness should not prevent me and my children from returning to London.'

Ross scraped his knife loudly across the plate as he cut some cheese. Deliberately, of course. Scratching the pastoral scene painted on the china. Amy gave a little snort of amusement.

'Come now,' Nathan objected, 'that's not very sisterly of you, Belinda. Do you not wish to tend Daphne through her illness?'

'I've already tended to her more than you have.'

Daphne ducked her head, the image of divided loyalties. 'Please, ma'am, let us not have any unpleasantness.'

Nathan took a sip of his wine and swirled it about his mouth. 'Mmm. I quite agree. We must make the best of a bad situation. And you know, I have already been seeking out tutors for young Freddy. Sensible men able to nip those... violent tendencies of his in the bud.'

Belinda swallowed. Please God, it would never happen, they were getting out tonight. But she still had a mental image of poor Freddy, caned and cowed. 'He did *not* harm your dog.'

'Then who did?'

'Please, ma'am,' Daphne begged her once more, 'do listen to reason. Master Freddy *can't* go back to London, not as he is. Telling such tales... when we all know Dawkins killed poor Mr Bainbridge. I'm sure he used to grumble often enough about his pay and the amount of work he had to do. Didn't he, Amy? You must have heard him in the kitchens too.'

Amy nodded while Nathan looked on approvingly. The smug blockhead. He really thought he'd done it; turned his wife against her sister. He saw only what he wanted to see.

Shakily, Daphne picked up her glass, slopping a little barley water on the tablecloth as she drank. 'I'm sure you'd much prefer a strict tutor living here than Freddy being sent off to school, wouldn't you?'

'There *are* a number of places he could go,' Nathan offered. 'Institutions claiming to be able to correct troubled boys. The old man made a list of them before opting to send me to his cousin in India.' He gave Belinda a pointed look. 'But those schools, you know... such a long way to travel. The dangers of the roads. And, of course, disease spreads around them like wildfire. You would not want to risk anything befalling Freddy before he could reach his majority.'

She did not have to simulate the fury on her face as she pushed back her chair. 'You will not get away with this. My family will want to visit us at some point. They will grow suspicious.'

'Really,' Daphne tried again, dabbing her lips with a napkin, 'it would be prudent for you not to make such a fuss over so little. I am saying this for your own good, ma'am. If neither you nor Master Freddy cause any problems... if he learns to speak *sensibly*... I am sure nothing bad will happen. Your brothers have their own concerns. We must trust Nathan to look after us now.'

She ought to be on the stage. If Belinda did not know better, she would think Daphne had changed sides.

Amy offered neither comment nor look; presumably she had needed to keep her own counsel many times during the execution of this plot. But Belinda could see Ross was struggling not to laugh. He faked a cough to pass it off.

That was what they thought of Daphne and her. Spoiled little rich girls to be mocked, without an ounce of sense or a backbone between them.

Belinda rose to her feet, shaking with rage. She could feel the cool outline of the nursery key in her pocket, pressing against her leg. Just a few hours until darkness. She need only hold her nerve a little while longer. 'I cannot believe you do not take my part, Daphne. After all we have been through together.'

'A true friend is the voice of reason, even when you do not wish to hear it. I would urge you to take my advice. It is kindly meant.' Daphne paused, wet her lips. 'After all, I should not like to be obliged to write to Mr Kipling and tell him your reason has deserted you in your time of grief.'

It was exactly what they had planned to say. Even so, the words ran like droplets of cold water down her spine. Belinda let her jaw hang open, swept her eyes from Daphne to Nathan and back again.

'Sit down, sister.' He waved, all graciousness now. 'You are making quite an exhibition of yourself. Of course, we understand the depth of your loss... It has undone you. But do *try* and show a little decorum.'

She thought of his own ugly sobbing at the funeral. How quickly he had hardened his heart and turned from that emotion. The figure sitting at the head of the table now had become as unfeeling as one of the wooden companions. Perhaps that was the only way he could live with the guilt.

'Pray excuse me,' she said tartly. 'I find I have lost my appetite.'

Turning from the table, she strode out of the dining-room and into the Great Hall.

The dog was there, stretched out on the oriental rug. His tail was bandaged more expertly now and would heal, in time. But that was not what drew her eye. It was the silent companion beside him.

Merripen. The boy from the diary who had been convicted for Hetta's crime, maiming the Queen's horse. Freddy claimed it was Merry who first warned him about Hetta's true nature. A good, well-meaning boy.

The board stood close, almost as if it were comforting the animal.

Cautiously, Belinda bent and fondled Dev's ears. 'Did Hetta cut your tail, boy? Was it really her?'

He whined back.

Such a tangle. If they put her on oath right now, Belinda could not say what she truly believed. But surrounding Merripen was that same crackle in the air, the same static charge she'd felt before. Despite every-thing she had learnt, there was enough superstition left in Belinda for her to lean in and whisper: 'Tell Freddy to be ready. Tonight. Keep him awake.'

Merripen's wooden face stared back at her, impassive.

Feeling like a fool, Belinda walked away and mounted the stairs for what she prayed would be the last time.

❊

She used to anticipate nightfall in this house with a cold dread. Now it felt as if the darkness would never come. She changed her clothes for a plain gown and hard-wearing boots, secured her jewels and the remains of her pin-money in her pockets. It took next to no time at all.

Of course there was more she should pack. Freddy might get cold or hungry and Lydia was bound to need a change of clouts. But the children's discomfort would have to be endured. All they could do was travel light and swift, praying that she could buy whatever they needed somewhere along the way. Getting out was the chief objective. Evading pursuit.

Belinda stood by the window to watch the sun set. She could not keep entirely still; found herself rocking on the balls of her feet. Having awaited this night for so long, she expected to see a blaze of colour, powder pinks and apricot, to herald the end of her last day at The

Bridge. Nature did not oblige. The sun simply receded under the horizon, darkening the sky in increments.

She sat on the edge of the bed and wished she'd taken longer to dress. Waiting only gave her time to think of everything that could go wrong. It reminded her of the last days of pregnancy; longing for the baby to arrive and yet fearing the ordeal of childbirth. Hours seemed to pass without the clock making a sound.

More than once she rose and pressed her ear against the door, listening for signs of the others retiring to bed, but it was impossible to hear anything above the thumping of her own heart. She had to hold her nerve. Leaving too soon would ruin everything.

While her mind dwelt on the very human threat to her children, her body had not forgotten its earlier fears. It still jumped at every creaking board, every bird rustling in the trees outside. When the remains of daylight finally dribbled from the room, the darkness seemed to breathe around her, sentient. She rose and lit all the candles but left her lamp. She wouldn't waste the oil by igniting it until the last moment.

She passed to the window again. The moon was full, as Daphne had promised. That would help in the long trek uphill to the gate and crossing the bridge into Fayford.

At last, at last, she heard the clock strike one. Exhausted, electrified, she rose from her dressing-room sofa and lit the lamp, then snuffed out all her candles. Surely it was late enough for everyone to be asleep? With the sun rising around half-past six, she dare not leave it any longer. She wanted to be well out of Torbury St Jude before daybreak.

Trembling, she approached the door and eased it open with one damp-palmed hand, using the other to raise her lamp aloft and illuminate the corridor lined with marble busts.

Her lungs emptied in a rush. A companion waited in the shadows: a footman in blue and yellow livery. Roberts. It must be; he had the same full lips, the same obnoxious smirk as the man downstairs. She caught only a glimpse of his knowing, sinister smile before her lamp guttered out.

Impossible. A lamp could not just blow out like a candle, it was protected behind glass and there was plenty of oil. She blinked, trying to accustom her eyes to the pitch black.

She could see nothing, nothing at all. Reaching out, she tried to feel her way along the wall, but she'd forgotten the marble busts were there. Her hand moved over cold, stiff features; death masks that wobbled at her touch and threatened to topple over. How many were there? She had never counted them. Here was the one with the missing nose and here—

She faltered. Something flat. Not made of stone but wood...

Hiss.

Recoiling, she cast out wildly. Blackness in every direction. Only sheer force of will drove her feet ahead to where she could not see.

Where were the companions? Were they coming closer?

Her breath sounded achingly loud. She had to get her bearings, she must not spiral into panic. Maybe Nathan had set the companions up outside her room for exactly this purpose: to frighten her and keep her contained in one spot if she did try to venture out. Of course it did not explain the lamp, but there would be a nightlight in the nursery; she could take that with her. This was a setback. Nothing more. She just had to keep going.

Belinda stumbled on. Her fingers met flock wallpaper. Which wall was this? She felt the edge of a gilt frame, thought perhaps it was the turning towards the staircase... The floor gave way under her, but she managed to lock her grip on the newel post before she fell down the first step. Her lungs felt like they would burst from the effort of swallowing a scream. Carefully, carefully, she descended. Each creak seemed to travel up her bones. *Stay asleep, stay asleep.*

She could not believe that she was doing this, that it was truly happening. She was still clutching the useless lamp tightly in one hand. She dare not drop it or set it down for fear of making a noise.

Her feet reached the landing before she was ready. She nearly tripped again. But on this floor, it was brighter. Waves of yellow lapped through the gap at the bottom of the nursery door to guide her steps. She fumbled in her pocket for the key Daphne had given her.

Here came the hardest part. She did not know if she could pull it off, but failure was not an option. She slotted the key into the lock; once again, her hands were too slippery to perform the manoeuvre with any grace. Although she turned the key as slowly as she possibly could, the lock gave way with a sudden pop.

Belinda froze.

There was no response – no sound of Amy turning over or waking up.

She was not sure how much faster her pulse could race before she succumbed to a paroxysm like Mr Knowles had. Inch by inch, the door creaked open.

The nursery appeared twice its usual length; a shadowy ocean she must cross. Biting her lip, she placed one foot carefully in front of the other. She could hear Amy breathing now, shallow and even, but did not stop to look at her. All her focus must be on keeping her footsteps soft. *Step. Step. Step.*

The little boys were together in the same bed. Amy's Thomas had his arm flung up over his face, but Freddy was wide awake. His blue eyes widened at the sight of her.

Hurriedly, she pressed a finger to her lips and begged him to read her thoughts. Lowering her hand, she gestured behind her.

Freddy seemed to understand. Imitating her stealth, he slipped out from under the covers. Thomas stirred but did not wake. Freddy crept around the long way, past the rocking horse, closer to her.

God bless that child. God bless his intelligence, his velvet tread. She wished she could take the same route as he just had, where she could be certain there were no noisy floorboards, but Lydia's crib was in the opposite direction.

Steeling herself, she started towards it. She had never seemed to move so slowly in all of her life. Every muscle quaked from resisting the urge to run.

Lydia snuffled in her sleep. How was it that her gentle infant noises had become so loud? Closer, closer. Belinda was nearly there. She parted the curtains. Her baby was in reach. She held her breath, extended a hand.

Lydia sneezed.

Heat flooded through Belinda.

Amy snorted awake with a confused noise. *No, no, no.* 'Freddy,' Belinda hissed. 'Run!'

She felt the movement of air as he fled. With a lurch, she grabbed for Lydia, who let out a startled mew. She thrust the baby haphazardly over her shoulder, too desperate to care.

'What the hell do you think you're doing?'

Amy's foot met the floor with a heavy bump as she got out of bed and came to stop her.

Belinda did not think. She whirled around and hit her with the lamp.

Something like cartilage gave way. Panicked, Belinda lashed out again, heard the glass mantle shatter, a tooth break. Thomas cried from the bed.

What had she done?

There was no hope of secrecy now. All she could do was try and run, praying her head start was long enough. But the men could saddle horses, ride after them...

She'd come this far, she was damned if she was giving up now. Dropping the broken lamp, refusing to look down at the felled body of Amy, she charged after her son.

There was a tread on the stairs above, a creaking like old bones. Belinda started to run, the light behind her fading with every step. She'd forgotten to grab another lamp. Lydia writhed and kicked.

'Freddy,' she whispered, 'where are you?'

The gallery was nearby. She had a terrible vision of herself crashing blindly through the railing, plunging down and landing on top of Lydia.

'Freddy, I can't see you!'

Without warning, weight shoved against her legs.

She nearly lost her balance. Reaching out, she felt warm fur.

It was only the dog, Dev. 'Shoo! Get out of my way!' He did, but in another moment he was back, nudging at her thigh with his nose. Trying to tell her something.

She still couldn't get her bearings. Where was Freddy? Where were the stairs?

There. She managed two steps before her foot slipped.

A moment of weightless panic. Instinctively, she curled herself tight around Lydia. The impact seemed to jolt her shoulder from its socket. Blows struck at her head, her back, her hips. Stars of pain were bursting in the darkness while Lydia wailed like a banshee. She had to stop the fall. If they kept sliding downstairs, they'd split their heads open on the flags of the Great Hall. Still clutching Lydia with one arm, Belinda grabbed furiously with the other hand. By some miracle, her fingers caught hold of a baluster. She jerked to a painful halt that made her wrist crack.

Belinda panted, pain in every joint of her body. She'd suffered a knock to the head and it took a moment for her vision to steady. Lydia was screaming, yet not visibly hurt. Thank God. But now Belinda had to get up.

There were voices above. She'd been discovered, but she was almost there! Forcing herself upright, she pounded down the final steps screaming Freddy's name.

No answer.

Her boots hit the flags of the Great Hall. Belinda staggered to the door and snatched at the iron ring, hoping against hope that Daphne had managed to unlock it as she'd promised. It gave an inch and then stopped on an uneven flag. Belinda put her sore shoulder to it, forced it open with a scream of agony.

Cool night air rushed in. Ragged clouds drew away from the bone-white moon. Freedom was so close...

'Stop right there!'

Her feet froze to the spot.

'Take one more step and I promise you will regret it.'

Belinda turned to look back over her shoulder. Her stomach hollowed out.

Nathan stood in the gallery above, ashen by moonlight. The sharp tip of his sword was pressed against Freddy's delicate throat.

CHAPTER 30

The blade was already dipped in blood – at least, Belinda assumed the liquid was blood. It looked like tar in the shadows. But Freddy had no cut, only a dimple in his skin where the point pressed.

Why was it bloody?

'Put it down,' Belinda pleaded. 'I'm coming back, just – put the sword down.'

She hastened back into the centre of the hall, leaving the door open so moonlight could shine in. Lydia screamed in her ear. Belinda squeezed but could not comfort her. It felt like the sword was at her own throat.

Nathan did not release Freddy. 'This ought to have been so simple, Belinda.' Although he stood crookedly without his cane to support him, his grip on the boy was firm. Freddy held himself petrified. His chin was raised, his blue eyes enormous. 'You had your life in London. Your friends and family. Why did you seek more here?'

Ross Roberts melted out of a dark corner and cracked his knuckles. Not locked in his room after all. He looked uncannily like the companion she had just seen, brought to life. She flinched away.

'I started off so generously!' Nathan cried, incredulous. 'It was reparation, not revenge, I sought. I even gave Wilfred the benefit of the doubt. People change,

I thought. He was only a boy.' He moved the blade, ever so slightly, tracing an impression on Freddy's skin. 'But Ross was right. Selfishness runs in the Bainbridge blood.'

Belinda saw Dev on the other side of the gallery. She nursed a wild hope that he'd leap to the defence of his favourite friend, but he didn't. He turned tail and ran away, a streak of white against the darkness.

'Please, Nathan.' Her voice sounded like someone else's. 'Think about what you are doing.'

He unsheathed a smile like another weapon. 'I am already damned, Belinda. Wilfred made sure of that. Even so, I did not set out to kill a child...' He shook his head. 'I ought to have let that sword fall on Midsummer Eve. Eh, Freddy? That accident was a stroke of luck I never looked for. I threw my chance away through a moment of sheer weakness. If I hadn't saved him, none of us would be in this mess. You and Wilfred would have returned to London, to nurse your broken hearts, and never set foot in this house again.'

He was right. Not even Wilfred could have stomached living in the place where their darling had died so tragically.

'You were always too soft with them,' Ross said. He was addressing Nathan, but he kept his menacing gaze on Belinda and her wailing child. 'The Bainbridges didn't just take my uncle's life. They took everything from Fayford, even tried to take the common land. Parasites!' he spat. 'But there won't be enclosures under my management. No sky-high rents to line the master's pockets. It's about time the rest of us got a share of the luxury.'

'You want the estate? You can *have* the estate!' She juggled Lydia into a new position, hearing her own panic in her daughter's screams. 'There's no need to hurt Freddy. We'll sign it over. Whatever you wish. I'll make Paul agree to it all. We want nothing to do with you or The Bridge. Turn it into "Roberts Place" for all I care! Just give me my children and – and Daphne. You'll never hear from us again.'

'I do not believe you,' Nathan said simply. He pressed the tip of the blade hard enough to draw a dribble of blood. Freddy gasped. 'This boy is not going to stay quiet. Are you, Freddy? Rumours will spread, and before you know it they'll be questioning the whole sorry past of this place. Dawkins, Mrs Knowles. Roberts. Tiffany. They all died while I lived here. Wilfred taught people to blame me for everything, and they will. I'm not going to hang, Belinda.'

A patter of feet. From the corner of her eye, she saw a white shape appear in the gallery. The dog had returned.

'You will certainly hang if you kill a little boy! What do you think people will say if the children under your care disappear? Do you think they would just let you inherit, no questions asked? It is over! Whatever game you were playing, you've lost, Nathan.' She did not want to aggravate him further, but she felt the truth of her own words. 'It's *you* who ought to be running. Go back to India or America as you once planned to do. Maybe the law won't find you there.'

'He's not going anywhere,' Ross growled. 'We need his money and his claim. This is *our* house now. Land managed for the people. Things will be fair for the first time. You Bainbridge coves aren't going to drive your fancy carriages over our backs any longer.'

'It's *not* your house!' Suddenly, Freddy found his voice, echoing high and petulant around the gallery. 'It's hers – it's always been hers.'

'Enough!' Nathan jerked him by the shoulder. 'I've made up my mind. If I've truly lost, Belinda, if all that is left to me is revenge – well, I'll take it.' He raised the arm holding the blade. Steel glinted in the moonlight.

Belinda tried to scream but her lungs were empty, there was only a choking sound and a—

Hiss.

Everything stopped. For a fraction of a second, she thought she'd made the noise herself. Yet it was coming from above, louder than it had ever been before.

Hiss.

Nathan glanced up, irritated. What he saw made his expression crumble. Even in the darkness, she could see the colour drain from his face.

She turned. Her knees seemed to buckle beneath her.

Wilfred.

Her husband: compressed into a board of wood.

He stood facing his brother across the chasm of the gallery, the shadowy balustrade rising to his waist. Every detail was correct. The green coat, the fob watch, the wig upon his head. Only the bright burn of his eyebrows had changed. They were lowered, glowering in fury.

Hiss.

Somehow, she tore her eyes away. Even in that short time they had multiplied. Companions she had never seen before ranged up the staircase and on either side of the fireplace, their faces brimming with hunger.

Nathan stared in disbelief. His jaw and hands fell slack. 'No. It's not possible...'

Freddy seized that moment to twist out of his grasp. Before his uncle could grab at him again, he shoved at Nathan's bad leg hard from behind.

The crack was deafening. Wood groaned and splinters pattered down on the stone flags as the gallery railing snapped.

Belinda shrieked, pulling back and trying to shield Lydia.

Nathan dropped. She did not hear him scream or even cry out in surprise. It happened too quickly for that. He was nothing but a rush of air, a blast of debris, until he made impact with the floor. She felt the vibrations in the soles of her feet.

Freddy thumped down the stairs and barrelled to her side. He started pulling her towards the open door, not even looking back to see his grim handiwork. 'Quick, Mamma! Hurry!'

She caught a flare of blood and the grin of exposed bone. She was vaguely aware of Ross, rushing towards the fatal spot. But Freddy's fingers were insistent, surprisingly strong. She surrendered to their tug and ran out into the night.

Gravel crunched beneath Freddy's feet, worked its way into Belinda's boots. The sky was clear enough to show pinpricks of stars and the pale orb of a full moon. Belinda hardly saw them. She drank in the cool air like water, fighting the urge to collapse. There was a high-pitched ringing in her ears. It sounded like screams.

She was not conscious of climbing the incline towards the gatehouse. It was only when the muscles in her legs seized that she became aware of the mist, rising up from the nearby river and marbling the air. She stopped to drag in breath. As she glanced back she beheld the manor at the base of the hills, gently cupped by trees. It looked almost peaceful from a distance. Copper lights burnt in the windows.

'Sawyer,' she breathed.

Freddy was already at the gates, rattling the iron rails. 'Mamma, help me open them!'

She said nothing. Everything was rushing back: thought, feeling, duty. She could not leave her sister. Whatever she had just seen, whatever it was that moved the companions, she would not abandon Daphne to its mercy.

And Wilfred. She closed her eyes against a memory of that tortured wooden face. *The people who die here are trapped in the house.* She'd give kingdoms to believe that wasn't true. But she'd seen him. He was *there*.

'Freddy, take your sister.'

He was shivering in his nightshirt and his bare feet were cut from the gravel. Her poor boy. 'We have to run, Mamma!'

'I know. We're going to. But I must go back for your aunt.'

'No!'

'Yes.' She placed Lydia into his arms. Exhaustion had claimed the baby and she'd finally screamed herself out. She looked so large, held by a child. A real weight to bear. 'I'm going to open the gates and you'll take Lydia to Fayford. Wait for me there. By the church. Find John Knowles if you can.' It was too much to ask of him, especially after all he'd been through tonight. All he'd done. Soon shock would set in. It was not fair to leave a terrified boy wandering the night with a baby in tow. But she did not see that she had a choice.

'Be careful, Mamma! Hetta's angry. She'll be even angrier now we've taken Lydia away.' His eyes were wide like a spooked horse's. In the darkness, the cut on his neck resembled a noose.

'I know, sweetheart. But I am angry, too.'

True to her word, Daphne had unlocked the gates. They squealed back on their hinges, tearing the letter B in two. Freddy slipped through the gap into the thickening mist.

Belinda prayed to God she had done the right thing.

She set off downhill, refusing to look back, knowing she would lose her nerve. Now she didn't have the children to perform for, she was afraid she might give in to the terror that had been trying to claim her all night. She could not make sense of what had just happened. How those companions had appeared so suddenly, all together at once, as if the dog had gone to fetch help.

Had they helped?

Her breath turned to smoke before her. She had no idea what she was running back into. Ross Roberts and Whitfield would not just stand aside and let her pass. Nathan must be dead, and Amy... God, she'd forgotten all about Amy. Hot queasiness took hold.

And that wasn't the only violence that had taken place before the confrontation in the Great Hall, was it? Nathan's blade had already been coated in blood.

The fountain glowed white up ahead. In a few more steps, she would be able to see through the windows of the house. There was a scudding sound and a white shape whumped past her, streaking uphill.

What was Dev running from?

As his paws pattered away, the night fell strangely still. The fountain babbled gently as if nothing had taken place. She'd left the door wide open but now it stood ajar, screening her view.

Belinda gritted her teeth and pulled it.

The fire had been lit, flooding the space with a shifting, autumnal glow. The first thing she saw by its light was the wreck of Nathan: one half of his face totally compressed into the stone flags, unrecognisable. Blood beaded his beard and threaded through the remaining, open eye. He'd landed on his side. The impact had reverberated through his body, pushing bones out of place and joints through the skin. Gruesome as it was, she did not feel the need to vomit as she had when seeing Dawkins. In place of the nausea was a macabre sense of satisfaction. It shamed her.

But where were all the companions? Where was Ross? She'd last seen him running towards the body as if to help his cousin. Her head swivelled this way and that, searching, finding only the same suits of armour, the swords on the wall and the stone flags red as a slaughterhouse...

There was no wood. As she stared at the puddle surrounding the corpse, she realised it ought to be littered with shards from the broken gallery. Splinters should be crunching underfoot, chunks of wood slowly absorbing the blood. Frowning, she glanced up to the jagged gap where the rail had split.

And now the bile came flooding into her mouth. Ross was there. So was all of the broken wood. The two had been combined.

He sprawled with one arm hanging over the side of the drop, a human pincushion. Spears prickled from his back, his legs, through both his eyes. The man who had claimed that this was his house twitched, impaled from every angle.

Beside him stood a wooden girl with her hair piled on top of her head and a rose pressed demurely to her chest. Smiling.

In that moment, Belinda realised she had never truly been mistress of The Bridge.

'Help!' It was more of a bleat than a cry.

She whipped around to see Daphne staggering towards the top of the staircase. Her dark hair was unpinned, her body clad in a nightgown. The bodice was pale and disordered, but the skirts... The skirts were hemmed with red.

'Daphne!'

She dashed to the bottom of the steps just in time. Her sister fell down the great sweep of stairs. Belinda managed to catch her before she could hit the floor.

'Daphne!' Belinda gathered her in her arms. She felt as limp as a rag doll. There was no way of telling where the hot blood was oozing from. 'What happened?'

'I distracted him.' Daphne tried to smile, red dribbling from the corner of her mouth. 'But he figured it out. He had his sword.'

'It's all right,' Belinda gabbled, searching desperately for the injury. 'You're going to be all right. Nathan's dead. You're free now. We all are. We're going home to London.'

Daphne's gaze swam towards her husband's crumpled body, but she did not appear to see it. 'Home,' she repeated dreamily, before her eyelids flickered shut.

Epilogue

Winter in the city was ever the same: smoggy, tasting of smoke and damp wool. The cold nibbled like mice. But an effort had been made to render the graveyard pleasant for visitors and inhabitants alike. Sand had been scattered to stop the paths from becoming too slippery, while the grass had been cleared of fallen leaves. Bare branches reached over the pair of sleepers Belinda had come to visit. The mounds of earth were soft and fresh, the headstones as yet untouched by lichen.

It did not seem real.

Every so often, she glimpsed Freddy through the mist, walking calmly amongst the graves with Dev at his side. He paused at each one and touched the stone. Occasionally, he spoke. She told herself he was talking to the dog.

Lydia sighed and burrowed deeper into her mother's shawl. Belinda rocked her, thinking sadly of the relatives her daughter would never meet. It had been difficult enough to process the fact of Wilfred's death, but at least there had been the discovery of his body and its committal to the family crypt. Belinda's father and her brother Paul had gone down to the bottom of the ocean with their ship. The hungry waves retained them. The coffins in these graves contained only keepsakes.

With all the loss, and risk of loss, she had faced in recent months, she realised these deaths were more than a deep bereavement: they signalled the end of an era. Her girlhood was truly over. Now she was no longer just the youngest child, the sole daughter, her mother's prop. There was space for her to be more.

'I think little madam is growing restless.' Her brother Luke appeared at her shoulder and pulled a funny face to make Lydia smile. 'I suppose we had better get her in from the cold soon.'

'You would be surprised by how resilient she is,' Belinda said. 'She has been through much worse.' She tucked the once-splintered arm, now fully healed, back into its swaddling. 'But it's good that she is strong. Lydia will have to rough it a little in her future life.'

Luke frowned. 'Do not say so. You know I'll give all I can to help financially. And I'm sure that someday soon there will be movement on selling The Bridge, or at least an offer to lease it.'

She shook her head. 'No, Luke. It was already infamous locally before all of this. Now... well.'

She had not been at the house for the removal of the bodies. Nor had she been able to provide a satisfactory account to those who had questioned her about the deaths. Not that anyone had thought Belinda culpable. She'd told them that Nathan had threatened Freddy with a sword and that he'd overbalanced without his cane, falling from the gallery. A white lie. There was little else for her to offer. She could not say for sure how Ross had died, or Whitfield, whom they'd found devoid of breath in a locked room with a pillow over his face. No one had mentioned whether there was a silent companion beside him, but she imagined there was.

Of course, Nathan's past spoke against him, as did his attack on Daphne. It was concluded he'd gone on a murderous rampage before his fall. The matter was closed.

Amy remained the only guilty secret burning like embers in Belinda's chest. She had not meant to *kill* the wet-nurse with blows from the lamp, simply to knock her out. But in her panic she'd bestowed a broken nose, a chipped tooth, and then a fatal fracture to the side of the head. Amy's son Thomas Whitfield, orphaned at eighteen months, was sent back to his aunt in Torbury St Jude. That was Belinda's burden to live with forever.

As were the questions.

No matter how many times she ran it over, she could not be certain how much of her nightmare had been caused by Nathan and his friends. Her brother-in-law *had* tried to frighten them away with ghost stories and cruel pranks. Yet there was truth behind his words. Unwittingly, he'd been right about the silent companions all along.

And one way or the other, he'd achieved his aim. Now Nathan would stay at The Bridge for all of time. By night, a companion with a cavalier beard and bright blue eyes might drag its wooden base across the floorboards, leaving long, white scratches. But he was not the only one trapped. Belinda could not forget the new companion who'd appeared so briefly on the opposite side of the gallery, distracting Nathan for long enough to let her son escape.

No; she could never sell that house. Not if there was a chance that Wilfred's spirit lingered there. She would let it become a mausoleum.

Luke sighed, resting his fingers in his waistcoat pocket. 'It seems a shame. That whole big mansion sitting empty.'

'It's *not* empty,' she said darkly. Luke raised his eyebrows. 'But I know you don't believe me on that score.'

'Perhaps I'll take Mamma to live there,' he jested. 'A few resident ghosts would encourage her out of the house pretty often, don't you think?'

She gave a wry smile and followed his gaze over to the chapel where Daphne's wicker Bath chair was parked on the frosted grass. The injuries inflicted by Nathan's sword had changed her life, but they did not stop her from indulging in her favourite pursuit of sketching. Even now she was working in fingerless mittens, setting down a new version of the world around her. A better one, perhaps.

Mamma kept a white-knuckled grip on the handle behind. She was pale, hunched over the back of the chair and staring fixedly at Daphne's pencil. Yet she was outside. Trying to live as other people did. When the calamity she had so feared struck her family at last, she'd made an effort to rise from the ashes. Belinda was proud of her for that. Still, it would take time.

'Actually, I don't think you will need to watch over Mamma. Daphne wants to stay with her. Form their own household. The pair of them have much to discuss.'

Luke fidgeted, uncomfortable. She supposed he did not like to admit the truth about Daphne's connection to them any more than Papa had, but he was outnumbered. Belinda had returned to London with the understanding that Daphne was to be treated as her sister from now on. And that acceptance seemed to have fixed something inside Mamma, too. She was speaking haltingly of the woman she had known, who gave them a child and lost her life so tragically. At last, Daphne was learning the truth of her own past.

'Won't you be with them?' Luke asked.

Belinda shook her head. 'No. I have my settlement from Wilfred and a little from Papa. After Christmas, the children and I will be moving to Bath.'

'Why Bath?'

The spa city was a little more expensive than she liked, but coin was what it took to secure rooms in freshly built houses of pure white limestone. Her children would grow up in a residence where no one else had ever lived before – or died, for that matter.

'I hear it is a good place for widows. A busy social scene and beneficial to the health. It will be a fresh start.'

Luke blinked at her, as if he was not sure what to make of this new, self-possessed sister who had returned from her haunted house full of ideas and demands. But he had always been the most easy-going of the three men in her family. He was not angry, only confused. 'Well... I hardly know what I shall do with myself then, if neither you nor Mamma need me. With the business all wound up, there are no ships to send.'

She laid a hand upon his shoulder. 'You can live, Luke. You were ever in Paul's shadow, but now is your time. Get married yourself – as heir, you can afford a family. Pursue an employment that truly interests you, not one duty binds you to. We are both at liberty now, you and I.'

He regarded her strangely, as if she were speaking a foreign language. She understood his caution. She was afraid herself, but after what she had faced at The Bridge nothing felt insurmountable.

'It must have been a philosophical sort of ghost bothering you,' he observed. 'What did it do, read revolutionary pamphlets aloud at night?'

She let him laugh, even laughed along herself. He would never understand but she did not need him to.

Beneath a skeletal white beech tree, Freddy had stopped and squatted on his haunches. There was a small, marble angel there. She could see his lips moving. Whispering to it.

'I am feeling the chill a little now,' she confessed. 'Perhaps we should head back.'

Luke went to help Mamma with Daphne's Bath chair. Belinda called to Freddy and whistled to the dog. Dev came bounding to her side at once. He sniffed happily at Lydia and let Belinda secure the leash.

Freddy remained where he was.

The cold seemed to settle in her lungs. 'Now, Freddy. It's time to leave.'

Reluctantly, he rose to his feet. He approached at a slow pace and kept looking back over his shoulder. Belinda forced the dog's leash into his small, gloved hand. She took the other in her own.

'What were you looking at over there?' She wished she hadn't asked, for she already knew the answer.

'I can still see them,' Freddy said, his warm breath forming a cloud. 'They... speak to me. It never used to happen, Mamma, not before I went to The Bridge.'

'Well, maybe you will outgrow it. The longer you stay away from there, the more the voices will fade.'

She spoke as one with authority. But in fact she had no idea what would happen.

Their whole future was a gamble, a wild roll of the dice. She could not be sure how much Freddy would remember of this terrible past year. Behind those blue eyes lay a host of traumatic impressions, as numerous as the companions themselves. Including the murder of his uncle – albeit in self-defence.

What would she tell her children of the grand estate they owned but must never visit? Perhaps she would not *need* to remind Freddy. But when she thought about explaining it all to Lydia, her heart stuttered. Would her daughter believe her? Or would she go seeking out The Bridge herself once Belinda was gone? What if Hetta tried to possess her again?

The family gathered to walk back through the lych-gate and out onto the street. Lydia giggled at the sight of the dog's short wagging tail. The wheels of Daphne's Bath chair purred along as she chattered with Mamma, trying to keep her focused and not panicking. Hope flared, as bright and brief as the winter sun through the smog.

It was a bad inheritance: there was no denying that. Whether it was Bainbridge wealth, East India Company wages or her father's trading fortune, the money she, Luke and Daphne had received was not clean. She did not know if they could undo that legacy of oppression. Or if they even deserved to. But Belinda was going to try her best.

With difficulty, they crossed the street, waiting for the endless flow of carriages and carts to ease before manoeuvring Daphne's chair over the uneven surface. Once they'd gained the other side, Luke strode on ahead but Freddy was still glancing back. Belinda searched the deserted graveyard. She saw only mist, swirling and shifting with a will of its own.

Freddy waved goodbye to nothing.

She pulled him along.

'Oh!' A sharp intake of breath up ahead. Mamma flinched as if burnt, clutching at her left hand.

The chair trundled along for a moment before grating to a stop.

Daphne tried to turn and see what was going on over its high back. 'Are you all right?'

'It's nothing, nothing,' Mamma cried, tearful. 'Only it gave me such a fright! Oh, my poor heart.'

Belinda hastened towards her, dragging Freddy in her wake. 'Mamma? What has happened?'

'It's that horrible wicker! So scratchy and rough. I do not know why they insist on making the chairs out of such a nasty material. Look what it has done!' She held out her arm.

Belinda's stomach lurched. A splinter of wood had pierced the skin at Mamma's wrist, between the start of her glove and the end of her sleeve, poking out like the spinous quill of a hedgehog.

So small and yet so sharp. The kind of weapon that killed slowly, with pinpricks.

Belinda let go of Freddy's hand. She yanked the splinter out and threw it on the pavement, where she ground it under her heel. 'Never mind. No real harm has been done.'

Mamma wiped her eyes and took up the handle of Daphne's chair once more. Freddy latched back onto Belinda's arm.

They all walked on, together, into the billowing smog.

Acknowledgements

My friend and agent Juliet Mushens is quite literally the saviour of this book. I was at the point where I was ready to set fire to the manuscript, bury the ashes in the back garden and pour cement on top. Within less than twenty-four hours of requesting her assistance, she came up with an idea which helped me turn the whole story around. Thank you Juliet, I would be in a puddle on the floor without you.

Huge thanks to all of the wonderful people at Bloomsbury Raven who have brought the book to life. My editor Alison Hennessey, who first launched the companions into the world and takes such glee in plotting nightmare fuel with me, Faye Robinson, Ben McCluskey, Amy Donegan, Charlotte Phillips, and Lynn Curtis for finding me an era-appropriate flower. Your enthusiasm and hard work are so appreciated.

Lastly, I want to thank all the booksellers and readers who championed my earlier novel The Silent Companions and made it possible for me to write this story. You are simply the best and I hope you enjoyed your trip back to The Bridge.

A Note on the Author

Laura Purcell is an award-winning former bookseller living in Colchester, Essex with her husband and pet guinea pigs. She is the author of five previous novels for Raven Books, among them *The Silent Companions*, which was a Radio 2 and Zoe Ball ITV Book Club pick, *The Shape of Darkness*, winner of the inaugural Fingerprint Award for Historical Crime Book of the Year, and *The Whispering Muse*, which was the 2023 winner of the Dracula Society's Children of the Night Award. Her short stories have been included in *The Haunting Season* and *The Winter Spirits* anthologies, which were both instant *Sunday Times* bestsellers. She also wrote 'Roanoke Falls', a dramatic podcast for Realm, working with John Carpenter and Sandy King Carpenter.